What Reviewers Say About Kim Baldwin's Books

"A hallmark of great writing is consummate characterization, and *Whitewater Rendezvous* does not disappoint…Captures the reader from the very first page…totally immerses and envelopes the reader in the Arctic experience. Superior chapter endings, stylishly and tightly written sentences, precise pacing, and exquisite narrative all coalesce to produce a novel of first-rate quality, both in concept and expression." —*Midwest Book Review*

"Nature's fury has nothing on the fire of desire and passion that burns in Kim Baldwin's *Force of Nature*! Filled with passion, plenty of laughs, and 'yeah, I know how that feels…' moments, *Force of Nature* is a book you simply can't put down. All we have to say is, where's the sequel?!" —Outlookpress.com

"…filled with non-stop, fast-paced action…Tornadoes, raging fire blazes, heroic and daring rescues…Baldwin does a fine job of describing the fast-paced scenes and inspiring the reader to keep on turning the pages." —*The L Life*

"The story had me on the edge of my seat with the multiple action scenes of firestorms and heroic rescues. With *Force of Nature*, Kim Baldwin has created another compelling read filled with multiple conflicts that interconnect well. With only her second novel, she is fast becoming a force as a lesbian fiction author." —*Independent Gay Writer*

"'A riveting novel of suspense' seems to be a very overworked phrase. However, it is extremely apt when discussing…*Hunter's Pursuit*. Look for this excellent novel."—*Mega-Scene* magazine

"A…fierce first novel, an action-packed thriller pitting deadly professional killers against each other. Baldwin's fast-paced plot comes…leavened, as every intelligent adventure novel's excesses ought to be, with some lovin'." —*Q Syndicate*

"Clever surprises and suspenseful drama resonate on each page, setting the wheels in motion for an exciting ride. Action sequences fire rapidly in succession leaving the reader breathless. The total effect will have you riveted to Kim Baldwin's book. Once you pick up *Hunter's Pursuit*, there is no putting it down." —*The Independent Gay Writer*

By the Author

Hunter's Pursuit

Force of Nature

Whitewater Rendezvous

FLIGHT RISK

by
Kim Baldwin

2007

FLIGHT RISK

ISBN: 10-digit 1-933110-68-6
13-digit 978-1-933110-68-4

This Trade Paperback Original Is Published By
Bold Strokes Books, Inc.,
New York, USA

First Edition: February 2007

Credits
Editors: Jennifer Knight and Stacia Seaman
Production Design: Stacia Seaman
Cover Design By Sheri (GRAPHICARTIST2020@HOTMAIL.COM)

Acknowledgments

For M.: You put up with more than usual in the writing of this book. Thank you for your endless patience, for pushing me for more pages, and for never complaining that I rarely offer to cook anymore.

For my dear friend Xenia: Your contributions to this book cannot be measured. I'm deeply grateful for your ideas and insights, bits of dialogue, unflagging enthusiasm for the project, and especially, for providing Alexi's "voice."

I have learned so much since being fortunate enough to sign with Bold Strokes Books, and I continue to grow with each project. My books always greatly benefit from the talents and expertise of this incredible, warm bunch of women, and I am so honored and proud to be associated with them. First and foremost, Radclyffe—publisher, inspiration, mentor, and friend. You have made the realization of my dreams possible, so how can I ever adequately thank you for that? To Jennifer Knight, senior consulting editor: my books and my craft are so much richer for your insights, ideas, guidance, and encouragement. Thanks also for Stacia Seaman's editorial expertise and meticulous eye for detail. And Sheri—wow! You really outdid yourself on the cover this time, mate. Such artistry. I'm so grateful.

To Connie Ward, I have double reason to be thankful. For your tireless efforts as BSB publicist, and most especially for your wonderful insights and encouragement while beta reading for me. Also to my beta reader Sharon Lloyd, co-owner of Epilogue Books, who seems to catch every typo and other careless omission.

I have a wonderfully supportive group of close friends who provide unwavering support for every writing project of mine. Linda and Vicki, Kat and Ed, Felicity, Tim and Scott (thanks much again for the medical expertise, Scott), Marsha and Ellen. You are family, and near or far, I hold you always close to my heart.

And most especially, to the many, many readers who support and encourage my writing efforts by buying my books, showing up for my appearances, and e-mailing me. Thank you so much.

Kim Baldwin, February 2007

Visit us at www.boldstrokesbooks.com

Dedication

For all the women
who inspire me
each and every day

PROLOGUE

There were three gunshots altogether. Loud, staccato reports that pierced the stillness of the night. Two in rapid succession, then one more after a moment's pause, as if the shooter had stopped to take a breath.

Alexi Nikolos was already pounding back up the familiar stairs by then, her heart beating so wildly in her chest she was almost dizzy from the burst of adrenaline. She clutched her Beretta with such tension that the rough crosshatches in the grip left a faint impression in her right palm.

It was after midnight and there were no lights on in the house, but Alexi knew every room, every stick of furniture, and each of the twenty-three steps that led to the upper level and bedrooms. As she got to the top and rounded the corner, a fist lashed out of nowhere and connected with her jaw. Her world went black.

When she regained consciousness, she was alone and the house was silent. Her gun was gone. She staggered to her feet and lurched toward the bedroom, wanting to shut down, to be anywhere else. Knowing what she would find, she forced herself through the doorway, hearing, as she did, the squeal of tires outside.

She flipped on the light and let out a keening animal wail of anguish.

Sofia Galletti was slumped in the corner, silent and still, the pale skin of her nude body stark against a growing pool of crimson. Blood splattered the cream-colored wall behind her, and two dark holes marred the plaster where the large-caliber bullets that had pierced Sofia's head and abdomen had ended their deadly rampage.

Alexi stumbled toward the woman she had made love to not an hour before and sank to her knees. With infinite tenderness, she cradled Sofia in her arms.

"I am sorry. I am so sorry." She whispered it over and over and over, as if she could take it all back—her carelessness, her selfishness, her stupidity at thinking that the rules did not apply to her.

She rocked Sofia gently, her mind refusing to accept what had happened, until so much time had passed that the warm flesh she clutched began to grow cold.

CHAPTER ONE

One Year Later

B layne Keller sighed wistfully as she slipped tickets and an itinerary into an airline folder and handed this to the meticulously groomed businessman sitting opposite her desk. In the eight years she had worked at the Balmy Breezes Travel Agency she'd booked thousands of vacations for clients, but this was the first time she had arranged a trip to her dream destination. Remote, exotic Fiji. Three hundred and thirty islands of tropical bliss. *The Blue Lagoon.*

It was an especially appealing excursion to think about with the record-breaking cold spell Chicago was enduring this February. When Blayne drove by the large digital thermometer on the bank building down the street that morning, it had read nine below zero, up from an overnight low of minus fifteen. The parking lot that serviced the travel agency and the soda wholesaler behind it was slick with ice, and she'd nearly fallen half a dozen times getting to the door.

Blayne had about $3,600 in her Fiji fund, a stash of cash stuffed into an old coffee bag in her freezer at home. But that was not nearly enough. Not for the kind of luxury adventure she had in mind. The business class airfare alone from Chicago was more than five grand. She had another couple of years at least before she could arrange her own sojourn to the South Pacific. Until then, she'd have to be content with spending her vacation time closer to home.

Her client got to his feet and she did the same, thanking him for his business and wishing him well for his trip.

"Gotta say, I envy you," she confessed amiably as he tucked the travel folder into the inside breast pocket of his crisp navy suit. "The diving and snorkeling in Fiji is absolutely phenomenal." She offered her hand and the man shook it, but his bored expression told her what he thought of her comment.

"Yeah, well, I don't know about that. Give me Vegas any day," he said. "This was the wife's idea. No place to me is worth being trapped on a plane for thirty hours."

Cretin. You don't deserve Fiji. Blayne kept the smile on her face only until the client turned to go, then she stuck her tongue out at him, an impulse that prompted a muffled snort from the dark-haired woman seated at the desk to her left. Fortunately, the man never looked back as Blayne silenced her friend, Claudia Cluzet, with a withering glare.

They were both thirty, and Blayne sometimes wondered how they had ever become close friends, they seemed so very different. For a start, their outward appearances were almost diametrically opposite. Blayne was petite and curvy, her Irish heritage spelled out in her shoulder-length strawberry blond hair and lightly freckled complexion. She was also feisty, outspoken, and fiercely independent, and she dressed for comfort much more than for style. Today she'd chosen black dress slacks and a loose-fitting turtleneck sweater in the muted gray-green color of high-quality jade, the same shade as her eyes.

She never tried to look provocative. But a few people, Claudia included, insisted she had an understated type of sex appeal. That she was graceful in the way she carried herself, and her ready smiles and sense of mischief made her attractive to others. Blayne never had any trouble getting dates, if that was a litmus test of her charms, but she was well aware that the serious good looks belonged to her friend. Claudia had the statuesque, wispy frame of a model, and her classic features and dark eyes and hair were reminiscent of a young Isabella Rossellini. Unlike Blayne, she dressed to impress and entice. Today, despite the cold, she wore a long leather skirt and a formfitting red sweater that focused attention on her nipples.

Blayne tended toward perky enthusiasm, where Claudia was languid ease. But they communicated in their own shorthand, developed over a decade of private jokes and shared confidences.

"Fiji, land of hot monkey sex on the beach," Claudia said smugly as soon as the man was gone.

"Claud, don't even…" Blayne threatened, propping herself against the edge of her friend's desk.

"That tongue of yours is getting a real workout these days," Claudia remarked in a seductive tone. She hiked her leather skirt above her knees and leaned back in her chair, moistening her lips in invitation.

Blayne obliged by leering at the expanse of skin exposed on Claudia's long legs. "You wish."

"God, get a room already," an exasperated Joyce Houseman interrupted from the hallway behind them. Joyce was a bleached blonde with breasts too perfectly round and pert to be anything but artificial. Every article of clothing she owned showed them off. In the midst of winter, she favored snug V-necked sweaters—today's was pink. Joyce was past forty and it was beginning to show, so she was fighting the advance of time with plastic surgery and too much makeup. "You two will *never* convince me you have nothing going on."

"Only in her dreams," Claudia replied.

"I'm not the one dreaming these days, sweetheart," Blayne countered playfully.

"Better late than never," Claudia shot back.

Joyce's scowl deepened. "What the *hell* are you guys talking about?"

Blayne and Claudia both cracked up.

"Should we be nice and tell her?" Blayne asked.

"If you must."

"About damn time." Joyce moved closer. "You're trying to tell me you two really haven't gotten together? Not ever?"

"No." Claudia stuck out her rosy lower lip in a pout. "Not yet."

Blayne reached over and ruffled Claudia's hair affectionately. With a trace of regret, she said, "And we never will."

"But you're both unattached, and you obviously have the hots for each other." Joyce looked bemused. "I don't get it."

"Well, to understand, you have to back up about ten years to the day I walked into my dorm room at Michigan State and found this magnificent specimen"—Blayne trailed her gaze up and down the length of Claudia's body appreciatively before continuing—"in my bed."

"Soon to be *my* bed," Claudia added.

"She announced she was my new roommate, but only if she could have the bed by the window. I wasn't about to argue since I got a delightful new view myself in the bargain."

"And?" Joyce prompted.

"*And*...I lusted after her like crazy," Blayne admitted. "She used to wear these tight white shorts that barely covered her ass."

Claudia laughed.

"But she was only into men then." Blayne sighed. "And totally oblivious to my fascination with her."

"Until the night you kissed me," Claudia supplied.

"Aha! I knew something must have happened between you," Joyce said with satisfaction.

"Still seems more dream than memory," Blayne continued. "Far too much to drink. Anyway, that ol' cat came barreling out of the bag *that* night, for sure."

Joyce turned impatiently to Claudia. "So? Come on. Did you kiss her back?"

"Well, yes and no."

"Mostly no," Blayne said. "It was over almost before it started."

"You caught me by surprise," Claudia said. "Long before I knew I could swing in that direction. And it wasn't exactly the time or place."

"What does that mean?" Joyce pressed. "Details! I want details!"

"Well, we were in the shower," Blayne said. "Naked, of course… and she had her arms around me…"

"That's more like it. *Now* I'm getting the picture."

"Not the whole picture you aren't," Claudia interjected defensively. "She stumbled in at four a.m., very drunk, and I put her in the shower to try to sober her up. I had my arms around her to keep her from falling over." She glanced toward Blayne. "Which is another reason I discouraged you that night. Not only was I not ready for it, I wasn't entirely sure you knew who it was you were kissing. You were pretty far gone."

"Well, for your information, I knew all too damn well who I was kissing," Blayne retorted. "I went out that night in the first place because I had it so bad for you I thought I'd go mad if I didn't get laid soon."

Claudia's eyes got big as she took in this tidbit from the past. "Did you really?"

"Yes."

"*So?*" Joyce demanded. "What happened?"

"Well, I was so shocked I guess I just kind of tried to laugh it off," Claudia said. "Blayne apologized the next day and blamed it on the alcohol."

Blayne sighed inwardly. She'd realized as soon as Claudia pulled back that her own feelings weren't shared. She supposed she'd known it all along, but she'd just wanted to kiss her so badly she couldn't help herself that night.

Joyce processed this for a moment, then asked, "What about now? You're both into women, aren't you? And you have this huge flirtation thing going all the time."

Claudia hesitated. "Let's just say our Blayne has not been lucky in love, so she's become a bit relationship-shy." She fell silent when Blayne glared at her.

"No. That's not the reason. The reason we're not together is that we've been friends too long and I won't let anything mess that up."

"So you keep saying," Claudia murmured.

Blayne shrugged and gave Joyce a resigned little smile, indicating the revelations were over. Joyce took the hint and said, "Better get back to the books. Holler when lunch is here. I'll pay whoever."

She strolled off down the hallway that led to the rear business office next to the employee lounge and restrooms. Joyce liked to joke that she could skip work and they'd never know she'd gone. Her office was just a few feet away from two convenient escape routes—a connecting door to the soda company in the back and an alarmed fire exit to the parking lot.

"You're so stubborn," Claudia commented once they were alone again.

"And you're just bi-curious," Blayne replied. "You keep ping-ponging from men to women. Any idea yet which it is you want to settle down with?"

"Does it matter? I'll be happy as long as I find someone I trust, can confide in, love, respect, am wildly attracted to…" Claudia ticked off the qualities on the fingers of one hand, then feigned surprise as she looked at Blayne. "And what do you know. You meet all those criteria!"

Laughing, Blayne got up and moved behind Claudia's chair so she could lean down and hug her around the neck. "Not going to happen, honey," she said affectionately, then she planted a kiss on the top of Claudia's head. "You know we make much better friends than we would lovers."

"I'm not done trying to change your mind about that." Claudia stretched and glanced at the clock on the wall. "Time for lunch, and it's my turn to go. Italian today?"

There were a number of ethnic restaurants within a short walk of the travel agency, and the three of them alternated on who got to choose the cuisine for the day. Joyce always ordered the same thing and Blayne knew the Firenze menu by heart. She pulled her wallet out of the top drawer of her desk, extracted a ten, and handed it to Claudia.

"I'll take that salmon and pasta dish with the dill cream sauce."

Claudia bundled up in a coat, hat, scarf, and gloves until only her eyes were exposed. "When I come back, let's plan a girls' night out," she said, her voice muffled by the scarf. "Somewhere with a heater better than in my apartment. A place with lots of booze." She headed for the door, firing one final thought over her shoulder. "Or lots of hot women. That would do too."

Blayne cracked up. Warning, "Watch the ice," she returned to her desk.

Pictures of Fiji stared at her from the computer monitor. Tanned, toned bodies in bikinis, fortunate tourists sipping fruity drinks. She tapped a pencil on her desk impatiently as a restlessness swept through her. It wasn't just a vacation she craved. She wasn't entirely sure what it was that she needed, she only knew she needed a change, and soon.

She liked her job, her friends, and even living in Chicago, though she'd never expected to settle in the Windy City. At one time, it had seemed her life was all laid out for her. After college, she'd planned to travel for six months and then return home to Ishpeming, Michigan, to take over managing Blarneys, the family pub she'd lived above all her life. Her parents had expected it and she wasn't averse to the idea. She loved small-town life and knew she would enjoy working in the congenial atmosphere of the authentic Irish tavern.

But a month before her graduation, Blarneys had burned to the ground, killing her parents and leaving her suddenly orphaned, homeless, and with an uncertain future, all in one swift awful nightmare. Claudia's father had offered her employment in his travel agency, and Chicago had seemed as good a place as any to start her life anew.

Since then it had been a comfortable existence, but it had gotten much too comfortable of late. She needed some fun. Some action. Some romance. Something spontaneous in her life. *Time to shake things up a little. I need to get out more.*

❖

Across the street from the travel agency, four men in business suits and overcoats sat shivering in a large panel truck that read *L. Wolfe and Sons, Plumbers* on the outside.

In the back with two other unhappy agents on temporary transfer from Washington, Special Agent Leslie "Skip" Topping wondered how long it would be before his walrus mustache froze over like a mountaineer's.

"Turn up the heater, will you, pal?" he called forward to the driver, a paunchy local agent dressed in the insulated coveralls a real plumber might be wearing on such a lousy day.

"Up all the way already," Johnny Trelaine responded.

Skip had a feeling the jerk was lying, sitting in his cozy little hole up front, making sure the three Washington ringers in the back were as uncomfortable as possible. It was pretty obvious he resented the hell out of the lead role they'd been assigned in this organized crime investigation, when it was FBI Chicago that had put the case together.

"Damn this cold." Special Agent Dennis O'Rourke blew on his hands. A ginger-haired agent Skip had known for years, he was having trouble operating the sophisticated recording equipment in front of him with his gloves on. So he kept taking them off, then complaining that his fingers were icicles.

Skip had a slightly easier task. He could manage his binoculars just fine with the heavy gloves he'd bought the second day of their surveillance, and there hadn't been much to see today anyway. Six apparent customers of the travel agency and three trucks in and out of the soda place. The bitter cold and icy roads had kept the streets virtually clear of traffic.

The bosses in Washington were optimistic the tip they'd gotten would pay off, and this miserable stakeout would provide them with evidence to finally nail Vittorio Cinzano. So far the ruthless mob underboss had proven to be an elusive target. Cinzano was careful to avoid being seen anywhere near one of his distribution hubs. And guys that high up in the Mafia hierarchy were rarely sloppy.

"Anything?" Special Agent George Dombrowski mumbled through a mouthful of glazed donut. It was his third, but he was one man who didn't need to worry about the calories. He was built like a brick wall, with a massive neck to match his overdeveloped arms and shoulders, and beefy hands that made the donut seem half-sized.

"At least we can hear something, finally," O'Rourke reported, fiddling again with the knobs on the recorder. "It's a woman talking. She wants someone to call her when the meeting is over."

Dombrowski paused over his donut. "That's all she said? To call her when the meeting's over?"

"All we got, anyway," O'Rourke confirmed. "Not enough to ID her. But it's got to be one of the three that work in the travel agency. They're the only women in the building."

"Which one of them do you think it is?" Dombrowski asked.

"No way of knowing with those damn windows where they are," Skip complained, not for the first time. The squat red brick building they were watching had two large picture windows in front, but they were set too high to see inside. "If I had to pick, though, I'd say the brunette."

Dombrowski chuckled. "We didn't ask which one you wanted to screw, Skip."

"Hell, they could all be in on it," O'Rourke said. "Maybe they're back there in the warehouse all the time. Maybe this is just the first time we've caught one saying anything."

"Heads up," Trelaine interrupted from the driver's seat. "Three subjects. Ford sedan approaching from the rear."

Skip shot to his feet and trained his binoculars on the battered sedan that drew alongside them. It slowed to turn into the travel agency parking lot, then disappeared behind the building. The windows were tinted, making it almost impossible for a positive identification of the occupants.

"That was Cinzano himself, God damn it!" Trelaine whooped. "In the back, left side."

"You sure?" Dombrowski asked doubtfully. "Couldn't see much."

"Could be him," Skip agreed. "Sedan looks about right. He'd want to be inconspicuous."

"I know I'm right. I've been staring at pictures of him for months," Trelaine reminded them, the usual edge of resentment missing from his voice.

Skip knew what he was thinking. *Play nice or get cut out of this.* "We'll know soon enough," he said. "Everybody shut up now, will you, so I can hear what's going on."

CHAPTER TWO

Vittorio Cinzano paused just inside the door to the soda distribution center that shielded half his cocaine empire. The warehouse was quiet, the massive garage doors to the parking lot closed and the forklifts idle. High, cellophane-encased pallets crowded the building, and Vittorio knew he looked out of place there in his expensive navy suit and silk tie, handmade Italian shoes, and cashmere-lined coat. But he always dressed according to his status and position and was conscious of his dark-eyed handsome looks when he chose his garments.

Six feet tall and in his early fifties, he thought he was aging even better than most Italian men. His brown hair was only just tinged with gray and he still felt women's eyes on him despite the recent accumulation of extra pounds around the middle, a consequence of his fondness for pasta. The only flaw in his classic profile was his crooked nose. Vittorio had occasionally contemplated plastic surgery so he could look like a mature movie star, but when he saw his nose he also saw his father and his heritage, and that was something he would never trade away for vanity.

He swung his gaze slowly past the loading dock at his end of the warehouse to the glass-fronted office virtually out of sight at the rear. He knew the traitor he had come to see was watching him on the security cameras, so he lingered a moment where he was, enjoying a small measure of satisfaction. He knew exactly how much he was making the man sweat.

He had been here only twice before, both times late at night when there'd been nothing in the building that could compromise him.

However, there was plenty to incriminate him in the surrounding pallets today, and he'd also come in broad daylight. But he judged it worth the risk. This was personal. Deeply personal. He had just confirmed that someone in his inner circle had betrayed him.

Aldo Martinelli had been a nobody, a low-level associate, until he had the good fortune to catch the eye of Vittorio's baby sister, Marie. Their marriage had been his way up the ladder, for family was everything to Vittorio. It had gotten Martinelli the esteemed position of *caporegime* and the cushy job of overseeing deliveries at the warehouse. Vittorio had even looked the other way when he learned his brother-in-law had taken a mistress, but only because Martinelli had been discreet about it.

Unfortunately Aldo had gotten greedy. Not content with the percentage Vittorio allowed him, he had upped the street price of their coke on his own and was pocketing the extra. It hadn't taken long for some of the customers to start complaining.

Vittorio had paid a surprise visit to the Martinelli home that morning to confirm his suspicions, and it had been a snap to do so. There was a Jaguar in the driveway, a massive new high-definition TV in the living room, and Marie had prattled on and on about the Florida condo they were about to close on. Martinelli had evidently been skimming for quite some time.

Vittorio had not let on to his sister that anything was out of the ordinary. But he knew she might just call her husband for some reason and mention the visit. So Vittorio had come to the warehouse straightaway, to give his brother-in-law an opportunity to own up to what he had done. He wanted to believe, for Marie's sake, that his *caporegime* could grow some balls and accept responsibility like a man. But he knew that the fat fuck he'd come to see was the type to run, or worse—seek protection in the wrong places—if he learned he'd been discovered.

Vittorio did not allow his face to convey any of his rage. Nor his voice. "See we're not interrupted," he instructed his driver.

The guy, one of two dozen goons who worked for him and who all looked uncannily alike, exited to stand watch outside. His bodyguard, another of the same, followed Vittorio toward the rear office.

Martinelli met them halfway there and greeted Vittorio with the customary embrace and kisses that bespoke their family connection and shared Italian heritage. Vittorio allowed it, then stood back, silently studying the man he had trusted enough to appoint as his captain. He gave nothing away in his posture or blank expression.

Martinelli had the same olive complexion as his boss, but the similarity ended there. Nearly a head shorter, he was balding and heavyset and had a vaguely porcine face with beady black eyes set too close together and an upturned pug nose with oversized nostrils. He was dressed in brown trousers and a tan shirt, the sleeves rolled up and the buttons stretched too tight. The clothes were appropriate, nice but not too extravagant. But Martinelli had gotten sloppy about the details and Cinzano never missed the details, like the pricey watch and the quality of the polished wingtips.

"Hey, Vittorio." Martinelli hailed him with false cheer, obviously trying not to show his nerves. He had a faint growth of beard, like he couldn't be bothered to shave the last day or two. "Didn't expect to see you today."

To his credit, he was trying not to let on that he knew he was in trouble, but the slight twitch in his left eye gave him away. That, and the sweat that was beginning to pour out of him. Vittorio had arranged for him to get a call earlier telling him to anticipate a meeting, but he would have expected it to be routine business with one of Cinzano's men. As soon as he saw Vittorio, he had to know he'd been discovered skimming some of the cut.

"We need a sit-down," Vittorio said. He glanced at the pallets around them, surveying the enormity of places where bugs might have been planted. It wasn't lost on Martinelli.

"The office?" he extended a palm in that direction. He had small hands, pudgy like the rest of him, and Vittorio was gratified to see that no matter how hard he tried, the traitorous *capo* couldn't hold the hand steady.

Vittorio led the way and his bodyguard waited for Martinelli to follow before bringing up the rear. They entered the office but Vittorio remained standing, ignoring the comfy couch along one wall and the large oak desk with Martinelli's leather chair on one side and two plush and inviting guest chairs on the other.

Martinelli turned on the radio and set it high enough to obscure any conversation. He was really sweating now. The dome of his head shone with it. He pulled out a handkerchief and quickly swiped at his face and forehead.

Still Vittorio remained silent. Watching. Waiting. Patient. Inscrutable. And intimidating as hell.

Martinelli moved behind his desk and gestured toward the couch. "Please, make yourself comfortable. Something to drink? I got some great old Scotch."

Evidently he thought there might be a small chance that if he acted all business as normal, his brother-in-law might remember they were family. Vittorio didn't move.

Martinelli's shaking became more noticeable, and there was a quaver to his voice now too. He was rapidly unraveling. "How are Nicki and the twins?"

"Fine." The clipped response cut short any further inquiry about family.

Vittorio remained outwardly impassive, glancing about the office, in no hurry to address what he'd come for. He was getting off on watching Martinelli talk himself into a hole. He loved this part of the life he led. Exacting his brand of justice. Setting an example. His sister was better off without this turd anyway.

Martinelli wasn't about to stop talking. It was better than the alternative. "Hey, how about something to eat? I...I can send Joyce out for something. Great Italian place down the block."

Vittorio allowed the blasé demeanor to vanish, making direct eye contact that pinned Martinelli in place. "I just lost my appetite. Do you know why?"

Sweat rolled down into Martinelli's eyes, making him blink. He wiped at his face with the handkerchief again and seemed to be having trouble breathing. Desperation flashed in his eyes, and he looked around, seeking an escape. It told Vittorio all he needed to know. He'd given Aldo a chance. He owed Marie that much. But he had to protect himself at all costs.

Vittorio made a subtle movement of his head, and his bodyguard moved between Martinelli and the door. The bodyguard, who seemed not the slightest bit interested in what was happening, towered over Martinelli and was muscle everywhere that the smaller man was fat.

"Sit down, Aldo." The abrupt command contained the first hint of

Vittorio's growing impatience, and his disappointment that Martinelli wasn't going to confess his misdeeds unless pressured.

Martinelli sank into the chair and began rearranging the stuff on his desk, obsessively tidying the papers into piles while avoiding eye contact. "I should call home. Marie has been asking me to invite you and Nicki over for dinner," he said, procrastinating.

Vittorio held his temper. "What do you need to tell me, Aldo?"

❖

"What the hell are they saying?" Skip Topping was standing almost on top of O'Rourke, trying to hear any sound that might be escaping the agent's earphones.

"Can't hear squat," O'Rourke griped. "They've turned on the damn radio. We should have broken it when we planted the bug."

"Yeah, like that wouldn't have been obvious," Trelaine commented from the front, plenty loud enough for the Washington boys to hear.

"I wasn't serious, asshole," O'Rourke shot back, frustrated by his inability to catch any of the conversation going on in the soda warehouse.

Aggravated, Topping said, "So we don't even know if it's him for sure."

"It's him," Trelaine insisted. "And something major is happening if he's paying a visit in the middle of the day."

❖

Claudia returned to the travel agency with their lunch, her face brick red from the cold. "Brrr. That's my last time going for lunch until April, at least," she vowed.

While she peeled off her winter outerwear, Blayne unpacked the sack of food, frowning when the contents yielded only three Styrofoam containers, plastic utensils, and napkins. "Forget something?"

Claudia gave her a questioning look. "Did I?"

"Drinks? You know the fridge is empty."

"Oh shit, that's right. Well, I'm sorry, but I'm not risking life and limb on those streets again. And besides, the food would be stone cold by the time I got back."

Blayne grinned conspiratorially. "There is another option."

"You're not," Claudia advised, but she knew damn well Blayne wasn't about to listen. She liked being naughty way too much. "Joyce will stop you."

"Yeah, what's up with that, anyway?" Blayne lowered her voice as though Joyce might overhear them. "I like Joyce and all, don't get me wrong. But she acts like this self-appointed watchdog. We used to go back there and help ourselves all the time when Pete was running the day shift."

"It *is* odd," Claudia agreed. "She sure flew off the handle the last time she found out you'd snuck a few cans."

"Yeah, I mean, so what? Who's going to notice?" Blayne shrugged. "Maybe she's in menopause or something."

"Well, it's pretty obvious she's dating that Aldo guy. He's in her office all the time. And I know she goes over there too." Claudia made a face like she'd smelled something repugnant. "You don't think she's worried one of us would be interested in him, do you? I mean, gross!"

"Can't be that." Blayne winced. "He gives me the creeps."

"Me too. But he does send business our way."

"Well, yes, there is that, I guess." Blayne stood and rubbed her hands together, anxious to embark on her soda-snatching adventure. "I'm going before the food gets any colder."

"You know, one of these days that cute little larcenous side of yours is going to get you into some real trouble."

"Today is not that day," Blayne declared confidently. "And I'm sure those guys don't give a damn. There's always an open pallet of soda out there. I'll just duck in, then pick up Joyce on the way back."

"I wish you wouldn't." Claudia knew her protestations were pointless. She wasn't sure what was behind Blayne's penchant for petty theft; she'd even tempted the Fates stealing little stuff like pens and paperclips in college. It was always something trivial, but her luck at escaping repercussions couldn't hold out forever. "Be careful."

Blayne gave her worried friend a thumbs-up and headed toward the rear hallway. She edged slowly and quietly as far as Joyce's open doorway and snuck a quick peek inside. A large travel poster hung under glass on the opposite wall, and the glass reflected the inside of the office like a mirror. Blayne could see Joyce faxing something, her back to the doorway.

Taking advantage, she slipped past and continued on beyond the lounge and restrooms to the big steel door that led to the soda warehouse. After easing it open a few inches, she paused momentarily to listen and caught the faint sound of a radio playing. That was all. *Perfect.*

A moment later, she was inside, heading for a vantage point she knew of, where she could see inside the glass walls of the office. She hurried toward it, keeping low and moving between the pallets. If anyone was about, she wanted to make sure they were occupied and wouldn't notice her.

The office walls didn't extend as far as the high warehouse ceiling, so the sound of the radio got louder as she drew closer. She started hearing something else too. Voices.

❖

Fear unlike any he had ever known pulsed through Aldo Martinelli. Every nerve ending was jagged and raw. He wanted to run *so bad*. His eyes went left, then right. But before he could move, the bodyguard shifted to stand directly at his side, cutting off any hope of escape.

He took a deep breath. *Think.* His mind raced. He had to offer an explanation. Any explanation. Anything to stall for time. Whatever excuse he could offer, he would offer. Because he knew as soon as he stopped talking, he was a dead man.

"Okay. So…okay," he stammered. "It's like this. I have to charge more to cover some extra costs that came up unexpected." It was not an acceptable explanation, but he wasn't in the big leagues in thinking on his feet.

"Since when do you make those decisions yourself?" Cinzano asked.

"I didn't think I needed to get it cleared with you," Aldo lied, glancing up at his boss. "I did it for *us*, for all of us."

Cinzano smiled as though he believed it, even accepted it perhaps, and Aldo almost relaxed a little. A glimmer of hope skittered up his spine. *Maybe*, he thought. *Maybe he doesn't know how long it's been going on.*

"The money isn't in yet," he said, looking away again. Perhaps his brother-in-law might give him a pass, let him make amends, for the sake of family. "Of course, when it is, I'll send a man right over."

The only sound for a long minute was the radio. Cinzano waited until Aldo looked at him before he spoke again. "So then how do you explain the new Jaguar?"

Aldo began to hyperventilate. All hope was gone.

"And I understand you are closing on some real estate in Florida," Cinzano continued.

Aldo tried to stand up but the bodyguard pushed him back down. He couldn't breathe. Couldn't swallow. He knew he was about to die. "Please, boss." His voice broke. "Vittorio. Please. I did it for Marie. Give me another chance." He hated sounding weak and pleading, but he'd do anything to stop what was coming.

Cinzano held a gloved hand out toward his bodyguard, and the bodyguard reached under his jacket and handed a 9mm Glock to him. Cinzano placed the gun on the desk in front of Aldo, facing him.

"God forgives. But I am not God. Do the honorable thing, Aldo."

❖

From twenty feet away, hidden behind a pallet, Blayne watched the unfolding drama through the office window, unable to move. Her heart pounded. Her body was energized and poised for flight. She wanted desperately to escape this madness, but fear instinctively froze her into motionless silence so she wouldn't draw attention to herself. Transfixed, her subconscious registering every detail of what she'd stumbled into, she watched.

The fat man sitting behind the desk stared at the gun, then reached for it as though hypnotized. But his hand stopped short and he looked up. Blayne could just make out the words. "You know I can't do this. Please. We're family."

The man in the suit showed no emotion, but Blayne could have sworn there was a certain expectation in his eyes when he looked from the fat guy to the gun and then back again.

Everything seemed surreal. She could not believe what she was seeing when the frightened guy behind the desk picked up the gun. He seemed to weigh it in his hand and study it, like he was also thinking about his choices. Everything about his body language said there was no way out. No more options.

And nothing left to lose.

He pointed the gun unsteadily at the guy in charge. "Just let me leave, boss. Let me go home." They were only a few feet apart, the width of the desk and a bit more.

To Blayne's astonishment the tall, elegantly dressed boss shook his head and took a step toward the desk, taunting his subordinate. Blayne automatically braced herself for an explosion as the fat guy pulled the trigger.

Click.

Click.

Click.

He rose, wide-eyed in shock. His lips started moving but no sound came out.

The boss looked disgusted. Blayne thought she glimpsed a faint nod to the muscle-bound hulk she assumed must be his bodyguard, but nothing was said. Everything played out before she could really understand what was happening.

The bodyguard moved faster than Blayne would have thought possible for such a big man. He pulled out a gun—it looked abnormally long because of the silencer on the end—put it against the fat guy's head, and fired, all in the space of a second or two. The only noise was a muffled *pop* as the bullet made a neat hole in the victim's right temple, then blew out the left side of his head.

Brain matter splattered against the glass and the dead man fell forward onto the desk. Blood poured out, soaking the neat piles of paperwork all around him.

The bodyguard unscrewed the silencer and stuck it into his pocket, then slipped the murder weapon into a shoulder holster.

The horror of the scene stripped away the caution that had paralyzed Blayne up to that moment, and her instinct for self-preservation took over. She turned to flee, but the flash of movement betrayed her.

"A woman! There!" a voice barked before she had traveled three steps.

A gun fired.

❖

"Jesus! Somebody's shooting! Move! Move!" O'Rourke bellowed as he ripped off his earphones.

"Call for backup," Skip yelled, scrambling out the back of the surveillance truck.

Trelaine got the vehicle started and stomped on the accelerator. Skip was already positioned outside the side fire exit when the van fishtailed on the ice in the parking lot in front of him. Dombrowski was advancing through the front door of the travel agency.

Their surveillance map showed an internal access to the soda warehouse at the rear of the building. They had to take the risk that Cinzano would choose to escape via the parking lot rather than wait around for a shootout once the FBI presence was announced.

Chapter Three

The first shot had shattered the glass window of the office. The noise was jarring, deafening. The second bullet splintered the edge of the pallet just behind Blayne and sent a spray of wood skittering across the polished floor. Panic gripped her and her next step faltered badly. *Jesus God. Oh fuck. Oh fuck.* She started to fall but caught herself just as the third bullet roared by right where her head would have been had she stayed on course. When the bullet buried itself in a pallet four feet away, an explosion of white powder dusted Blayne as she regained her footing and stumbled by.

Her blood buzzed loudly in her ears and her heart pounded against the walls of her chest, but she became aware that the running footsteps she could hear behind her were retreating, not advancing. The realization wasn't enough to make her slow her steps, however. She didn't dare believe that she was truly out of danger.

She was nearly to the connecting door when it burst open with a crash and a massive brute of a man in a dark blue suit came rushing in, gun drawn. As soon as he spotted her, he pointed the gun at her head. She stopped in her tracks, light-headed with adrenaline and certain her death was at hand. *No wonder they weren't chasing me. They knew he would get me.* The man quickly scanned the area around them.

It seemed to take forever for him to say the words that allowed her to breathe again. "FBI! Face down, on the ground!"

"Yes, okay." Relief poured through her as she dropped to her knees. "Two men are in here and they have guns," she volunteered in a low voice as she got down on the ground. "They...they killed a man in the office."

"That's enough. Quiet now," Dombrowski said. "Hands behind your back."

She did as he ordered. The concrete was cold against her cheek as she lay flat and put her hands behind her back. When he started to put handcuffs on her, Blayne's mind and gut recoiled at the prospect of being restrained. She was the victim here.

"Hey! I *saw* it," she informed him. "They tried to kill me. I wasn't *in* on it."

"Quiet," Dombrowski repeated, in a voice that demanded compliance. "Don't move." He fastened the cuffs and then headed toward the office, gun at the ready.

Craning, Blayne saw the boss and his bodyguard nearly run headlong into another Italian who'd come running at the sound of shots. The three of them burst through the door to the parking lot and came to a dead halt.

Almost immediately, Blayne heard someone shout, "FBI. Drop your weapons." And from the silence that ensued she guessed the murderer and the man giving the orders had been arrested.

As her adrenaline rush faded, she felt the cold permeate her body from the concrete beneath her and took deep breaths, trying to clear her head and settle her nerves.

It took a couple of minutes for her monstrous captor to return. "We got them," he volunteered. He helped Blayne to her feet but kept the handcuffs on her.

The connecting door to the agency opened and Joyce and Claudia came in, followed by another FBI agent with a walrus mustache like something from a Wild West photo. Both women looked anxious and worried, but Claudia's face visibly relaxed when she spotted Blayne. Joyce, however, looked beyond Blayne, toward the blood-splattered office, her anxiety palpable.

The agent with the mustache said, "I'm Special Agent Leslie Topping and my colleague is Special Agent Dombrowski. We are going to need statements from all of you."

"What the hell..." Claudia stared at the handcuffs clamping Blayne's wrists. "What is this!"

"Claud!" Blayne began. "There was—"

Agent Topping cut them both off. "No talking." He took Claudia by the elbow and led her away toward the office, along with Joyce.

Blayne started to follow, but Agent Dombrowski held her back. "We don't want anyone talking to each other just yet." He let the others get well ahead before following with Blayne.

Joyce let out a wail of anguish when she spotted the dead man slumped over his desk through the glass shards that remained of the office window. As it became obvious that half of his head was gone, she gagged.

"Who was this man to you?" Agent Topping kept one hand firmly around Joyce's elbow to prevent her from going into the office.

Joyce sobbed uncontrollably, near hysterics, paying no regard to the agent at all. Her thickly applied mascara and eyeliner left ugly tracks down her cheeks, but she was, for the first time in the years Blayne had known her, totally unmindful of her appearance. "Oh God, Aldo," she wailed, eyes fixed on the widening pool of blood around him. "What the hell did you do?"

Dombrowski steered Blayne away from the others, putting a row of pallets between them as he hustled her past and toward the door at the rear. It did not escape her notice that although she was handcuffed, the agent was treating her with kid gloves, his grip on her arm surprisingly tender, like a father walking his daughter down the aisle.

They were nearly to the door when she began to hear sirens, lots of sirens, still distant. Dombrowski pushed open the steel door and let Blayne precede him through it.

She was startled to see *him* just outside. The tall Italian boss turned at the sound of the door, and a sadistic smile spread across his face as he looked Blayne in the eyes. He was in handcuffs and another agent was standing close by talking to someone on his cell phone, but Blayne still felt incredibly threatened. She leaned thankfully into the solid wall of Agent Dombrowski as he walked her past the cold-blooded killer.

Just as they drew level, the mobster said so quietly that she barely heard it, "Blayne Keller, right?"

The menace on his face sent a chill through Blayne. She knew that look. It was exactly the look she'd seen a moment before he killed the man in the office. It conveyed an unmistakable message. *You are going to die.*

❖

More than four hours later, the shock and fear generated by the day's events began to give way to annoyance and frustration as Blayne repeated for at least the twentieth time every detail she could recall of what she had witnessed. She was exhausted, both physically and emotionally. She had cooperated fully, answered all of their questions more than once, and was anxious to get out of the police interview room and go home.

The feds had kept the witnesses and wiseguys apart for the few minutes it took for the cavalry to arrive. Several squad cars, crime scene techs, and the medical examiner's van all converged on the soda warehouse within a half hour of the shooting. After a short and slightly heated exchange between the feds and local cops, Blayne had been loaded into one squad car, Claudia and Joyce into another, and the mobsters into two more. They were all driven to the First Division Headquarters of the Chicago PD on South Michigan Avenue.

There Blayne was patted down by a female police officer and placed in a windowless room on a miserably uncomfortable wooden chair. Two police detectives came in, though one did all the talking, and she began to repeat her story over several cups of some of the worst coffee she had ever had.

At long last the detectives announced they were done questioning her for the moment, but before she could relax, they were replaced by Agents Topping and Dombrowski, who asked her to start all over again.

"You've got to be kidding me," she complained, letting her irritation show. "I've done nothing but go over and over this for hours. Look, I'm doing my bit. I'm being the good citizen, but this is getting ridiculous."

"The CPD has jurisdiction over the homicide," Dombrowski explained. "We're handling other aspects of the case. We need you to go through it all again."

And so she did, and she found that in the repeated telling of the details of the murder, she became, each time, a bit more inured to the horrific event. She even began to let go of some of the trepidation she had been feeling since the man involved had said her name. He was in custody, after all, she kept telling herself.

But once the agents were satisfied with her account of the murder, they began questioning her about other matters entirely, things the Chicago cops had not. It was only then that she began to get a clear picture of what had really transpired that day, and how much danger she was now in.

First they asked her about what she knew of the soda warehouse, its employees and customers, and about Joyce's involvement with the dead man. Then they asked her whether she had ever noticed anything unusual or strange about Aldo Martinelli or the people who worked for him, and she told them that he had referred a lot of men to the agency for travel arrangements.

"There is one guy," Blayne volunteered, "who comes in every couple of weeks to pick up tickets he orders online. What's odd is that although the destination is always the same—Miami—the tickets are never in the same name twice. And he always pays in cash."

The two agents glanced at each other and Blayne had a strange sense of foreboding at the pleased look that passed between them.

"We're going to show you some pictures," Topping said. "Have you pick out anyone who looks familiar. You know, someone who may have come into the agency, or perhaps somebody you saw in the parking lot."

"First let's get you something to eat," Dombrowski offered. "And we'll try to find a place to continue this where you'll be more comfortable."

Blayne's heart sank at the news, for it sounded as though she might be tied up here for several more hours of questioning. But at least it was the first time since she'd been brought in that anyone seemed concerned about how she was faring through all of this. "A double cheeseburger and fries," she called out as Dombrowski headed for the door. "And a large coffee. That stuff you've got here is undrinkable."

They got her what she ordered and they found an unused conference room where she could relax on a couch while she looked over the thick books of photographs. During the next two hours, she picked out the Miami ticket client and a handful of other men Aldo had referred to the Balmy Breezes.

The next book they gave her had a photo of the man who'd ordered his bodyguard to shoot Joyce's boyfriend. It was not a mug shot, like most of the others, but a slightly grainy photo that had been taken with a telephoto lens. In it, he was dressed very much like he'd been dressed today, in a tailored suit and expensive overcoat.

"That's him." She didn't touch the photo itself. "The man from today. The one who seemed to be in control of what was going on."

This was greeted with a long pause. "Who is he? And how did he know who I am?"

She'd asked these questions several times already, of the cops and the agents both, always getting the same response—that she was there to answer questions, not ask them.

But this time, the agents exchanged a look of tacit agreement and Dombrowski said, "His name is Vittorio Cinzano. He is a big man in organized crime here. An underboss."

"Organized crime? You mean the Mafia?" Blayne felt so clammy she knew she'd gone white at the news.

Oh shit. She knew next to nothing about the Mafia, only what she had picked up from TV shows like *The Sopranos* and films like *The Godfather*, and the occasional news report. But it was enough to know that she was in a very serious situation here if Cinzano knew her identity, even if he was in custody.

"He probably knows you because he owns the building you work out of," Topping said. "Not on paper, of course. Nothing traceable, because they run a cocaine business out of there. Or did."

Blayne's forehead furrowed in confusion. "That can't be right. Philippe Cluzet owns the travel agency, and at least our half of the building. He has for twenty years or so."

"He *runs* the agency, yes. But he sold out his share of the property to a European consortium nearly a year ago."

Blayne was shocked. And she was certain Claudia didn't know. She would have said something if her dad had sold the building.

"Cinzano is an important guy, and we've got him cold with what you saw." The agent stroked his long ruddy brown mustache with the kind of satisfaction Blayne associated with pompous pseudointellectuals. "He'll be looking at federal charges, including racketeering, as well as whatever the DA comes up with in connection with the homicide. And there'll be the bodyguard's murder trial. So you're going to be the star prosecution witness in at least three trials."

It began to sink in. *She* was going to be the *key witness* in the trial of a Mafia underboss. *Holy shit.* That would put her in a world of danger. Blayne wanted to do the right thing, but at what cost?

"What if I don't agree to testify?" she asked nervously.

Topping answered like he'd been expecting the question. "Then we would bring obstruction of justice charges against you at the very least. And Cinzano's men would be out on the street looking for you, of course."

Her head swam, and that feeling of foreboding rushed back. "He knows who I am," she repeated, more to herself than the agents.

"Yeah," Dombrowski said sympathetically. "You'd last maybe a week."

"That was really pretty sloppy of him," Topping said. "They never make threats like that themselves. He had to be awfully pissed at the way you compromised him. Plus he's got a big ego. He thinks he's untouchable."

"But you got him cold, you said. So he can't get out, right?" Blayne wanted some reassurance from these men that she wasn't in as much danger as she feared. But she knew the answer even before she asked it.

"No, I don't think the judge will grant bail on what we have on him," Topping agreed.

"But we have to be honest and tell you that doesn't mean you're not in a great deal of danger," Dombrowski said. "We're going to have to keep you in protective custody."

"What?" Blayne went rigid. She certainly hadn't considered *that*. The mere words *protective custody* made her feel vaguely claustrophobic. She bristled at the thought of any loss of her independence.

"That doesn't mean you'll be locked up," Dombrowski hastened to add. "It just means you'll have to stay somewhere safe, not your house, and you'll have to be under constant police protection. And you can't go back to the travel agency, at least not for the foreseeable future."

"I can't go home? Can't go back to my job?" This was getting worse by the minute. Her whole life was suddenly in upheaval. Blayne got a bad case of the shakes and suddenly felt like she'd been kicked in the stomach. Without warning, she lost her burger and fries into the nearest wastebasket.

Chapter Four

Dawn would not break over Thessaloniki for another two hours, but Alexi Nikolos was already up and pacing on her balcony in the chill morning, restless, despite the fact that Greece's most popular female singer was just inside, asleep in her bed.

It wasn't that their evening together hadn't been enjoyable, though Alexi had not gone out looking for companionship. Dimitra Lambros had been amusing, fun, and extremely responsive beneath her, just the way she liked, but then again Alexi had always been partial to the passionate women of her homeland. The mistake she'd made was in bringing her home to her villa, because now she had to find a suitable way to get her to leave.

Alexi rarely sought out someone for sex. She never had to. Wherever she went, men hit on her and beautiful women seemed to want to make themselves available to her. Gay or straight, it didn't seem to matter. So although she rarely slept with the same woman twice, there was never a lack of bed partners.

Her appearance was what first drew them in. Although not a large woman, only 5'6" and slight of build, Alexi knew how to make the most of her commanding presence. She was confident, smart, and sexy. And really more handsome than beautiful, though she was certainly that too. She had a rather androgynous body, with a small ass and few curves to speak of save for her well-shaped but not overly large breasts. Her shoulders, arms, and legs were tautly muscled from regular workouts at home, and the flat plane of her stomach always elicited sighs of envy from the women she slept with.

But while her body might tread the sometimes thin line between masculine and feminine, her face was all woman. She had the bronzed complexion of her Mediterranean homeland and classic features. A strong jaw beneath a straight nose and high cheekbones. Full, expressive eyebrows, long, dark lashes, and a pronounced, dramatic widow's peak. Her medium brown hair, cut in loose waves, hung below her shoulders. Her lips, full and rosy red, formed a perfect Cupid's bow. Kissable lips, most women said.

Alexi was aware of her beauty from any angle, but the feature that always drew the most compliments could only be admired face-to-face. Her eyes were the deep rich blue of the Aegean, a gift from her maternal grandmother. Alexi enjoyed gazing into them herself. Because of the resemblance, they brought back happy childhood memories.

The women she chose to keep company with were drawn in by her looks and then fascinated by her charm and the polite attention she gave to everyone as a matter of course, a product of her formal upbringing and an ingrained part of her personality. They were one-night stands, but she made sure they never felt as though they were. First she would romance them in a way that few people did these days, listening attentively and laughing at their jokes as they shared a candlelit dinner and dancing. She would pay them compliments and treat them like queens, and when she took them to bed, the entirety of her attention was on their pleasure and not on her own. So she always left them wanting more and never knowing that no matter how magical the evening might have seemed, Alexi had no feelings at all for any of them. Sexual encounters were simply one way for her to relieve the boredom that had taken over her life.

Dawn was as long as she could bear to wait before having her home to herself once more, so she went about evicting her guest. Sitting on the edge of the bed, she gently caressed Dimitra's back until she roused.

"Good morning," she said in Greek: *Kalimera.* The tone of her voice and the expression on her face could easily have been mistaken for affection, and often was. "I've brought you some coffee." She set a mug on the bedside table.

"Why don't you come back to bed, and we can think about coffee later?" The singer threw back the covers, exposing her full breasts, curvaceous hips, and the dark triangle of hair at the apex of her thighs.

She parted her legs and ran her hand invitingly up her thigh to the tender, swollen areas still damp from Alexi's expertise the night before.

"I would love to," Alexi responded gently. "But I'm afraid I have to be somewhere." She stood and took a few paces away to forestall any further efforts to seduce her.

"Will you call me?" Dimitra asked, taking the hint and getting up to dress.

"We'll see."

Alexi made sure their good-bye was pleasant but noncommittal. She was honest in her recreational dealings with women. No false promises meant no hurt feelings.

Last night's distraction had scarcely departed before Alexi's phone rang. It was unusual for her to get calls this early, unless it was from overseas. *Probably some American who cannot tell time*, she surmised, another unworthy ne'er-do-well seeking money from the philanthropic foundation she ran. So she answered in Greek instead of English, just to annoy them.

"*Parakalo.*"

There was a long silence on the other end before a deep male voice asked, "Alexi? Is that you?"

Her hand tightened around the telephone. She recognized the caller; she had a talent for accents and languages, speaking five herself. But she didn't answer immediately, for it conjured up painful memories.

When he repeated her name, she finally replied, "Theo. To what do I owe the pleasure?"

Her polite tone did not entirely mask the sarcasm she felt, but Theodore Lang was not as adept at picking up nuances as she was and missed it. The last time she had seen her former associate, they'd both been stationed in Chicago. Unless he had been relocated, that meant it was now after midnight where he was.

"You're a difficult woman to track down," he said. "And this is a business call I didn't want to make at the office."

She was intrigued. "Business call?"

"Yes. How would you feel about taking on an assignment?"

"Who's asking?" she replied.

"You'd be reporting to me. Paul was bumped back to inspector last month. I've taken over the Chicago office."

"Why ask me?" She made her tone perfunctory. She didn't want

Theo thinking she would just come running the moment the welcome mat was out.

"Someone from the Joint Task Force on Organized Crime is leaking information to the mob."

He had to know this would push her buttons. Alexi contemplated the prospect of returning to witness protection. It did have a certain appeal, despite the way things had ended. WITSEC was the one thing she had done that she felt really suited her, and it had certainly never been boring. Yet it was also where she'd made the worst mistake of her life.

"And why should this appeal to me?" she asked.

"Because we just lost one witness and another was attacked in a safe house."

A breath hissed from deep in her throat. "Any ideas so far?"

"I think it's one of the FBI guys, and not someone from this office, but I can't eliminate anyone at this point." He tried flattery. "D.C. wants the best and I want someone I can trust. That's why I'm talking to you."

"There is something else. Don't be coy with me, Theo."

He hesitated, but only for a split second. "It involves the Salvatore family."

They both lapsed into silence as she digested this information. She walked to the balcony and stared out at the clear blue waters of the Aegean, already missing her beloved Greece.

"When do you want me?"

❖

No way. No fucking way.

Blayne stared into the mirror, unable to recognize herself. Her hair was dyed black and cut very short in a spiky hairstyle she despised. She had a realistic-looking tribal tattoo on her right bicep and a scorpion tattoo on her neck. Attached to her lower lip were two small rings that looked like authentic piercings, and there was a slightly larger one in her right eyebrow that pinched uncomfortably.

Her eyes had been made up in thick black goth makeup, and she had ruby red lips. *I'm a punk raccoon looking for love.*

The woman who had taken two hours to dye her hair and make her up had not let Blayne near a mirror until the work was done and she'd packed up her makeup kit and fled. Now Blayne knew why. It was all she could do not to wash it all away so she could find herself again beneath the garish circus paint.

There was absolutely *no* way she was putting on the clothes. What the hell were they thinking? Punk. Goth. Grunge. *Make up your mind already. And all of it is* so *90s.*

She said aloud to herself, "Guess I should have expected this, letting total strangers decide how I'm going to look."

It wasn't that she considered herself fashion conscious by any means, but no one could look good in what they'd given her to complete her disguise. Hugely baggy jeans, an obscenely studded military-type jacket, clunky Doc Martens boots, and an oversized black T-shirt that read *Some Days It's Not Worth Chewing Through the Restraints*. The FBI agent who picked that one out must have had a good laugh. She wondered if it was Topping. The man seemed to have no sense of humor at all. She liked Dombrowski much better and wished he were still with her. At least he had let her in on what was happening some of the time.

At the outset of this nightmare, the day she'd witnessed the murder, she'd been allowed to make a quick trip home under the protection of three FBI agents. Under instructions to collect any personal belongings that were important to her, she'd packed two bags with clothes, toiletries, photographs, papers, and whatever else she thought she might need or want. She'd put her Fiji fund into a large envelope and stuffed it into the back pocket of her jeans.

For the next three days, she'd stayed in a not-too-shabby hotel suite on the outskirts of Chicago, under the watchful eye of a dour female special agent named Monica Wright. Another agent was always stationed outside, in a car or van, and Blayne was not allowed to leave or contact anyone, even Claudia.

No one would tell her what was going on, or whether Claudia was also under protection. Blayne had hated the restrictions and complete disintegration of every routine and sense of normalcy in her life, and showed her irritation in flashes of Irish temper.

The arrangement hadn't lasted long. On her third boring evening in front of the television, Dombrowski had showed up and ordered her to get changed and pack all her things as quickly as possible. When

Blayne quarreled and demanded to know what was going on, he looked her in the eyes and said in the gentle way one would break the news to a close friend or relative, "Joyce Houseman has been murdered."

Blayne still couldn't believe it. Joyce's body had been found on a street near her apartment. She'd been shot. No witnesses. Worse still, Philippe and Claudia Cluzet hadn't been seen in a couple of days.

"You think something bad has happened to them, don't you?" Blayne had asked, thinking, *No! Not Claudia.* There was a knot in her chest that made it hard to breathe. She couldn't imagine life without her best friend, and Philippe had become like a second father to her. They were the only family she had.

Dombrowski had reassured her that they were following up every angle and they would find Claudia and Philippe. Meantime, she had to get to a more secure location right away. So Blayne had relented, and five minutes later she was packed and they were ready to go.

When they got down to the lobby, the desk clerk was checking in a middle-aged couple with two cranky kids in tow, and there were a few other guests about, but nothing had appeared out of place. A tired businessman with an open briefcase in his lap chatted at one of the pay phones. A couple of Hispanic men in their sixties bickered good-naturedly over a game of chess. A young couple preoccupied with kissing each other headed out the front door to catch a cab. No one paid the three of them any attention, and they set off toward the side door to the parking lot, walking at a nice steady clip but not hurried, nothing that would draw undue attention to them.

There were no windows on that side of the building, so once they reached the big metal fire door, Wright held Blayne back until Dombrowski could confirm they were clear to exit. Everything had seemed fine. Only it wasn't.

Blayne still couldn't remember the exact sequence of events. One moment they were crossing the well-lit parking lot, the next Dombrowski's head snapped around and he alerted Wright to two teenagers rounding the corner of the building.

The word that sprang to mind was *punks*. They wore baggy jeans and oversized sweatshirts, the hoods partially obscuring their faces. They were everywhere in Chicago these days—nameless young men who relied on petty crimes to pay for whatever they were injecting, smoking, or inhaling. That was all that mattered to them. How to finance the next fix.

Dombrowski had parked the dark SUV in the spot nearest the door, and they quickened their pace toward it. The punks exchanged a couple of quick words and Blayne became aware that they were staring intently at her. As if they recognized her. Or thought they did.

"Get her in the car! Now!" Dombrowski reached for his gun as the punks reached for theirs.

Wright had the door half open when the first shots rang out. Shielding Blayne's body with her own, she pushed her forward, knocking the wind out of her, which only heightened Blayne's sense of helplessness. Dombrowski was returning fire and got one of the shooters in the head just as the kid was about to pull the trigger. He hit the other in the chest, but not before the teenager had fired a round himself.

That bullet grazed Wright's shoulder and shattered the tinted window beyond, showering Blayne with shards of glass. None of this deterred Wright from covering Blayne with her body and ignoring her protests. Pinned by the agent's weight and panicking over the attack, Blayne had struggled until Wright barked, "Stop it!"

The authority in her voice stunned Blayne into submission. The close call had scared the shit out of her, and all she could feel was the rush of fear and adrenaline. After Wright moved off her, she'd had to look herself over to be satisfied she hadn't been hit. She couldn't stop trembling.

"You saved my life," she'd stammered. "Thanks."

"That's what I get paid for," the agent replied drolly before gracing Blayne with her first real smile in the three days of their acquaintance.

They both stared at the blossoming bloodstain on Wright's left shoulder.

"Not too bad," Wright reported of the two-inch tear the bullet had made in her flesh.

Blayne could hear sirens in the distance, and the local cops soon showed up to secure the scene. A half hour later, ensconced in a replacement sedan, she was driven away from the downtown headquarters of the FBI's Chicago division and soon found herself on the ramp to Interstate 55, heading southwest. With her was a new female agent who'd been called in to replace the wounded Wright. And because Dombrowski had discharged his weapon in the line of duty, he was also off the case. Agent Skip Topping was accompanying Blayne.

Five hours later, just as the sun was coming up, they'd arrived at Scott Air Force Base and Blayne got to see her lovely new home, a blandly furnished housing unit in an isolated section of the base. Her seclusion was much the same as it had been at the hotel, but with significantly more Spartan accommodations and tighter security. She had three rooms, no view, and plenty of time to think about how fucked up her life was.

She hadn't been able to sleep properly since.

At nine the morning after her arrival, a distinguished-looking gentleman in a suit the color of charcoal had arrived at her door and displayed his badge and credentials. His name was Larry Elkins and he was with the U.S. Marshals Service. He was polite, and friendly, and it was immediately apparent that he'd done this many times before.

They settled themselves on a battered couch with a loud avocado-colored print dating from the 1970s, and Blayne looked him in the eyes. "I hope you're going to give me some answers about what's going on."

"Yes, I'm here to discuss what's next for you," he answered helpfully. "But I'd like to ask you a few questions about the events of the last few days first, if you don't mind. I've been briefed by Special Agent Topping."

"You're with the Marshals Service?" Blayne had heard of it, but mostly in connection with the increase in air security following the 9-11 terrorist attacks. The government was putting more undercover U.S. marshals aboard aircraft to protect against future attacks. She couldn't imagine what that had to do with her, and why this man had to hear her story all over again.

"Yes, ma'am. I'm an inspector with the WITSEC division."

He was in his forties, she guessed, by the hint of gray at his temples, though he kept his body in superb condition with regular trips to the gym. Puzzled, she asked, "WITSEC?"

"It stands for Witness Security. You've perhaps heard of it as the Witness Protection Program?"

"Oh, right, yes. I've heard of that."

"WITSEC was founded to protect witnesses in major crimes from intimidation before they testify, and also from retaliation after the trial is over," he explained. "The FBI called us in on your case. Obviously, you are a likely candidate. But before I make any recommendations about bringing you into the program, we need to talk."

The Witness Protection Program? *Holy fucking shit. No fucking way.* "Isn't that where you get a new identity and relocated and all of that?" Blayne asked. "I don't need that, do I?" The thought that she might have to start all over again somewhere, like she had before…but this time, all alone. It was depressing beyond words.

"That's what I'm here to determine," he said. "Clearly, you are at high risk of further attempts on your life. You'd be much safer far away from here until the trials. And regardless of the verdicts, probably safer afterward if you are elsewhere as well."

The ensuing three-hour interview had covered not only the events of the recent past but also, it seemed, the entirety of Blayne's life up to that point. Inspector Elkins said he would recommend quick approval of her acceptance into the WITSEC program. The final determination, he told her, was up to the U.S. Attorney General, but he anticipated no problems with the request and said it would then be up to her to decide whether to accept the government's offer of protection.

If she did, she would be taken to a secure WITSEC facility for several days of orientation and then relocated to a new state with a new identity in exchange for a sworn statement agreeing to testify.

"WITSEC has helped roughly eight thousand witnesses and ten thousand family members relocate under new identities," he said. "And not one participant in the program who has followed our security guidelines has ever been harmed while under our active protection."

The careful wording of his declaration suggested that those who *didn't* follow the program's rules might have met a different fate, but he volunteered no details.

"The final decision is up to you. It's not an easy one, because one of the conditions of the program is that you cut all ties with your friends and acquaintances. That's the hardest part for most of our witnesses. But frankly, Miss Keller, I don't think you have much choice if you want to stay alive."

Blayne thought about his words again as she opened the wallet they had bought her and looked at her new driver's license, social security card, and the $500 they'd given her for incidentals. Everything else would be handled once she got there—money, a place to live, a new job. Wherever *there* was.

Cut all ties with friends. She closed her eyes and Claudia's face returned in a kaleidoscope of memories. Cutting up in college. Getting dressed to the nines for a date. Consoling her heartbreak. Flirting with her at work. Claudia was the only friend who mattered, anyway. *Where are you, Claud? I need you. You can't be dead.*

Did it matter whether she stayed or left, without Claudia? Was Inspector Elkins right? *Did* she have a choice?

Blayne picked up the hideous T-shirt and held it up against her tank top. It was big enough for two of her, and fell to well below her ass.

There was a knock at the door. When she opened it, Special Agent Topping stared at her a long moment, taking in her new persona. He nodded approvingly at the T-shirt in her hands, a wry grin on his face. A few feet away, the new female agent was trying her damndest not to laugh. *Yup. Topping did the shopping.*

"I'm not wearing this," Blayne said, waving the shirt. "Or the pants. I can't keep them up. I look fucking ridiculous."

"You look nothing at all like yourself, which is exactly what we're going for," Topping said patiently from across the threshold. "We'll wait. You have five minutes." He pulled the door shut again before she could protest.

Blayne smoldered a minute, flipping him a finger that he failed to appreciate before stalking off to change.

I hate this. I hate this. I just fucking hate this, she muttered to herself as she threaded a belt through the oversized pants. She stuck her Fiji fund into one of the many pockets and her new wallet in another.

Then she donned her new studded military jacket and took another reluctant look in the mirror. *A punk raccoon looking for love, wearing an army tent that once belonged to Liberace.* She sighed. She'd always thought she was a pretty plain Jane when it came right down to it. Oh yeah, there were days when she dressed up nice and put on some makeup. That got a few compliments, but all in all, she was average, she'd decided. And right now, this getup was so patently ridiculous she craved average. *I can never look in a mirror again.*

She went to the door and opened it. The agents were poised just outside.

"Ready to go, Elizabeth?" Topping asked.

She glared at him and bit back a response.

The former Blayne Keller, now Elizabeth Weaver, picked up a duffle bag containing all her earthly possessions, took a deep breath, and stepped into her new life.

Chapter Five

Thirty-six miles west-northwest of Scott Air Force Base, Alexi Nikolos sat leafing through a magazine in the first class lounge at the Lambert–St. Louis International Airport, killing time. She wore a tailored red silk blouse under a black leather coat that fell to mid-thigh, and tight black trousers slung low over her narrow hips. The trousers flared to accommodate the leather boots beneath.

Three men and two women had hit on her on the flight from Greece to Chicago, and another man and one very cute flight attendant on the short hop from Chicago to Saint Louis. *Shame about that one.* She'd been back in the U.S. barely two days, just long enough for her briefing from Theo, done in secrecy at his home. She was still a bit jet-lagged, though she normally functioned quite well on only a few hours of sleep.

She checked her watch. It was just after ten a.m. *They should be leaving the base now, and arriving in forty minutes or so.* That would give her a half hour to study Special Agent Skip Topping before they got on the plane.

Theo suspected that it was one of the three D.C.-based FBI special agents on loan to Chicago—either Topping, Dombrowski, or O'Rourke—who was behind the leaks to the mob. They were working the case with WITSEC as part of a Joint Task Force on Organized Crime and had access to the information that had been compromised.

Thirty minutes at the gate and then two and a half hours on the plane should be enough time to gauge something about Topping, she figured. She was also curious about what her observations would tell her about the witness he was protecting, Blayne Keller, a.k.a. Elizabeth Weaver. She had a dossier on the woman and one on Topping, compliments of

Theo. Both files were in the leather satchel at her feet, with much of the information already committed to memory.

Topping was supposed to deliver Blayne to the U.S. Marshals Denver District Offices as soon as they landed. If there was any threat to Blayne en route, or any sign that he was the dirty one, Alexi would intercede.

It was time to take up a position at their departure gate. The lounge had been cozy, but she needed to clear her gun with the airline so she could carry it on board with her, and even for a U.S. marshal, that always took a few minutes these days. Besides, the passengers for Mid-Knight Airlines Flight 23 to Denver would be starting to check in soon and she wanted to study each one as they arrived.

❖

Once they reached the *Only Ticketed Passengers Beyond This Point* security checkpoint, Agent Wright's replacement left and Blayne was stuck with Topping. The concourse was jammed with people hurrying to their flights, stopping for a bite of lunch, or shopping at one of the vendors for a souvenir St. Louis Gateway Arch or paperback to read on the plane.

"There are so many people," she remarked shakily as they neared their departure gate. "It doesn't seem safe. Isn't there a better way to get me there? Less public?"

Topping rarely answered any of her questions, so she was a bit surprised this time when he did.

He stopped walking and faced her but didn't look down at her. He was constantly scanning the area around them for trouble as he spoke. "Yes, there are other ways, but the Salvatore family knows how we usually operate. That's why we're leaving from Saint Louis instead of Chicago, and why we're going commercial. It's easier to get lost in a crowd."

"I see."

He glanced at her. "Our flight has only sixty-four ticketed passengers on it. We've vetted every one of them, along with the flight crew, cleaning crew, and vendors servicing the plane."

Blayne breathed easier as they resumed their trek to the gate, but as long as he was in the mood to answer questions, she'd shoot him the one that had popped into her head. "What about late arrivals? People paying to get on at the last minute?"

"None allowed on this flight." His clipped tone indicated that was all the information she was going to get.

"What happens when we get to Denver?"

He ignored that question completely and kept walking. She dropped her bag and stood her ground.

❖

The pair looked to Alexi like a puppy running after its master, the tall agent with the walrus mustache striding purposefully toward the departure gate, used to using the bulk of his body and height to intimidate. Always aware of his charge out of the corner of his eye, he seemed just a hair away from showing his annoyance at her persistent nipping at his heels. Agent Topping, Alexi concluded, was an arrogant asshole, who appeared competent at his job but neglected to include a touch of human compassion.

Yes, he seemed vigilant enough, constantly looking around as if expecting trouble. His gaze was everywhere, and in a subtle way, not exaggerated, nothing to draw undue attention.

Now the witness—she was another story. Blayne Keller was not at all what Alexi had expected. Her first thought was that the dossier she had on the woman certainly must have gotten her birth date wrong. She looked twenty, not thirty. Her second thought was *Poor kid, what the hell have they done with you? I think they went way over the top this time. You look ludicrous.*

But she was a feisty thing, despite the crazy getup. Not the typical lamb of a female witness being taken into the program, though she had to be just as scared and uncertain as the rest of them. Apparently that was not enough to keep her from standing up for herself with Agent Topping.

Alexi watched with interest as Blayne dropped her bag and then waited patiently for Topping to rejoin her, and he did, irritation making his mustache twitch. She couldn't hear what they were saying, but their body language told her that Blayne was questioning Topping and growing increasingly perturbed when he kept brushing her off.

After a rather heated exchange, Topping got his charge started again toward the check-in counter. She looked anything but happy about it.

Topping was anxious to board. Alexi could see that in the way he was pushing the witness along and in the nervous movements of his hands. Jingling his keys one minute, clenching and unclenching one fist the next.

His growing impatience with the young woman he was guarding was evident, too, in his stern expression and rigid posture as they stood at the counter. She was obviously still trying to get him to talk to her and he was totally shutting her out.

Blayne Keller certainly was persistent, Alexi had to give her that. She wouldn't stop trying.

The two of them took seats twenty feet away, near enough that Alexi got a good surreptitious view of both over the top of her magazine.

The witness was all jangled nerves and no longer hiding it well. She kept her head down, eyes on her feet, as if afraid of being recognized, and she fidgeted constantly with her clothes, almost telegraphing the fact that they were not her own and that she wasn't the least bit comfortable in them.

Alexi kept an eye on the uneasy pair while still doing quick assessments of the other passengers now congregating at the gate. Everything looked normal so far, but she never let her guard down.

A Mid-Knight Airlines gate agent, a curvaceous redhead with great legs, opened the door to the gangway that led to their plane and then announced over the loudspeaker that boarding for first-class passengers and those with special needs would begin momentarily. As soon as she began talking, Topping said something to his charge, and they both got up and headed toward the gangway door. Alexi made no move to immediately follow. She knew where they would be sitting and she wanted them to get settled before she got on board herself.

Flight 23 was aboard an Airbus 340 whose eventual destination was Hawaii. It would be pretty full during the final leg of its trip between Denver and Honolulu, but it was nearly empty during this initial hop from Saint Louis to Denver, which was precisely why the FBI had chosen it. Topping and Blayne had seats together in the left rear, near the tail, and there were a number of empty seats all around them in every direction.

Alexi had booked a seat on the aisle in the section just ahead of them, near the wing, and she'd made sure there was no one ticketed right next to her as well.

She waited until the final boarding call was announced before she picked up her satchel and headed toward the gangway.

❖

Eduardo Sanchez had awakened that morning to the same problems that had been plaguing him for nearly two years. How to keep from losing his home, his wife, and his kids when he spent most of what he earned as a Mid-Knight Airlines baggage handler on gambling. He was about to take care of all those problems, at least for a long while. He kept telling himself that so he didn't have to think too hard about the small black valise in his hand, and what might be inside.

The telephone call that morning had been brief and to the point. If he agreed to put a bag on a certain flight, he would receive fifty thousand dollars, half of it up front. It would be difficult with the increased security measures enacted after 9-11, but he had been at his job for more than two decades and knew how to get around them. So it didn't take him long to agree. But now, with a thick wad of cash safe within his pocket, he began to think he might be making a mistake.

He couldn't help but wonder what the suitcase held and whether he would ever be able to go to confession again if his action lead to the kinds of consequences no one could forgive.

Too late for second thoughts now, he told himself. *Just do it.* He added the black valise to the luggage in the cargo hold of the Airbus 340 and secured the door.

Chapter Six

B y the time Flight 23 was halfway to Denver, Blayne's jaw hurt from grinding her teeth. She was stressed to the max and supremely frustrated by her unsuccessful efforts to break her escort's stoic silence. She had stared at his profile so long trying to get him to talk to her that she had every detail memorized. The more he ignored her, the more she wanted to rip that mustache off his face.

There was no one else near enough to talk to and she was too keyed up to read a magazine. She just *had* to get up, move around, *do* something, or she'd go mad. That caged-animal feeling was back with a vengeance.

"I need to stretch my legs," she announced and waited for Topping to stand up so she could get out into the aisle. Despite the countless empty seats in their section, he had insisted on having her sit beside him.

"Not a smart idea," he answered. "I'd rather you wait until we land. It'll only be another hour or so."

"Come *on*," she insisted. "I'm just going to walk up to the restroom and back." She half stood in her seat so she could count the heads rising above the seat backs between their seats and the lavatories. "There are less than a dozen people back here. I'll be there and back in two minutes."

He still made no move to get up, but she could tell from the expression on his face that he was at least considering it.

"I had two cups of coffee this morning before I left, and now two more, and it's all hitting me at once," she threatened. "You can come with me if you have to, but I have to *go*."

"All right. All right." He stood and stepped out into the aisle.

She pushed past him before he could change his mind. He was still issuing orders like she was five years old as she started forward.

"The nearest one and right back. Stay in sight and don't talk to anyone."

But Blayne took her time, proceeding slowly up the aisle, savoring the tiny bit of freedom. As she passed by the handful of passengers between her and her destination, she glanced briefly at each of them, reassured that no one seemed the slightest bit interested in her. A woman, head down, engrossed in a magazine. A middle-aged couple, playing a game of cards. A young mother and her fussy toddler twins. A paunchy businessman, fast asleep and snoring softly.

She lingered in the restroom, staring at herself in the mirror, still shocked by her transformation. It made her dizzy, the unfamiliar landscape of her current reality. She needed her anchor—the one person she could rely on. The one person who had helped her make sense of her life the last time she lost everything and had to start over. Claudia.

Where are you? You can't be dead. You can't be. Tears welled up and spilled down her cheeks. *Wouldn't I know? Wouldn't I feel it if the only family I have left was gone forever?*

She refused to accept the possibility that Claudia and Philippe were dead. Topping was obviously going to tell her nothing of their fate. Perhaps she wouldn't know until the trials, when she returned to Chicago. Certainly many months from now, at the earliest. That thought of not knowing what had happened really depressed her. But perhaps it was better than learning they were dead, extinguishing all hope entirely.

Sighing, she wiped her cheeks and unlocked the door. She knew Topping would come looking for her if she delayed much longer. And indeed, he was watching intently as she stepped back out into the aisle. Thankfully, he was also somewhat preoccupied chatting with a cute dark-haired flight attendant, so Blayne didn't rush to get back to her seat.

❖

Alexi was initially surprised to see Blayne Keller venture to the facilities alone, but she supposed she might also have let her off the leash if she'd been Topping, given the scarcity of passengers in this section of the plane.

She followed Blayne's progress out of the corner of her eye and managed to appear preoccupied as she passed by. She adopted the same approach when Blayne ambled back down the aisle, but she could not resist trying for a quick close-up glimpse of the witness. Alexi was surprised to feel an unexpected jolt of sympathy when she registered the traces of tears on Blayne's face. For just a moment she forgot herself and didn't immediately look away.

Their eyes met.

Blayne stopped in her tracks with four feet or so of distance between them. Despite her edgy anxiousness and the disconcertment she felt at being stared at under the circumstances, she couldn't help but stare right back at the woman whose compelling gaze had arrested her. She even forgot her hideous hair and makeup for a moment. She sure liked the way this woman was looking at her. *God, you're beautiful. Any other place and time, to find such a woman taking an interest...*

Before she could complete the thought, she was thrown from her feet as a tremendous force seemed to smash against her. The plane shook violently and a foggy mist filled the cabin. Blayne knew she screamed with fright but she could not hear herself. An excruciating pain rocketed through her eardrums and she was flailing against the seats around her, dragged as if by a current. At exactly the same moment, she felt a hand clamp down on her wrist and she was hanging there, torn between two equal and opposite forces.

Somehow it seemed the viselike grip also put the brakes on time. At first, all Blayne could hear was the ringing in her ears, then the noisy straining of her heart, all as if underwater. Then she could make out people screaming, babies crying, overhead luggage bins slamming open, the drone of the engines, the roar of air rushing by. Everywhere, debris flew, large and small. Pieces of the plane, buzzing wires, magazines and pillows, shoes and purses, carry-on bags, and cans of soda turned into deadly projectiles.

A can of ginger ale grazed her temple as it whooshed by, and for the first time her mind seemed to process information. There was a hole in the plane. They were going down. She tried to look around but all she saw was something metallic coming straight for her, then she fell into a dark vortex and her last thought was *I'm dead*.

Alexi stared down at Blayne's limp body. Blood almost seemed to gush from her head. But she was alive. Alexi could feel her pulse. The oxygen masks had deployed, dangling about her in every direction, a sea of orange cups. But in order to reach hers, she would have to let go of Blayne. It wasn't an option. She tried to suck in air, but her lungs screamed for more, and she prayed she wouldn't lose consciousness. If she did, Blayne wouldn't stand a chance.

The lights flickered on and off and finally went out in their section, except for the emergency trail of small bulbs along the aisles. It was still plenty light enough to see well; they were up above the clouds and it was the middle of the day. But most of the window shades had been pulled down for the in-flight movie, so the contrast was extreme between Alexi's section and the gaping hole behind her where the sunlight streamed in. In the blink of an eye, Special Agent Topping and the flight attendant had been sucked out into oblivion, along with the seat that Blayne had been sitting in.

Flight 23 had already started its long descent into Denver and was at 15,000 feet when the bomb went off, but the air temperature at that altitude was still a bone-chilling minus fifteen degrees. It was hard enough keeping hold of Blayne against the vacuum of air pulling her away. When she added the drop in temperature and the loss of cabin pressure to the mix, Alexi wasn't sure how long she could remain like this. Her heart was racing and her body was pumped full of adrenaline, but she knew this burst of energy wouldn't last long.

She winced against the pain in her ears as she stared in horror at the hole. It seemed enormous. So much blue sky. Ceiling panels hung down, swinging wildly in the turbulence. *Ohi gamoto. This plane will never land like this.* Alexi was fairly certain of that, yet it did not deter her from her efforts to save the woman whose weight was straining her shoulder unbearably.

There was less general panic around her now, though both toddlers just ahead of her were still howling. People were grabbing for the masks, putting them on, checking for injuries. Alexi couldn't hear what anyone was saying over the roar of air from behind her. She glanced up the aisle and squinted against the bits of flotsam still swirling about them, but saw no help forthcoming. The flight attendants were busy elsewhere, it seemed, and for the moment it was every man or woman for herself.

Without warning, the plane abruptly tilted downward at an angle much too steep to be safe, and Alexi and Blayne were both thrown forward. Blayne slid a few feet down the floor of the aisle, and Alexi strained against her seat belt.

She managed to brace herself against the seat back in front with her right hand while still keeping her grip on Blayne, but the muscles in her left arm trembled from the strain. She braced her legs to keep Blayne from sliding farther as the unhampered pull of gravity sent her stomach into her throat, like she was on some crazy free-fall amusement park ride. Gritting her teeth, she tried to ignore the screams of the other passengers as Flight 23 hurtled toward the earth.

The downward pitch of the plane was so severe that Alexi was certain the pilots had lost control, that they were done for. *God help us*. It had been many years since she had been to church, but she found herself repeating prayers she'd learned as child to Agios Dimitrios, patron saint of Thessaloniki.

Just when it seemed they could not possibly make it, the Airbus began to pull out of the dive, the engines straining, and Alexi realized it was suddenly easier to breathe. The screams and the panic around her subsided as the plane leveled off, but even over the roar of air, Alexi could hear the mother four rows ahead, her wail nearly equal to those of her toddler boys.

Blayne was still out cold, and Alexi was beginning to lose feeling in the hand that anchored her. She wasn't sure how much longer her back and shoulder would hold out, either.

"Ladies and gentlemen, this is your first officer," a male voice boomed over the loudspeaker. Very composed, Alexi thought, under the circumstances, though it was hard to hear over the noise of air. "Please remain calm. Don't panic. Stay in your seat with your seat belt fastened. You shouldn't need your oxygen masks now. The flight attendants will be coming around—let them know if anyone is injured. We'll be landing shortly."

And indeed Alexi just then spotted a male flight attendant, a thin, sandy-haired man in his late twenties, making his way toward her, checking on passengers as he did. He seemed harried, but efficient and reassuring. When he got near enough to see Blayne in the aisle, and Alexi holding on to her, he started toward them.

He was about even with the lavatories when he spotted the hole. His eyes widened and his steps faltered. Completely awestruck, he stared open-mouthed at the spectacle for a moment, then recovered his composure enough to reach for the in-flight phone nearby.

After a brief conversation, presumably relaying the extent of the damage to those in the cockpit, he resumed his trek toward Alexi and

Blayne. The vacuum effect from the hole had decreased considerably, but he still gripped the seats on either side to anchor himself.

"Has she been out the whole time?" he asked as he reached Blayne.

"Yes," Alexi answered. They both had to shout even at that near distance to be heard over the din.

He glanced up again at the hole and the carnage of twisted metal around it. Alexi could see a slight tremor in his lip when he spoke. "What happened? Do you know?"

Before she could answer, the young man glanced around as though he'd just realized what—or rather who—was missing. "Have you seen Brenda? Your flight attendant? She's tall, brown hair?"

"Gone. I am sorry," Alexi told him. "She was standing right where the bomb went off."

"Shit!" His hands began to shake, and he stared at the hole again. "A bomb did that? You sure?"

"I'm a U.S. marshal. I am pretty sure." Alexi tilted her head toward Blayne. "Help me get her up and buckled in here, next to me."

The first things Blayne became aware of were arms supporting her, encircling her, and the fact that she had a whale of a headache. When the arms loosened their grip, she opened her eyes to find a young man's face before her. Unfamiliar. "Are you all right?" he asked.

Am I? She felt...sore. Bruised. And cold. *I'm freezing.* She saw a small piece of paper go flying by. Became aware of how noisy it was. *What the...?* It registered, finally, that something was very, very wrong. Blayne turned around and at first her mind refused to accept what she was seeing. All she knew, all she could focus on, was that Agent Topping wasn't where he was supposed to be. So she needed to find him. Her hand reached automatically for her seat belt to unfasten it.

Alexi could see from Blayne's glazed expression that she was disoriented and clamped a hand on her arm to prevent her rising from her seat.

The grip on Blayne's arm—the simple human touch—helped ground her, orient her to the reality of her situation. She looked back at the hole, disbelieving. *I really* am *on an airplane with a big-ass fucking hole in it. One big enough to drive a truck through. I'm not just dreaming this.* She came fully awake and fully aware then. *Fuck. Oh fuck. Oh fuck.* Her heartbeat sped up and she felt as though there was a sudden weight on her chest.

How the hell are we still in the air? She realized she had regained consciousness just in time to experience what was probably a very scary way to die. *We surely can't stay up much longer like this. Any minute now and we're going to fall right out of the sky.*

"Are you all right?" the man repeated.

Blayne turned back to gape at him as though he'd just asked the most ridiculous question possible. "All right? All right?" she was shouting, and just on the verge of hysteria. "How the hell can anybody be all right? We're going to die, aren't we?"

She fought the panic that clutched at her body and mind, swelling up in her like a poison in her bloodstream. *I'm about to become fish food.* Her insides rolled and churned.

"Oh fuck, I'm going to be sick."

A bag appeared in front of her just in time, held by the young man, and Blayne lost the contents of her stomach into it. Hunched over in the seat, she felt a hand on her back, a comforting hand, a soft caress of reassurance, and Blayne looked up to find...*her.*

There was strength and reassurance in the vivid blue eyes she met, and Blayne sure needed a big dose of that right now.

"It is a lot to take in," Alexi said reassuringly, continuing her caresses along Blayne's back. "But we seem to have stabilized, and the pilot just announced we will land soon."

"That's the last thing I remember," Blayne said, her mind working to fill in the blank spot in her memory. "Looking at you."

"I remember too."

"If I hadn't paused just then..." Blayne turned back toward the hole. *Right where I was sitting. I should be dead. I would've been, a minute later. Or a few minutes earlier.* She struggled to breathe. Her heart was suddenly pounding furiously against the walls of her chest.

Alexi could almost see the wheels turn as Blayne's mind cleared and she began to realize that the hole was caused by a bomb, meant for *her*, and that the agent protecting her was gone. Dead.

The flight attendant absented himself to dispose of the sick bag just as the first officer's voice vied once more with the intercom static.

"Ladies and gentlemen, we're about to make an emergency landing in Colorado Springs. Please remove all sharp objects from your person. Glasses, pens, pencils. Then assume the brace position."

Alexi took deep, regular breaths to try to remain as calm and focused as possible. *If* they made it out of this alive, she would have to come up with a plan, and fast, to keep Blayne safe. But she had no control over the runaway beat of her heart. It was certain they were about to die, and it was making itself known with such force in her chest that she could do no thinking at all at the moment.

Blayne listened and followed along, as did the woman next to her. In the din of the rushing air, she had to concentrate intently to make out the instructions, and in an odd way that helped keep her calm.

"Tighten your seat belt. Bend forward as far as possible, with your head touching the seat back in front of you. Hands one on top of each other, on top of your head. Don't interlock your fingers. Tuck your forearms in against each side of your face. Now angle your lower legs behind your knees. Okay. Stay like that, and try not to tense up. Here we go."

Blayne held her breath and closed her eyes, her heart pounding furiously in her chest. *It's going to break up when we land. We're too close to the damn hole.* She grabbed automatically for the comfort of her Catholic school upbringing. *Our Father, who art in heaven, hallowed be Thy name...*

Chapter Seven

Alexi raised her head to glance out the nearest window as the plane descended the final fifty feet. Against a gorgeous backdrop of mountains, she could see emergency vehicles rolling along beside the runway, their lights flashing. Red and white fire trucks with *Colorado Springs Fire and Rescue* on the sides, police cars, and a handful of ambulances. A scant few seconds before the wheels hit the tarmac, she put her head down once more and forced herself to remain loose, muscles relaxed.

The Airbus bounced and the rear section around the hole creaked and groaned so loudly it sounded like the plane was barely holding together.

Blayne tensed, waiting for everything to fall apart or for them to explode in a ball of flame. *Hail Mary, full of grace...* Her nerves were shot and she was wound up so tight she had no idea if it was a prayer or a scream.

The wheels thumped down again, and this time held fast. The sound of the brakes erased all other noise, including the frantic chatter in Blayne's head. The aircraft slowed and the noise began to abate, but it was not until the plane had nearly come to a complete stop that reality dawned. She was alive. They were all alive.

As if the same thought hit everyone at the same time, the passengers burst into cheers and sobs and frantic applause. Alexi and Blayne gazed at each other with the giddy relief of those who've cheated death and didn't expect to. Abject terror had turned to shaky joy, and Blayne impulsively reached for Alexi and embraced her tightly.

Alexi initially stiffened at the unexpected contact, but after a moment hugged Blayne back, her normal reserve crumbling in the face of these very strange circumstances.

"Ladies and gentlemen." The first officer sounded so calm that they might have been landing on any normal commuter flight on any day of the week. "Thank you for remaining calm. Please remain in your seats. We will evacuate the injured first, by ambulance. The rest of you will be taken by bus to the hospital to be checked out. You may take your purses with you, but please leave all carry-ons on board. Airline officials will contact you at the hospital to take care of you from there."

Blayne glanced back at the hole once more, and the wreckage beneath it where her assigned seat had been. *That bomb was meant for me. They found me. They know where I am. They always know where I am.*

With a sudden, sick certainly, she realized that the mob was going to stop at nothing until they made sure she did not testify. They were willing to kill a whole plane full of people just to get to her. And somehow, even with all the increased airport screening, they had nearly succeeded. The realization was mind-boggling.

They weren't supposed to be able to find me. Topping said that... Topping. His face was still so vivid and clear in her mind. *Dead. Protecting me. And I gave him such a damn hard time. He was only doing his job.* She felt a wave of guilt and remorse, and wondered whether he had a wife and kids.

Alexi knew they would soon be taking Blayne away in an ambulance. That wasn't a bad idea, she decided. The diversion to Colorado Springs was a lucky break because it would take Cinzano a while to get someone here. *I will ride with her in the ambulance and come up with a plan while she's getting checked out.* She didn't think Blayne's injuries were too serious, although the concussion was a concern and she might need stitches. But she seemed quite lucid. *We can be on the road in an hour or two.* Now that they could finally hear each other speak, it was time to identify herself.

Alexi touched her arm, and got her attention. "Miss Keller... *Weaver*," she said deliberately. "My name is Alexi Nikolos and I am with the U.S. Marshals Service. You will be under my protection from now on."

Blayne stared at her with a stunned expression. "You...you know who I am?"

"Yes. I know everything. I'm an inspector with the Witness Protection Program. You can trust me."

Blayne said nothing for a long moment. Her mind was spinning. She closed her eyes and gripped the armrests to steady herself. She wanted to believe this woman, but she was shocked by the revelation that Alexi wasn't some random passenger on the plane. And so much had happened in recent days she was now suspicious of everyone.

How the hell did they find out what plane I was on? Surely that was information that wasn't readily available. Topping had been reluctant even to tell *her* anything until the very last second, saying it was for security reasons. They were obviously going to great lengths to keep her safe. But the mob had still found out what plane she was on. That meant one of the presumably few who knew—FBI or whoever—had told them.

She stared at Alexi. *She has an accent, does that mean anything?* She couldn't tell what kind, but it put her even more on edge. The mobsters were all Italian. How could she know Alexi was who she said she was? And was it just coincidence that Alexi was seated just far enough away from the bomb not to be injured by it?

Everything was happening too fast. "Why should I believe you?" Her aggravation leaked into the tone of her voice. "Why should I trust any of this?"

Alexi reached under the seat for her satchel, but her hand found only empty space. She half stood and peered at the seats behind and in front of them. It was gone—one of the myriad of bags sucked out through the hole. The satchel had her identification in it, her files on Blayne, and her wallet. There was no way to prove who she was. *Damn.*

The doors to the plane were open now, and emergency crews were starting to come on board to assess the passengers. "Unfortunately, I cannot identify myself at this time," she told Blayne. "So you will just have to take my word for it. You must come with me, Miss Weaver."

Blayne's sense of alarm increased. *How convenient.* "What do you mean, I don't have a choice? I don't remember being arrested, so I *do* have a choice. I have no desire for a babysitter. I'd rather take my own chances. Surely I can't do worse than *this*." She gestured in frustration at the hole.

"I understand that you feel you would rather do this on your own, but I cannot allow it. I don't think you realize that things *could* get a lot worse. You have to come with me."

"Worse than this? How much worse can it get?"

"You have been very fortunate until now to have survived all this, largely thanks to the agents protecting you. But luck runs out, and these people will not stop until they succeed in what they have set out to do."

Blayne half stood, ducking her head to avoid hitting the overhead compartment. "Once again, I do intend to continue alone, and I hope I stay lucky, because it seems as though it's the only thing I have going for me."

Alexi rose as well and stopped Blayne with a hand on her elbow. "Miss Weaver—"

They were interrupted by a paramedic and a tall gray-haired man in a suit who wore a gold badge at his belt. "Ladies, please remain seated," the police officer said.

"Excuse us, but she seems to be disoriented," Alexi said. "She was knocked out for several minutes. Lost blood. Struck her head, *there*." She reached out a hand to touch Blayne's injured temple, but Blayne shied away as though burned. "She's confused."

"No, I'm not!" Blayne glared at Alexi in disbelief. "I'm not disoriented or confused. Why would you say that? I just need to get off this damn plane!"

Alexi's mind worked furiously. Blayne seemed determined to run and she had to prevent that. She looked at the EMT in a conspiratorial way, then in a calm, even tone, said to Blayne, "Yes, this gentleman will help us off the plane and make sure we get you to a hospital. I think you need an ambulance."

"No, I don't!" Blayne snapped. "I'm *fine!*"

"Ladies, will you follow me, please?" The EMT led the way, the policeman brought up the rear, and they left through a set of stairs that had been wheeled into place beside the Airbus.

Outside, a chaos of activity greeted them. Fire trucks encircled the crippled Airbus, their lights flashing red and white along the smooth surface of the plane. The sounds of approaching sirens and shouted instructions filled the air. Babies cried. A woman screamed hysterically. In a blur of action, emergency personnel ran about, attending their well-rehearsed duties aiding the injured, calming the distraught, and securing the plane. A flight attendant stood a few yards from them transfixed, staring back at the plane. Blayne slowed her steps and turned to look too. From the outside, the hole seemed so impossibly, inescapably big and terrifying that her body clenched and her vision swam and she stumbled. She would have sprawled headfirst onto the tarmac had Alexi Nikolos not caught her.

The strong arms that encircled her waist were instantly reassuring, but as soon as she was upright, Blayne pushed them away without a word and followed the EMT toward a row of ambulances parked on the edge of the runway.

He tossed a question at her as he opened the rear doors of his rig. "We'll take you in this one, Miss…?"

She had to answer. The cop was standing right there. "Amanda Jones." *Now that's original.* But it was the first name that popped into her head. She wasn't about to give out either her real one, or her new WITSEC identity. Either might be used to track her down.

Alexi was impressed. *Smart girl.*

"But I *don't* need an ambulance," Blayne insisted.

"You should let a doctor look at you. You're not thinking clearly after that hit you took," Alexi said.

"Why do you keep saying that?" Blayne was fuming. "There's nothing wrong with my thinking."

"It really is best you get evaluated, Miss Jones," the EMT said. "The airline wants everyone to get checked out. All the passengers and crew are going to the hospital. It's just a matter of whether you go by bus or by ambulance." He grinned encouragingly and pointed toward the stretcher in his rig, "This is a lot more comfortable and we can keep an eye on you. Please?"

"No. No stretcher," Blayne said automatically, then she reconsidered. *But if you ride in an ambulance, you can get away from her.* "Uh, okay. It might be best."

She climbed into the rig and the EMT got her comfortably situated before excusing himself to go make sure no one else needed immediate attention.

Blayne closed her eyes and tried to relax. It was still noisy, but the rig effectively cut out a lot of the din and allowed her a moment's peace. *Okay. I'm rid of her. Now what am I going to do?*

At the back of the ambulance, Alexi waited for the EMT to close up the doors, then said, "I need to ride with my sister. I'd hate for us to get separated, especially since she's been acting kind of funny since she hit her head."

"Oh! Your sister! I didn't realize. Of course." The EMT started to reach for the rear doors again, but Alexi stopped him.

"I thought I would leave her alone a minute," she said. "Let her calm down—you know? It has been a pretty harrowing day."

"Of course. Go ahead when you're ready, then. I'll find my partner. Shouldn't be long."

He headed back into the commotion and Alexi glanced around. No one was paying her any mind. She opened the rear doors of the ambulance, scrambled inside, and quickly shut the doors behind her.

"What the hell do you think you're doing?" Blayne snapped. The EMT had strapped her loosely onto the stretcher. She unbuckled the top straps so she could sit up. "Get out of here! I'm not riding anywhere with you!"

"Yes, you are." Alexi planted herself on the bench seat that ran along one side of the rig, a couple of feet from Blayne's head.

"You can't come in here. I'm going to tell them…tell them—"

"Tell them what? You're not going to tell them anything, Miss Weaver. I've told them I'm your sister and that you are confused. They will believe me over a distraught woman who's been hit in the head."

Blayne shook with rage. "You told them *what?*"

"Accept it, please. You are under my protection now."

"First you tell them I'm delusional, and then you claim to be my sister, and you expect me to believe a word you say? Trust you to make decisions for me? *Now* who's delusional?" She shot daggers at Alexi with her eyes and with quick, angry movements unsnapped the remaining straps confining her. *Where are you planning to run?* she asked herself even as she did. She felt trapped. "I told you I want nothing to do with you! Leave me alone!"

Alexi was surprised and even a bit amused by the outburst, but showed neither emotion. This woman had a fire in her, that was for sure. She had to admire that. "Please calm down. You know, your hysteria is not going to work in your favor if you plan to try to convince anyone you are all right."

Blayne clenched her fists and ground her teeth. Alexi Nikolos infuriated her more every time the wretched woman opened her mouth. "Even if I *believed* you—which I *don't*—I'm *done* putting my life in the hands of the feds. You've done a pretty shitty job of keeping me safe."

Blayne's words struck an old wound in Alexi, but she did not allow her emotions to register on her face, and when she answered it was with the same controlled, even tone that she always used. "I would say we have done our jobs very well. It is Agent Topping who was killed, and Agent Wright who took a bullet. Not you."

A flush of shame colored Blayne's cheeks. "Okay, maybe that was a bit harsh. But who exactly told them what plane I was on, huh? Tell me *that*!"

The door to the back of the ambulance opened, abruptly ending the exchange. The sandy-haired flight attendant who'd helped them on the plane stuck his head in. "There you are! Glad to see you're both okay. I just wanted to say thank you for taking care of her," he told Alexi. "Lucky we had you on board."

"Just doing my job."

The paramedics returned, cutting off any further opportunity for escape, and soon they were en route to the hospital. Blayne answered all the usual health questions as one of the EMTs patched the cut on her temple, but she wanted to be left alone to collect her thoughts. To figure out what the hell she was going to do. How was she going to get rid of this woman? And after that... *Yeah. After that, what? I'm alone now.* Even when she lost her parents, she still had Claudia. But now...now she was *really* alone, for the first time in her life.

Alexi watched the paramedic tend to Blayne and tried to figure out a way to get the witness to believe her, trust her. *I do not blame her skittishness after all she has been through. But she sure is not making a difficult situation any easier.* She could almost taste the woman's anxiety, *feel* her fear as Blayne tried to put what had happened into perspective and make decisions on what to do next.

Alexi felt protective of her, which was not a surprise, of course. That *was* precisely what she was here for, after all, it was her *job*. But she also felt an unfamiliar urge to *comfort* Blayne, hold her hand or something. She guessed it was because despite all of Blayne's big talk and bravado, there was a certain vulnerability about her, just under the surface.

Alexi shrugged off the urge, however. She knew what could come from giving in to those impulses, and she needed to focus all of her attention on keeping her charge out of harm's way.

Would she be able to do her job? Keep Blayne safe? She'd thought so. But now the doubts were creeping in. She had studied every single person getting on the flight, and she knew the FBI had vetted all the vendors and crew. Yet she hadn't seen this coming. And certainly Topping hadn't either. This was going to be one hell of an assignment. She had no resources, and she had not only the mob to worry about, but a scorpion within her own ranks.

Can I do this? Can I keep her safe? She knew she didn't really have a choice. Someone was telling the mob where Blayne Keller was every step of the way. *I'm her only hope.*

❖

WITSEC Chief Inspector Theodore Lang was getting into his car in the agency's parking lot when his BlackBerry vibrated against his hip.

The caller was Paul Fletcher, the man he'd replaced as head of WITSEC's Chicago office. Fletcher had been bumped back to inspector and was assigned to the Joint Task Force on Organized Crime.

"We have a problem," Fletcher said. "The plane carrying Skip Topping and Blayne Keller just made an emergency landing in Colorado Springs. News reports say there was an explosion on board."

"An explosion?" Theo mentally kissed good-bye to the birthday dinner his wife had been planning for the past month. He didn't often allow himself a night out on the town. At fifty, a man in his line of work had to be very fit and look ten years younger than his age if he wanted to keep climbing the career ladder. This was even more so for an African American. Theo followed a disciplined diet and exercise regimen to keep himself at the top of his game.

"Initial reports suggest maybe a bomb," Fletcher confirmed. "We can't reach Topping on his cell, and there's no word on Keller yet. We're making calls and we have someone en route."

Theo was tempted to ask Fletcher to check on Alexi as well, but he didn't trust anyone with the knowledge that she was on the case. He'd have to make some discreet phone calls himself.

"Keep me posted," he said, already planning how he was going to handle the evening. "I'm heading home."

❖

Vittorio Cinzano was led from his cell in Division 11, a state-of-the-art facility and the newest addition to the sprawling Cook County Jail complex. Designed for maximum security detainees, the more than seven hundred cells in Division 11 were double-occupancy, but Vittorio was housed by himself. A sheriff's deputy escorted him down the long corridor toward a small room with two chairs and a table, where his attorney, Michael Florio, awaited him.

Vittorio was used to getting his own way, and the inscrutable demeanor he maintained was beginning to slip under his incarceration. Every day, his irritation and impatience became a little more evident in his terse tone and body language. And so, too, did his humiliation at having to trade his custom-tailored suits for this obscene orange jumpsuit. It took all his self-discipline to maintain the dignity of his name and his position under the circumstances. He wanted results and he wanted them yesterday.

His lawyer had better have some good news for him.

Vittorio was gratified to see the faint smile on Florio's face when their eyes met. They were left alone, but their actions were monitored by a female deputy through a thick Plexiglas window.

"Sit down, Michael." Vittorio gestured toward one of the folding chairs on the visitor side.

Florio waited for his boss to claim the other before asking, "How are you holding up, Vittorio?"

"How the fuck do you think I am holding up? I can't go anywhere without them following me."

Florio did not respond, and when Vittorio spoke again he softened his tone. He had talked to his wife the day before, and she had assured him all was well, but he relied on his attorney to give him an honest assessment.

"How is Nicki? Have you talked to her today?"

"She's fine. Seems to be hanging in there," Florio responded.

"And Marie?"

"Still in seclusion at your mother's. Won't talk to me or anyone else right now."

"I expected that. So, is there any news?" Vittorio asked.

"Yes, we should be hearing something soon. I think you'll be satisfied."

"You're good to me, Michael." Vittorio kept his manner casual. But it took an effort. Without a witness, they couldn't hold him for long, and the day of his release couldn't come soon enough.

Three days after the shooting of Aldo Martinelli, he'd received the information he was waiting for in a jailhouse phone conversation with his attorney. As such, he knew it was privileged, but he and his lawyer still spoke in a cryptic shorthand. It was second nature, anyway. A way of life for someone in Vittorio's position.

He'd made it clear to Florio on the day of his arrest that he wanted all three women from the travel agency eliminated, along with Philippe Cluzet, the building owner. First they'd dealt with Aldo's *goumada*, Joyce. She probably knew too much because that fat fuck never could keep his mouth shut. It wasn't her fault, and Vittorio had behaved like an honorable man and instructed the clip to be quick and clean. She never saw what was coming.

The witness they were now hunting had to go for obvious reasons. Fortunately one of their friends in high places understood where his interests lay, so they knew every move that woman was making.

Philippe Cluzet and his daughter both had to go as well. Vittorio had no choice. Cluzet had only reluctantly cooperated with the sale of the building, and though he'd sworn never to tell anyone about what he knew about the soda operation, who could know what a father might tell his daughter?

Vittorio's orders went against the mob's long-standing policy of using threats and intimidation alone against civilians. The cops didn't mind wiseguys killing each other, but when an innocent died, there was a lot of heat in a hurry. Way too much heat, on *all* the families, and that made it difficult to do business. Vittorio, however, was not about to be compromised. He followed the unwritten code of conduct only when it suited him anyway, and this time he was in serious danger of losing his freedom for a long while.

"Bail?" he asked.

"Probably not until we get everything resolved," Florio replied. "But we're ready to proceed as soon as the timing is right."

As a sick smile spread across Cinzano's face, Michael felt his cell phone vibrate and glanced at the number displayed. Cautiously, he said, "I need to take this call outside." He knew his boss would understand. Some things could not be discussed inside prison walls.

Cinzano gave a dismissive wave. Excitement gleamed in his dark eyes. Michael hoped to Christ he'd be returning with good news.

As he exited the visiting room he picked up the call and instructed, "Hold on a minute," waiting until he was in the parking lot before he said, "Okay. Go."

"There's been a serious complication," the voice on the other end relayed. "The airplane has landed. We're going to Colorado."

"Colorado?"

"Colorado Springs."

Michael glanced at his watch. "Anything else?"

"I'll let you know." The phone went dead.

He phoned his secretary. "Cancel my appointments. I'll be out the rest of the day."

CHAPTER EIGHT

Y ou've got quite a bruise here," the doctor said as he gently palpated where a water bottle had slammed into Alexi's back. "I'll have the nurse get a cold pack for that, but I don't think it's anything to worry about. Anything else hurt?"

Alexi had pulled a couple of muscles in her back and shoulders trying to hang on to Blayne, but in order to minimize her time in the emergency room she didn't want to dwell on her condition. She had protested being separated from Blayne once they got to Memorial Hospital, but without revealing that she was a U.S. marshal she couldn't force the issue. Blayne was in radiology having a series of head X-rays, and the admitting staff had said Alexi would be allowed to join her "sister" once she was checked out herself.

"I am fine," she told the doctor. "Any word on what is happening with my sister? Amanda Jones?"

"I'll ask. You can put your shirt back on." The doctor paused halfway out the door. "Oh, the police want to talk to everyone. They've got a couple of cubicles to go before they get here. Should be just a few minutes."

He had barely gone before the nurse appeared with a cold pack and a thick roll of bandage. "I'm going to wrap this to keep it in place. You should leave it on at least twenty minutes. Lift your hands, please." She positioned the ice pack and asked as she started wrapping, "Were you on that plane? That plane on the news?"

Alexi was instantly alert. Of course it was on the news. Everyone had a cell phone and camera these days. "What are they saying?"

"CNN has been on it for the last half hour. I can't believe the hole in the plane. Wow. Just *amazing*. They're looking at whether it was a terrorist attack because they think it may have been a bomb." The nurse was excited. Obviously it was the biggest news in Colorado Springs in years. "The waiting area is full of TV and newspaper reporters trying to interview passengers, but no one out there was near where it happened. Were you?"

"No," Alexi lied. Admitting the truth would make her a priority with the local cops. She couldn't have that. Now that the story was on the news it was more important than ever that she get Blayne the hell away from there as soon as possible.

"I'm going to find my sister," she told the nurse as soon as the bandage was secured. "Then we will talk to the police. Can you tell me how to get to radiology?"

❖

Blayne waited for the radiology technician to leave with the X-ray films, then she snatched her ugly-as-hell jacket off the chair and headed for the door. She patted her pants pocket, feeling for the envelope containing her Fiji fund to reassure herself it was still there. There would never be a better time to slip out. The area around the emergency room had been swarming with police and reporters when she'd been wheeled off to radiology, but now she was in a quiet wing a floor away, and she hadn't seen *that woman* for a good half hour.

She felt extremely conflicted about Alexi Nikolos. There was something…*reassuring* about her, she had to admit. She *seemed* trustworthy, and the flight attendant had made it sound as though Alexi had taken good care of her. Knowing who she was made Blayne reinterpret that first look between them. She'd been so certain it was a look of attraction, of interest, but she was woefully mistaken. Alexi was just doing her job, that's all.

The thought was strangely depressing, on top of everything else. Blayne wondered if Alexi was even her real name. There were way too many unknowns about the woman for her liking, and even if Alexi was only trying to keep her safe, she was employed by the same people who couldn't seem to keep her whereabouts a secret. Alexi would be reporting in, notifying them that she was alive and had Blayne with her.

The information would soon be out there and yet again whoever was leaking it would tell Blayne's enemies.

Yup, I'm definitely better off on my own.

She cracked open the door, peeked out, and spotted a nurse heading away from her, to her left. The other way was clear, and at the end of the hall was a sign that said *Stairway. Perfect.*

Blayne made it downstairs and exited through a side entrance, successfully avoiding both the press and the police. Now she had to find some transport. There was a bus stand near her, but no one waiting there and no bus in sight. So she walked the perimeter of the hospital and was relieved to see a taxi pulling up in front of the visitors' entrance to drop off a fare. She hurried over with a wave and a shout and managed to get the driver's attention before he pulled away.

"Hi. Where to?" He was a beefy Scandinavian type in his forties. His radio was tuned to a classical station, and that was a pleasant surprise.

Where, indeed? Somewhere far away the hell from here. "Got a state map?" Blayne asked.

❖

Cursing, Alexi continued around the perimeter of the hospital, vigilant to each person, car, every hint of movement within sight. No one and nothing escaped her careful and quick scrutiny. As she rounded a corner her eyes were drawn to a glint in the distance—a flash— sunlight hitting metal. The studs on the back of Blayne's jacket as she got into a taxi.

"Stop!" she yelled, sprinting across the lawn. The cab was the only vehicle currently in the U-shaped drop-off zone in front of the visitors' entrance, but before she got within a hundred feet it pulled away. The driver hadn't heard her.

Breathing heavily, she glanced around, desperate for a way to follow the car before it got out of sight. She couldn't believe she had allowed this *amateur* to give her the slip. She had been out of the game too long, apparently. In a parking lot to her left, a thirtysomething man with a dark beard and shoulder-length hair stood beside a dark green Lincoln Navigator, fishing through the pockets of his white lab coat for his keys.

She came up behind him just as he found them, and snatched them out of his hand. "I am a U.S. marshal in hot pursuit, and I am commandeering your vehicle." She hit the Unlock button on the key-chain control and slid onto the front seat of the SUV almost before the man could register what was happening. "I'll leave word where to pick it up at the hospital."

"Wait!" He thrust out his arm and held the door open. "I want to see some ID."

"Take your hand off the door, *now!*" She fired up the engine and shifted into reverse.

The tone of her voice was enough. He stepped back and watched his Navigator speed away.

❖

Blayne studied the map the taxi driver had handed over. The main highway through Colorado Springs, I-25, ran north into Denver, the plane's original destination—*that way's definitely out*—or south to Pueblo and on into New Mexico. It was a start. A first decision. It felt good to make one on her own.

As the taxi headed west toward the interstate, she watched the meter tick away her precious funds. She hated the cost per mile, but speed was of the essence.

Let's see. About 45 miles, it looks like, to Pueblo. Then what? Stay on the highway or get off? Stick with the cab or switch to something else? Buses were too slow. Planes were fastest, but she couldn't think about getting on one of those again anytime soon. And that would require she show identification, anyway. A train, maybe.

"Is there an Amtrak line around here?" she asked.

"Yeah," the driver said. "There are two. If you want to head south, you hit the Southwest Chief. It goes through La Junta, that's about a hundred miles southeast. Or it stops down in Trinidad, that's about a two-hour drive." He glanced in the rearview mirror at Blayne. "The California Zephyr is closer, but that's north, out of Denver."

"No," Blayne said. "Head south."

The cabbie seemed not too concerned that she had no definite destination in mind. "You got it."

The more she thought about the Amtrak alternative, the less

she liked the idea. The mob might be watching the stations or have somebody on each train. That would be easy enough to do, and then she'd be trapped on a moving vehicle with someone who wanted to put a bullet in her head.

"Do you have a range or something? A limit on how far you'll go?"

"I'm willing to negotiate something."

Blayne pulled out her new wallet and the Fiji fund, and out of view of the driver counted her money. Four thousand one hundred and twenty-nine dollars, when she added her holiday stash to the money the feds had given her. It sounded like a lot, but not if she had to disappear and start over somewhere. And certainly not if she was going to spend hundreds on a taxi ride.

Can't get a rental car without a credit card. I wonder how much I can get a beat-up junker of a car for? Fifteen hundred, maybe. That's not bad. Keep to the back roads. It sounded like a pretty good plan. The snag was, it was almost dark, and the used car places in Pueblo would already be closed.

It was the best she could think of at the moment. The taxi meter ticked away, audible only during pauses in the classical music. She could swear the thing was speeding up in its mission to devour her dollars.

"How much to Pueblo?" she asked.

❖

Alexi caught up to the taxi as it was getting on the expressway, and followed at a distance while she explored the interior of the SUV. She was irritated as hell that Blayne's conduct had forced her into taking the car. *Only a quarter of a tank of gas. Not great, but could be worse.* There was a map of Colorado above one of the visors. But no cash, credit cards, or cell phones in the pockets or storage compartments. She hoped the driver of the vehicle wasn't at that moment contacting the police. If she got pulled over, she might lose Blayne while trying to verify who she was.

Where is she going, and what do I do when I catch up to her? She was impatient to gain Blayne's cooperation so she could start figuring out how she was going to keep them safe. She had a lot to work out.

Like how she was going to get some funds and where she was going to take Blayne. The usual safe houses were no good. *Who can I trust? Do I dare even tell Theo where we are?*

She rubbed her eyes and tried to ignore the fatigue that was starting to assert itself. She felt overwhelmed and even disoriented, like her internal compass didn't work anymore.

It was a feeling that took her back to her childhood. To all the years she'd spent in boarding schools, isolated from her family. Initially, the disorientation and rejection she'd felt at being sent away had sent her into a spiral of depression. But her father insisted the experience would make her independent and resourceful. And it certainly had done that.

She had learned to put her emotions aside and to view every situation and challenge head-on. Logically. Fearlessly. Just assess the risks and take appropriate action. It was why she became a standout at WITSEC.

But her long-held confidence in her abilities had taken a big hit when Sofia was killed, and she was only now realizing to what extent. She found herself battling uncertainties she thought she had long ago dispensed with, and she knew how dangerous it was to indulge those doubts. The mob was determined to take out her witness, and Blayne was determined to run. She had to be at the top of her game.

It was well past dusk when the taxi reached the outskirts of Pueblo, slowing down as it passed a bright string of restaurant and hotel signs at one of the exits. Alexi understood exactly what was going on. The passenger was trying to make a decision about where to spend the night. She would choose something off the main road because her instincts would drive her toward seclusion and privacy.

Predictably, the taxi took an exit to an area less well lit and proceeded past a few fast food and chain restaurants scattered amidst various budget hotels and motels. It slowed yet again at a used car lot with padlocked chains across the entrance and exit. The prices were scrawled across the windshields in huge white and yellow numbers.

$800. $1,500. Blayne probably had access to that kind of money, Alexi thought, so she would hole up nearby and plan to return first thing the next morning for whatever Nissan or Ford looked like a good buy. It wasn't that late, not even quite eight o'clock yet, but the day must have taken everything out of her. She would want to make a plan. Study a map. Consider her options. There was a Motel 6 a bit farther down the road. If Alexi were a gambler, she'd have put her life savings on this one.

She watched the taxi continue on to the three-story motel. Blayne would not be pleased to see her and she would likely not be shy about saying so. A confrontation was probably inevitable but Alexi had to avoid a scene that would draw attention to them, so she hung back, content to wait for an opportunity.

The cab let Blayne off right in front of the office and she went directly in to register. A few minutes later she came back out, walked to a nearby room on the first floor, and let herself in. At all times, there were too many people about, in the parking lot, on the stairwells, near the soda machine, by the office. Alexi couldn't risk it, so she waited until things quieted down, using the time to study the map.

When there was no one in sight, she got out of the SUV, walked to Blayne's door, and knocked. She hoped Blayne would open up without looking, but she wasn't optimistic that would happen. The curtain at the window beside the door was pulled back, and she saw Blayne's eyes widen in disbelief. But the shock was quickly replaced by a flash of temper.

"God damn it! Leave me alone!" Her voice was muffled through the thick glass between them, but since she was shouting every word was clear.

Alexi glanced around. No one in sight. "Please let me in, Miss Weaver." She said it louder than she wanted to. A necessary risk.

"No!"

"I am not going away."

Blayne appraised her for a long moment. "Suit yourself."

"I will not keep shouting at you like this," Alexi said. "I am going to get an audience out here, and we do not want that, believe me."

"There is no *we*," Blayne retorted. "I told you, leave me alone! I'm not going with you!"

Alexi tried to keep her irritation in check, but it was getting tougher by the moment. She was tired, and hungry, and she knew they were in far too much danger to be wasting time like this. "If you do not open this door in two minutes, I am going to kick it in."

Blayne's eyes narrowed. "I'll call the front desk and tell them you're bothering me."

"No, you will not. They'll ask too many questions."

The two women stared at each other. Blayne's jaw was set, her face tight with anger, as though it was all she could do not to reach through the glass and throttle Alexi.

Alexi remained outwardly impassive, but she was fighting mightily the urge to shake some sense into Blayne. "At least open the door with the chain on so that I can talk to you without drawing attention to us."

The curtain closed. It took another minute for the door to open, and it was with the chain on. But Alexi knew then she'd won. She stuck her right boot into the opening.

"I don't need your protection." Blayne had taken a couple of steps away from the door, to be out of Alexi's reach. But she stood where they could see each other. "I can get away from them by myself and I'll be safer."

"Really?" Alexi responded pleasantly. "Let's just reality check, shall we? So far, nearly every decision you have made has been a bad one, one that will ensure you get caught. Those bad decisions, by the way, are the reason I am standing here. It is mere good luck that I arrived first, and not a hit man."

This seemed to register and Blayne took a step closer to the door. "What do you mean?"

"You take a cab, use the only smart way out of town, and stop at the first motel you come to? You think the men hunting you don't have connections in cab companies? The driver will tell someone where you are, and you will be dead long before that used car lot opens down the street."

Blayne's eyes widened in alarm and shock. "How did you know what I—"

"As I said, you are predictable." Alexi heard voices approaching. People on the levels above, heading down the outdoor stairwell toward them. She had to get in the room, and fast. "Miss Weaver, I mean you no harm. If I wanted you dead, you would have been dead already and I would not be standing here like an idiot trying to negotiate my way through a chain. You are wasting precious time. Open the door." The last three words were unmistakably a command, not a request.

The blunt words seemed to reassure Blayne and she finally unhooked the chain just as the upper-level guests emerged from the nearest stairwell. Alexi stepped inside the room and quickly closed and locked the door behind her. When she turned to face Blayne, she found that the witness had retreated to a chair, one of two flanking a small circular table by the front window. She took the other.

"Thank you for opening the door." She referenced Blayne's bandage with a tilt of her chin. "How are you feeling?"

Emotions played across the delicate features of the woman in front of her as she fingered the square of gauze at her temple. She was obviously still seething, but Alexi's accurate assessment of her plan to escape had really frightened her too.

"Shitty headache. How did you know what I was going to do?" she asked, half the fight gone.

"You are doing the obvious things an innocent person would do."

Blayne leaned back in the chair and gripped the armrests. *Am I? She certainly found me. How the hell did she find me? I paid the taxi and hotel in cash.*

"All right. Let's say maybe I haven't made all the best choices. So, I'm listening. What's *your* inspired master plan for getting me out of here, huh? Dazzle me."

Alexi got back on her feet. "The priority is getting you as far away from here as fast as possible. In the way they are least likely to be able to track us. I have a car outside."

"Not so fast." Blayne didn't budge from where she was. Her independence had been much too short lived and the knowledge that the mob was right now probably closing in on them scared her, but she wasn't ready to place her life in this woman's hands without some terms. "I'm not saying I believe you're who you say you are, but I'm willing to go with you. As long as you know this is *not* long term. I'm not going back to WITSEC under any circumstances, or to any constantly-under-guard thing. No military bases. I just can't do it."

Alexi had been trying to come up with a good explanation for why she wouldn't be taking Blayne to the nearest federal facility. She couldn't acknowledge that even the feds couldn't be trusted, that there was a leak within the task force somewhere. Blayne had probably figured that out already and had lost confidence because of it. Fortunately, Blayne's stubborn pronouncement provided a way out.

Frowning as though only reluctantly accepting her terms, Alexi said, "I understand your hesitation after what you have been through, Miss Weaver. So...for now, I will agree. No military bases, no WITSEC, no cops. Shall we go?"

❖

Blayne noticed right away that something was decidedly wrong about the vehicle they were in. It was clearly no rental. A variety of small personal items overflowed the cup holders and console storage areas. Sunglasses, lip balm, tissues, maps, pens. A CD out of its case. *Yummy Yummy* by the Wiggles. The *Wiggles?*

She glanced in the backseat. There were more Wiggles CDs on the floor, and several toys appropriate for a toddler. The SUV had a lived-in feel to it, and it didn't seem to suit Alexi at all. Blayne got a sudden hollow feeling in the pit of her stomach.

"Whose car is this?"

"I did not ask his name. There wasn't time."

"You *stole* this car? Oh my God! Brilliant! They'll never track us in a stolen car! What the hell kind of an agent are you? Stop right now and let me out!"

But Alexi kept their speed a constant forty, grateful there were few other cars on the two-lane and no imminent stop signs or traffic lights. "I commandeered this vehicle. It was not my first choice, but you gave me few options." She glanced over at Blayne, who was eyeing her with mistrust. "Although I have the legal authority to do what I did, the authorities will probably be looking for this car, so I am going to get rid of it soon. I do not want to be slowed down answering questions about who we are." She glanced at her watch. It was almost eight thirty.

"If you get rid of this, then how are we going to travel?"

"You will see."

Blayne was already regretting her decision to go with Alexi. "That's exactly why I despise this under-protection crap. Having everything about my future kept from me! And why I'm going to allow it only as long as I have to." She stared out the window as they turned off the secondary streets Alexi had been taking onto Highway 50 West and headed toward the town of Florence, some thirty-five miles distant. "I am so tired of having someone else decide what, how, when, and where the hell my life is going next. It's *my* fucking life!"

Alexi didn't respond. She let the silence lengthen, glancing at Blayne now and then. The witness was agitated and angry, her breathing rapid. She had been through so much, seemed so vulnerable, that once again Alexi found herself having to fight the urge to reach out a hand to comfort her. "Miss Weaver, you have had an impossibly stressful day. Why do you not try to get some sleep?"

"Yeah, *right!*" Blayne's tone was almost a snarl. "I can just curl up in the back of this stolen car and nod right off. Nothing like being a human target to make you all sleepy."

Alexi felt the sting of the rebuke like a slap. "Do as you please. I think it wise to get some sleep, but suit yourself."

They were approaching a gas station/convenience store that was invitingly absent any customers at the moment. Alexi glanced at her fuel gauge. They were down to less than an eighth of a tank, so they needed to make a stop soon anyway. She would like to have waited for Blayne to reach a calmer frame of mind, but they hadn't the time for that. "How much money do you have?"

"Money? Why?"

Alexi pulled into the driveway of the store and parked the Navigator at one of the pumps. "My wallet was with my identification in my bag," she explained as she switched off the engine and pocketed the keys. "Which was sucked out of the plane. I need money for gas."

"Oh, this is rich!" Blayne exclaimed, shaking her head. "So you say you're a federal agent, but really…the only thing you have in your possession is a stolen car. And…and you say you're going to help me… and then you ask for my money!" *What the hell have I gotten myself into?*

"This is an unusual situation. But I have a plan. Now please, may I have the money?"

"I have a plan," Blayne mimicked, her voice dripping with disdain. She reached into her pocket for her wallet, but half turned away from Alexi to open it, in an effort to keep the contents secret. She'd transferred some of her own money into it; there was more than a grand in there now. The rest was in the envelope stuffed into her back pocket. "They gave me five hundred," she said as she reached in to extract a couple of twenties.

"How much do you really have? All totaled?"

Blayne paused and looked at Alexi, her temper rising again. "I *said*, five hundred."

Alexi held out her hand. "Miss Weaver, hand me your wallet."

"I will not!"

"You will force me to take it from you, then."

"Look, I'm not going to give you my wallet. I'll give you whatever you need for gas…" She plucked out two… *No, make that three twenties,* she decided.

Alexi reached around to the small of her back while Blayne was preoccupied and fumbled momentarily at a clip on her belt. From the front, it looked like any ordinary women's belt, plain black leather with a decorative gold buckle. But it had been adapted for plainclothes law enforcement personnel to hold some of the tools of their trade.

When Blayne turned to hand Alexi the twenties, she found her wrist immediately encased in a handcuff. Before she could react, its twin was secured to the SUV's steering wheel and the wallet was snatched out of her hand.

"What the fuck!" She stared at the handcuffs in disbelief as Alexi got out of the car. "You can't *do* this! Take these off right now!" She rattled the cuffs, testing them. *I knew I shouldn't have opened that door and let her in. Fuck! This can't be my life!*

"I am sorry. But you are a flight risk."

"I came with you willingly, damn it!"

"But you were about to take off again."

Blayne seethed, her jaw clenched, her eyes slits of anger. "I didn't say anything…"

"You did not have to," Alexi cut her off. "Now remember, we cannot draw attention to ourselves. I will be right back." She shut the door to the Navigator and pumped several gallons into the tank, watching Blayne all the while, thankful that she didn't blow the horn or do something equally stupid.

She could see that Blayne was furious. Every now and then she could hear a muffled curse through the glass, and the rattle of the handcuffs as Blayne pulled at them in frustration.

Oh yes, it is certainly going to be great fun being tied to this firecracker for the next however many hundreds of hours.

She kept an eye on the SUV through the store's front window while she bought a few items and quickly perused the local newspaper. There were several possibilities in the classifieds, so it only took five minutes and three phone calls to get what she wanted. She scribbled directions on the edge of the newspaper, tucked it under her arm, and headed back to the SUV with her purchases.

Blayne didn't want to sound like a brat, but she lit into her as soon as she got the door open. She'd had several minutes to work up a head of steam. "Took you damn long enough! I saw you in there, reading the paper."

Alexi regarded her benignly and held up one of two large paper cups of coffee. "Do I dare give you this, Miss Weaver? It is very hot. And I have only this one change of clothes." She offered a half-smile of apology.

Blayne's anger subsided a little. In addition to the coffee, Alexi had a small bag full of food dangling from one hand. Potato chips and a two-pack of Hostess chocolate cupcakes peeked out of one side. Her stomach growled at her to be grateful.

She rattled the handcuffs. "Since we're into the bondage stage of our relationship, don't you think you can start calling me Blayne?"

It was so unexpected that Alexi burst out laughing, nearly dumping coffee onto herself, and Blayne had to join in after a moment. It was the first time either of them had really laughed in days and she felt somehow much the better for it.

"I am happy you are the forgiving type," Alexi said as she slipped into the driver's seat and unlocked the handcuffs.

Blayne rubbed her wrist. "Don't do that again."

"Do not give me reason to."

"I didn't give you a reason this time!" Blayne argued.

"Yes, you did. You are very easy to read, Miss Weaver...Blayne. Very predictable."

"Will you please stop calling me so fucking predictable? You've been doing that all night."

"It just illustrates why you need me," Alexi replied evenly. "If I can read you, so can others. Your naïveté is nothing to be defensive about. You are just a kid, and you are acting impulsively because you are frightened. It is understandable, given what you have been through."

"A *kid*? You have some hell of a nerve. Talk about fucking condescending!"

"I meant no offense," Alexi replied. "Look, we are both tired. May we start over? I am pleased to meet you, Blayne. I am Alexi."

She offered her hand, and Blayne took it after a moment's deliberation. The handshake was brief but firm, the eye contact more sustained as the two women studied each other. *So damn cocksure of herself,* Blayne thought. She found Alexi's confidence both aggravating and comforting.

They were back under way a couple of minutes later, some of the tension defused. There was no more talk between them for a while, both women too engrossed in taking the edge off their hunger with ham and cheese sandwiches and the rest of the convenience store bounty.

"Where are we going?" Blayne finally asked when they reached Florence and paused at a quiet neighborhood park, an expanse of greenery with basketball courts and children's playground equipment.

"To trade vehicles." Alexi was pleased to see the car—a red 1990 four-door Geo Prizm parked under a street lamp beside a blue late model Ford pickup. Two men in their twenties leaned against the Prizm's hood, smoking.

Alexi parked in a patch of darkness beyond the men. "Hunch down, out of sight," she told Blayne. "I want you to stay here with the doors locked until I come back. Don't say anything. Don't do anything. And keep down." She got out quickly and hit the Lock button on the remote.

"Good evening, gentlemen," she said as she walked around the Prizm, studying it from every angle. When she spoke, there was no hint of the accent that was usually a part of her speech. She sounded like she was from the next town. "Like I said, guys, I'm in a hurry. Got the keys?"

She started the car and gunned the engine, listening for problems, and checked the gauge to make sure the tank was full as she had instructed. Satisfied, she swapped seven hundred and fifty dollars cash for the title, and then turned down the men's offer of help in getting the car home, saying her husband would be arriving to help her at any moment.

Once the men had departed in their pickup, she returned to Blayne. "All clear. Time to leave."

They bagged up the rest of the food, retrieved the map, and headed to their new ride. Blayne opened the door and recoiled at the first whiff of stale cigarette smoke. The Prizm stank of it.

"Of course. Nothing can be easy," she grumbled, not entirely to herself.

They got in and buckled up, and as soon as Alexi started the engine, she lowered her window a couple of inches and cranked the heater up to high. It had been a mild early March day, with temperatures nearing fifty, but it was getting much colder now, down below freezing, and neither woman had the warmest of coats.

Alexi retraced their route until they were back on Highway 50, and this time headed east. In no time, they came upon a sign that said *Pueblo—24 Miles.*

"Pueblo?" Blayne cried, aghast. "We're going back to Pueblo?"

"We are only passing through, and you are going to be lying in the backseat when we do." Alexi glanced over at her. "Would you climb over there now, please?"

"No. Not until you tell me why we're heading right for where *you* said we had to get the hell *away* from."

"Are you always going to be so stubborn?"

Blayne had to smile a little at that. "Probably. I'm Irish."

"If you get into the back, I will tell you some of what I have planned."

"Deal." Blayne climbed over the seat and slouched down so she was mostly out of sight, but still able to watch Alexi.

"We went west initially because that is the way they will expect us to go, and I reinforced that notion by leaving the SUV where I did. But our actual route will be in the direction they will least suspect. Back toward Chicago."

"Chicago!" Blayne sat up. The horror of Martinelli's murder replayed in her mind, and in no time, her heart was pounding. "You can't be serious! I'm not going back to Chicago!"

"It is the safest direction at the moment," Alexi said patiently. "And we are not going into Chicago, just nearby so that I can replenish my resources."

Blayne slumped back down, feeling only slightly less alarmed by Alexi's choice of escape routes. *Back to Chicago.* Even if it was dangerous, at least it was familiar. *It'll probably be a lot easier to find out what happened to Claud from there. I can call our friends. Stop by some of our haunts. See if anyone has heard anything.*

She studied Alexi's profile in the dim light from the dashboard, still not entirely convinced she was who she said she was. *Worst-case scenario, she could wait until we get close to Chicago, handcuff me to the car again, or take me straight to the marshals and I'll be history.*

But as long as she could make sure Alexi would trust her enough to leave her for a few minutes, Chicago was also the perfect place for her to disappear. At least she knew the terrain. She started compiling in her mind a list of people Claudia might have contacted. Yes, Alexi's choice of direction was sounding better all the time.

I just have to find a way to ditch her. And from what I've seen so far, that's not going to be easy.

CHAPTER NINE

It was after midnight, but Theo answered on the second ring.
"Lang."

"It is Alexi. I have Blayne Keller."

"Thank God. Where are you?"

"On the move." Alexi stared past the store clerk to the Prizm bathed with the bright overhead lights beside the gas pumps. They'd left Pueblo behind four hours earlier and were now eastbound on Interstate 70, just over the Kansas state line.

"Where are you headed?"

"Somewhere safe."

"Alexi, you can tell me. This line is secure."

"I cannot depend on that. No one was supposed to know what flight we were on."

"Give me something," Theo insisted. "What's your plan?"

"My plan is to keep the witness safe until trial. That is all I can concentrate on right now, because she is resistant to protection and determined to disappear. If we push her too hard, we are going to lose her testimony."

"But if we don't know how to reach you, then we can't guarantee her court appearance," Theo said. "Without her, they might not be able to hold Cinzano."

"It is her choice, Theo. She wants nothing to do with WITSEC right now. I am trying to change her mind, but she lost trust in us after the explosion."

He sighed resignedly. "All right. What do you need?"

"I'll let you know. You'll need to assign someone else to find your leak. I have my hands full with this, and I don't think she will accept anyone else guarding her."

"Understood."

"And Theo, for obvious reasons, I would ask that you continue to keep my involvement in this case to yourself."

"The task force pretty much knows already, Alexi. A flight attendant remembered you, and the guy whose car you took. The hospital workers put you two *sisters* together, of course."

Damn.

"They'll get your name from the airline or Saint Louis airport when they reach the right people," Theo continued. "I presume you had to show your papers to get your gun through?"

"Yes."

"So they'll know who you are soon. And then Paul will call me, asking questions. So far I haven't volunteered or verified anything."

"All right," Alexi said. "Keep that up as long as you can."

"Of course."

"One more thing. The SUV I took is now in Florence, Colorado. A place called Denton Park. I *want* you to get that information to the Task Force, but in some roundabout way if you can."

"Florence. Denton Park. You got it. Anything else?"

"No. I'll be in touch."

"Frequently, I trust. Good luck, Alexi."

The second call Alexi made was to an old contact she hadn't talked to in many months. Ray Hill was a small-time forger who had been caught up in a major counterfeiting sting. He'd testified against his partners in order to avoid prosecution, and Alexi had guarded him during the trial. They had become unlikely friends.

Hill had relocated to Milwaukee after his associates were put away—close enough to Chicago to still do business there, but not close enough to run into anyone who might hold a grudge—and he had changed his specialty from money to documents. Alexi hoped he was still doing business, because he was fast and meticulous and never asked questions.

It took five rings for him to answer, and his voice was groggy from sleep. They exchanged pleasantries for several seconds, then she told him what she wanted.

"This is a rush job, my friend."

"Not a problem," Ray said. "Driver's licenses, passports, credit cards. It'll only take me a couple of hours once I get photos."

"You will have to take those yourself. We will be in Milwaukee in a day or two. In the interim, there is another favor I would like to ask."

"Whatever you need, you know that."

Once Ray was briefed, she made her final call—collect—to her attorney in Greece. She instructed him to wire a hundred thousand in cash to Ray as soon as the banks opened. It would pay for the forgeries and leave her with plenty left over to hide them away for a while. The money was to come from one of her personal accounts, and not the multimillion-dollar philanthropic foundation she administered, but it was still an insignificant amount to her.

Money had never been her motivation for joining the U.S. Marshals. Alexi came from a family of wealth, a Greek shipping dynasty going back several generations. She had been raised in privilege and schooled in the best European boarding schools and American Ivy League universities. It was expected she would run the Nikolos Philanthropic Trust when the time came.

And she did her duty, taking up the reins of responsibility and fulfilling her familial obligations. But she knew the trust was her father's moral compensation for what else their money had paid for. The politician's entertainment, the policeman's silence, the judge's leniency. She had her own way of atoning for the past that had shaped her birthright.

Alexi returned to the Prizm balancing grocery sacks full of provisions with a tray containing two large coffees. She'd made an effort to find all the sugary and chocolate items Blayne had requested. Her charge was showing signs of cooperation at last, and Alexi wanted to reward her, but she knew she could take nothing for granted. Blayne was still apt to bolt at any time.

She wasn't used to having to convince a witness to accept her protection. But she was confident she was up to the challenge. *I just have to make it much more desirable for her to stay with me than to strike out on her own.*

Blayne saw her coming and this time, instead of shouting at her, she got out to help, then settled back into the front passenger seat to examine the purchases. On top of the first sack were the Twinkies she'd requested, carefully placed so they wouldn't get crushed. Beneath them, a variety of other junk foods. Cupcakes, cookies, chips, nuts, and pretzels. And a very impressive assortment of chocolate candy bars.

"Nice." She plucked out a package of Twinkies and a Milky Way bar, and set the rest in the backseat.

Alexi handed one of the coffees over and Blayne took a long sip, then opened the second sack. It held maps, sunglasses, toothbrushes, and toothpaste. Dental floss, tissues, lip balm, shampoo and conditioner, tampons, deodorant, lotion. A box of pre-moistened towelettes. A first aid kit. Flashlight and batteries.

"Did I overlook something you might need right away?" Alexi asked, reaching past Blayne to extract the maps. "Allergy medicine, anything like that?"

"No. Looks like you got all the essentials." Blayne set the bag in the back with the food, then took another sip of coffee while she studied Alexi. "Sure you don't want me to drive?"

"I'm certain." Alexi unfolded a map of Kansas. "We will go a few more hours, and then stop at a motel. Get a shower and a decent meal."

"You're spending my money rather fast. Can't have much left."

Alexi looked up from her map. "It only has to last until tomorrow."

"What happens tomorrow?"

"We pick up money and new IDs in Milwaukee."

"Milwaukee?" Blayne frowned. "Is that as close as we're going to get to Chicago?"

"Yes. We are going to divert through Rockford." Alexi started up the car and got back on Interstate 70, continuing east.

Rockford, Blayne mused. *That might be my chance to get away.* They'd be just ninety miles west of Chicago. Easiest for her if she could take the Prizm and leave Alexi behind. She'd have to look for the right opportunity. Or maybe just *any* opportunity.

"You need to pick a new name," Alexi said. "Elizabeth Weaver is known. Any ideas? Nothing that can be used to trace you. No family or friend names."

"I have to change both first and last again?"

"Yes. Blayne is too unusual to keep."

Blayne was quiet for several minutes. Not an easy task, to pick a name she could adopt and feel comfortable answering to. It had taken her a while to come up with Elizabeth Weaver, and now she had to start all over again.

I'll keep with something Celtic, she decided. If she had to give up the name she was born with, at least she could still respect her heritage. There were many good, sturdy Irish surnames that appealed to her. O'Leery, or perhaps Callahan, or Murphy. *Yes, I like Murphy.* The first name was harder. It had to *fit,* had to really suit her, and most names that she thought of off the top of her head just didn't. She certainly wasn't a Mary or Wendy. She wanted something a bit more unusual, like Blayne was. After a moment, it came to her. Fiona. *Fiona Murphy. That's not bad.* "Fiona Murphy. How's that?"

"That will be fine."

Blayne opened her Twinkies and polished off the first one in three big bites. "You have to limit how much of this stuff you give me," she said before tackling the second sweet cylinder of spongy cake. "I've always tended to overload on junk food when I'm stressed. I gained twenty-five pounds during my last year of college and had a hell of a time getting it back off."

"You don't look as though you have ever had a weight problem." Alexi couldn't suppress a grin at the dollop of cream poised on Blayne's upper lip, like a small white mustache.

"What?" Blayne's forehead furrowed.

Alexi reached over and rubbed her thumb lightly over Blayne's lip, scooping up the cream. She did it really without thinking, and then, as she turned her attention back to the road, she stuck her thumb in her mouth to lick off the sticky spill.

Watching, Blayne felt her stomach do a little flip-flop. It was a totally innocent gesture, she was certain of that. But for some reason it struck her as entirely sensual. Alexi underwent a transformation in her eyes at that moment.

For the last several hours, despite some lingering reservations, Blayne had been seeing Alexi as her intrepid protector. The woman certainly had been acting the part. Determined. Strong. Brave. Unflappable. Totally in control. And despite her doubts, and the fact that she hated giving up control, Blayne had to admit she was impressed. She felt, at last, that she was in capable hands. For the time being, anyway.

During that first eye contact between them, just before the bomb went off—she'd known that she found Alexi damn attractive. And she had thought, for a moment, that the interest was mutual. But once she'd found out Alexi was only doing her job, she'd managed to put the woman in proper perspective and not think of her *that way*. Alexi had made it easier with her calm, cool, and detached demeanor.

And now she has to do that one damn sexy gesture, and I can't stop staring at her. There was enough light from the dashboard to pick out the curve of Alexi's lips, the strong jawline. *Yup. One nice-looking woman, that's for sure.* But Blayne had no doubt the attraction was one-sided. Alexi had done nothing to indicate that she was even gay, much less that she had any interest in *her*.

How could anybody be interested in me the way I look now, anyway? She glanced down at her oversized clothes and frowned. She needed to make some changes, and soon. *First off, I'm getting some new clothes. And some hair coloring. I can look different without looking freakish.*

Blayne opened another pack of Twinkies. "Alexi Nikolos, WITSEC inspector. Greek, obviously. That's about all I know about you. I could trust you easier if I knew some more about you."

Alexi glanced over at her. "What do you wish to know?"

"Mmm. How old are you?"

"Thirty-nine." Alexi dug into the bag of snacks and pulled out a granola bar.

"How long have you been with WITSEC?"

"Fourteen years."

"How did a Greek girl end up as a U.S. marshal?"

"Went to school here and stayed."

"Dangerous line of work."

"I find it rewarding."

She certainly doesn't volunteer a lot. Blayne was the curious type, used to asking questions when she met someone and used to them answering in much more detail. Most people liked to talk about themselves, but evidently not Alexi. She was polite and accommodating, but not terribly forthcoming.

"Hobbies?" Blayne persisted. "How do you like to spend your free time?"

Alexi smiled at the question and Blayne wondered what had popped into her head. *She doesn't smile very often.* Not that there had been anything much for either of them to smile about. And even now it was a just a maddening glimpse of one, a momentary upturn at the corners of her mouth, here and gone.

And Blayne was somehow certain her eventual answer to the question had nothing whatsoever to do with why she had smiled.

"I don't really have any hobbies. How about you?"

Turn the question around and get the attention off you. Okay, I'll play along. We've got a few hundred miles to go. "Mmm. Well, I'm a fiend on a jet ski. And not bad on a snowboard."

"Perhaps that familiarity with adrenaline rushes helped you today," Alexi said. "All in all, you have been managing pretty well throughout your ordeal. Not giving in to panic. You should be proud of yourself."

"I still can't believe that plane kept flying." Blayne closed her eyes and the image of the gaping hole in the fuselage flashed in her mind. *Impossible we survived that. Impossible.*

"We were very fortunate," Alexi said. "I can only recall a couple of occasions where an aircraft has managed to land with a big hole in it."

"I don't think I can get on another plane any time soon." Blayne stared out the passenger window into the darkness beyond, her gaze unfocused.

"I hope that won't be necessary," Alexi said. "I will do my best to avoid it."

Blayne glanced back at her. "Can *you* get on a plane right now?"

"If I had to, to keep you safe, most certainly." That trace of a smile returned, once again only briefly. "But I must admit I would rather not. Not any time soon."

Blayne was pleased at the admission, for it was the first small crack in Alexi's perfectly confident exterior. It made her more human, somehow.

"I suggest you try to sleep, if you can," Alexi said. "I would like to make a couple hundred more miles at least before we stop."

As though her body heard the suggestion and embraced it, Blayne yawned an enormous yawn. "I won't argue." She wiggled through the narrow gap between the front seats, brushing up against Alexi as she did so, and plopped down onto the bench seat in the back. "Wake me if you want me to drive, all right? I'm happy to, any time."

"I'll keep that in mind."

The next thing that Blayne knew they were stopping again, this time in front of a Days Inn motel. It was still dark outside. She sat up and glanced at her watch. Four thirty. "Where are we?"

"Salina, Kansas." As soon as she had shut off the engine, Alexi stretched her arms and yawned. "Sun will be up before long, but I need a few hours' rest, and I know you can use it too." She looked in the rearview mirror at Blayne, barely visible in the light reflected from the motel sign they were parked under. "Please tell me I can trust you."

"I am far too tired to run." *At the moment.*

Chapter Ten

It was nine a.m. when Alexi awoke to the sound of water running and found her left wrist handcuffed to the sturdy metal headboard.

She was a light sleeper, and she had surreptitiously tucked her handcuffs beneath her pillow, but Blayne had managed to find and secure them without waking her. *Pretty deftly done. Perhaps I have underestimated you.* She had to admire Blayne's pluck and abilities.

And the phone that had been on the nightstand beside her bed was gone. Alexi supposed she should have seen it coming, but she had convinced herself that Blayne was so exhausted she would save her next escape bid for a time when she had some energy. They'd both crashed on the double beds the moment they'd walked in the door and fallen asleep fully clothed, minus only their coats and footwear.

Alexi's coat was hung over the back of a chair, and her boots were placed neatly side by side against the nightstand, toes facing the bed. Blayne's things, strewn on the floor the last time Alexi saw them, were gone.

The water shut off and a few minutes later Blayne appeared in the bathroom doorway. She had her jacket and Doc Martens on, and the keys to the Prizm in one hand. "Now you get a chance to see what that feels like." She tilted her head toward the handcuffs, smiling mischievously. "Sorry to have to do this, really I am. But I told you I was going to go it alone once we got a safe distance away."

Blayne felt a vague sense of disappointment that Alexi appeared totally nonplussed by the turn of events. "I'll call the office and tell them to come check on you when I get a few miles down the road."

"I understand you feel powerless right now and wish to regain some control," Alexi said calmly. "But you do not want to do this."

"I have to take what opportunities I can. I'm sure you'd do the same thing."

"I believe I am more practiced at considering all the contingencies." With her free hand, Alexi reached between the mattress and box spring and pulled out a familiar-looking envelope. "I dare say you will need this if you plan to get very far."

Blayne's eyes widened and she patted the pocket where her Fiji fund had been. "Damn you! You took it while I slept!" She fumbled for her wallet, which she had found in Alexi's coat, and opened it. It was empty. "Fuck!"

Alexi shrugged and shoved the envelope of money into the pocket of her trousers. "Insurance."

"That's mine. I earned it. Every penny. Three years of saving for a South Seas vacation."

"You will be reimbursed. I will see to it personally. No matter what you do."

Blayne hesitated, then started angrily toward her as if to take the money back, but Alexi stiffened in readiness, and Blayne paused.

"Come on," Alexi coaxed her. "You know you can't go on the run with a few dollars and some Twinkies."

Blayne's aggravation flashed in the gray-green depths of her eyes. But something else was present too.

Glimpsing her uncertainty, Alexi changed her tone to one of caring. "Please, Blayne. I just want to keep you safe. Stop this foolishness."

Blayne considered her options. *Even if she is handcuffed, with all that training to be a marshal...* She knew better than to underestimate Alexi. "I don't think so. Money or no money, at least I have the car. Make hay while the sun shines, and all of that..." She started to go but paused at the door. *God damn it all.* "That *is* my money. I earned and saved every dime!"

"I told you, you will be reimbursed," Alexi said. "Now come unlock these handcuffs."

"I'm sorry. I can't do that." Blayne put her hand on the doorknob. "Are you *sure* you won't reconsider and toss me some cash? You claim to be concerned about my welfare. Don't you hate to think of me stuck somewhere with no money, no food, no gas?"

"I cannot let you leave alone, Blayne," Alexi said. "Please do not force me to create a scene that compromises our safety."

"Won't do you a bit of good to holler," Blayne said smugly. "There are hardly any cars in the lot, and none nearby. I think all the rooms around us are empty."

"Miss Keller, *please*." Alexi's patience was wearing thin, and it was evident both in her tone and in her unwavering glare. "You have to stop making these impulsive, rash decisions. You need to think about what you are doing."

"Okay, that's it. Time to go. I think you've given me the 'you're just a stupid kid' speech more than enough." *I hope there's some fucking gas in the car*. She cracked the door and glanced outside. There was no one in sight.

She stepped over the threshold and glanced back at Alexi. She felt that sudden lurch in her stomach again. Under other circumstances, seeing a striking-looking woman like that, handcuffed to a bed…well, it certainly had other possibilities. "I'll call when I settle somewhere. Thanks for…" Blayne trailed off in disbelief as Alexi went from relaxed nonchalance to a blur of efficient motion.

Alexi reached into her right boot and withdrew her Sig-Sauer P229, which carried a magazine of twelve rounds. It was the service pistol of the U.S. Federal Air Marshals—easily concealed because of its size—and Alexi favored it when she needed a boot gun. In the time it took her disobedient charge to say three words, Alexi drew the gun, aimed, and fired, splitting the handcuffs in two.

Blayne flinched at the noise, and before she knew it, Alexi had snatched up her boots and coat and was barreling toward her at full speed. Her face a grim mask, she snatched the keys, grabbed Blayne by the elbow, and propelled her toward the Prizm. She yanked open the front passenger door.

"Get in." Unmistakably, a command.

Blayne complied and Alexi hurried around to the driver's seat. She threw her coat and boots into the back and shoved the key into the ignition. They shot out of the parking lot just as the desk clerk stepped outside of the office to investigate the noise.

In two minutes, they were on I-70 headed east. The first sign they came to said *Kansas City—165 miles*.

Blayne felt it wise not to say anything. Though she could tell Alexi was trying to appear her usual controlled self, her clipped tone of voice was only one of many signs that she was mightily pissed. She stared straight ahead, taking deep breaths. Blayne could detect small twitches in the muscles in her jaw.

She had to admit that seeing Alexi in action was pretty impressive. *Whatever the challenge, she meets it head-on and knows just how to deal with it. Is she ever unprepared for anything?* It was hard not to trust her. Not to feel *safe* with her. She was certainly a formidable woman.

Even as angry as she was now, Alexi was clearly focused, thinking ahead, and in control. But strong emotions were there, simmering just beneath the surface, and Blayne found the glimpses of them unexpectedly appealing. The longer they were together, the more Alexi intrigued her. *Maybe I need to keep an open mind about this protection thing, as long as it's her.* It seemed a timely moment to remind herself once more that Alexi *had* saved her life, and if she wanted her dead that just didn't make any sense. Alexi was also armed. She could have put a single shot in Blayne's head any time she wanted.

Perhaps she *should* stick with Alexi awhile. Just never let her guard completely down. *It's obviously going to be difficult getting away from her. I just piss her off more each time I try. And perhaps she is better equipped to deal with all of this than I am. Wouldn't hurt, I guess, to see how Milwaukee goes.* It would also give her a chance to get some of her money back and some new ID.

And it will give me some time to get to know her. She studied Alexi surreptitiously for at least a half hour as they drove in silence, and when she detected the beginnings of relaxation, she dug into the pocket of her oversized jeans for the keys to the handcuffs.

"If you put your hand over here, I'll get that off of you."

Alexi glanced over without a change of expression.

"Sorry," Blayne said.

Alexi nodded once and offered her left wrist. Blayne removed the metal bracelet and tossed it onto the rear seat.

The silence between them grew. It was another half hour before Alexi spoke again. "This distracting cat-and-mouse game between us has to stop. It takes up far too much energy and exposes us to too much risk. I need to focus on keeping you safe, not on how to keep you from getting away from me."

"What makes you think you can keep me safe?"

"I have faith in my abilities. I am good at what I do." Alexi reached over into the sack at Blayne's feet and pulled out the two pairs of sunglasses. "Take your pick."

Blayne chose a wraparound set, leaving a pair of rectangular wire frames that seemed perfectly suited for Alexi's face.

"Blayne, there are no guarantees here. I cannot promise you that no harm will come to you. But I am much better equipped than you to deal with the people who are after you. Especially if you decide you do not want to go into a protective facility or safe house."

"I guess I'm finding it hard to disagree with that."

"You do not have to accept the program or relocation. For now, I would be happy if you just agree to let me make the decisions for you, and stop trying to get away."

They were approaching an exit ramp populated with numerous restaurants and gas stations, and Alexi took it. "We need gas and food. Will you be putting us at risk again, or not?"

"Not," Blayne said. "At least until we hit Milwaukee. I'll give you that. My word on it."

❖

Despite her promise to stick with Alexi at least until Milwaukee, Blayne found herself on a very tight leash when they stopped in Des Moines. She had begged to shop for clothes; she couldn't stand to wear her goth disguise for another minute. Alexi said she needed a change, too, but insisted they stick to small strip mall places so that she could keep Blayne in sight at all times.

Blayne went in and out of the dressing rooms, choosing jeans, sweaters, and shirts. Alexi had asked that she get only a few clothes, and quickly, as they had a long way to travel that day. As far as she could tell, Alexi never tried on anything for herself, but when Blayne placed her selections on the counter Alexi set a small pile down next to them. The contrast in their choices could not have been more obvious. Where Blayne had chosen a lot of bright colors and patterns, all of Alexi's clothes were in conservative dark tones. "I guess there's not much of my money left now," she remarked as Alexi paid for their purchases. This earned a somewhat irritated look.

"As I have said, you will be reimbursed."

Blayne felt some sense of confidence that all the money *would* be paid back, providing she kept in touch with authorities so they would know where to send it. She was still debating with herself whether she was going to testify. Probably yes; her conscience would nag at her if she didn't. But she still abhorred the idea of having to move and live in fear, always looking over her shoulder. Using a name not her own, and having to sever all ties with her friends. Which really meant with Claudia. She was really the only friend who mattered. *If something has happened to Claud and Philippe, is it really such a big deal whether I stay in Chicago?*

"Can we stop at the Walgreens next door?" Blayne ran a hand through her hair as they left the store, still not quite accustomed to its short length. "I'd like to get some hair coloring, maybe something remotely resembling my real color."

"Which is?"

"They always called it strawberry blond when I was growing up. Kind of a light reddish blond."

They deposited their clothes in the trunk of the car before venturing into the drugstore. "I would like to suggest you consider a darker red, at least." Alexi said. "So you are not quite so instantly recognizable."

"I'll think about it."

Blayne settled on a L'Oréal offering called Light Golden Copper Brown, a two-tone color that was darker and richer than her own. Her complexion would blend well with it, she thought, and yet it was also quite different from any photographs they might have of her. She had begun to accept that perhaps Alexi did have her best interests at heart and was providing her with good advice. On hair color, she could compromise.

Blayne wandered the aisles of the Walgreens, Alexi close behind, and selected a few other items before they departed. Cosmetics, perfume, her favorite skin care products, more snacks, bottled water, and a couple of paperbacks. They filled up the gas tank again, Alexi took another look at the map, and they were back on the road in less than an hour, all told.

"Next stop?" Blayne dug through the drugstore bag and pulled out a bag of CornNuts. Soon she was crunching noisily away.

"We will stop as we need to for gas and food, but otherwise go straight on through to Milwaukee. Looks like it is another six hours or so, so it will be ten or eleven p.m. at least before we get in there."

"Then what?" Blayne offered Alexi one of the bottled waters, and it was accepted with a slight nod of thanks.

"We will stop at a motel near where my friend lives. Get a good night's sleep, and you can color your hair and change your appearance. First thing tomorrow, he will take our pictures, and in a few hours, we will have new passports and can head up into Canada."

"Canada?"

"Yes. Some cabins or something. I will know a good place when we find it."

Blayne had to admit Alexi's plan didn't sound half bad. "Does WITSEC have some arrangement with Canada?"

"No. You told me you wanted no involvement with the program, so I am avoiding our normal places." Alexi kept their speed just over the limit. "For the time being, Blayne, I am not telling my superiors where we are. I want you to be able to trust me."

Blayne was surprised by the admission and felt intuitively that Alexi was being straight with her. *Sure to hell hope I'm right.* "Thank you for that."

They got into Milwaukee a few minutes after eleven and checked into an Econo Lodge near the airport. It took a good half hour of repeated shampooing for Blayne to get out most of the temporary black hair dye. Several more minutes to scrub off the raccoon makeup and the tattoos. Then another three-quarters of an hour to color her hair, but she was happy with the result. She could recognize herself again and felt decidedly less freakish, though she still bemoaned the loss of her shoulder-length hair.

And she was ecstatic to be rid of those godawful baggy clothes that made her feel huge and ungainly. Normally she slept in the nude, but she had picked up a baby blue tank top and matching shorty briefs at the strip mall to wear to bed. Blayne put the sleepwear on and ventured out to join Alexi.

Alexi had caught the end of one of the local newscasts and was switching repeatedly between channels, finding nothing to hold her interest, when she heard a sound behind her. She had seen a few transformations in her years with the Witness Protection Program. But nothing like this. Her breath caught in her throat at the sight of Blayne towel-drying her hair in the bathroom doorway.

A twentyish, feisty punk had gone into the bathroom. *Where did the kid go?* Blayne was certainly all woman now. All soft curves, in just the right proportions, and the minimal clothing she had on showed off her amazing assets from every angle. The baby blue briefs draped a firm, round ass and shapely hips, and the tank top hugged her breasts, the bump of nipples faintly visible beneath the thin fabric.

She draped the towel over her shoulders and glanced over at the television to see what Alexi was watching, which gave Alexi the opportunity to stare unabashedly at her a few seconds longer. She took in the damp and tousled hair, the coppery brown color perfectly suited to Blayne's fair and lightly freckled complexion and the shadowed green of her eyes. Without the tattoos, fake piercings, and absurd goth makeup, she was adorable. No, more than that. *She's sexy as hell.*

Blayne smiled, and it lit up her face, imbuing it with such sweetness Alexi wondered how she could have missed the attractive woman hiding beneath the clothes and makeup.

"What the hell are you watching?" Blayne asked, finally resting her gaze on Alexi.

It was only then that Alexi realized she had paused on a late-night infomercial, this one trying to sell a collection of rather demonic-looking international dolls of the world. Flustered, but careful not to show it, she clicked off the set.

"Nothing on at this hour, I am afraid. We should get some sleep anyway."

"Yeah, I'm ready to crash. That's for sure." Blayne stretched her arms above her head, exposing the pale, smooth skin of her stomach, and Alexi decided it was a damn good thing they had been able to get a room with two beds.

True to her word, Blayne was sound asleep soon after her head hit the pillow, but Alexi found it harder to drift off. She found the new Blayne disconcerting and she knew she needed to get a handle on her attraction at once. Her weakness for a shapely feminine figure had already cost her much. She would not allow history to repeat itself.

At first light, she awakened and had her own shower, and by the time she was dressed she found Blayne ready and waiting for her, in jeans and a green turtleneck sweater that matched her eyes and was altogether way too formfitting. *Giati Thee mou. Give me strength.*

❖

Theo Lang was accustomed to late-night phone calls, so he answered on the second ring, fully awake. It was Paul Fletcher with an update.

"Skip Topping is dead and Keller is alive. We're not certain of her whereabouts, but it looks like she's with a U.S. marshal." Fletcher paused.

Theo knew he was waiting for the reaction, trying to gauge how much his superior knew.

"Topping was sitting right where the bomb went off," he said when Theo was silent. "And it *was* a bomb, they're pretty certain. Keller was supposed to be there too. But we know now that she was up and walking and was taken to the hospital after the landing. She skipped out before police could talk to her."

"That's all we have?" Theo probed, sensing Fletcher was holding something back, no doubt saving the best till last.

"The U.S. marshal on the plane was Alexi Nikolos," Fletcher announced, then paused again, as though expecting his boss to either express surprise or offer verification.

Theo did neither. "Anything else?"

"She commandeered a vehicle at the hospital. We got a tip and found the car southwest of where the plane landed. If they keep in that direction, they might be headed to Utah, or Vegas. Maybe even Mexico."

"Are we sure she's with Keller?"

"When she took the car, she told the driver she was in hot pursuit. So we're operating under the assumption she is either already with Keller or is following her."

"All right. Keep me informed." It was Theo's dismissal, but Fletcher was obviously determined to find out who had brought Alexi in on the case.

"Should I make some phone calls to try to verify that Nikolos has been reinstated? And, if not, why she's involved in this?"

"No," Theo said. "I will see to that aspect of the case."

"All right. Whatever you say."

Theo could sense Fletcher's disappointment. He and Alexi had not gotten along when he had been her superior, but her personnel files contained few details about her departure from WITSEC, just as Fletcher's file contained few details about why he'd been demoted from the top spot in Chicago a few months later.

Everyone in the Chicago WITSEC office had been shocked by both events. Alexi Nikolos had been a highly regarded inspector, held in esteem by her peers. And Paul Fletcher had been viewed as a more than capable division chief, organized and evenhanded, approachable, and quick to offer praise and encouragement.

Fletcher had seemed to take his demotion in stride and had voiced no complaints about his reassignment to the Joint Task Force on Organized Crime. Alexi hadn't complained either, at least not to Theo, or confided in him about the reasons she'd left.

But then again, he reasoned, both of them had been very well trained never to show their emotions, never to reveal too much about what they were feeling and thinking and planning. He wondered, not for the first time, exactly what had happened, and whether the abrupt changes in the two officers' fates was related somehow.

❖

A short while later, another call was made from a public phone near the WITSEC offices to a cell phone. The men speaking were familiar with each other's voices. They had spoken many times, but only one had any idea who the other was.

"Blayne Keller is alive, but we don't know where she is," the caller reported. "She may have a U.S. marshal with her, but it's on the hush-hush. Something's not right with this. It's become too risky for me to call you."

"Perhaps you don't understand what risky *is*," Cinzano's man responded casually, but with deadly implication. "Now tell me everything you know."

CHAPTER ELEVEN

The two women got to Ray Hill's place shortly after eight.
"Hey! There she is! How ya doin', Lex?" Hill was a short and stocky man, with tattoos all over his arms and neck. He greeted Alexi with a kiss on the cheek and a bear hug that lifted her off her feet.

"As good as can be expected when I have to come see you," she responded warmly. "But any excuse to see you will do. You look great."

Blayne was startled by the contrast between the two, and their obvious connection despite it. The biker tough guy and the charming WITSEC inspector. Alexi was dressed down, in blue jeans and a cream-colored shirt beneath her leather coat, but whatever she wore, there was an element of classic elegance to her appearance. The jeans fit her perfectly, hugging her slim hips and flaring just enough to accommodate her boots, and she'd managed to find a shirt that looked nicer than the usual off-the-rack stuff found at strip malls. The fabric was cut well, and it was finely detailed with wide cuffs and mother-of-pearl buttons.

Hill had a two-bedroom condo over a car repair joint. It didn't look like much from the outside, which was typical of Ray and one reason Alexi liked dealing with him—he never drew attention to himself. Once they were inside, however, it was evident the forger made a comfortable living. There was an impressive high-definition television along one wall, and the living room was crowded with the various tools of his trade—photography equipment, two copy machines, a laminator and credit card embosser. His desk overflowed with blank birth certificates, passports, and other documents.

"Come on in. Have a seat." He snatched up some of the dirty clothes and empty takeout cartons that were scattered about, and Blayne and Alexi sat in comfortable leather easy chairs the color of mud. "Oh! I ran that errand for you, Lex." He reached under his desk for a paper grocery bag, half filled and folded closed, and handed it to Alexi. "No problems, just like you said. Now, you wanted the full works, right?"

"Yes. Passports, driver's licenses, birth certificates, credit cards. My friend here will need documents under the name Fiona Murphy, and I would like you to do my set under Jacquelyn Andrews."

"I'll get those photos done, and I'll have everything for you by ten thirty, eleven tops."

"Excellent. So how have you been, Ray? Staying out of trouble?"

"Flying under the radar, so far." Ray retrieved two cameras from the clutter on his desk, one digital and the other an instant-photo type. "What's up with you? Sure been a long time."

"I have been out of the country."

"Well, nice to see you back. Don't be such a stranger, huh?" He positioned himself beside the blank wall he used as a backdrop. "Who's first?"

Alexi turned toward Blayne. "Fiona?"

The photos took only a few minutes, and then they were back in the Prizm with at least a couple of hours to kill. Alexi stashed the bag of cash in the trunk. "Shall we find a nice place for a leisurely breakfast?"

"Sounds great. So…how do you know this guy Ray?" Blayne asked. "I mean, is this the way you usually get passports and stuff for people?"

"Usual is such a relative term. Usual means to go to city hall and then several days' wait, and I don't think you want that."

"Oh! I get it!" Blayne said. "All that stay-out-of-trouble stuff. This is illegal, isn't it? Did you arrest him or something?"

"He was a witness I was assigned to protect."

"Well he seems healthy enough, so I guess I can consider him a good reference for your abilities, then."

Alexi had to smile at that.

"So if he's not exactly a straight-arrow kind of guy…tell me, can he also get me a gun?" Blayne asked.

"A *gun?*" Alexi repeated. "You are definitely *not* getting a gun. No way."

"And why not? I've shot a gun before. My dad was a hunter and had rifles and pistols both."

"Blayne, you are not getting a gun. You have no need for one."

"I'd like to be able to protect myself," Blayne argued. "What happens if you're not around?"

"I will always be around. You do not need a weapon, as long as you allow me to protect you."

Blayne didn't argue the case further. But she also did not abandon the idea of trying to pick up some kind of weapon for herself, with or without Alexi's help.

They found a small café with an unexpectedly creative menu that included four varieties of eggs Benedict and homemade cinnamon rolls and pastries. It also had fabulous coffee, so they lingered over their first decent meal in days.

Alexi had to keep reminding herself not to stare at Blayne, but the transformation still astounded her and she caught herself repeatedly stealing covert glances at Blayne's body, breasts, and face. It was irrational, she knew, but still she marveled at how a simple change in hair color, makeup, and clothes seemed to turn Blayne from irritating to irresistible.

"You know…" Blayne paused to sip her fourth cup of coffee. "I understand the need for new IDs, and I'll be careful when I need to be. But I want you to still call me Blayne when we're alone and when it doesn't matter."

"All right. As you wish."

Blayne decided it was time to take another stab at getting the taciturn WITSEC inspector to open up. "Is Alexi short for Alexandra?"

"Yes."

"Any brothers or sisters?"

"A younger sister. Her name is Vasiliki."

"What's she like?"

Alexi smiled as she considered how to answer. "Irrepressible."

Interesting answer. "Is she here or in Greece?"

"Neither. She lives north of London."

"Parents?"

"No. Both deceased."

"Mine are gone too," Blayne said. "They died in a fire while I was away at college." It had been so many years ago that it no longer ripped her apart to talk about it, and she hoped that opening up about herself would encourage Alexi to reveal a few personal things as well.

"I am sorry. That must have been extremely difficult."

"Yeah, it was. We lived above an Irish pub that my parents opened when I was just a baby. Blarneys. I was going to go back to work there after I graduated."

Most of the information that Blayne was volunteering was in the WITSEC file on her, but Alexi let her talk anyway. *Maybe she needs to.* And it never hurt to know as much as you could about the witness you were protecting. She wouldn't mind a few more insights into how Blayne's mind worked. It might help her predict what Blayne would do. She certainly hadn't seen the handcuffs coming.

And, to be honest, Alexi didn't mind at all listening to Blayne talk about herself. She was rather intrigued by her unpredictable charge and was also relieved that a rapport seemed possible between them. Blayne's change in appearance seemed to have brought about a change in attitude too.

"So, you've been in law enforcement a long time," Blayne said. "Ever done anything else?"

"Nothing noteworthy."

"Ever want to?" Blayne pressed.

"No. Not really."

"Ever answer in more than brief phrases when someone asks you about yourself?" Blayne allowed her frustration to creep into her voice.

One side of Alexi's mouth tipped upward in a half-smile. "No."

That made Blayne laugh, and she let the questions go for a while. So far, she'd struck out in her efforts to get Alexi to engage in the kind of social chatter that most people she knew engaged in. She usually had no problem getting clients at the travel agency to talk ad nauseam about their trips, their jobs, and their families. The challenge was in getting them to stop.

Alexi was always polite and accommodating, but she answered every question with a minimum of information, or she engineered a clever shift in the conversation. She was an enigma, nearly impossible to read. Blayne found her lack of expression and emotion both intriguing and enormously frustrating. And she couldn't stop thinking about that moment when Alexi had touched her lips and then licked the cream off her thumb. *Damn, that was sexy.*

As they left Milwaukee, after collecting the documents from Ray, Blayne wondered briefly whether she'd made the right decision in sticking with Alexi. *You'll just be getting farther and farther from Chicago from now on. It will be harder to find out what happened to Claud.* She'd been too tired the night before to make a run for it but had been sorely tempted that morning. Tempted enough to search Alexi's clothes for the keys to the Prizm while she was in the shower. But also content enough to stay when she realized they were not to be found. *Took them in the shower with you, did you? Well, I guess I can't say that I blame you.*

Blayne made several more attempts to engage Alexi in conversation as they drove along the shore of Lake Michigan. They passed into Michigan's Upper Peninsula at Menominee and continued to hug the shoreline, moving northeast on M-35. There was sparse traffic on the two-lane and the sky was a brilliant blue, and with the sun sparkling off the big lake like diamonds, the drive was not at all unpleasant.

"You know, I grew up pretty close to here," Blayne said. "Ishpeming. It's not very big. Just a couple of hours north."

"Did you like growing up in a small town?"

"Yes, very much. Knowing everyone, and everyone knowing you. It was great." Blayne fell silent for a long while, casting her mind back. "I suppose it's too close to Chicago and too traceable to think that I might be safe moving back there."

"I am afraid so."

"Figured. It's not like I have a lot of friends back there now anyway. Most of the kids I went to high school with moved away, like I did. But at least it's familiar."

Her memories of home, and their proximity to it, made Blayne nostalgic for the carefree days of her youth. Since she was having no luck getting Alexi to talk about herself, she gave up that effort for the time being and decided to try to distract herself with one of the paperbacks she had bought. But it was hard to concentrate. She would scan a page or two, then stare out of the window and immediately forget what she had read.

Watching sadness sweep over Blayne's face as they rode along,

Alexi decided that some cheering up was in order. "What are you reading, might I ask?"

"*Broken Prey*," Blayne answered. "John Sandford. Know him? He writes suspense-thrillers."

"You haven't had enough of that in your own life?" Alexi asked drolly.

That got the smile she was hoping for.

"Touché," Blayne said.

They pulled into Saint Ignace, the tourist-driven town on the north side of the Mackinac Bridge, just after eight p.m. and found a motel room overlooking the water.

"I saw a steak and seafood place coming into town," Alexi offered after they had unpacked their few belongings. "Interested in some supper?"

"Don't have to ask me twice."

❖

La Famiglia was a well-appointed, intimate restaurant with subdued lighting and soft jazz and a wall of windows overlooking the Straits of Mackinac, which gave every table a spectacular view. There was a full moon, and it reflected huge and silver off the water, and the lights on the Mackinac Bridge twinkled in the distance.

Alexi regretted her choice of establishments immediately. It was exactly the sort of place she would normally bring a woman if she wanted to bed her later. And that was certainly not the case tonight. She was already attracted to Blayne, and this would do nothing to stem those feelings. But it was too late for a change of venue, so she just had to be careful not to let her interest in Blayne show in any way. *Which shouldn't be too difficult.* She was accomplished at hiding her feelings.

The hostess seated them in a private corner by the window, a cozy table for two, and a short while later Alexi was feasting on fresh grilled whitefish while Blayne dug into a medium-rare filet mignon.

Blayne sighed at the irony. Here she was, enjoying dinner in the most romantic restaurant she'd been in, in several months. Sharing a bottle of wine with a beautiful, charming woman who impressed and intrigued her no end. *No one should look that good by candlelight.*

But things were not as they appeared. There was certainly no romance involved here. *Damn shame she's not the least bit interested. Has hardly looked at me and hasn't even commented once on what a nice place this is.*

Blayne was a bit of a lightweight when it came to alcohol. She usually didn't have more than one or two drinks when she went out. But she desperately needed to unwind tonight, so she ignored her usual limits. After all, she reasoned, she'd been through hell, was running for her life, and her future was as uncertain as it could possibly be. She still didn't know what had happened to Claudia, she had no job and no home, and now her hormones were getting all stirred up over someone who probably wasn't even gay. If that wasn't enough reason to knock back a few, what was?

They were seated perpendicular to each other at the small square table, Alexi to her left, and as they made small talk Blayne found herself leaning closer than strangers should. Alexi said something about taking another shopping excursion in the morning before heading into Canada, but Blayne barely registered what she was saying. A seductive sax riff was playing in the background and the wine was loosening her inhibitions. She couldn't stop staring at Alexi's lips, wondering how soft they would feel against her own.

Halfway through her fourth glass of wine, after they had been silent for a while, Blayne decided it was time to find out a little more about the enigmatic Alexi Nikolos. She had to say something, anything, because if she didn't, she just might have to give in to a growing impulse to kiss her.

"So, do you bring all your witnesses to such romantic restaurants?"

It had not escaped Alexi's notice that Blayne had been looking at her lips for the last half hour or so, staring more overtly with each glass of wine she consumed. She had been aware of it because she had been stealing frequent glances herself, more surreptitiously, of course, of Blayne's smile, her delicate hands, and the curve of her breasts, which were far too tantalizingly outlined by the formfitting green turtleneck not to be noticed.

But the question still caught Alexi off guard with its bluntness. She looked around as if noticing the surroundings for the first time. "It was not a conscious choice. Does it make you uncomfortable?"

"Uncomfortable is certainly *not* the word I would use." Blayne's response was filled with innuendo, said with an inflection that begged Alexi to ask what word she *would* use, but she did not rise to the bait.

"I chose it because it had more cars in the parking lot than any of the other places," she said. "Which is usually a pretty reliable way to go when you are in a strange town."

Blayne's face registered disappointment at the prosaic answer, but Alexi pretended not to notice. She sipped her Lambrusco with no change in expression. She was on her third glass, but she had been raised on wine and it had little effect on her. A damn good thing, because she needed to be in total control right now.

I swear she's flirting with me. Isn't she? Oh, this was not good. Not good at all.

"Tell me about yourself," Blayne requested. She was getting a bit too inebriated to notice that with each question, she was leaning closer to Alexi.

"What do you wish to know?" Alexi said it casually, but inside, she dreaded what was coming. She kept her eyes trained on the water outside.

"Anything." Blayne leaned forward a little more. "*Everything.*"

"You have to be more specific. Tell me what it is you would like to know and I will choose whether I will answer." Alexi tried not to squirm, but she could feel Blayne was staring at her. She hoped that Blayne hadn't picked up on her attraction.

"Are you married?"

Uh-oh. "No, I am not."

"Seeing anyone seriously?"

"No." *I don't like where this is going.*

"So…what type of person are you attracted to?"

Shit. How do I answer this? I'm attracted to thirty-year-old feisty redheads at the moment, apparently.

Blayne's voice had gotten nearer with each question. They were breathing the same air.

Alexi didn't dare look her way, afraid that Blayne might see something in her eyes. "I do not have a 'type.' It depends on the individual."

"You sure don't volunteer much about yourself, do you?"

Alexi leaned back in her chair to put more distance between them. Casually swirling the burgundy contents of the glass she held loosely in one hand, she glanced at Blayne. "Only when it is necessary and appropriate."

"Well, I would deem it *very* necessary on this occasion." Blayne licked her lips, and Alexi found the gesture entirely too provocative. "After all, the more I get to know you, the easier I can trust you."

"I am private by nature. I assure you, I am well qualified to protect you and dedicated to my responsibilities."

Blayne swayed slightly as she leaned in several more inches toward Alexi. "Well, maybe this occasion needs to be both necessary *and* appropriate, then. So when is it appropriate for you to open up to someone about yourself? Hmm?"

Alexi considered her answer. The truth was, she really never opened up to anyone completely, outside of her immediate family. Never divulged the most innermost parts of herself to either friend or lover.

She glanced at Blayne again and was surprised by the intensity of her gaze. Alexi remained outwardly relaxed, but it was only with deliberate, conscious effort. The one sign of her discomfort at Blayne's insistent attention was her occasional tendency to run one hand through her hair. It was a gesture Alexi would have immediately recognized in someone else, a sign of attraction, but she failed to accept its significance when she did it herself.

"It is appropriate when I am connecting to someone on a personal level and not a professional one. When I intend to establish a long-term relationship of some kind." Blayne felt a hollow pang of disappointment in her chest at Alexi's clear and rigid delineation at what their relationship was to be. *Or, more accurately put, what our necessary association is to be.* But she was still not entirely deterred from her efforts to get to know Alexi better, because she had noticed that Alexi never made any reference to dating men. *It depends on the individual, does it? That's carefully evasive about which way you swing.* So perhaps all was not lost yet. She finished glass number four and reached for the bottle to pour herself some more. It was empty. "Damn."

"Perhaps you have had enough for this evening. We should get some rest so we can get an early start." Alexi reached for the check.

"No." Blayne put her hand on Alexi's arm to stop her. "Please. Not yet. Just a little longer. One more glass." She was adorable in the candlelight, her face shining in her slight intoxication, her lower lip extended in an exaggerated pout.

"All right. One more." Alexi hailed the waiter and ordered a glass of wine for Blayne and coffee for herself.

Blayne was staring at her again. She could see it in her peripheral vision, and she wasn't sure what in the hell she should do about it except to try to keep from fidgeting under that intense scrutiny.

Blayne's insistent attention was extremely disquieting, and the look in her eyes said *I want you.* But did it mean Blayne was gay? Perhaps it was just the alcohol. Or maybe Blayne was lonely and confused, and this was just her way of distracting herself during this extreme time of high emotions.

Sometimes near-death experiences themselves could trigger unexpected things in the body. Alexi herself had, on occasion, felt herself unexpectedly aroused when her body was pumping with adrenaline on the job. But it really didn't matter *why* Blayne was flirting so outrageously with her. Or that she was very tempted to flirt back. She had to act completely oblivious to what was going on, though she could very well read the clear body language. Under no circumstances could she allow herself to become involved with a witness again. Period. That was that.

"You are a very appealing woman, Alexi." Blayne placed her hand on Alexi's arm again.

Her mind worked to come up with a way to crack Alexi's implacably cool exterior. She could sense a fire raging beneath the surface, a passionate nature barely contained. Maybe it was just wishful thinking. But she was becoming increasingly frustrated by her inability to get any kind of any emotional response from Alexi or even an acknowledgment of what she was really getting at.

She took another sip of wine. "Mysterious. Evasive. Elusive. You know, I happen to find all of those traits extremely compelling."

"Perhaps that's because you have had too much to drink," Alexi replied. *What an insane and impossible situation. This gorgeous woman is practically throwing herself at me and I cannot do what I want to do. Damn it all.*

"Why? Am I misbehaving?" Blayne said, her eyes twinkling with mischief. "Or am I being too honest?"

"Neither. You are just tipsy, tired, and in need of distraction."

"Hmm. Slightly tipsy, maybe," Blayne agreed. "But I know what I'm doing, or trying to do…and I'm obviously not getting through. What am I doing wrong? Is it because I'm a woman?"

Alexi tried to appear nonplussed by the question. *Why the hell did I let her have any more wine? This cannot be happening.* "Your gender is not relevant. Your mental and physical state is. It is not just the alcohol. It is the stress of the whole situation, also. Your judgment is impaired."

"I may be tired and this whole situation may be insane, but my judgment is just fine," Blayne argued.

"I beg to differ. If there were nothing wrong with your judgment you would not have given me such a hard time all the way here." Alexi met Blayne's eyes steadily, seeing an opportunity to convince her to finally accept her protection, and also to get the conversation diverted to another topic. "From the moment that we met I have been trying to persuade you to allow me to keep you alive, and I have actually saved your life, also. However, you have done nothing but doubt my intentions. In my book, that is bad judgment."

"I've had every reason to be suspicious of you," Blayne replied testily. "Of *anyone*, considering what's happened. That doesn't mean I don't know what I'm doing." She cocked her head to one side, studying Alexi. "Why the hell can't you handle a compliment?"

She is like a dog with a bone. How can I get her to stop? "As I said, I cannot trust your judgment. Besides, you are not in any position to be declaring an attraction, and I am not in any position to be able to accept it."

Blayne perked up at that statement. "So, if my condition and your situation were different, would that change anything?"

"I do not work with hypothetical situations. We need to concentrate on keeping you alive, and not indulge in pointless speculation."

Her reply was a frustrating and vivid reminder to Blayne that Alexi didn't see this as a romantic restaurant, full of possibilities. It was work. And she was on guard. Always. "Don't you ever relax?"

"Only when I can afford to. And now is not that time. Your life is too high a price to pay for the sake of some fleeting experiment." Perhaps that trivialization would hit home where common sense had so far failed.

Blayne barely seemed to register the comment. "Look, I'm certainly glad you take your job so seriously. But surely we're safe now. Can we just have some fun? Even if it is just an…experiment."

Alexi struggled to maintain her composure, but it was getting increasingly difficult. Blayne's persistence was starting to have an effect on her physically. *Oh, I understand exactly what you mean. And we certainly could have some fun together, if things were different. Lots and lots of fun. But I cannot let this continue.*

"Listen to me. This happens all the time, witnesses being infatuated with the agents protecting them. Rather like a patient falling for her therapist. It will pass. Now, please finish your wine, because we both need to get some rest."

She snatched up the check and signaled the waiter they were ready to pay, hoping to forestall further conversation.

But Blayne was not about to let the topic rest after a comment like that. "Pardon me, but that's just bullshit. I know damn well when I'm attracted to a woman, and I have since the age of fourteen." Her anger was rising, and it was clear in her voice. "I understand if you're not attracted to me, but don't think that you know me and what and how I feel. You were hired to protect me, not to analyze me."

Alexi knew there was truth in that statement. Perhaps she had indeed overstepped her bounds. But she *was* speaking from experience—several of the witnesses she had protected had come on to her, or developed crushes on her, men and women both. And it was entirely possible Blayne was falling into the same pattern.

Blayne apparently didn't think so. And if she were truly honest with herself, Alexi might admit that it felt different to her too. But there was no use acknowledging that. There was simply no way she would get involved with a witness again.

She kept her voice even, with some difficulty. "I am sorry if I've given you the impression that I am trying to analyze you and tell you what to feel. It was not my intention. And if I have insulted you in any way please accept my apologies."

Her polite and totally emotionless answer only infuriated and frustrated Blayne even more. She felt like grabbing the WITSEC agent and planting a big kiss on her, telling her to analyze *this*, just to see if she could get a reaction, any reaction, because her words and her outright flirting weren't doing the trick.

Yeah, maybe she'd do just that. She took another long sip of wine to steel her courage as Alexi paid the check.

❖

He had stayed at his computer at the Chicago Joint Task Force on Organized Crime far longer than usual, hoping for more news on Blayne Keller and Alexi Nikolos. But to remain at his desk so long after his shift was risky under the circumstances. The graveyard-shift guys were starting to give him odd looks, so he finally gave up and headed home shortly before eleven p.m.

When he let himself in, his wife was putting the leash on their Jack Russell, who was whining for his nightly neighborhood stroll.

"Just in time," she commented as she kissed him hello. "He was getting so impatient, I was about to take him out myself."

"No need," he said. "Come on, Frisco." Still in his suit and tie, he headed out with the dog.

As he passed in front of a darkened storefront a quarter mile from his home, a well-dressed man stepped out of the recessed entryway and fell into pace beside him. He masked his surprise and kept on walking. He had never seen the man before, but he knew immediately the voice would be familiar.

"Like clockwork. You are always so predictable," the stranger said.

"What the hell are you doing here?"

"Well, I'm sure not here to join you for a romantic moonlit walk. We want to know why you haven't contacted us." The stranger suddenly veered off from the man's usual route, so they would now be heading away from his house. Even the dog seemed momentarily surprised. "Act natural and keep on walking," he said.

Reluctantly, the man followed. "I haven't called because there is nothing to report. We don't know where she is."

"So you're telling me your whole task force cannot track down one woman?"

"Yes. Exactly. She's pulled out of the program. We've lost contact with her." The dog stopped to do his business, and the men paused awkwardly, both of them glancing around. They were in a mixed area, part residential but with a few neighborhood businesses, all closed. There was sparse traffic, and no other pedestrians at that hour.

"But you will continue to look for her," the man said when they resumed walking. The inflection made it more statement than question.

"Yes. She'll turn up."

"We expect to be informed about her every move."

"It's very risky for me to contact you," the man said. "I think they may be watching me. Or at least trying to find the leak."

"We have paid you sufficiently to solve that problem," the stranger said.

"Yes, you have. And you won't let me forget it."

"See to it, then. Now go home."

The stranger continued on in the direction they were heading, and the man and his dog turned and headed back the way they had come.

The two miles back to the motel were not nearly long enough for Alexi to calm the inner stirrings of her body. She saw Blayne to their room and unlocked the door, but did not follow her inside.

"I have something to do," she said from the threshold, and Blayne paused and turned around with a disappointed expression. "Please do not leave the room or make any phone calls. I will be close by, and back soon. Get some rest."

She left without giving Blayne a chance to object, but remained just outside the door for a long moment in case Blayne was tempted to follow her. When she did not, Alexi headed to a place in the shadow of a large tree where she could wait, unobserved, in the darkness and still see the door to their room. She pulled the collar of her jacket up and hugged her arms to her sides. She wished she had dressed more warmly now, but she was counting on the fact that the alcohol Blayne had consumed would put her to sleep before she got unbearably chilled.

What a nightmare. How the hell am I going to protect her, be with her day and night, with her trying to seduce me? This is torture.

CHAPTER TWELVE

Alexi rubbed her eyes, trying to shrug off the drowsy aftereffects of a night spent tossing and turning, unable to sleep as she fought an inward battle of physical arousal versus mental resolve. When she'd returned to their motel room, she had found Blayne passed out, fully clothed, looking so innocent and vulnerable in slumber that it was all she could do not to touch her fingertips to the soft coppery strands of hair that rested against Blayne's cheek. *I'll keep you safe.*

The more she got to know Blayne, the more protective she felt toward her. *She has had such a lot to go through. To endure all this with no family to support her, and now cut off from all that is familiar. No wonder, then, that she has developed an attachment for me, but that attraction is misplaced.*

She kept reminding herself that was all that it was. Blayne was just naïve about what was going on. She would come to realize she was merely reaching out toward the one person who could make her feel safe. And then the infatuation would fade, as quickly as it had begun. *Pity, too.*

It would certainly make it easier for Alexi to focus on her job if Blayne wasn't throwing herself at her the way she did last night. But Alexi also found herself lamenting the day that Blayne realized her feelings weren't real but only transitory. *Regretful we could not have met under different circumstances.*

She didn't care to examine why she was feeling somewhat wistful about this missed opportunity. She had enjoyed wonderful evenings with countless women, had sex pretty much any time she wanted it, and never before had wasted energy thinking about a woman she could not have. There was always another woman around the corner.

Alexi was beginning to feel restless to get back on the road. She glanced at her watch. Nine a.m. She'd give Blayne another half hour. Looking out over the water once again, she recalled their evening and Blayne's blatant flirting. *I wonder if she will remember everything she did. She was getting pretty intoxicated there toward the end.* And even more than that, she wondered whether Blayne would try to pick up where she left off.

Blayne replayed the night before in her head as she studied Alexi in profile. She was, at turns, chagrined by her bold behavior and excited by the memory of how Alexi had made her feel. She still couldn't believe that she'd fallen asleep waiting for Alexi to return to the room, even with her frustration boiling over. She had been *there*, all primed and ready to go, all set to finally taste those lips she had stared at all night, and before she'd even realized what was happening, she was alone. *Fuuuck.*

Now it was morning and her head hurt like a sonofabitch. She winced at the bright light streaming into the room. Alexi was standing at the window looking out over the water. And this morning, the alluring inspector was certainly a feast for the eyes, dressed in tight, hip-hugging jeans and a red, long-sleeved T-shirt. It was an entirely casual ensemble, but it showed off Alexi's sculpted body so well that Blayne found it to be extremely sexy.

Such a nice ass you have there. Don't turn around. Don't turn around. Don't turn around.

The events of the night before came rushing back again, this time with stark clarity. *Oh shit. I didn't.* She pondered what Alexi had said. *An understandable infatuation, my eye. I know what I feel. And it's no patient-therapist kind of thing.* The idea that Alexi had had witnesses get crushes on her before stirred a twinge of something unfamiliar in Blayne, something unsettling. *I bet people are throwing themselves at her all the time, on and off the job. So why would I expect her to think this is any different?*

But it *was* different. For Blayne, anyway. Drunk or sober, she found Alexi very compelling, and she was unabashedly staring at Alexi's ass when that beautiful face turned in her direction.

Alexi knew she should totally ignore Blayne's blatant ogling. Acknowledging it would only likely encourage more bold flirtations. But the lingering, appreciative look felt like a caress, and she had to turn away while she got her body under control. "Good morning. We should get going soon."

"Okay. I won't be long." *I'm not at all done with you, yet*, Blayne thought, as she got out of bed and headed off for a long, hot shower. Or maybe, she mused ruefully, a cold one would do her more good. *Nope, not done with you by a long shot. Just let me get rid of this headache so I can figure out a way to get through to you.*

There was an awkward silence between them while they packed up their meager belongings and headed for the Prizm. "Are you ready for some breakfast?" Alexi inquired as they buckled up.

"Oh, God, no. No food." Blayne winced. "But coffee would definitely be appreciated. Mass quantities of coffee. Intravenously, if possible."

Alexi smiled. "The mass quantities at least, I can do." They headed for the nearest fast food joint, just down the street. "I was going to suggest we do some more shopping this morning, because I think our opportunities will be more limited where we are going in Canada. But perhaps you would like to wait until we get to Sault Ste. Marie?"

"Most definitely." Blayne tilted her seat back to ease the pounding in her head. "See if they'll give us a little bag of ice too, will you?" she asked as they pulled up at the drive-through. "And then we need to stop at the convenience store over there for some ibuprofen."

❖

A couple of hours and several cups of coffee later, they were in Sault Ste. Marie and the drugs and massive infusion of liquids had started to work their magic. Blayne felt almost human again.

Alexi parked the car in front of a Wal-Mart and said, "Get whatever you will need for the foreseeable future. Clothes, personal items. We will probably be tucked away somewhere remote, so something to keep you occupied too. Music, books. Don't worry about the cost."

"Does that mean you're giving me my money back?" Blayne asked as they headed into the store.

"I think it prudent for me to continue to handle the finances," Alexi replied. "For now." She pulled out a shopping cart and they set off down the nearest main aisle.

"I'm not going to go anywhere, you know," Blayne said. "Not any time soon. You don't have to watch every move I make in here."

"Better that we stick together."

Blayne stopped in her tracks, forcing Alexi to stop as well. "I'm serious, Alexi. I'll accept your protection, but you have to give me room to breathe. I think we're safe here, don't you?"

Alexi considered her answer. "Relatively, yes. If it is that important to you..." She could tell from Blayne's body language—hands on hips, feet firmly planted—that this was no small matter, but a test of trust.

"It is."

"All right, then. I will leave this cart with you and get my own." Alexi stepped back from the one she was pushing. "How long do you need? A half hour? Forty-five minutes?"

Blayne looked surprised but pleased at the quick concession. "Make it forty-five. Trying on clothes and picking out a few CDs will take some time."

"All right. I will meet you up by the cashiers, then." Alexi headed toward the front of the store, but doubled back once Blayne was out of sight. She would allow Blayne the illusion that she was not being watched, but the reality would be entirely different.

Blayne went to electronics first, and Alexi watched her select a portable DVD/CD player and several movies and music CDs to go with it. Then it was on to books and magazines, then health and beauty aids.

It was there that Alexi first realized Blayne was shoplifting.

The cavernous store was nearly empty, so she couldn't get close enough to see what she had taken, or exactly where on her body she had put it, but Alexi knew from the quick glance around and the way Blayne positioned herself that something funny was going on. *What the hell does she think she is doing?*

The next stop was sporting goods, where Blayne once again did her glance-around before lifting an item from off the shelf and tucking it somewhere on the front of her body.

Damn it. What foolishness. She hadn't told Blayne, of course, that she had a sack full of money in the trunk, but she thought she had been clear that money was not a concern. *Why is she doing this?* She had put most of her selections in the cart to be paid for, which made Alexi all the more curious to know what it was that she didn't want to be seen purchasing.

This has to stop. Right now. If someone catches her, what a nightmare. Alexi began to wonder what else she might have missed. She had to admit Blayne was pretty good at it. Very quick and subtle. And she didn't look guilty at all. Who knew what she might have tucked away in her jacket, her pockets, and wherever else.

She followed Blayne to women's clothing and watched her pull several items from the racks—jeans, shirts, sweaters, dress slacks—and stack them across the shopping cart. When Blayne headed into one of the dressing rooms with her armload of clothes, Alexi was dead on her heels. She pushed her inside and locked the door behind them before Blayne had a chance to react or protest.

"Okay, let's have it," Alexi demanded.

"What the hell? Have what?" Blayne dropped her stuff and faced Alexi with a scowl. "You scared the shit out of me."

"I want to have whatever it is that you have been stealing."

A flush of embarrassment colored Blayne's cheeks. "Stealing! I have no idea what you're talking about," she sputtered.

"I mean it. Hand it over." Alexi advanced quickly on Blayne and shoved her against the wall of the dressing room. Her throat was tight with anger. "Stop lying to me."

"Damn it!" Blayne tried to push Alexi away, but Alexi was ready for it, and her reflexes were astounding. Before Blayne knew what hit her, both her arms were pinned above her head and Alexi was frisking her. Her flash of outrage and natural instinct to fight faded quickly, however, under the delicious distraction of Alexi's touch and the close proximity of their bodies.

Alexi smoothed her hand over Blayne's coat and checked the pockets. She was furious that Blayne would take such stupid chances, to risk getting arrested for shoplifting. She supposed that was why she had been a bit rougher with Blayne than she needed to be in pinning her to the wall. But her frustration and Blayne's refusal to cooperate had made her overreact.

Once the coat was checked, Alexi patted down the front pockets of Blayne's jeans and discovered a hard, smooth object in one of them. She reached inside with difficulty—the jeans were tight to begin with—and extracted a Swiss Army pocketknife.

"What is this?" Frowning, she held it up in front of Blayne's face.

To her surprise, Blayne was no longer furious or fighting. Nor did she seem the least bit repentant. Instead, she was smiling. Smiling rather naughtily, as a matter of fact. And the look in her eyes was reminiscent of the way she'd been leering at Alexi the night before. It was disquieting, to say the least.

"Looks like a knife to me."

Alexi tried to ignore the way Blayne was looking at her, but it was not easy. What had begun as a standard procedure search, something she had done almost without thinking hundreds of times, had suddenly taken on sexual overtones. She was all too aware that the both of them were breathing hard. That their bodies were nearly touching. That the air between them had gone heavy with flushed desire.

"Better keep searching," Blayne invited. "There's more to find."

Alexi's right hand—the hand that held the pocketknife—started shaking. Perhaps this had been a really bad idea. But she couldn't stop now. She tossed the knife onto the pile of clothes and reached around to pat down Blayne's back pockets, trying not to visualize, as she did so, how cute Blayne's ass had looked in those skimpy baby blue briefs.

"Take your time. No need to rush," Blayne said, her voice slow and lazy and full of seduction. "It pays to be thorough, you know."

Alexi tried to purge her mind of who she was touching and where she was touching her, fought to obliterate her growing arousal and concentrate on the familiar and methodical routine of frisking someone. But nothing about this felt routine any more.

She bent forward slightly to run her hand lightly up the inseam of Blayne's jeans to her crotch, cupping her briefly, intending to continue on, down the other inseam. But as soon as she reached the apex of Blayne's thighs, Blayne moaned and leaned forward, pushing into her touch, and she put her mouth on Alexi's neck.

All thought fled from Alexi's mind, and the hand that was pinning Blayne's wrists to the wall started to tremble as Blayne's lips and tongue traced a path of wet heat along her jawline.

"Christ," Alexi said under her breath. "Stop. Blayne, please." But she didn't pull away—she couldn't—and neither could she move her hand, now steadfastly refusing to budge from the warmth of Blayne's center. In fact, against her will, she found herself briefly arching her neck to allow Blayne's mouth greater access.

"Keep going," Blayne murmured between kisses. She was now thoroughly into being restrained. It added an exciting twist to this unexpected encounter. Finally, she had some proof that she could get Alexi interested, plenty interested.

She could feel the rapid, pounding beat of Alexi's heart when she pressed her mouth against the pulse point at the base of her throat. The driving tempo matched her own heart's rising excitement. Her blood was roaring in her ears. She thrust her hips forcefully into Alexi's touch and a strangled groan escaped Alexi's lips as she jerked her hand away.

"No!"

Blayne pulled back a few inches to look down at their bodies, dumbly wondering where Alexi's hand had gone. Her gaze fell on their breasts, mere inches apart. Their coats were open, and she could see the outline of Alexi's erect nipples through the red T-shirt she had on. They matched the prominent display of her own, through the thin fabric of her green button-down. *Oh God, that's damn hot.*

"Don't stop," she whispered as she leaned forward into Alexi again so she could feel their breasts press against each other. When they did, a surge of heat rushed through her and settled low in her belly. "Please don't stop."

Alexi might have tried to tell herself that she was only following routine, finishing what she had started, if she had been capable of conscious rumination. But that whispered plea compelled her hand back to Blayne's body. She skimmed her fingers over Blayne's breasts to check the crevice of her cleavage, then looked down with heavy-lidded eyes to confirm what she had felt. The stone-hard bumps that were Blayne's nipples, pressing against her bra. A black silk bra—the edge visible because she had left three buttons unbuttoned on her shirt.

Her hand stilled as she stared at Blayne's breasts, uncertain of her next move, reluctant to disengage. It was all she could do not to unbutton the rest of those buttons. Her mind had gone hazy with desire, and as she gazed into the depths of Blayne's eyes, she could not resist the open and unguarded yearning she saw there. She had to kiss her. Had to.

But before she got the chance, two sharp raps on the dressing room door startled them back to reality. Someone rattled the knob.

"Anyone in there?" A woman's voice.

"Yes," Alexi responded shakily, stepping back from Blayne. She ran a hand through her hair—the hand that had caressed Blayne's breast—to try to stop its trembling. "We will be a few more minutes."

They stared at each other as the woman outside retreated, and Blayne took a step toward Alexi. The hungry look of arousal in her eyes had not diminished, but Alexi had regained a measure of control.

"No, Blayne." Her voice held less than its usual measure of absolute authority, but she had managed to don a credible façade of detachment. "No. I am sorry. That should not have happened."

"I know you were getting off there as much as I was," Blayne said with conviction.

"I apologize for my part in it. It will not happen again."

Want to bet? Now that she knew Alexi was attracted to her, now that she had experienced the fire beneath the surface, Blayne had every intention of seizing any other opportunities that might come her way. And if they did not, she just might create some. *How can what just happened...or didn't happen...be sexier than most of the sex I've ever had?*

"Please tell me why you stole the knife," Alexi said. "And hand over whatever else you took, because I know you put something else into your clothes." *Please do not make me search you to find it, because I cannot.*

"I told you I want something to protect myself, and I knew you'd probably object," Blayne said. "It's not a big deal. I wasn't going to try to use it to get away from you or anything. I mean, it's a Swiss Army knife, for God's sake."

"What else did you take?"

Blayne stared at her for another long moment before she let out a long sigh. She reached behind herself and pulled a rectangular box out of the waistband of her pants, near her spine. "This." Her cheeks flushed and she averted her eyes as she handed it over.

Alexi forced herself not to smile. It was a small massage wand. The box proclaimed it a great and portable way to relieve sore and aching muscles, but the shape of the device left no doubt that it could be used for other, more pleasurable purposes.

"Well, you know...last night...you got me all stirred up and all, and nowhere to go with it," Blayne said sheepishly. "I thought there might be future, similar occasions." She looked up at Alexi with a wry grin and fire in her eyes. "Course, I had no idea you'd get me going again before we ever got out of the store."

I have got to get out of here. She can't keep looking at me like that. "Is that everything you took?"

"Yup. But you are welcome to keep searching if you don't believe me. I think you missed a spot."

Alexi kept her face expressionless, but her heart was pounding. She needed some space to get herself together, and right now. "Try on your clothes. I'll be just outside." She headed for the door, but paused before she opened it and didn't turn around. "You can get whatever you like. No more shoplifting. That was another bad judgment call."

Damn. Blayne watched her go, and it felt as though all the heat departed the small enclosure. *Oh well. Keep your chin up. If you can get this close in a dressing room, just imagine what can happen in a remote hideaway in Canada.*

No words were exchanged between them as they checked out. Blayne put both the knife and the massage wand in with her items, and Alexi didn't flinch as they were rung up.

Alexi's selections included a small locking suitcase for the money, and two large duffel bags for their clothes. She packed them all and stuck them in the trunk before they drove the short distance to the border.

"Get out your passport," she instructed Blayne as they neared the checkpoint. "Remember, from now on, you are Fiona Murphy and I am Jacquelyn Andrews. Please let me do all the talking unless you are asked a direct question. We are longtime friends from Chicago who are heading to Toronto for a few days' vacation."

They made it through without any problems and stopped at a restaurant on the other side to get breakfast and so that Alexi could make some phone calls. She didn't dare contact Theo directly anymore. It was too risky. She would have to relay information through Ray.

She would have him let Theo know they were safe, and in Canada, but that was all, and she wanted an update on the search for the leak and any news about the case against Cinzano.

❖

Ray had done as instructed but he did not have good news for her. Lang had been unhappy with the go-between arrangement and wanted more specific information on their location. He'd had no luck in nailing down the leak, and he had nothing but discouraging news about

Cinzano. The district attorney had warned the task force that without the guarantee of Blayne's testimony, a judge might agree to a motion that had been filed by Cinzano's attorney to get him released from jail.

Damn. That will certainly delay any trial. Who knows how long we will be cooped up together? Days, weeks...months? The memory of Blayne's body pressed up against her returned and she tried to ignore the sudden twitch of feeling in her lower abdomen.

She returned to the Prizm, unfolded a map of Canada, and studied the area.

"Have you picked a destination?" Blayne asked.

"Only a route with good possibilities. I will know the place to stop when I see it. Somewhere remote. Private."

She had long ago decided that whatever hideaway she chose should not have a telephone to tempt Blayne, and now she added a second prerequisite—they certainly would need separate bedrooms. Her loss of control in the store unnerved her. She had come dangerously close to kissing Blayne, and she knew that sharing a cabin with the feisty redhead was going to be one long exercise in frustration.

Mentally chastising herself for her weakness, she vowed once more not to allow the past to repeat itself. But it was going to be torturously difficult if they were stuck together and Blayne kept flirting with her. She had to minimize the opportunities for Blayne to get to her that way.

"Remote and private." Blayne nodded thoughtfully. Remote and private with Alexi sounded damn fine. Just as long as she could get to a phone. Because she knew she couldn't truly relax until she made some calls herself, to see if she could find out anything about Claudia.

CHAPTER THIRTEEN

W hat a fabulous place," Blayne said as they surveyed their surroundings from side-by-side Adirondack chairs on a screened-in porch. *Couldn't have picked a more romantic setting myself. It's perfect.*

Moondance Resort comprised a log cabin lodge and dozens of cabins, all scattered throughout hilly, mostly wooded acreage that surrounded a picturesque private lake. Alexi was able to book them the two-bedroom A-frame that was farthest from the lodge, where the only phones for miles around could be found. Their cabin sat on a small rise overlooking the lake, and the huge window in the upstairs front bedroom offered a view of anything approaching by water or road. Alexi had also arranged for a rental boat with a fast motor, ostensibly for fishing, so that they would have an alternate route away from the cabin. It would be delivered to their dock that afternoon.

"Fresh air. Breathtaking views. And a sexy woman to share it with." Blayne glanced at Alexi, who was avoiding her eyes. "What's wrong with this picture? Oh yeah." She snapped her fingers as if the answer had suddenly come to her. "You seem to be far too able to resist me."

"Blayne," Alexi said reproachfully. "You have to stop this. Here and now. Nothing is going to happen between us. Nothing."

"I wouldn't put money on that. I can be pretty convincing. And you did pick a place where we are going to be spending a lot of time together, with little else for entertainment. No phone. No TV."

"Speaking of which," Alexi said, "I would like your word that you will not sneak away to the lodge to make any phone calls while we are here."

"I promise."

The immediate answer made Alexi suspicious, though she had come to believe that when Blayne gave her word, she meant it. "Thank you. It is necessary."

"I do believe that you have my best interests at heart." Blayne stretched languidly and long. "Well, some of my best interests, anyway. Perhaps you could do more for my physical interests, but there's time for that. Plenty of time."

Her voice had a husky breathiness to it that washed over Alexi like a verbal caress and forced her up and out of her chair. "I am going to unpack. Then we can head over to the lodge for some dinner." She had to be alone for a few minutes to get herself together. It was becoming increasingly difficult to act nonchalant about Blayne's come-ons.

"Whatever you say. I'm not going anywhere."

Alexi heard the underlying promise in the statement, and she was both relieved and disturbed by it. It was great that she could apparently stop expending so much time and energy trying to keep Blayne from running. But it was obvious that Blayne was determined to continue her efforts at seduction, and that was just as dangerous a distraction. She could allow nothing to divert her focus and attention from the job she had to do.

While Alexi was avoiding her, Blayne put her feet up, wrapped her jacket tightly around herself, and stared out over the lake. Not only was she feeling safe for the first time in days, she was actually quite content with her current situation. It certainly could be a whole lot worse.

If only she knew what had happened to Claudia.

She knew Alexi wouldn't approve of what she was planning, and that helped her tamp down the niggling of guilt she felt about her promise. There would be no harm in what she was going to do, she was sure of it. Now she just had to figure out how to do it without Alexi being any the wiser.

So far the only thing that had seemed to crack Alexi's concentration was blatant flirting. *Okay, then. I have a plan.*

Blayne had gotten the layout of the lodge during their short visit there to register. While Alexi had been dealing with the front desk clerk, she'd wandered through the lobby, always within sight, feigning interest in the wildlife art on the walls and the view out of the windows while noting each phone, elevator, exit, and every other conceivable resource.

When they returned for dinner she was pleased to discover that the lodge dining room, though not quite as cozy and intimate a place as they'd eaten in the night before, was certainly adequate for what she had in mind—lit by candles and quiet enough for private conversation.

"You sure know how to pick 'em," Blayne commented as they were led to a lovely table for two near one of the south-facing windows. "I haven't been wined and dined in such nice places since I can't remember when."

"Perhaps we should skip the wine tonight," Alexi commented as they took their seats.

"Aw. Don't be a spoilsport. I'll be *good*, I promise."

Alexi was hearing every sentence out of Blayne's mouth as a double entendre, which, she was certain, was the intention.

"A couple of glasses, then." She knew she couldn't tighten the reins on Blayne too much. But she loathed the idea she might have to once again fend off the kind of advances she had faced the night before, or worse. She would have to take the initiative in the conversation more, keep to safe subjects. Or perhaps even better, throw Blayne off guard a little. "Blayne, I am curious about something."

"Shoot." Blayne leaned forward expectantly.

"How long have you been shoplifting?"

Blayne frowned. "I told you. I took the knife because I wanted something to defend myself with, and I knew you'd probably have a problem with it."

"I am not talking about this one incident. It was rather obvious that you had done it before. Perhaps a lot. Yet I view you as an otherwise intelligent woman and not in dire need financially. So I just wonder why."

Blayne squirmed in her seat as she considered her answer. "It's not a big deal. Once in a blue moon, I take something from a store. It's never anything expensive."

"Is it a compulsion, would you say?"

"No. Not at all. Look, I know it was stupid. A foolish risk. I'm sorry."

"Have you done it a long time? Or is this a relatively recent thing?" Alexi could tell from Blayne's nervous fidgeting with her hands that she was uncomfortable with the line of questioning. A part of Alexi regretted it, but she also had to admit she got a certain satisfaction out of rattling Blayne a little after enduring what she had.

The waiter arrived to take their orders and brought back a bottle of Chardonnay. After a few sips, Blayne answered, more seriously than Alexi expected.

"When I was growing up, my closest friend for many years was a girl who lived two blocks away. Bridget. She was everything that I wasn't then. Completely fearless and irresponsible." Blayne took another long drink of wine as images from her childhood flashed through her mind. "She was always daring me to do things. Dangerous things, usually. Running through traffic, walking across thin ice, climbing the tallest tree. I swear, looking back, she was, like, the world's youngest adrenaline junkie." *God, how many times did you almost get us killed?*

"And she dared you to shoplift something," Alexi supplied, after Blayne had lapsed into silence for a long moment.

"Yes. When we were nine. Candy from a drugstore. I guess that's how it started."

"Why now? Still?" Alexi asked. "Do you know?"

She shrugged. "No. Like I said, I don't do it much."

"Whatever happened to Bridget? Do you still keep in touch?"

Blayne shook her head. "No. She drowned in a gravel pit when we were thirteen. A place we'd snuck into a lot to go swimming." Her gaze was vacant, unfocused. "She asked me to go with her that night, but I didn't. She went alone."

"And you regret not being there."

She nodded thoughtfully. *Yes, I do. Every time I think about it.* "I guess maybe I take things because I remember her every time I do." She looked over at Alexi. "Never wanted to think about it too much."

An ache of loneliness swept over her as she flashed back to the countless times that Claudia had cussed her out for shoplifting and asked her why she did it, especially back in her college days when it had been a more frequent occurrence. *I have to know what has happened to you. I just can't believe you're dead.*

That brought her back to her plan of action for the evening, which Alexi had successfully diverted her from far too long already.

"So now that we've figured out my shoplifting, let's figure out why you are so adamantly opposed to giving in to my efforts to seduce you, shall we?" Blayne batted her eyes playfully, and Alexi couldn't entirely suppress a small grin. But it was there and gone in an instant. "I know you are interested in me."

The waiter arrived with their food, and Alexi was grateful for the timing because it gave her time to formulate a response. "I unfortunately got carried away in the moment. It was not personal, it just happened, and I am sorry if I gave you reason to believe that it was anything other than momentary confusion."

"Confusion, my ass. You wanted to kiss me. I know you did." Blayne refused to be deterred. "And I bet you still do."

"You state that I am interested in you. You do not *ask* if I am. Had you asked, you would have known by now that I have *no* romantic intentions with you. And *will* not, regardless of how much you flirt with me."

"We'll see. Apparently you haven't met stubborn Irish determination head-on before." Regardless of Alexi's efforts to put her off, Blayne just wasn't buying the "I'm not interested" façade. She had seen the look in Alexi's eyes, and she recognized that look. And her gut told her there was definitely something personal growing between them.

"I suggest you use that stubborn determination to stay out of trouble," Alexi said.

"Oh, there's enough to spread it around for whatever I need it for, don't you worry."

"Eat your dinner. It is getting cold." Alexi needed something— anything—to defuse the growing sexual tension in the air.

Blayne smiled and picked up her fork. "Fine. As long as you know that your efforts to change the subject or dissuade me aren't going to work for long." She dug into her trout almondine with gusto, eyeing Alexi all the while. Alexi appeared outwardly composed, as always. But she would hardly meet Blayne's eyes, and Blayne took that as a good sign that she wasn't as blasé as she appeared.

They finished dinner and ordered coffee and dessert, tiramisu for Alexi and strawberry shortcake for Blayne.

"Want to taste mine?" Blayne cocked one eyebrow as she offered Alexi a forkful of plump red strawberry goodness.

Alexi glanced over and watched as Blayne licked a smear of whipped cream off her upper lip. Her belly twitched at the provocative gesture, but her outward expression did not acknowledge it. "Thank you, no," she managed.

"Sure? I think you'd like it a lot." Blayne put the proffered forkful into her own mouth and chewed slowly, relishing the flavor. "Mmm. Sweet. Succulent. How can you say no?"

Alexi didn't respond. Blayne's seductive glances and overt machinations were having a definite effect on her body, like it or not. And her mind as well, conjuring up unbidden images of what she could do with some whipped cream and an evening with Blayne looking at her like that. She poked at her tiramisu. *Why am I having such a hard time with this? I have certainly resisted a woman's advances before.*

Before she knew what was happening, she felt Blayne's fingers at the base of her throat, and she drew back involuntarily until she felt a tug at the back of her neck.

"Hey! It's okay," Blayne said. "I just wanted to see what this is." She held in her hand the simple cross that Alexi wore on a gold chain. "I've noticed you wear it all the time."

"A gift from my mother," Alexi managed. She had been startled, and that combined with the sensation of Blayne's hand against her skin got her heart pounding. "Excuse me, please, I need some air." She got to her feet and looked around for the waiter, who was nowhere in sight. "Are you finished?"

"Yes, of course," Blayne said. "I need to run to the restroom anyway. I'll do that and sign for the check. And meet you where? The terrace?"

Alexi hesitated. "No, I'll come with you."

"You just said you needed some air, and I definitely don't need a chaperone to the ladies' room," Blayne insisted.

"Better we stay together."

"Alexi, you are not going to come with me every time I use the john. I mean, I'll put up with a lot, but that's crazy."

Alexi studied her face. "No phone calls. Just there and back."

"I promised you earlier no phone calls. I'll see you on the terrace before you know I'm gone." Blayne glared at her and flagged the waiter down.

Alexi still felt uneasy as she headed toward the doors to the adjacent paved patio, but she rationalized that there was a difference between protecting someone and needlessly invading their privacy.

She crossed the terrace and rested her elbows against the smooth stone railing that ran waist-high around the front and sides. It was a clear night, but there was a brisk chill in the air, so no other guests had ventured outside. Alexi was grateful for the solitude.

God, why do I let her get to me like that? Blayne's face in the dressing room flashed into her mind. Then the image of her in her skimpy briefs and tank top, just out of the shower. *Well, what is not to like, really. Am I not human? Do I not have needs? Problem is, I cannot solve that the way that I usually do.*

It was, ordinarily, an easy hunger to satisfy. She could find a desirable, willing participant and take care of things almost anywhere. But it was not so easy when she was on round-the-clock duty and holed up in the middle of nowhere. *I need to get laid. That is all I need. That will take care of things and allow me to regain my focus. But it appears unlikely that can happen any time soon.*

Until it did, Blayne would continue to get to her. Even without her blatant come-ons, it would be difficult enough to act uninterested when what she really wanted was to give in to the enticements.

Back to the cabin to separate bedrooms, where she would have a night to try to regain her equilibrium somewhat. That was the plan. She glanced at her watch. Nine thirty. Still early. Blayne was right about one thing. They were going to be spending a lot of time together, without a lot to amuse and entertain them but each other and a few paperbacks. And she felt too restless to sleep and too pent up to concentrate on reading.

She had seen a Tavli set among other card and board games in a big trunk in the cabin. That might serve useful in getting Blayne occupied in something other than sex. And she imagined that Blayne might be an amusing adversary at the game. She was bright, and determined, and certainly capable of formulating a strategy for success.

Speaking of Blayne…she had had plenty of time to do what she needed to do. *Where is she?*

❖

Blayne got their bill taken care of with a quick signature, remembering only at the last second to sign as Fiona Murphy. Then she made a beeline for the lodge's guest services desk, which was across the lobby from the reservations counter.

Seated behind the desk was the same fresh-faced right-out-of-college blond Adonis who had been there when they arrived. *Great.* "Hi there." She put on a big smile when he looked up from his magazine, and he reciprocated.

"Good evening! How may I help you?"

"Didn't I see you wearing an MSU sweatshirt last night?" Blayne asked. "What's a Sparty doing so far from home?"

He laughed. "That tells me you are the rare guest who is not here for the fishing, or you'd know. But welcome, fellow grad." He stood and extended a hand. "William Levine, Telecommunications, class of '05. Call me Bill."

She offered her own and they shook hands. "Hi Bill. Fiona Murphy, Public Relations, and I no longer admit to the year."

He laughed again. "What can I do for you, Fiona?"

"Well, I am absolutely *desperate* for two minutes online." She eyed his computer longingly. "*Please*. You *have* to help me out. I just realized I never forwarded an e-mail that my office needs tomorrow for a big sales pitch. It's a *huge* deal."

"Well, I don't know…" He glanced around. The reservations clerk was occupied with a young couple and was paying them no mind. "I'm really not supposed to…"

"Two minutes or less, I promise. I'm a fast typist. One e-mail. *Please?*"

"Oh, okay. Really fast, though, please." He tilted the monitor toward her and slid the keyboard where she could access it.

"Like the wind," she promised. "I can't thank you enough."

She hadn't been lying about being a fast typist, one perk of having typed thousands of reservations over the last eight years. She sent the e-mail to Claudia's address and a half dozen others in her Yahoo address book, all mutual friends of theirs. Short and sweet, it asked if they knew anything about Claudia's current whereabouts and begged them not to tell authorities that she had been in touch. She hit the Send button and signed out of her account.

"You're a peach, Bill." She slid the keyboard back and gave him a thumbs-up. "Kept me from getting into hot water later. I owe you one."

"No problem. Have a nice evening, and enjoy your stay."

"I will. Oh, by the way…I don't suppose there's any chance I can check my e-mail again in a day or so and see if there's any word on how this all turned out?"

He chewed on his lip. "Well, maybe I can give you another couple of minutes, but there would have to be no one else around."

Not telling me something I don't already know. "I completely understand. Thanks again."

She found Alexi alone on the terrace, a beautifully romantic setting though the still-dormant rose garden around them would not bloom for months. The stars were abundant and the sounds of owls calling to each other could be heard in the distance. But she had no time to properly exploit the potential of the picturesque setting. No time even to fully appreciate it before Alexi was steering her by the elbow back toward the door she'd just come through.

"Let us go back to the cabin, if you do not mind. I have gotten a bit of a chill out here."

"Oh. Sure." *Back to the cabin with you sounds like a dandy idea. Just dandy.*

❖

Theo Lang was in bed and just drifting off to sleep when the phone jolted him back awake shortly before midnight.

"We've located Blayne Keller." Paul Fletcher's voice was excited, though still professional. "She sent an e-mail last night to two of the friends we were monitoring. Took us some time to trace the IP address, but it just came through. A hunting and fishing lodge in Canada. About six hundred miles. Ten hours by car."

Theo turned on the bedside light. His wife Selma, lying beside him, groaned. "What did it say?"

"Keller asked whether they had heard from Claudia Cluzet and told them not to tell us she'd sent the e-mail. Nothing in there about Alexi Nikolos."

"Get directions on how to find the place and arrange a helicopter that can leave at first light," Theo instructed. "Let's say, at six. And get whatever flight clearances I need."

"You? You're going?" Fletcher's inflection indicated he thought that Theo was kidding, or perhaps it was intended to urge him to reconsider. "And who else?"

"Just me. I'm going to handle this personally, Paul. How many people know about the e-mails?"

"Just me and the graveyard boys. Harry and Erik. They beeped me and I called you right away."

"I'm going alone to try to talk Keller back into WITSEC. If too many people show up, she'll bolt," Theo said. "Keep this just between the three of you. And call me back at five with the arrangements."

"Whatever you say."

❖

It was risky to venture from the Joint Task Force office with only the three of them there. He would likely be missed if he was gone longer than a few minutes, so he made the phone call from a gas station only two blocks away, checking carefully to make sure he wasn't followed.

The familiar voice answered on the second ring. "Yes?"

"She's in Canada. A lodge called the Moondance Resort, in Ontario."

"Excellent."

"We have a man going up by chopper in the morning." He looked at his watch. It was nearly midnight. "Take Lang four or five hours...so he lands by ten or eleven," he mumbled to himself, and then spoke more loudly into the phone. "If you're driving up from here, you need to leave ASAP to get there before he does."

"Anything else?"

He considered telling Cinzano's man about Alexi Nikolos, but decided against it. He'd given them plenty already; better to save it for when they squeezed him again. "No, nothing else." *Maybe now they'll leave me alone for a while.*

The line went dead.

He headed back to the office, wondering which of them would reach the lodge first—Theo Lang, or the mob.

CHAPTER FOURTEEN

Alexi excused herself as soon as they returned to the cabin on the pretext she was going to put on another layer of clothes to ward off the chill. But in truth, she was trying to put as much distance between them as possible until she could figure out a way to get Blayne to stop pursuing her. She lingered in her room, looking out over the lake, enjoying the splendid view of the canopy of stars above. It was a wonderfully romantic setting, she had to admit. Exactly the kind of place she'd bring someone if she were in the mood for a long weekend of sexual escapades.

Which made it all the more difficult to ignore Blayne's efforts to arouse her interest. Whatever she might *think* she should do, her body was refusing to be deterred. It demanded satisfaction. *Later.* She headed back downstairs to find to her horror that Blayne had made good use of her absence.

The cabin great room already had a cozy ambience all on its own, with its large comfy couch and matching chocolate-brown easy chairs, framed nature photographs on the walls, and earth-toned rugs and furnishings. A fully stocked kitchenette was tucked into one corner, separated from the rest by a waist-high counter lined with bar stools.

Blayne had managed to up the romance quotient significantly in the ten or fifteen minutes she'd been left alone. She had lowered the lights, lit a few candles, and started a cheery fire in the red brick fireplace. A Norah Jones love ballad was playing on her new CD player. And she was looking sexy as hell, stretched out on the couch, smiling at Alexi as though she could eat her alive.

Alexi fought back the urge to lower herself onto that waiting, willing body, claim that mouth, and calm her own relentless craving for release. *No one should have to resist such temptation.*

"Wish we had something for a nightcap." Blayne ran her fingertips lightly and provocatively along the back of the couch as though it were Alexi's body.

Oh, yes. Adding more alcohol to this scenario would most certainly help matters.

Alexi took a deep breath and tried to keep her voice neutral. "Since you are evidently not sleepy…" She opened the games trunk, which served as a makeshift end table for the couch, and withdrew the familiar board that she had spotted there earlier. "How about a game?"

"I have some fun and games in mind, for sure," Blayne responded. "But backgammon isn't one of them."

"We call it Tavli." Alexi reached into the trunk for the checkers and dice that went with the game. "It is the oldest recorded game in history, you know. And a favorite pastime where I come from. No… actually, more a national obsession."

It wasn't what Blayne had in mind for the evening, but she thought it might be an avenue to get to know Alexi better. It was one of the first tiny pieces of information about her homeland or history that she had offered without prompting. It was a start.

"How young were you when you learned to play?" Blayne asked as Alexi set up the board on the coffee table.

"Six."

"Who taught you?"

"My father."

"So you're probably even better at this than you are at everything else, then," Blayne observed.

Alexi shrugged noncommittally. "I know the game well." She pulled an easy chair over to face the couch, so the board sat between them.

"Well, I never played very much, and not for many years. I'm not sure I even remember how to move, so I'm afraid I won't be a very worthy opponent for you."

"That is not important. And I bet a lot of it will come back to you." Alexi hunched over the board. "You are the light stones, and you move in this direction…toward your house, here, according to the roll of the dice. Once you get all fifteen within the bar"—she gestured as she spoke—"you bear them off, or remove them. I move in the opposite direction." She went on to explain other fundamentals of the game, along with a bit of strategy.

"I think I get it." Blayne found herself remembering more than she thought she would about the game. And it was well that she did, for she only heard about half of what Alexi was saying. It was impossible to be completely immersed in backgammon when such a beautiful woman was sitting four feet away, lit by the warm golden light from the fireplace.

They rolled the dice and Blayne won the right to open the first game. She started her stones around the board. "So tell me, Alexi...what other games do you play? Hmm? You know, if any other pleasurable pursuits spring to mind while we are alone here together, you'll find I am a willing and eager student."

"Tavli is likely the only pleasurable pursuit I will engage in during my time in your company, Blayne, as I have repeatedly told you." Alexi gripped the dice loosely in her right palm, enjoying the familiar play of the two smooth cubes against each other before she sent them flying. "I will not allow anything to distract me from my responsibilities."

"You know, I just bet that you are one of those people who can easily do two things at the same time," Blayne said. "I'm not really concerned that my safety will be compromised if you come over to this side of the table and make out with me in between games."

Alexi acted as if she hadn't heard, but the image that sprang to mind got her heart thumping hard in her chest. "I believe it is your turn."

"We haven't established the stakes yet." Blayne uncrossed her legs, leaned back, and draped her arms over the back of the couch. Her inviting body language and the gleam of naughty mischief in her eyes were impossibly irresistible.

"Stakes?"

"Yes. Gotta make it interesting. Now, I know you are going to whip my ass, so your reward should be relatively minor if you win. But I'm such an underdog that I should get a pretty big payoff if I manage to beat you."

Alexi knew the answer would be provocative, but she was unable to keep from asking the question. "What do you propose?"

"Well, let's see. If you win, you get...hmm...I know. Perhaps a nice massage. How does that sound?"

Alexi's whole body clenched at the thought of Blayne's hands, everywhere, exploring and pleasuring her body. Kneading. Rubbing. Stroking. *Jesus. What I would not give for a lot of that right now.* But that was certainly not an option. Not with Blayne's hands, anyway. Her own hand, a little later, right where she needed it, now that was another story.

"That sounds like a not entirely appropriate reward." Alexi got up to put another log on the fire, though her skin already felt overheated. She remained before the hearth, stirring the embers with a long metal poker, grateful for the opportunity to regain some equilibrium. "Doing the dishes or making the coffee is perhaps more reasonable."

"Oh, don't you think it's fun to be unreasonable once in a blue moon?"

"Blayne. Truly, you must stop this." *Before you drive me so crazy I have to excuse myself for a few minutes.*

"Well, if you win, we can go with the dishes and coffee thing if you like. But I will leave open your ability to renegotiate. Now, if *I* win…that would be a much bigger accomplishment, of course, so it should have a commensurate reward." Blayne paused until Alexi turned back around and looked at her. "A kiss. One kiss."

Alexi's first impulse was to refuse. She didn't want to encourage Blayne. But she knew it was a safe bet. "I will accept your condition, in the interest of getting back to the game. But I should tell you that I am confident there will be no kissing." She took her seat. "Roll the dice."

She would take no chances. Her plan at the outset of the evening had been to let Blayne come close the first couple of games, and then win the third or fourth to boost her confidence. But with a kiss at stake, Alexi would make sure she always had a reasonable margin of victory.

The first game took ten minutes. The second, just about as long.

Blayne's frustration grew with each move. Though she wasn't a bad player, it was obvious right away that Alexi was a master at the game and was allowing her an occasional opening only to keep things from ending much too quickly. *She never hesitates. As soon as it's her turn, boom, next move, right there. She's probably already got the whole thing played out in her mind.*

She knew she was well outmatched. Alexi would never have agreed so readily if she thought there was any possibility of losing.

But she had to have that kiss. By any means necessary. Her whole body was humming for it. And she knew her only chance stood in doing all she could to distract Alexi while she prayed for a few favorable rolls of the dice.

"That fire sure has warmed things up in here," she said as Alexi set up the board for the third game. "I know you don't mind if I get more comfortable." She waited until Alexi glanced up at her. When she did, Blayne reached down and unbuttoned the third and fourth buttons of her navy blue blouse, exposing her cleavage and the lacy top of the crème-colored bra beneath.

She was gratified to notice a slight increase in the rise and fall of Alexi's chest, and even more so, that Alexi's attention was no longer on the game board—it was instead fixed rather soundly on her breasts.

Blayne still lost that game, but it was much closer. Encouraged, she undid the rest of her buttons. "*Damn* hot in here, wouldn't ya say?" she asked in her most seductive tone. "You know, if you want to take something off, I certainly won't object."

Alexi froze, hand poised in midair. Blayne saw the slight trembling in that hand and watched Alexi's gaze traverse the length of her body, and she felt somewhat more optimistic about her chances in game four.

Luck was with her. She rolled two high doubles to start off the game with a bang, and her efforts to distract Alexi seemed to be working like a charm—her moves were no longer quite so quick and automatic. And here and there, a few small errors crept into her play. It was close, very close, right up to the end. Alexi seemed to realize then that she stood a chance of losing, and began paying more attention to the board and less to Blayne's bra.

It came down to the luck of the final throws, and fate was against Alexi. She threw ones and twos when she needed all fives and sixes, and Blayne threw three sets of doubles.

Blayne stood, a cocky grin on her face, and rubbed her hands together in eager anticipation. "I'll collect now, if you please."

Alexi was stunned. Bewildered. *I lost. How could I have lost? Damn.* Her mind and body seized upon the kiss she'd *like* to plant on Blayne, the kiss she could never let happen. She felt that kiss down to her toes, throughout her body, as though it really was happening.

She needed to get upstairs. And fast. Her mouth wanted Blayne's, and the rest of her wanted to peel off that bra she'd been staring at. Her control was slipping. But first, it was payback time. Blayne had made her suffer all evening. And now it was time to return the favor. Oh, she would pay up. She was a woman of her word, after all.

Alexi stood on shaky legs and moved slowly and deliberately around the table between them as Blayne turned to face her, shirt flying open even further, exposing the rest of those magnificent breasts and allowing an unimpeded view of the pale smooth skin of her stomach. She was torn between the urge to run…and to take, hungrily, what was being offered to her. But she knew she could do neither.

Blayne had been so intent on winning the game that she failed to see the full effect of her scheming until Alexi came around the table and paused. Their bodies were less than a foot apart and Alexi's expression wiped the grin right off her face.

Alexi was looking right *through* her, lids half closed with arousal, pupils dark and enormous, nearly obscuring those brilliant blue irises. She looked as though they'd already been half the night in bed together and she was getting ready to take her again.

Blayne's breath caught in her throat. Every nerve ending was poised, anxious, for that first touch. She watched Alexi moisten her lips provocatively with her tongue. *Kiss me already*, her body screamed.

Alexi brought her right hand up, slowly, between their bodies, skimming her fingers up Blayne's stomach, over the small divide of bra between her breasts, into the crevice of her cleavage, toward her neck. Her eyes never left Blayne's as she did; she was thoroughly enjoying the effect she was having. *Not very nice, what I am doing, but she deserves it.*

When her fingers reached Blayne's face, her touch became lighter still. Her thumb traced lightly over Blayne's lips, then away, teasing her, returning to push slightly into her mouth before retreating yet again.

She watched Blayne's breathing become labored and her eyes begin to glaze over. *Perfect. Now I think you will understand what you have been putting me through for the last couple of days.*

Blayne tried through sheer force of will to move Alexi's lips closer to hers. She didn't say anything lest she interrupt the deliciously torturous anticipation of the moment. The feel of Alexi's hand on her mouth. Suggestively invasive. She thought she surely would burst if Alexi didn't kiss her soundly, and soon.

As though she had heard, Alexi's light touch turned suddenly solid. Both of her hands came up to cup the sides of Blayne's face and she stepped forward until their bodies were touching, and the shock of the full-on contact set off a torrent of butterflies in the pit of Blayne's stomach.

She closed her eyes as Alexi pulled their faces together, and wished for time to stand still.

But an instant was only an instant any way it was measured. And she might have sworn it had not happened at all, it was so brief and so light, but her body was so *ready* that the world slipped away except for that warm and glancing caress upon her mouth and she knew she had not imagined it.

She blinked, and it was over. Alexi had stepped away. After so much anticipation, after such arousing tactile foreplay, the absence of what she wanted, needed, *expected*, hit her like a sudden cold shower.

"What?" she stuttered. "You...you can't...that's not fair."

"You do not seem too concerned about playing fair." Alexi calmly closed the grill on the fireplace and blew out the candles. "I am going to turn in and I advise you to do the same. I will see you in the morning."

"I...you...*damn it!*"

Alexi headed upstairs, managing to contain herself only until her bedroom door was closed and locked behind her. She came in seconds.

CHAPTER FIFTEEN

Alexi's first thought when she spotted Blayne shortly after dawn the next morning was *serves you right*. Blayne had pulled one of the oversized easy chairs over to the picture window that faced the lake and was slouched down into it, feet up on a hassock, sipping from a large red mug. It was obvious from the circles under her eyes that she hadn't slept much. And though it was only seven, the coffeepot on the counter was already down to its final dregs.

"Rough night?" Alexi asked with exaggerated cheeriness. There was no way she would let Blayne know that she too had tossed and turned all night.

"Such a comedian." Blayne did not look up at her. She was dressed in jeans and fuzzy blue slippers and had on a thin navy sweater with a low V-neck. It exposed the pale skin of her chest and hugged her body so snugly it was clear she wore no bra. Her hair was sleep-tousled, and Alexi thought it was adorable.

She herself had not emerged from her room until she was perfectly put together. Her brown hair had been brushed until it shone, and she was nattily attired in black jeans and a tailored black blouse with wide cuffs. She made a fresh pot of coffee and waited until it had brewed to pull the other easy chair beside Blayne's. *Do not stare at her breasts. Do not stare at her breasts.*

They sipped coffee for forty minutes without saying anything, watching the forest outside come to life. Birds flitted about, resting in the trees and scratching along the ground for something to eat. Two does stepped out of the woods near the lake, moving slowly, pausing here and there to seek out something to graze as they made their way to the water.

"What would you like to do today?" Alexi asked.

Blayne snorted derisively. "That's a loaded question."

"Not if you do not choose it to be. Would you like to go to the lodge for some breakfast?"

"Maybe later." Blayne got to her feet. "Despite the fact that I'm exhausted and a bit pissed off at you for last night, I'm apparently still in need of a long cold shower." She headed upstairs without a look back.

Alexi nodded in agreement after she had gone. *Good thing there is no chance we will run out of cold water in this place.*

Blayne reappeared an hour later, looking a lot less bleary-eyed and eminently more presentable for going out in public. Her coppery hair was styled, she had applied a touch of blush and some color to her lips, and she was dressed in new charcoal gray slacks and a burgundy sweater. The effect was most appealing, and Alexi wondered whether it was all part of Blayne's campaign to entice her interest. If so, it was definitely working. She looked *hot.*

"I guess I could force down some eggs and toast now," Blayne said by way of greeting. "Since I'm apparently not going to get my other appetites satisfied any time soon."

Alexi ignored the pointed reference and retrieved the keys to the Prizm from the counter. "I will stop at the front desk while we are there and order groceries to be delivered so we can eat some meals here." She picked up a tablet and pen and handed them to Blayne as they headed for the car. "Start a list of what you would like."

The Bell 206B Jet Ranger III helicopter could only fly three hours on a tank of gas and it was more than five from O'Hare airport to the lodge, so they had to stop at the Otsego County Airport in Gaylord, Michigan, for refueling. While they were waiting, the pilot studied a map of Canada. He and the chopper were both on loan to WITSEC from the Chicago Police Department.

"How long before we get to the lodge, do you think?" Theo Lang unfastened his seat belt so he could look over the pilot's shoulder at the map.

"Less than two hours, looks like," was the reply.

Theo glanced at his watch. It was nine thirty and they would reach their destination within two hours. Hopefully before Alexi and Blayne Keller had departed for points unknown. "Once we get to the lake, look for a clearing opposite the lodge. Up on a hill, they said. I'll hike in from there."

"Any idea how long you'll be?" the CPD pilot asked.

"Well, I hope to wrap it up quickly, but it's hard to say." He wondered how he was going to convince Keller to return to the program, and how Alexi would react to the news their security had been breached.

Badly, he thought.

❖

The dark sedan clipped along just over the speed limit as it ate up the miles on the Canadian two-lane highway. Traffic was sparse and the weather was clear, and they had made excellent time from Chicago, encountering no difficulties with customs at the border.

Three of the four burly occupants were asleep, and the one in the front passenger seat was snoring so loudly that the driver, Frankie Sloan, was beginning to grind his teeth in irritation. Unfortunately, Mr. Buzz-saw was the man in charge on this job, so there was not much he could do but endure the noise.

He glanced at the map, then at the digital clock on the dashboard. Ten a.m. They'd be getting to the lodge in an hour or so, he figured, maybe a little more, so he could get away with waking Rosco and the others pretty much any time.

❖

Blayne was mostly quiet during breakfast, a departure from their last couple of meals together. Alexi chalked it up to lack of sleep and the rising sexual chemistry between them. She was grateful not to have to be fielding any of Blayne's increasingly irresistible come-ons, especially with her looking so delicious this morning in her new clothes. Tired or not, Alexi seemed to be in an almost constant state of mild arousal around Blayne at the moment. *God, do I need to get laid. Push all this out of my head and put my focus back where it belongs.*

While they ate, they drew up a list of groceries they would need, enough to get them through a week or more of meals and snacks.

"I'm going to check in with guest services," Blayne said as Alexi waved the waiter over to get their bill. "I want to see what all there is to do around here. Maybe inquire about some fishing gear. I'd be happy to drop off the grocery list at the front desk."

"That is all right, I will do that while you see about the other."

Blayne forced herself not to press the issue. *Damn. I can't get back on the computer without her seeing me if she's standing at the front desk. Maybe I can come back this afternoon. Say I'm taking a walk because I need some alone time.* It wasn't stretching the truth too much. She'd certainly needed some alone time the night before after Alexi had retired to her room. But she'd found the orgasm she reached with her new massage wand vaguely unsatisfying, and she'd been unable to drift off to sleep afterward as she usually did.

The almost animalistic attraction she was developing toward Alexi mystified her. Ordinarily she wasn't comfortable getting intimate with someone right away. She liked to take her time, get to know them, see if they clicked before she went very far. Oh, she'd certainly had a one-night stand or two, who hadn't? But not since college. In recent years, she usually had a handful of dates with someone before deciding to share her bed.

And she still knew virtually nothing about Alexi Nikolos. In fact, Alexi was stubbornly circumspect and annoyingly determined to fend off her advances. *What's up with that, anyway? I don't throw myself at women. But I sure am doing about everything I can to get her to bed, despite the obstacles.* And they were safe now. Surely Alexi could loosen up a little.

Damn it. I know she's interested. She'd seen it in Alexi's eyes in the dressing room, and again last night, right before that maddeningly brief kiss. She could still feel Alexi's hands gently cradling her face. *What the hell is the problem with a quick bit of fun in the sack? A much better way to pass the time than backgammon, that's for sure. And no one ever needs to know.*

While she was dressing that morning, Blayne had decided to do whatever she could to try to *get* to Alexi, the way she had been *getting* to her during their last game of backgammon. Those glimpses of the fire beneath Alexi's cool exterior were far too rare. Most of the time, she was a stone, controlling her emotions and reactions so well that it was nearly impossible to determine what she was thinking or feeling.

But I know she was feeling what I was last night. I know she wanted to kiss me...really kiss me.

She yearned to see more of that passionate nature in an unguarded moment. And most of all, she wanted to see if she could stir Alexi's blood the way Alexi was stirring hers.

There would certainly be plenty of opportunities if they were cooped up together like this for the foreseeable future. *Romantic dinners and evenings by the fire. Oh yeah. Plenty of opportunities. I just have to be patient.*

After Alexi had signed for the check, they strolled to the lobby together, Alexi heading toward the front desk and Blayne toward guest services.

Bill hailed her while she was still several feet away, and she cringed, hoping Alexi didn't hear. "Back again! Fiona, right?"

"Hi, Bill." She kept her voice low. "I just came to see what all you offer in the way of things to do around here."

"Sure. Let me give you this." He handed her a colorful brochure peppered with pictures of fishermen, hikers, birdwatchers, and couples in kayaks and canoes. Inside were brief descriptions of the amenities and outdoor activities available through the lodge. *Hmm, in-cabin massages. I could use a little of that right about now, but unfortunately it's Alexi's hands I'd like to have on me and not some masseuse's.*

All the same, Blayne was impressed with all the classes and special events available to guests. There were fly-fishing, birding, and cooking classes, wine tastings and eco-tours, spa treatments, family fishing derbies, and poker tournaments. *Quite a range of activities. This has got to beat the hell out of whatever WITSEC had planned for me.* She still wondered about that. She had been born and raised a Yooper, with a passion for the unspoiled natural beauty that was Michigan's Upper Peninsula, so this Canadian wilderness was welcome and familiar.

She'd been worried from the start that WITSEC would plant her in some hot, desolate environment, devoid of any real change of seasons—Vegas, or Phoenix, or Miami. She could not be happy long in a place like that. But this? She could get used to this. *No* problem.

"Thanks a lot. This looks great." She glanced toward the front desk. Alexi was still preoccupied with the clerk, but had one eye on her as well. "Well, better get going. See you soon." *Hopefully very soon.*

"Take care, Fiona. Go Spartans!"

As she crossed the lobby toward Alexi, she took a few moments to admire the coiled beauty of the WITSEC inspector. She looked absolutely relaxed, casually leaning against the counter, amiably chatting with the clerk. But Blayne had spent a lot of time watching her lately, and she was beginning to recognize subtle things about Alexi that told the real story. No matter how nonchalant she might appear to be, the reality was she was always alert. Always keenly focused on her surroundings. She managed to keep an eye on everything and everyone without it appearing obvious she was doing so. At least she was always that way when there were other people around.

When they were alone, now that was another story. She had managed on at least a couple of occasions to get Alexi thinking personally—*very* personally. *The way she was looking at me just before she kissed me. Damn, do I want her to look at me like that some more.*

Alexi straightened as she approached and concluded her conversation with the clerk. Whatever she said made the young woman laugh, and Blayne felt a flash of something—a flutter of regret. She wished she had been the recipient of Alexi's clever remark.

"See any classes or anything you wish to take advantage of?" Alexi tilted her head toward the brochure and events calendar in her hand.

"Oh, don't you be talking about wishes and taking advantage... unless you really mean that." Blayne wagged a finger at her reproachfully, suggestively, and was gratified to see a faint flush tint Alexi's cheeks.

"I...I did not mean..."

"Yeah, yeah. You never do." Blayne's smirk of pleasure at ruffling Alexi's composure was interrupted by a sudden yawn she could not suppress. Her sleepless night was beginning to catch up with her. *Maybe a nap when we get back to the cabin. Then, this afternoon...I'll see if I can ruffle her up some more.*

They rode the short drive back to the A-frame in silence.

Alexi tried desperately to dispel the provocative image that had sprung to mind when Blayne said the words *taking advantage*. They were back in the dressing room, but this time, she wasn't frisking Blayne, she was fucking her, up against the wall, and Blayne was loving every minute of it.

Her body resonated with arousal, *painful* arousal, and she didn't dare look at Blayne on the ride back. *How the hell am I ever going to get through this? She can turn me on with words alone.* The first thing she had to do when they got back was to get a few minutes to herself, in her room. *Appears I am going to be doing a lot of that.*

She parked the Prizm in front of the cabin and they stepped out into the late morning sunshine. She was so intent on her imminent orgasm that she didn't immediately see the dark silhouette waiting for them on the screened-in porch.

Blayne had taken three steps forward and was almost directly between her and the intruder before his movement caught Alexi's attention. The sudden realization that someone was waiting for them made her heart leap into her throat. "Blayne! Down!" She reached behind her for her gun, which was stuck into the waistband of her pants.

Blayne turned uncertainly in her direction.

"Down!" Alexi repeated as she darted forward to shield Blayne with her body.

"Alexi! Stop! It's Theo!"

She had the gun pointed at him, ready to fire, but his words penetrated and his voice was instantly familiar, so she froze and tried to will her heart to slow down. "Damn it, Theo! You nearly got yourself killed!" She turned to Blayne, whose eyes were wide in shock. She looked ready to bolt. "It is all right. He is my boss."

Blayne's fear transformed to anger when she realized there was no imminent threat. "How the fuck is he here? You told me you weren't going to tell anyone where we were!"

"And I did not," Alexi assured her. "I do not know how or why he is here, I assure you, but I sure as *hell* intend to find out." She put the gun back in her pants, and they resumed their trek to the porch. Theo met them at the door.

"Sorry to take you by surprise." Their visitor extended a hand toward Blayne. "Miss Keller, I'm Theodore Lang. I'm the head of WITSEC'S Chicago division."

Blayne eyed him suspiciously, nodding that she understood. But she made no move to shake his hand, and he let it drop.

"How did you find us, Theo?" Alexi said without preamble, her irritation evident. "And how long have you known where we were?"

"We've known since midnight."

"We?" Alexi asked.

"Three at the task force headquarters," he clarified. "Which means I cannot guarantee your safety here."

"*How*, Theo?"

His eyes shifted to Blayne. Alexi followed them.

"What? Why are you looking at me?" Blayne fidgeted under their scrutiny.

"You promised me you wouldn't call," Alexi said. "I trusted you."

"I didn't!"

"Go pack your things, Blayne." It was not a request. "We need to leave. And bring me your passport."

"I said I didn't call anyone!" Blayne argued, not budging. It was important to her that Alexi believe she had kept her word.

"You can trace an e-mail as easily as you can a phone call, Miss Keller," Lang said patiently.

Blayne felt suddenly light-headed. "Oh, shit."

"*Pack*, Blayne." Alexi's voice was clipped. "Quickly, please."

"All right. I'm going." Blayne headed upstairs toward her room.

Alexi turned to follow but Lang stopped her with a hand on her arm.

"We need to convince her to get back into the program, Alexi." He pulled a folded document from his inside breast pocket. "These are her papers. I have a helicopter waiting, but I want her to sign before we get on it."

Alexi scanned the standard agreement. Blayne would be admitted into the Witness Protection Program in exchange for her promise to testify. Papers were usually given to the witness during their formal orientation, but Blayne had never made it that far. "I do not think she will sign these, Theo."

"She has to. Cinzano's attorney has filed a petition to get him released," Lang said. "You know we'll never convince a judge to keep him unless we have a sworn statement from her that she'll testify."

Blayne rejoined them, her duffel bag packed and ready to go. She handed her passport to Alexi.

"You have two minutes to try to convince her, Theo." Alexi gave him back the WITSEC documents. "Which is how long it will take me to pack."

Alexi headed upstairs, half of her hoping that Blayne accepted the offer so that they could take the chopper out of there, the other half wanting the situation to remain as it was. Just her and Blayne.

"Miss Keller," Lang addressed Blayne as soon as they were alone. "I know you're reluctant to return to the program, and I understand why. But we can protect you much better than Alexi can by herself. And we need your agreement to testify in order to keep Vittorio Cinzano in jail until the trial." He unfolded the papers in his hand and handed them to her. "If you sign these, we can be on a helicopter headed out of here in five minutes. You'll be in a new, safe location by tonight."

Blayne glanced through the document. "I *am* going to testify," she told him, but in truth she still wasn't entirely sure about that. Her intentions were good, but more and more, she wanted to distance herself from all of the danger and uncertainty that awaited her in WITSEC. Alexi had made her feel safe again, and she was reluctant to do anything to change the status quo. "But I'm not going to sign anything."

She handed the papers back. "When I agreed to let you people make all the decisions for me, I was shot at and nearly killed by a bomb aboard a plane. Since Alexi has been taking care of me…Well, I'm the one who screwed up, not her. I like things the way they are."

"We have far more resources than she does alone," Lang argued. "She can't protect you better than we can within the program."

"If you're so capable of protecting people, what about Claudia Cluzet? Have you kept her safe? Do you even know where the hell she is yet?"

Lang frowned. "No," he admitted. "No leads on her or her father."

Damn. She fought back sudden tears. *Oh, Claud.*

"By rights, actually," Lang said, "WITSEC was never responsible for protecting the Cluzets. It was the Chicago PD's—"

Blayne cut him off. "Like I said, I'm not going into the program. I'll take my chances with Alexi."

"Miss Keller," he snapped. "Be reasonable."

"I've made up my mind."

Upstairs, Alexi threw the last of her things into her duffel and retrieved the money bag from under the bed and added their passports to it. She was furious at Blayne for sending the e-mail, but relieved that Theo had gotten to them before anyone else.

She turned to head back downstairs, the bags slung over one shoulder, but something made her take one last look out of the big triangular window that had served as such an excellent vantage point.

There was a dark sedan parked in the near distance, on the little two-track that ran up to the cabin.

Her blood ran cold.

A sudden flash momentarily blinded her, a glint of sunlight off metal, and when she blinked past it, her eyes focused on a man with a gun, approaching the porch through the trees.

Her heart thudded heavily in her chest. *Blayne!*

Chapter Sixteen

A lexi took the stairs three at a time and bolted to the porch, throwing down her bags and drawing her weapon en route. She found Blayne on the floor, Lang hunched over her, gun in hand, trying to protect her. "Shots," he rasped when he saw Alexi.

Staying low and moving fast, Alexi half pushed and half pulled Blayne into the cabin, as Theo lingered briefly behind to cover them. Just as they reached the doorway, a bullet hit the doorjamb near Alexi's head and splintered the wood. Another grazed Lang's left arm, just below the elbow, and took out a small chunk of flesh. He groaned and scrambled inside after them.

They'd heard no shots being fired. Their assailants were using silencers.

The door had barely closed behind them when it was peppered with gunfire. Alexi wrapped her arms around Blayne and brought her roughly down onto the floor.

Blayne got the wind knocked out of her but lay where she was. Alexi's body shielded her on one side, the counter on the other. She gasped for air, trying not to panic. All of her senses seemed heightened as her mind and body struggled with opposing urges to flee and fight. She felt Alexi's weight shift slightly to allow her to catch her breath.

"You all right, Theo?" Alexi asked in a low voice when the shooting subsided. A dark stain was blooming around the neat bullet hole in the arm of his coat.

"Not serious." He scrambled forward and crouched beneath the front window.

"Where is the helicopter?"

"Just over the rise behind us." Theo risked a quick glance outside from one corner of the window. "You can't see it from here, but it's not far. The pilot is Chicago PD. When we fire back, the shots will bring him in."

"He knows the situation?" Alexi asked.

"Enough to tell the good guys from the bad guys." Theo seemed about to say something else when one of the rear windows suddenly burst inward in a shower of glass, and they all hugged the floor again as the shooting resumed.

Chunks of wood from the back door flew through the air to land all around them. More bullets pierced the front door. Determined they would walk out of here, Alexi curled protectively around Blayne's back and signaled Theo. A brown-haired man in a dark winter jacket was poised just outside the porch door, gun in hand, intently focused on who might be lurking just inside the screen.

Theo raised his weapon and fired twice through the window, but the thick double panes deflected the bullets and the man ducked down out of sight, unhurt. He met Alexi's eyes and shook his head. His bullets left large holes and spiderweb cracks in the glass above his head.

Two more large-caliber bullets came through the back door. One shattered the ceramic base of a lamp three feet from Blayne and Alexi.

Theo's shots will be heard across the lake, so the gunmen will need to finish this fast. Alexi figured there were probably no more than four of them, since she had seen only one car outside. She had to take preemptive action. She could not wait until they shot their way in. Her body was energized and her senses were on hyperalert, analyzing every detail of her surroundings while she considered avenues of escape and likely scenarios.

"When I tell you…go around the counter, and lie flat, up against it," she instructed Blayne in a low voice. Their bodies were snuggled tight together, her breasts pressed against Blayne's back, her face in the curve of Blayne's shoulder. It was one of her favorite positions when she was fucking someone with a dick, and that familiar body memory flashed into her head when Blayne half turned so that their cheeks met and pressed against each other.

She shoved the image out of her mind as quickly as it had intruded, pushed it out with a fierce determination. *Thinking like that will get you both killed. Focus.* They were in a lull between shots. She knew it would not last.

"Go!" she told Blayne, shielding her as she moved around the counter.

Once Blayne was lying flat, she took up a position next to the rear window that had been shattered.

Before she exposed herself to get a look, she listened.

It took a few seconds to filter sounds over the pounding of her heart and the other ambient noise—the faint hum of the refrigerator ten feet away. Then she heard it. A very subtle metallic tapping, just outside. It lasted only a few seconds. The nervous tapping of a ring against the handle of a gun, perhaps. Human, whatever it was. And so close she knew someone was standing directly through the wall. She raised her pistol until it barely cleared the lower left corner of the window and fired three times, angling the gun slightly with each shot, knowing at least one of the bullets would find a target. A heavy thud of impact confirmed that a body had hit the ground, and she heard a long groan.

Alexi listened intently for several seconds, but could hear no further noise from outside and risked a quick glance up. A flash of movement in the woods warned her and she darted out of the way as a bullet whizzed by and sank into the wall behind her. She was back up and firing almost at once, but the man was gone, concealed behind the side of the cabin that had no windows and no door. *Eight bullets left.*

Theo was alternately keeping an eye on the front of the cabin and on the rear. His vantage point allowed him a clear view of anything passing by the window Alexi was crouched beneath. Alexi had to split her attention three ways—on her own window, on Theo's, across the cabin to her left. And on Blayne, to her right.

Cinzano's men hit both the front and back of the cabin almost at once. Alexi saw movement in the window above her boss's head and fired. Theo reacted by darting out from beneath. In that moment, as they were both distracted, one of Cinzano's men leaned into the window above Alexi's head.

"Alexi! Watch out!" Blayne screamed, and Alexi reacted on instinct, whirling about and firing blindly, hitting the man in the chest just as he pulled the trigger of his gun. The bullet flew by so near Alexi's ear that she swore she heard it, ricocheted off the metal refrigerator, and broke a coffee mug on the counter above Blayne's head, as cleanly as if it had been a trick shot in an old Wild West movie.

Cinzano's man slumped over the windowsill and his gun, a Beretta

92F equipped with a silencer, slipped from his hand onto the floor. Alexi snatched it up and quickly checked the magazine. There were nine bullets remaining.

It was poetic justice, she decided as she hefted the familiar weight of the 9mm pistol. The same model had been taken from her a year earlier by the same kind of killers, the night she'd failed to save Sofia Galletti. It wasn't going to happen again.

Two shots were fired from outside her window, audible shots this time, neither apparently aimed at the cabin or its occupants. She darted a glance outside. Fifty feet away, at the edge of the woods, a man in a navy jumpsuit took aim at a clump of thick shrubbery next to the cabin and fired.

"The cavalry has arrived." Alexi watched the pilot take another shot. He had one of the assailants pinned down. This was their chance. "We have to make a move. Your pilot is keeping at least one of them busy."

Theo sized up the situation. "How about I go out the back, shooting? He'll cover me until I get to the trees. We draw them toward the chopper while you get Keller out the front and to the car."

"Yes, good. I will give you a head start and cover you from the window. One second." Alexi darted over to where she had dropped the bag containing the money and their passports and slung it securely over her back. "Blayne, get ready to move. When we go out the front, stick close to me. Fast and low, right to the car."

"I understand." Blayne got into a semicrouch.

Theo hustled to the back door and signaled Alexi. She hurried back to the window and leaned out, firing toward the corner of the cabin to provide cover as Theo ran.

The exchange of gunfire started in earnest and as soon as he'd reached the pilot, Alexi ducked and scrambled to the front door, urging, "*Now*, Blayne."

The command was unnecessary, for Blayne was already moving in a low crouch around the counter to join her.

Alexi cracked open the door and stepped onto the porch, keeping low. She detected no movement, no sound, and could see no figures among the trees. The car was parked twenty feet away, under a huge oak. A gun in each hand, she gestured Blayne forward and they crept to the door of the porch, then burst out and bolted for the car.

They were halfway there before Alexi realized someone was

shooting at them. She never heard the shot, but just ahead of them the Prizm's front window suddenly cracked. Still running, she whirled around and returned fire toward the point of origin.

Blayne dove through the front passenger door, and Alexi threw open hers and followed suit. Another bullet tore a hole in the front window, now so crowded with cracks it was difficult to see through.

"Stay down!" Alexi ordered as she grappled for the car keys.

Another bullet hit the car, this time the front grill. Alexi glimpsed telltale metal in the trees and was able to pinpoint the shooter. She rolled down her window and fired, left-handed, with the Beretta. Once, twice, and the man went down.

She slammed the key into the ignition, and started to turn it, and only then did it register that something was different. Even with the bag of money on her back, she knew. She was sitting a bit too far forward. She froze.

"Out!" she hissed at Blayne. "Out of the car! Now!" She opened her door.

"What?" Blayne, not comprehending, looked up at Alexi from her hunched position, half on the floor and half on the passenger seat.

"Out! The car has been rigged!"

Alexi was already around to Blayne's side of the car before she was all the way out. She tugged her several feet into the woods and down behind a massive log, where they paused, both of them breathing hard.

"How do you know the car is rigged?" Blayne asked.

"The seat had been moved." Alexi scanned the woods around them. Intermittent gunfire could still be heard on the other side of the cabin, getting farther away by the moment.

"We need to get to the helicopter before they take off," Alexi decided aloud. "The long way around."

She had scarcely spoken the words before an enormous explosion shook the ground under their feet and a fireball almost as big as the cabin itself shot up from the top of the ridge, spewing thick black smoke into the clear blue sky. It could only be the helicopter. *Ela gamoto! Theo.*

With the pilot and Theo presumably dead, Alexi knew their assailants would be hunting them down to finish the job.

"Come with me." She grabbed Blayne's hand and pulled her to her feet and down the two-track driveway. Once they reached the dark sedan, Alexi put bullets in two of the tires with the Beretta, grateful for the silencer. They then cut through the woods toward the lake as fast as they could run.

"There! Down there!" Alexi heard a man shout just as they were about to board the fishing boat she had rented. She whirled around and saw two goons, similarly dressed in dark, nondescript jackets and jeans, running full tilt in their direction, guns blazing.

"Get in!" She tried to shield Blayne's body with her own as she raised her guns to return fire. But before she got a chance to squeeze either trigger, she heard Blayne cry out and a sudden splash soaked her as Blayne toppled into the water. *Oh God. She's been hit.*

A bullet tore past her into the boat, inches from her feet. She returned fire with both guns, forcing the mobsters to dive for cover behind trees. As they did, she jumped into the boat and reached for Blayne, who was resurfacing just beside it.

"Are you hit?" she asked frantically, still firing intermittently with her free hand. She had lost count, but she knew she had to be nearly out of ammo in both guns.

"No." Blayne threw both arms over the edge of the boat. "Fucking lost my balance when a bullet clipped the boat as I was getting in. Sorry." She hauled herself aboard with Alexi's help.

Alexi pulled the trigger of her Sig-Sauer as the two assailants came out of hiding and started toward them again, but the magazine was empty. "Start the boat and get us out of here," she told Blayne as she tossed her service pistol aside and reached for the Beretta.

She raised the weapon, praying it had a round or two left. Blayne started the motor and gunned the boat forward. Alexi's aim was impaired by the forward lurch of the boat and there were only two bullets, but her return fire managed to gain the time they needed to speed out of range.

"I will take over now." She laid a hand on Blayne's shoulder and knew instantly that getting her warm and dry had to be high on their priority list. She was soaked to the skin and shivering badly. The water was still as icy as midwinter, and she was lucky she had only been in it for seconds. But first, they had to get a car.

As Blayne sagged into the nearest seat, Alexi said, "When we get to the lodge, I am going to commandeer another vehicle. We have to get out of here as soon as possible."

"No argument from me." Blayne hugged herself, trying to keep warm.

"You should be proud of yourself, you know. You did very well back there. Kept your cool. Followed my instructions. And your warning saved my life. You showed a lot of courage."

Blayne looked up at her. "It means a lot to me that you think so. But you had your body between me and the bullets most of the time."

Alexi shrugged. "It is what I am paid to do."

"Thank you anyway. And I mean thank you for everything. I'm sorry I ever mistrusted you."

"You had good reason to be skeptical." Alexi gave her an encouraging smile. "I am glad we have the same agenda now."

Blayne smiled back and gave her a half-salute. "Just tell me what to do and I'll do it."

❖

A short while later, after relieving an elderly fisherman of his Subaru Outback, they were traveling east on a badly paved but virtually empty two-lane road, well in excess of the speed limit.

Alexi cranked up the heat and pointed all the blowers at Blayne. "We will stop soon to get you some dry clothes. I am afraid you will have to take what you can get."

"Hey, I'm so glad to be alive, I'm far from complaining." Blayne held her hands up in front of the blowers. *That makes four times now I've cheated death. Maybe I should buy a lottery ticket.* "You think Inspector Lang and the pilot are dead?"

Alexi didn't answer immediately. "I hope not. Will you check the glove compartment please and see if there is a map?"

Blayne pulled out a recent map of Canada and a cell phone. She pointed out the road they were on, and Alexi studied the surrounding area until she found what she was looking for.

"Chapleau. It is not far, and it has an airstrip." She stepped on the gas.

"Airstrip? Surely you don't mean for us to get on another plane."

Alexi glanced across at her passenger, who was chewing nervously on her lower lip. *God, what nice lips she has. They look so soft.* "Blayne, we have to put a lot of distance between us and these guys, and quickly. My plan is the best way."

"I just can't imagine it." The thought of getting on an airplane sent

Blayne's stomach into a roll and her heart rate into the stratosphere. Images of the gaping hole in the Airbus flooded her brain. She started to hyperventilate, but Alexi put a hand on her shoulder, and that had an immediate calming effect.

"I know it will be difficult. But it has to be done." Alexi didn't withdraw the hand for a long moment. She had the irresistible urge to caress Blayne's back. *To reassure her*, she told herself. *The human touch has a calming effect*. But she knew she was kidding herself. Any excuse to touch her, that was the real story. She resisted the urge.

"I know what you say is true…" Blayne couldn't look at Alexi, afraid that any movement she made might end the touch that anchored her. That made her feel less vulnerable. "But the thought of flying again so soon just terrifies me, I have to admit. I don't know that I can do it."

The words spilled out of Alexi before she really thought about them. "I will find ways to keep you distracted, I am certain. Whatever it takes."

Blayne snorted and looked down at her feet. "It will take more than backgammon." She hated showing such weakness in front of Alexi, who had just called her courageous. *Not very brave now. She was on the same plane I was, but she's not hesitating to do it again.*

"Like I said…" Alexi repeated.

The hand that had been on Blayne's shoulder moved to her chin, coaxing her into eye contact.

Somehow Alexi kept her attention on the road but also made sure her gaze steadied Blayne. "*Whatever* it takes," she said in her most provocative tone. She would suffer for this, she knew, but she was also certain it was probably the best way to get Blayne on that plane. "Do you not think I am capable of maintaining your full attention?"

Blayne swallowed hard. She couldn't believe what she was hearing. A warm rush of arousal caused by the look in Alexi's eyes immediately dulled her fear of flying. "Uh…that would be no problem for you, I'm sure."

Alexi smiled and placed both hands back on the wheel. "Good. So, tell me. Have you ever been to Europe before?"

❖

Theo Lang winced as the doctor finished stitching the cut in his chin. Despite the anesthetic, his jaw hurt like a son of a bitch. It was bothering him more at the moment than his broken arm or fractured ribs, all the result of being blown ten feet in the air when the helicopter exploded. All things considered, though, he was lucky. The pilot could run faster, so he'd been several feet closer to the chopper when the mobsters hit the gas tank. He'd suffered third-degree burns in addition to a concussion and several broken bones.

"All right, Mr. Lang. That does it. We'll get you moved to a bed in ICU soon."

"Need to make a phone call," Theo slurred through what remained of his teeth. His jaw was wired shut, so telling people what he wanted was a challenge.

The doctor raised a couple of half-hearted objections, but within minutes, Theo was connected to his superior, an assistant director of the U.S. Marshals Office in Arlington, Virginia. The nurse held the phone to his ear.

His attempt to identify himself came out *Heeo Ang* the first time so he said it twice, enunciating as best as he could. "I'm in a hospital."

When his boss acknowledged that he understood, Theo grated slowly, "Narrowed the leak to three men," he said. "Harry Granger, Erik Riker, or Paul Fletcher."

❖

I should not have to be the one to report such bad news, Frankie Sloan thought to himself. Two of their guys dead and two cops injured. They were plainclothes, but he was sure that's what they were—that would bring the heat in on this, big time. And worst of all, the broad got away. He would have to be the one to make the call because Rosco Rosetti, the only other survivor of this nightmare piece of work had refused to, and he was scared of Rosco. But he was even more afraid of the boss.

At least he knew how the two women had gotten out of there. When he and Rosco made it to the lodge parking lot to hotwire a new ride, they'd run into an old man all bent out of shape that two broads had taken his brand new Outback and the police still hadn't showed. Frankie pulled out his cell phone and dialed.

❖

"*Oh* no. No way." Blayne gazed around the airstrip, a primitive facility with two asphalt runways and a pair of wind socks. There was nothing like a building or hangar or fuel depot, just a few feeble-looking small planes untidily parked, one angled behind the next. "You're out of your mind. I'm not getting in one of those flying shoeboxes. The wind blows wrong and they can come down."

Alexi studied the small prop planes parked off to the side, and optimistically noted that one had printing on the side. "They are just as safe as larger aircraft," she said, hoping it was true. "WITSEC uses small planes frequently and has never had a problem. Besides, I only plan on us taking one as far as Toronto."

She parked the Outback as close as she could get and grabbed the cell phone out of the glove box before heading toward the single-engine Cessna Skyhawk. Blayne stayed in the Subaru, shaking her head.

The sign on the plane read *Cochran Charters. Fishing, Hunting, Sporting Adventures*, and gave a local phone number. Alexi dialed it on the cell. "Hello. Are you available for an immediate flight for two to Toronto if I can pay in cash?"

After making rapid arrangements for the charter, she told Blayne, "The pilot is meeting us in an hour's time." They had time to pick up a quick lunch and clean clothes, and for Alexi to tie up some loose ends. She knew she would likely have problems at customs if she tried to get on a plane with all the cash she had on her, so she stopped at a bank to arrange a wire transfer to one of her UK accounts.

Though she had lost her American passport in the airplane explosion, she still had her Greek passport—locked in the safe in her office in Thessaloniki. She would need it to access her accounts, and it would be a much better passport to use for European travel.

She also needed a weapon overseas, since she could not take her own with her on the plane without proper identification. So she called her administrative assistant and asked her to book a two-bedroom suite at a hotel in London and to express her passport there, along with a copy of her WITSEC credentials and the Smith and Wesson .357 Magnum revolver she kept in her safe. She would call back to check on the arrangements as soon as they landed.

Her next call, to Canadian authorities, was to ensure that the

Outback was returned to its owner. She also alerted them to the two guns they would find inside. The final call she made was to the lodge, where she learned from the manager that two men had been taken by ambulance to the hospital.

"I am certain that is Theo and the pilot," she told Blayne as she returned the cell phone to the Subaru glove compartment. "The men I hit were dead, and the other two were certainly healthy-looking when they were shooting at us."

Blayne didn't reply beyond a nervous nod.

"You can do this," Alexi said, sensing she needed reassurance. "It is just a few hours, and then we will be well out of their reach. You will be safe until the trial."

"I always wanted to get to Europe," Blayne said. "I just never thought it would be this way. I was saving for a trip to Fiji."

"Ah, I see. The envelope of money you had?"

"Yes."

"Why Fiji? If I might ask?" Alexi was happy that Blayne seemed to be coming to terms with the idea of getting on another plane. Truth was, she wasn't any too anxious to be back in the air herself, but she had decided her plan was a good one.

"Blue water, great beaches, warm sun, lazy days," Blayne mused. "And some really hot bodies to stare at all day."

Alexi laughed. "Actually, you have just described my homeland, and it has much more to offer than that, in my opinion. It is also more affordable."

"Well, I must admit I did look longingly at pictures of Greece whenever I'd book a trip there for somebody else," Blayne admitted. "Beautiful place."

"That it is."

"That where we're going?" Blayne asked hopefully.

"You never know where we might end up. We will see what destinations are available." She raised a hand in brief salute to an apple-cheeked man with a thick growth of salt-and-pepper beard. Their Cessna pilot, she assumed.

He yawned as though he had just rolled out of bed, which did not help Blayne's confidence in him one bit. "Jesus, Alexi, I just don't know about this," she said under her breath.

"We're going to be fine. No one has two air emergencies in one week. It's a statistical impossibility."

She said it with such confidence, Blayne could force her legs to climb the steps up. But as they buckled in, her hands shook, and she couldn't seem to think of anything—picture *anything*—but the sight of the enormous hole in the Airbus as they walked to the ambulance.

Alexi reached over and interlaced her fingers with Blayne's. It seemed a natural thing to do.

Grateful for the contact, Blayne closed her eyes and tried to take deep, even breaths. *How is it that you can keep me calm in the chaos when nothing else helps?*

For a very long while, it had seemed as though her attraction to Alexi had been entirely physical—sparked by Alexi's fabulous body and beautiful, classic features. Her smile, her eyes. That undeniable, simmering sexuality so well hidden most of the time. It sure gave her ideas. Lots of ideas. She had imagined them in all sorts of positions, doing all manner of things to each other.

But this latest attempt on her life had shown her that the feelings she was developing went far beyond just the physical. She respected and admired Alexi for her constant strength and quiet courage. Her resourcefulness and determination. And her thoughtful kindness, too, at moments like this.

Alexi's mysterious and taciturn ways had been intriguing in the beginning. But more and more, Blayne really wanted to get to know the woman beneath the tough exterior. And she wanted Alexi to trust *her* in the way that she had come to trust Alexi. *I know that everything she does for me is her job. But I think it's also personal with her. I can see it there, sometimes. God, I hope it is. I hope it's not just wishful thinking.*

Alexi squeezed her hand, as though in affirmation of her thoughts, and she warmed at the timing. "Better?" she asked.

Blayne opened her eyes and smiled at her. "Yes. Better. Thank you."

Alexi smiled back. "My pleasure. Better for me too."

Blayne wanted to say something else, something that expressed how thankful she was and how lucky she felt, and maybe even that she'd been a fool. She'd been uncharacteristically rude and obnoxious to a woman who had gone beyond the bounds of any job just to keep her safe. But she had trouble finding the right words and they were taking off, and it was all she could do to breathe. Instead of thinking about their wheels leaving the earth, she centered her thoughts on the woman next to her, drawing on her strength and taking comfort in her tenderness.

She didn't want to think about the future, or the next hurdle, or the people chasing them. She just wanted to exist in the now, feeling like her hand belonged in Alexi's.

CHAPTER SEVENTEEN

"Ineed a distraction." Blayne leaned toward Alexi as she said this, so the remark carried a certain intimacy. "Show me what you got."

Alexi looked momentarily stunned. "Could you repeat the question?"

"I believe distraction is your department, isn't it? You did say *whatever it takes*. I have those words burned into my memory," Blayne reminded her.

Alexi cleared her throat, considering a response. *I knew I should never have said that. What the hell was I thinking?* At least Blayne had waited until they had finished their meal. The lights in first class had been dimmed and the beds made up for those intending to sleep.

"Well?" Blayne demanded playfully. She was actually much more relaxed than she thought she would be, thanks to a couple of drinks, a nice meal, and the comfort of blankets, pillows, slippers, even pajamas if she wanted to embarrass herself. The British Airways complimentary amenity kit included an eye mask she had no intention of using. While sleeping might be one way to make the flight go faster, she was not about to waste time that could be spent collecting on Alexi's promise.

"Yes, I did say that." Alexi forced herself not to squirm. She didn't dare look at Blayne. From her seductive tone of voice, she knew what she would see in her eyes. And she didn't know if she could stand looking at that for the next several hours without touching her. "And I am a woman of my word. So what did you have in mind?"

Blayne threw a blanket over Alexi, grateful there were few other flyers in first class and that the pod-style seating screened the passengers from one another. She and Alexi had one of several pairs of seats designed for couples traveling together. But the airline wasn't taking any chances. If togetherness lost its charm, you only had to hit a button and a privacy screen rolled up.

Beneath the blanket, she put her hand on Alexi's thigh, halfway between her knee and groin. "This would sure distract me. How 'bout you?"

Despite her best intentions to remain unaffected, Alexi could not help but jump at the touch. Then she immediately took Blayne's hand in hers to keep it from moving any farther up her thigh. With her other hand, she gripped the armrest so tightly she was afraid she might tear it right off.

"This is…" *Completely unfair. Totally impossible. Excruciatingly wonderful. Damn it all to hell.*

"This is…?" Blayne leaned over the divider between them and snuggled in until her breast was pressing against Alexi's arm and her face was just a few inches from Alexi's ear. "Cozy? Inviting? Overdue?" she whispered seductively.

"I was going to say…this is…" Alexi struggled for some neutral response. "A good time for you to rest," she managed weakly.

Blayne laughed. "Yeah, right. That's exactly what you were thinking." She planted a soft, lingering kiss on Alexi's cheek. "Liar."

Alexi didn't move. Her mind seemed to suddenly desert her, leaving her body to fend for itself. And her body was welcoming Blayne's advances and urging her on.

"I know you're attracted to me," Blayne whispered in her ear. "I can tell you want me as much as I want you, no matter what you say." She punctuated this statement by sucking on Alexi's earlobe.

"Blayne," Alexi said hoarsely, "You…" *You do not know how right you are. You turn me on so damn much I cannot complete a sentence.* "You…cannot." It was a half-hearted response, lacking any sort of conviction whatsoever.

"Oh, yes, I can, and so can you." Blayne ran her tongue lightly along Alexi's neck. "You said *whatever* it takes to keep me distracted. All you have to do is just sit back and enjoy. At least for now."

Alexi had no power to stop her growing arousal. Nor could she manage to say or do anything to discourage Blayne's mouth from what it was doing. Her body wanted to move of its own accord, lean into Blayne's touch, and most of all…she wanted to touch Blayne back.

Meet those lips with her own. It was taking every ounce of willpower for her not to respond, and she had no idea how she was going to be able to keep this up all the way to London.

Without warning, Blayne's hand slid from beneath hers, moving firmly up her thigh, higher now, dangerously within reach. She trembled, every nerve ending on edge. *Christ.* As her breathing quickened she could feel Blayne's smile against her neck.

She couldn't help herself. She leaned her head back and closed her eyes as Blayne's hand moved deliberately, slowly, fingers spread to touch the greatest area possible. *Just for a moment, let me feel this. Enjoy this. Then I will stop her. But just for a moment.* The tantalizing strokes traveled down her thigh, then up the inseam of her pants, before skimming over her sex with frustratingly little pressure and beginning the same route again. At the same time, Blayne's teeth nipped lightly at her neck, and her tongue wetly claimed the pulse point at the base of her throat.

One pass of Blayne's hand, then two. Three. Each elicited a subtle lifting of her hips to meet it. *She is going to make me come if she keeps this up.* Her mind was hazy, out of control, in full surrender to Blayne's touch.

A soft chime penetrated her consciousness and forced her eyes open. The passenger in the window seat ahead of them, to the right, had summoned the flight attendant and she was already heading their way. Alexi sat up abruptly, distancing herself from Blayne's mouth as she snapped back to full awareness. Her hand stopped Blayne's, with more conviction this time.

She was breathing heavily, so intensely aroused she had trouble focusing. *Too close. That was way too close. Gamoto, what this woman can do to me.*

As the flight attendant exchanged words with the passenger, Blayne leaned in to whisper in her ear. "You can't seriously tell me you want me to stop."

Alexi's jaw clenched when she felt Blayne's warm breath against her face. Her body was throbbing, and there was only one thing to be done. "Excuse me," she whispered, barely recognizing her own voice. Rising hurriedly, she slipped past the flight attendant, grateful to find an unoccupied restroom a few rows ahead.

Once she'd locked the door on temptation, she stared at herself in the mirror. The extent of her need was written on her face so clearly it startled her. The plane shifted slightly in a small bit of turbulence, and she spread her legs to steady her balance. Still breathing heavily, she quickly undid her pants and used her left hand to brace herself against the sink, while her right brought her body the only satisfaction possible. It was quick, and necessary, and not nearly enough. It was Blayne's hand she wanted to be getting her off, not her own.

She washed up and decided to wait until her breathing had calmed before venturing back to her seat. In those moments with herself, she berated her weakness and vowed never again to allow Blayne to get her to the point of no return.

❖

It took Blayne several long seconds to fully comprehend that Alexi was *gone*. Had left her high and dry just as things were finally getting interesting. *Well, not so dry, actually.* Alexi was halfway up the aisle before it really registered, because Blayne was nearly intoxicated by desire and had successfully blotted out much of where they were and who was around them. By the time she figured out what was happening, Alexi was too far away for her to raise a protest without disturbing the few other passengers in the quiet cabin. *Fuck.* She knew damn well what Alexi was about to do. And that certain knowledge was the final straw.

When Alexi had unexpectedly begun to relax under her caresses, had closed her eyes and accepted what she was doing without argument, Blayne's body had come alive, every cell tingling with anticipation. The first time she tasted that soft, bronzed skin, her heart began to pound. And each time Alexi's hips rose slightly to meet her touch, her own arousal redoubled.

So by the time they were interrupted, Blayne was already close to the edge, ready to explode herself, just from the thrill of finally being able to touch Alexi. *And now this. She can't do this to me! She's going to come back all spent and satisfied and leave me frustrated. I just know that she is. Fuuuck.*

Alexi had been gone only a short while before Blayne decided that she wasn't about to be left stranded like that. *Two can play at that game.* She headed up the aisle herself and into the vacant lavatory opposite the one Alexi had claimed.

God damn it. So close. It was patently inhumane, she decided, to get that aroused and then have to stop. She knew Alexi wanted her. She studied her reflection as she unzipped her jeans. *I have to admit, I wear that just-rolled-out-of-bed look pretty well.* She had that heavy-lidded, sexually charged look of someone who had already been laid, and happily so, but the reality was altogether different. She was desperate to come.

She unfastened her pants and let them fall to her knees, unwilling to encounter any further obstructions to her release. She used both hands, one to knead her breasts roughly, tugging at the nipples…and the other to slide into the wetness that had formed between her legs when she had run her fingers over Alexi's sex.

Damn, that was hot. She closed her eyes and imagined her hand was back on Alexi, continuing in that seductive circle along her thigh. And she tried to tell herself that the hand she felt giving her pleasure was Alexi's hand. That is what she wanted. No, *needed.* It had gone beyond want a long time ago.

But her body just wouldn't believe her mental promptings.

She only succeeded in perhaps slightly increasing her arousal factor, and at great cost in terms of her frustration level. It was nice. It was pleasant. But she couldn't come, no matter how much she wished for it. No matter what formerly foolproof technique she tried. It only left her wanting more.

She washed and pulled her pants up, and took another look at herself in the mirror. That hazy look of desire had been replaced by the restless, vacant stare of a caged animal. *Damn, do I need to get off.*

In the lavatory across the aisle, Alexi took a deep breath and studied her reflection one last time. *Better.* Certainly a radical departure from the look she had come in with. To all outward appearances, she was her old self, a passable deception. Though she'd achieved what she'd come in for, her body still vibrated with need. The need to touch Blayne, to control her climb to ecstasy, to make her body thrill with want, to watch her come.

That was one need that had no chance of ever being satisfied. And that realization made her much sadder than she would have dreamed possible. She took a deep breath, unlocked the door, and opened it…to find Blayne just exiting the restroom opposite hers.

Their eyes met, and they both froze.

The look on Blayne's face threatened to implode Alexi's fragile composure. *Oh please, Christ, do not do this to me.* There was a hunger in her eyes, a hunger Alexi wanted desperately to satisfy. It was that unmistakable look that a woman gets when she is close to the precipice, wet with excitement, when nothing in the world matters but coming.

More than anything, Alexi wanted to pull Blayne into her cramped lavatory cubicle and quench the thirst that consumed the both of them. Push her up against the wall and hold her there with her body until neither could breathe.

But that would never do. She tried to force the image from her mind, but her body didn't want to let go.

Blayne stepped across the aisle, eyes boring into hers. She looked neither left or right, not caring if they were overheard. "Tell me…" she said, clearly annoyed, "How the hell you can look as though you don't feel what I know you're feeling?"

"We should return to our seats now," Alexi said, keeping her voice even. "With a firm resolve on both of our parts not to let anything like that happen again."

Blayne took a half step nearer until she was invading Alexi's personal space. Her eyes never left Alexi's. "Dream on."

Blayne's proximity and that damned look in her eyes was unraveling Alexi's composure. She reached out, grabbed Blayne's upper arm, and steered her toward their seats. "Go," she said in a low voice. "We cannot attract too much attention."

"This is not over," Blayne whispered.

Alexi sighed. *It never is.*

❖

Vittorio Cinzano drummed his fingers on the table, staring with disdain at the cocky guard watching over him, memorizing his face. *Smile, asshole. Keep smiling. I'll shove your teeth down your throat myself.*

Florio would get some of his anger as well, for making him wait. Which was no problem. He certainly had plenty of it to go around these days.

The door to the small meeting room opened and the attorney entered, carrying a briefcase. He nodded respectfully at Vittorio. The guard stepped out, and Florio took the seat opposite his boss.

"Better have some good news for me, Michael. I am done with waiting."

"I have," Florio said hastily. "We have a judge who understands our situation, and a favorable decision is expected today or tomorrow."

Cinzano smiled for the first time in many days. "And the other?"

"Progress there too. We have them at the Toronto airport. I should know more on that soon."

"Excellent, Michael. You keep your job for another day."

❖

So damn stubborn, Alexi concluded, watching over Blayne as she slept. *You will be my undoing, I suspect, with your absolute refusal to be deterred.*

When they had returned to their seats, Alexi had resolutely reached for her earphones and selected a movie, and then encased her body in one of the white British Air duvets, more to ward off further intimate touches than to fend off any chill. Her body temperature needed no assistance on that score.

Blayne had tried to start things up again, with suggestive looks and straying hands and none-too-subtle propositions, but Alexi had firmly ignored her, pretending complete absorption in the movie. Obviously aggrieved, Blayne had folded her arms across her chest and pouted for several minutes. And then finally she had turned her seat into a bed and succumbed to sleep.

Alexi remained awake, keeping vigil over her charge, and thought about what she needed to do once they got to London. She knew the city well and would be grateful to be back in familiar territory. First, a call to her assistant, then to the hotel to pick up her passport and gun. A stop at the bank for some ready cash. Then some shopping for clothes and other necessities.

She knew that Blayne would be jet-lagged when they arrived, but she was not about to let her nap when they got to the hotel. She wanted Blayne dead tired when they retired to their rooms for the evening, so out of it she would crash for several hours.

Because Alexi had plans for some company that night, a London lady friend who could hopefully accomplish what masturbation had not. Get her mind off fucking Blayne and back onto protecting her.

CHAPTER EIGHTEEN

I just want to get out and walk around and explore." Blayne's face was nearly pressed up against the taxi window as they drove by Trafalgar Square.

Alexi had told the driver to take a long, circuitous route to their hotel in Knightsbridge so that Blayne could get her first glimpse of some of the major monuments she'd been looking forward to seeing. Big Ben and the Houses of Parliament, Westminster Abbey, and St. Paul's Cathedral.

Though the language was familiar and the culture similar, Blayne was immediately fascinated by her first taste of Europe. Everything was very different. The road signs and automobiles, the sights and sounds, and the surreal quality of driving on the left side.

"Let us check in at the hotel first," Alexi said. "I have identification there that will allow me to access my funds. That way we can combine sightseeing with shopping. I do not know about you, but I am ready for a change of clothes and I know some great places here, starting with Harrods. Nothing much they do not have."

"Sounds like a plan," Blayne agreed. "Can we go by Buckingham Palace? Oh! And the British Museum?"

Alexi smiled. "Wherever you like." *I want you absolutely exhausted when you turn in tonight.*

Her assistant had booked them a spacious, airy suite at the Henry David, and at Alexi's request had arranged for fresh flowers, a fruit basket, and assorted chocolates to be waiting for them. There were plush terry robes and matching slippers, a full line of complimentary toiletries, and an impressively stocked refrigerator/bar.

"This is unbelievable." Blayne opened the French doors to the balcony and stepped out to appreciate their view of the greenery of Hyde Park. The balcony was surrounded by ornate cast iron and furnished with a breakfast table and two reclining lounge chairs. "I've certainly never stayed in a hotel anywhere near this plush." *So damn romantic. What a waste.*

She wished this could all be easier. It was hard to stay angry with Alexi. Even though she still felt intensely frustrated, and on some level rejected, Blayne could see Alexi was only trying to behave responsibly. The threat to her life was real and immediate, yet she'd done nothing but distract Alexi almost from the start. There was no denying the attraction she felt, and she was pretty sure the feeling was mutual, but she had allowed it to become a game she wanted to win, a competition to see whose will was stronger. All she'd succeeded in doing was making it essential for Alexi to resist her.

She had to change that, Blayne decided. It was time to let Alexi do her job and appreciate her for what she was already giving, instead of trying to force her to give more. She had no right to complain about Alexi's behavior, Blayne thought with a trace of shame. Alexi had helped erase a great deal of her fear and anxiety and had made their escape together feel more like a vacation adventure than a run for their lives. In fact, Alexi had spoiled her from the moment they arrived in Toronto and boarded their flight.

At first Blayne had assumed she was receiving some kind of special treatment from WITSEC. As she and Alexi settled into their comfortable, wide leather seats and a flight attendant instantly arrived to take their drink orders, Blayne remarked, "This is really nice. Why didn't WITSEC fly me first class the last time?"

"The government does not fly people first class, as a rule."

"Didn't think so. Why now?"

"Well, you have been through one ordeal after another. And the worst was aboard a plane. I know it is taking a lot for you to do this, though you are concealing it pretty well."

Blayne studied Alexi's face. She didn't want to think at all about that flight, but it was unavoidable, and looking at Alexi against this backdrop, she couldn't help but recall in vivid detail the moments before the explosion.

"That bomb didn't get me because I was preoccupied with you, you know… I stopped in the aisle because you were looking at me."

Blayne remembered the moment when their eyes met. She could have sworn she felt something special in that exchange. Something more than just Alexi recognizing her as a WITSEC witness.

Alexi looked as though she was about to respond, but the flight attendant had interrupted them with the customary seat belt, oxygen mask, and life-vest speech, and two minutes later they were taxiing down the runway.

"You hide everything a little too well, in my opinion," Blayne said carefully. "Tell me, are you nervous about flying again?"

"Of course," Alexi replied. "It was a terrible experience. But right now, we are a lot safer up here than we are down there."

"Looking back, I guess it's not such a bad thing I was knocked out during part of it."

Alexi was silent for a few seconds, then said, "I am glad you were not seriously injured."

While en route to the hotel many hours later, Blayne thought about that statement. She wished there were some personal sentiment behind it, but she knew Alexi meant it only as a courtesy. She was always courteous, always polite. Always considerate. Like booking them first class seats to London. They couldn't have been cheap. Neither was the Canadian lodge. And waiting in the UK or wherever for the trial instead of some Smalltown, USA, was also going to be expensive. She supposed Alexi must have jumped through a lot of bureaucratic hoops to get all this.

Blayne stared out the window of their big black London taxi. "Just how is it that the government is willing to fly me to London first class and put me up in Europe when I haven't even signed a statement that I'm going to testify? Not that I'm complaining, but I mean, is this where my tax dollars go?"

Alexi couldn't suppress a half-smile. "Well, not exactly, no. Your tax dollars are not paying for this trip."

"What is, then? Now I'm really curious."

"Your protection is being privately funded."

"Privately funded?" Alarm bells went off in Blayne's mind. The first possibility she considered was that Cinzano himself might be paying Alexi to get her out of the country so that she couldn't testify against him. *No. Impossible. He wants me dead, that's certainly clear. I can trust her.* She felt ashamed of herself for thinking such a thing, even in passing. Alexi had more than proven herself.

Alexi watched a myriad of emotions cross Blayne's face, and she knew she would have to tell her the truth. Blayne was considering other, darker possibilities, that was clear from her suddenly fearful expression. And even if her disappointment about the interlude on the plane was clouding her judgment, she still needed to know her trust was not misplaced.

"Do not worry." Alexi turned a little more in the capacious backseat of the cab. "I am paying for this trip, and your protection. Most of it, anyway."

Blayne's eyes got wide. "You?"

Alexi nodded. "It is not a lot of money to me. So it is nothing to concern yourself about."

"In other words, you're wealthy?" Blayne was intrigued by this latest bit of news. Not that money mattered much to her, except maybe as a means to travel occasionally. But she hadn't gotten the impression that Alexi was some spoiled rich woman. *Quite the contrary, really.* Although her formal manner and unflagging courtesy suggested a privileged upbringing, she seemed at heart a very down-to-earth woman, generally without pretense.

"Very comfortable, shall we say." Alexi smiled.

"I figured there had to be money in that sack that Ray gave you."

"Yes. He is a trusted friend."

Alexi had a sudden impulse, but before she gave into it she briefly weighed the pros and the cons. She reached into her pocket for one of two thick envelopes of money she had retained, opened it, and began to count out several bills.

"I believe I promised you I would reimburse your savings." She handed a short stack of notes to Blayne. "It was around four thousand, was it not?"

"Well, actually, that included the five hundred the FBI gave me," Blayne said in a low voice as she leafed through the bills. "I had about thirty-six hundred of my own money in there."

"That is two thousand," Alexi said. "I will give you the rest once I have made arrangements here in London."

Blayne hastily split the stack, putting as much as she could comfortably jam into her wallet and the rest into the left rear pocket of her jeans. "You're just going to give it to me like this? Aren't you afraid I'll use it to take off on you?"

"I hope that you will not." Alexi put the rest of her money away. "I believe you know now that you are safer with me than alone."

"Okay, got me there. Certainly can't deny that," Blayne admitted.

"I do not want you having to shoplift things because you cannot afford them, especially in a foreign country, where such behavior is often looked upon more harshly than in the United States," Alexi explained. "And if anything should happen to me, or happen to separate us, I want you to have some resources, since we are so far from all that is familiar to you."

"It's quite a show of trust on your part," Blayne observed.

"You have earned it in recent days."

"Well, I'm not sure what to say. Except thank you."

"I advise you to hang on to your money and let me pay for what we need as we go along."

"I can live with that." Blayne could not help but search Alexi's face for the woman she'd seen emerging from the lavatory during their flight. There was no sign of that brimming desire. Alexi was back to her calm, capable, in-charge self. It was infuriating and frustrating. She wished Alexi would show emotion more often. Excitement. Frustration. Desire. Anything. Blayne now had proof the feelings were there, even if they were constantly suppressed.

She wondered how she could break through that barrier. *Not by running at it headlong.* Maybe she would just relax and enjoy while they were in London. Alexi was great company. The best she'd known since finding Claudia all those years ago.

Damn it all. Where are you, Claud? I miss you so much. I bet you could tell me what to do about this frustrating but gorgeous U.S. marshal.

Blayne felt a hand on her shoulder and found Alexi watching her with a concerned expression.

"Are you all right? You got a very sad look on your face, just then."

Blayne forced a smile. "Thinking about Claudia."

"You are close?"

"Very. College roommates and best friends. Sisters, really. My only close family—she and her father, I mean—since the fire." Blayne blinked back tears that sprang up unexpectedly. "I hate not knowing what's happened to them."

"It must be very difficult. Especially on top of everything else you have to deal with," Alexi said. "It would be a great comfort, I know, to share some of your worries with a friend."

Blayne met her eyes. "*You've* been a great comfort. Much more than that, of course. I don't know how I could've ever come through this alone. I have no problems admitting that now. Sorry I was so stubborn in the beginning."

"You were following your instincts at self-preservation," Alexi answered. "That is a good thing."

"You know, I...I have come to think of you as a friend, Alexi. A trusted friend. I hope that's okay." She studied Alexi's face, hoping to find it was welcome news and that Alexi didn't suspect her of some ulterior motive.

But Alexi, as always, was difficult to read, and she didn't answer right away. When she did, her voice was exceptionally soft, with an element of uncertainty and vulnerability that was rarely evident. "I am pleased to hear that."

"Great."

Alexi blew out a breath and looked out over the park. "Shall we take in some of the sights, then?"

"Love to."

❖

It was eleven forty, and Frisco was even more hyper than usual, having had his nightly constitutional delayed by his master's lengthy phone conversation. By the time they finally set off around the block, the Jack Russell was nearly jumping out of his skin, anxious to see what new scents had been delivered to his domain.

They had gone a good distance before a stranger joined the walk and they abruptly veered off their normal route. Frisco sniffed the air anxiously. He scented fear coming from his master, and that put him on edge as well. He growled protectively.

"Hey, what's the matter with your dog?"

"Nothing. He gets that way sometimes with strangers. Heel, Frisco."

"So? Why is it you have not been in contact?"

"It's too damn risky to be talking to you right now," Paul Fletcher said. "Besides, apparently you know more than I do."

"Explain."

"I just got off the phone with that lodge, and that was the first I heard of what happened up there. Apparently two of your guys got killed, which I'm sure you already know…and my boss got injured, but I haven't heard that officially. Which means I'm pretty sure they suspect I'm the leak."

Despite the chill air, Fletcher had begun to sweat, suddenly even much more alert to their surroundings than he was before, especially to every van and panel truck parked within a reasonable distance.

"That is unfortunate if true," the stranger said.

"Which is why I haven't contacted you, and why you shouldn't be here."

"We will be in touch. Now go back the way you came."

Fletcher turned and headed home. He made it only halfway there before a dark sedan cut him off, pulling into a driveway just ahead of him to block his view. Two men he did not recognize got out and reached for their identification badges.

"FBI. Paul Fletcher?"

❖

Alexi had, at one time or another, seen all of the sights in London that she ever cared to see, having been to the city countless times for business and pleasure. But seeing it all again with Blayne was much more fun than she had imagined it could be. What had started out as a way to exhaust her charge had turned into a day she never wanted to end. Blayne was splendid company, her enthusiasm for every new sight and sound and experience delightfully contagious.

They strolled through the British Museum, admiring Egyptian artifacts and Michelangelo's drawings, the Rosetta Stone, and an Easter Island statue. Next stop, a walk up the Mall to Buckingham Palace to watch the changing of the guard, then a quick jump on the Underground to visit Covent Garden and a variety of shops along Oxford Street, accumulating an increasing number of shopping bags as they went.

Through it all, Blayne remained vibrant and enthusiastic and energized. She seemed different, more relaxed. Alexi was pleased. She had done the right thing by bringing her abroad. The distance had made her feel safer, just as Alexi had intended, and in turn she was less on edge, less determined to prove she could impose her will, in every way. She was so pleasant to be around Alexi nearly forgot why she was trying to wear her out.

When they could carry no more parcels, it was back to the hotel for a quick change before dinner.

"How shall I dress?" Blayne poked eagerly through the multitude of bags and boxes she had scattered all over the plush couch in the living room of their suite.

"Well, if you are up to it, I thought we might catch a play in the West End after dinner. So I would say dress accordingly. Did you buy some nice evening wear?" Although they had spent hours shopping, Alexi had not seen half of what Blayne had purchased. Often they were each busy with their own selections, and on one or two occasions Blayne had been adamant that she wanted to conduct her own transactions in private. To avoid another shoplifting episode, Alexi was more than happy to oblige.

"I think I can find something appropriate," Blayne said with an impish grin.

Her expression unnerved Alexi, for it was that same "I've got plans for you" look that she had on her face during the Tavli game. And she knew how *that* had ended—with her rushing to her room, desperate to put her hand in her pants. *Well, at least tonight, I have someone I can call if she gets me in such a state again.*

They retired to their separate bedrooms to change.

Alexi chose a classic but elegant ensemble, the clothes well tailored for her tautly muscled physique. Black dress trousers over black leather boots. A finely made Italian cotton dress shirt, white, with wide cuffs and a large collar. And to finish the look, her well-loved black leather jacket, which had held up amazingly well through all of their traveling.

The white shirt was a nice contrast to her bronze complexion, and the monochrome color scheme made her Aegean blue eyes even more vividly striking. Satisfied, she stepped out into the living room and stood, transfixed, watching Blayne unobserved as she preened before a full-length mirror, turning this way and that, checking her appearance.

Her hair and makeup were flawless. A bit of rouge, some color to her lips and eyes, her coppery short cut styled and primped in a way that framed her face perfectly and made her appear older and even sexier than usual.

But it was the dress that really did Alexi in.

Blayne had chosen a black cocktail gown, cut low to expose a generous display of cleavage and made of a shimmery material that clung to every curve like her body had been poured into it. The hem ended slightly above mid-thigh, and a slit up the side left little to the imagination.

To complete the look, she wore a delicate gold necklace with matching earrings, thin gold bracelets, and low black pumps that brought her roughly to Alexi's height. She looked exquisite, irresistible, and eminently fuckable, and Alexi was not certain how she would survive the night.

As though Blayne could feel someone watching her, she turned in Alexi's direction, and her smile lit up the room. "You look…just incredible, Alexi. Wow."

Look who is talking. Oh, you are one seriously dangerous woman, Blayne Keller. Seriously, seriously dangerous. Alexi tried to clear her head to think up an appropriate response, but her body was reacting to the provocative crease of cleavage, the perfect round ass, and definite come-hither expression, all for her.

A self-satisfied smile came over Blayne's face as she sauntered seductively across the room to meet her. "Like what you see?"

Alexi struggled for a neutral expression as she cleared her throat. "You look very nice."

"Not so much of a *kid* now, eh?" Blayne teased. "Isn't that what you called me?"

Alexi had to smile. "An erroneous assessment, I admit." *You are every bit a grown woman tonight. And if we do not get out in public right this minute, I cannot be held responsible for my actions.*

She gestured politely toward the door. "Ready to go?"

❖

The pain medication had kept him in a semidrowsy and lethargic state since the explosion, but Theo Lang insisted he be kept informed about the major cases involving his department and the Joint Task Force. So when a nurse roused him at six a.m. to tell him that FBI Special Agent George Dombrowski was on the phone for him, he knew something major had happened and tried his best to focus.

"Lang," he said through his broken teeth. The nurse held the phone awkwardly, trying not to touch his battered face but keeping it close enough for him to hear.

"Dombrowski here, Theo. We've had several major developments. First and foremost, Philippe and Claudia Cluzet have been located and are now in protective custody in Indianapolis."

"Indianapolis?"

"Yes. Philippe got tipped that Cinzano had a contract out on them both, and he and the daughter took off. They've been living in a motel, but his cash finally ran out and he had to use a credit card."

"Who tipped him?" Theo asked.

"Someone close to Cinzano, but he's not saying who yet," Dombrowski reported. "Cluzet is scared. He says he sold part of his building to the mob because they threatened him. But he got to like the money he was scoring from the arrangement, and Martinelli sent business his way. Seems like he made some friends among the wiseguys he made travel arrangements for. We're still talking to him, but it looks like he'll have some valuable information for us."

"Maybe they should be in the program." Theo spoke slowly, overenunciating every word. "I can send an inspector down there any time, so keep me posted."

"Will do."

"You got Fletcher yet?" Theo managed. The nurse gave him a weary look and shifted the phone to her other hand.

"Yes. He's talking his ass off, trying to make a deal. He's been under the mob's thumb for more than a year, since he was in your job, but claims he's been wanting out for a long time. They were paying him big, and we think they may have been blackmailing him with something, but he's not saying what yet. He did admit to the leaks. And by the way, he says they forced him to push Alexi Nikolos out of WITSEC after the Sofia Galletti murder."

That explained a lot. Fletcher probably got demoted because somebody upstairs got wind things weren't right but had no proof. So there was a connection between their changes of fate after all.

"Did he say why they wanted Nikolos gone?" Theo asked.

"Thought she was learning too much about the family," Dombrowski said.

"Anything else?" The pain medication was pulling him back to sleep.

Dombrowski hesitated. "Yeah."

Theo became more alert immediately, sensing the agent had saved the weightiest news till last. "Just say it."

"Cinzano's getting sprung this morning," Dombrowski blurted. "Probably within the next hour or two."

"Damn," Theo cursed.

"Also...Keller and Nikolos took a British Air flight from Toronto to London, traveling under forged passports."

"London! They're in Europe?" Theo was so agitated by the news it came out *Undun! Air in Erip?* But Dombrowski was good at translating.

"Yes. We're starting to call hotels."

Theo searched his memory. Something about London and Alexi was niggling at him, but the pain medication made it impossible to retrieve it from his memory.

"Mr. Lang." The nurse scowled.

"Better go," Lang mumbled, already half asleep. "Ask my secretary to look through Alexi's personnel file for any known family, friends, or business dealings in the UK, and to call me with whatever she finds."

"Will do." Dombrowski disconnected.

A plan was beginning to take shape in the back of Theo's mind. *Yup. That has definite possibilities.*

❖

Alexi spent most of dinner trying to look everywhere but at Blayne's cleavage, counting the minutes until they could leave the all-too-romantic restaurant she'd chosen for the welcome diversion of some theatrical entertainment. But it was impossible to ignore entirely how alluring Blayne was in that delicious second skin of a dress. It accentuated her breasts far too well.

They talked about their day and the sights they had left to see. "Aren't you going to call your sister while you're here?" Blayne asked over dessert. "You did say she lives north of London, didn't you?"

"In York. Two hours and some by train, three or four by car. And yes, I have considered it. But there is perhaps a risk in contacting her." Alexi set down her fork. She hadn't seen her sister in several months, and truthfully would love the opportunity to spend time with her. "Only a slight one, I think, but Cinzano has an unbelievable reach, as evidenced by his ability to put a bomb near your seat. And to find us in Canada. It is possible that he knows that I am with you, and also possible he could track down my family. If by chance he learns we took a plane to London, it is conceivable he might have someone watching my sister or monitoring her calls."

Blayne's eye widened. "You think that's possible?"

"Anything is possible," Alexi responded. "Likely? Probably not. But I have to guard against whatever is possible. It is not worth the risk to your safety. Or hers."

"But I know you'd probably like to see her, wouldn't you?"

Alexi shrugged. "Another time."

"You know…" Blayne bit her lower lip thoughtfully. "I find it hard to believe that you can't come up with a clever way to get word to her somehow…without them knowing it's you. If they *are* listening, I mean. Maybe get her to meet us somewhere?"

Alexi leaned back in her chair and was quiet for a long while. A visit with her sister sounded even more attractive than usual right now, though she wasn't sure why. And it might not be a bad idea to get her away from her house, if indeed it was being watched. And she knew a way to do it. "That is not a bad suggestion, Blayne."

She paid their bill and they caught a taxi to Leicester Square, where they scored two seventh-row center seats to *Les Miserables* at the half-price theater ticket booth. The musical started in a half hour, and it was only a short walk up Shaftesbury Avenue to the Queen's Theatre, so they were settled into their seats in plenty of time.

"So have you seen a lot of musical theater?" Alexi asked. The curved seats, normally quite comfortable, were not designed to accommodate weaponry near one's spine. Her gun was pressing uncomfortably into the small of her back, but she wanted to wait until the lights dimmed to move it.

"Oh, yes, I love it." Blayne skimmed her program. "I see…*saw*…a lot of the nationwide touring shows with Claudia as they came through Chicago." Thinking of Claudia infused sadness into what had been a wonderful day and evening. One of the most memorable in her life, in fact.

Blayne had booked so many trips to London for other people that she knew quite a lot about the attractions of the city. It was like making a dream come true to finally see it all firsthand, and seeing it with Alexi had made the experience all the more special.

They had wonderful chemistry, and Alexi had never looked hotter than she did right now. *She sure has a way of wearing her clothes.* Blayne had noticed heads turn their way when they entered the restaurant, men and women both, and when they crossed the lobby of the theater to get their tickets. *You can't help but look at her.*

And her own black dress had been the perfect choice. Alexi's gaze had not strayed far from her breasts and ass all night.

The lights dimmed and the show began, but Blayne could not keep her mind entirely on the misfortunes of nineteenth-century France with such a beguiling woman so near.

She reached over and took Alexi's hand in hers, and was immensely pleased that Alexi did not withdraw.

❖

Why am I holding her hand? Alexi kept asking herself, only vaguely aware of the singing and dancing now in full swing on the stage. *Because it just feels right* seemed the only answer that fit, and she didn't understand that at all. Holding hands was the sort of sentimental twaddle that she never engaged in, unless it was to suit some purpose.

But then again, many of her reactions and responses to Blayne were atypical of her usual behavior. *I am developing feelings for this woman,* she realized. *And I cannot fuck them away like I usually do.*

She knew it was her pattern, and she was not apologetic about it. She treated the women she bedded very well. They always had a wonderful time and always wanted more, but they knew from the outset that it was just for an evening. Once she had taken a woman, she could distance herself from her. It was a pleasant act, a nice evening, now concluded. No strings.

With Blayne, there was nothing but denied desire. She had not been able to have sex with her immediately and get her out of her system. And that had made it possible for an attachment to be formed and for feelings to develop.

The realization was extremely unsettling, because Alexi knew those feelings would likely continue to grow the more time they spent together. She was in trouble, and the more she felt for Blayne, the less able she would be to resist Blayne's constant efforts to seduce her.

We cannot go on like this. She hoped that her plans for later tonight would alleviate the situation somewhat. At the very least, it had to help defuse the sexual urgency that was making it difficult for her to concentrate on her responsibilities.

Lost in her thoughts, she failed to immediately react when Blayne started moving their enjoined hands. Before she knew it, her fingers were resting on Blayne's upper thigh, her *naked* upper thigh, beneath her dress. And Blayne's hand was atop hers, trapping it there.

Her sex twitched and grew hard. *Gamoto.*

Blayne shifted slightly so that her hips pushed upward, encouraging firmer contact. She knew she shouldn't be doing this, but despite her good intentions about not pressuring Alexi, she yearned for her. Alexi's hand on her thigh was warm, and soft, and unbearably close to where she needed it most. Blayne sucked in a breath and held it. The drumming of her heartbeat was so loud in her ears it played a convincing counterpoint to the rhythm of the music on the stage as she waited to see what Alexi would do.

Lifting her hips once again to press against Alexi's touch, she half turned to watch her. Predictably, Alexi's focus remained fixed on the stage, but the tension in her body was unmistakable. There was no doubt that Blayne was having an effect on the intrepid WITSEC inspector. The rapid rise and fall of Alexi's chest was testament to that.

She shifted her hand to edge Alexi's fingers a few inches closer to the apex of her thighs, and that finally provoked Alexi to turn in her direction.

Despite the dim lighting, Blayne could see the hunger in her eyes. And something else too. Something that looked like pain.

"Please," Alexi whispered. "No."

Blayne leaned toward her until their faces were only a few inches apart. "Please *yes*," she answered in a low voice as she pulled Alexi's hand still closer and opened her legs a few inches. Alexi had only to extend her fingers and she would be able to touch the evidence of her arousal. Her panties were uncomfortably damp.

Time stood still as she waited for Alexi's reaction. In the dark silence of a shift between scenes, as the audience waited for the stage lights to come up and the play to resume, she heard Alexi's rapid, labored breathing, and her heart soared. *Yes. Oh, yes. Tonight is definitely the night. God, I will be so ready by the time we get back to the hotel.*

But even as the certainty of it sent a shudder of delight through her body, Alexi withdrew her hand and sat up stiffly in her seat.

As the evening continued, Blayne tried to return to the undemanding physical closeness they'd had earlier, but Alexi evaded her attempts at hand-holding and sat statuelike, refusing to acknowledge her. Blayne could tell, however, that her mind was not on the play at all, for she failed to laugh at the clever lines and bits on stage that engaged everyone else and was noticeably behind in the applause at the end of every scene. *She has got to be just as horny as I am. There is just no way that she is not. Maybe she's just waiting for some privacy.*

So, in the taxi going back to the hotel, she still had high hopes that they would only need one of the two bedrooms in their suite tonight. But Alexi dashed those expectations the moment they stepped over the threshold.

"It was a pleasant evening, Blayne. But I am very tired and ready to turn in." She kicked off her boots and wearily removed her jacket. "I advise you to do the same. It has been a very long day and it will do you well to get adjusted to the time change."

Blayne frowned in disappointment, but Alexi never saw it. She said her piece and retired to her bedroom without looking back or awaiting any kind of response.

Damn. Damn. Damn. Blayne sucked in several deep breaths in an effort to dispel the anger and frustration coiling low in her belly. *She did it again. I swear to God that woman is going to make me implode if she keeps this up.*

CHAPTER NINETEEN

Vittorio Cinzano smoothed his hand over his hair and gave his reflection in the tiny mirror its first smile of approval in several days. Getting back in his suit made him feel almost like his old self again, but he was still impatient to regain his freedom. *That fucking bitch will pay for putting me through this.*

His first priority would be to assign whatever resources it took to put an end to this bullshit, once and for all. Information could always be had, and anyone could be found, if the price was right. He had no intention of spending another night locked up.

He heard the now-familiar clang of metal that foretold the imminent arrival of his jailers and smiled. *Finally. Time to go home.*

❖

Theo's stature within WITSEC helped cut through a lot of red tape, and he was on a Learjet headed for Chicago less than forty-eight hours after the explosion that had left him unable to eat solid food for nearly two months.

A private air-transport service, *Ambulair Unlimited*, was contracted to supply him with an RN, a secure and comfortable hospital bed, and every sort of medical paraphernalia that might be required en route. A cardiac monitor and oxygen, bandages and IVs. His secretary had also made calls to expedite his processing through customs at both Sault Ste. Marie and in Chicago. As a result, he was settled into his new accommodations within Northwestern Memorial Hospital's step-down ICU before the end of the day.

Theo could hardly wait for a time when he'd finally be done with intensive care and as far away as possible from the naso-gastric tube that had been threaded up his nose and down into his stomach. It was uncomfortable as hell, and it tethered him to a noisy pumping machine he wanted to throw out the window.

He asked the doctor examining him, an attractive Hispanic woman, if the machine was really necessary.

"Yes, I'm afraid so," she responded. "With your jaw wired shut, there's a danger you could vomit, and choke…so we need to keep your stomach empty until you can begin to tolerate clear liquids." She held up a pair of wire cutters that had been placed beside his bed when he had been moved to the ICU. "It's also why we always have these nearby. So we can get your mouth open in a hurry if we need to free your airway."

"And how long before I can actually go home?" he asked.

"A few days, maybe a week. Sooner if you have someone at home who can assist you as needed."

"I do."

"Then I would guess three or four days, perhaps. We'll decide based on your progress."

Theo fell silent, crystallizing his plans. The latest report from Dombrowski had been most encouraging. Philippe Cluzet had given them just what he needed to entice Blayne back to the States. Now all they had to do was come up with a way to get in touch with Blayne and Alexi and the rest would fall into place.

Dombrowski had been apprised of Theo's move and was led into the room as soon as the doctor had completed her preliminary evaluation.

"Welcome back," he greeted Theo as he pulled the nearest visitor chair closer to the bed. "Well, you look like hell. How you feeling?"

"Fucking fabulous. What a comedian."

The response was intended to produce a chuckle, and it did. Theo actually liked Dombrowski quite a lot, and in the course of their association on the Cinzano matter had considered more than once trying to lure him over to WITSEC full time. He added a rare and necessary human touch to the cases he worked, a real deep-seated concern for the innocent civilians he came in contact with.

"So, I'm here," Dombrowski said unnecessarily. "Just tell me what you want me to do."

"You're going to deliver a message for me," Theo said, pacing his words so he could cope with the misery of speech. "I'd put one of my own people on this, but my sources tell me you're the right man for this job because she trusts you."

Dombrowski perked up. "She?"

"Blayne Keller. The other agents tell me she took to you. Trusted you. They right?" Theo studied the agent's face.

"Well, I think we hit it off pretty well, sure," Dombrowski agreed.

"Great. Because I think I've come up with a way to get her back here and into WITSEC so we can proceed against Cinzano. Here's what I want you to do."

❖

Alexi closed her bedroom door and leaned back against it, taking deep breaths. Her body was stretched tight and screaming for attention. She knew she should allow a reasonable amount of time for Blayne to go to sleep, but every minute of delay was a struggle.

Forcing herself to wait fifteen minutes before she telephoned, she was careful to keep her voice low. As she hoped and expected, it took no convincing at all to arrange for a discreet rendezvous in less than an hour. Enough time, she hoped, for Blayne to fall fast and soundly asleep.

She was so pent up and ready to blow she could not stop pacing. Release was imminent, and her body knew it. It was only a matter of time. But as the minutes ticked by, she began to get the first hint of doubt that her plan would achieve all she hoped for.

Although she tried to think about the woman she had called, a leggy blond model named Kristy Holbrook, her mind kept fixating on Blayne in the other room and on the image of her stripping out of that tight black dress that had been driving her mad all evening. *Stop torturing yourself. Think about the woman you can have, and not about what can never be.*

She had met the British fashion model several months earlier when she was in town on business, staying at a hip five-star hotel called the Metropolitan. Kristy was there for a shoot at the hotel's famous guests-and-members-only bar, the Met, where the waiters wore Armani and patrons relaxed in plush red leather booths affording exceptional privacy.

After a couple of drinks and dinner, they had spent the next forty-eight hours in Alexi's room doing nearly everything imaginable to each other. And she had called Kristy on a few occasions since, when she was passing through London. The twenty-three-year-old model was beautiful, passionate, and always eager to please. And best of all, like Alexi, she viewed sex as something that should be fun and uninhibited, and always uncomplicated. For that reason, hers was one of only a handful of phone numbers Alexi had bothered to memorize.

Kristy Holbrook was nothing at all like Blayne, tall and slender, not petite and curvaceous. And where Blayne was fiery red in temperament, Kristy was all polite British reserve. Until, of course, one got to know her intimately.

Yes, she should have had no problem at all getting worked up about bedding Kristy. Their liaisons had always been wonderfully satisfying. Alexi kept telling herself that, even as she spotted Kristy through the security spy-hole in the door emerging from the elevator across the hall. She was wearing a wool navy trench coat and calf-high boots. And probably next to nothing underneath, if past experience was any indication.

Alexi opened the door and stepped out, pulling it nearly closed so that she could greet the model outside the suite.

"It's been too long," Kristy purred before planting a kiss first on one cheek, then the other. She was nearly four inches taller than Alexi, but her wispy frame made the difference seem less. "How nice to get your call."

"How splendid that you were free this evening," Alexi responded warmly. "I always so enjoy our time together."

"As do I."

Alexi would have preferred to have done this anywhere else, but no reasonable alternative was possible. She could not leave Blayne unprotected. "Please do not think me rude if I ask that we be especially quiet." She held out a hand and Kristy took it. "You know how much I enjoy your…enthusiasm. But I have a business associate in the next room and I want to ensure we do not disturb her."

"Difficult, but not impossible." Kristy pursed her lips in a feigned pout.

They slipped into the suite and Alexi led her into her bedroom, pausing en route only long enough to quietly retrieve two glasses and two cognacs from the minibar. But it quickly became apparent that Kristy had no desire for a nightcap.

Alexi turned away toward the dresser only a minute at most to pour their drinks, and by the time she had pivoted back around, a drink in each hand, Kristy had shed her coat and boots and was comfortably supine on the bed, dressed only in a sheer black thong teddy.

Alexi let her gaze slowly travel the length of Kristy's lithe frame, up her endless legs, lingering on the patch of fair hair beneath the sheer mesh before continuing on to the small pert breasts, barely a handful each but perfectly proportioned and visibly eager for her touch.

Kristy put a finger to her lips, promising quiet, before she crooked the same finger provocatively in Alexi's direction, beckoning her forward.

Alexi set the glasses back on the dresser and began unbuttoning her blouse as she crossed to the bed. Kristy watched appreciatively as she opened her crisp white shirt, revealing the lacy bra beneath.

"Lovely." Kristy licked her lips. "Take your time."

Alexi was never one to deny a beautiful woman in such a situation, so she complied without argument, feeling a strange and unexpected sense of relief to get a moment of hesitation before their imminent coupling.

This didn't feel as it should. As she expected it to. As it always was for her with a woman. This was the moment she began to lose herself in the act, surrendering her mind to her body. Caught up entirely in the exquisite feel of a beautiful, soft body beneath her mouth and hands, writhing and responding to her touch, heightening her own excitement to a fevered pitch, until she was delivered from the torture of unbearable *need.*

And her particular need tonight was unlike any state of arousal she had ever known. It was a need borne of days and days of denial and extreme self-restraint, of too much self-control and fruitless efforts to remedy the situation by touching herself. It was a need so great it pulsed within her and pushed at her relentlessly.

But even as she slowly stripped off her top, then reached between her breasts to unfasten the clasp of her bra, she wondered whether, for the first time, it mattered whose body was beneath her.

"God, you are so beautiful, Alexi," Kristy whispered. Her pupils were dark and her face was flushed. She sat up and reached for the clasp of Alexi's trousers. "Come here. I love to do this part myself."

Blayne stared at the ceiling of her bedroom, wondering how the hell she could feel so wide-awake. She'd had a nap on the plane, but it was only three or four hours at most, and in the sixteen hours or so since then they had been on the move, nonstop.

When Alexi had retired for the evening, Blayne had remained where she was for a full ten minutes at least. Stewing. Steaming. Furious at being left aroused and unfulfilled yet again. Then she had given up and gone to her room, not at all enthused about further efforts to alleviate her restless energy with masturbation.

God. Why do I let her do this to me every single fucking time? And why does it bother me that she doesn't give in? It's not like I've never been turned down before.

But it did bother her. A lot. Perhaps, she considered, because she wanted Alexi more than she had wanted anyone in a very long time. And perhaps too because she felt certain that Alexi craved this as much as she did. All it would take was the right set of circumstances and they could move beyond the dynamic that was holding them back. Blayne was not going to be on the run forever. Alexi would not be guarding her for more then a few months. They could look ahead. Blayne wanted to break through to her enough to show her it was possible.

After another half hour of tossing and turning, she went to the window and looked out. The lights of a lively pub beckoned from down the block. *I'll tell her I can't sleep and talk her into a nightcap. She wouldn't want me to go alone.* Her mind made up, she reached once more for her cocktail dress. She'd make sure to sit so Alexi couldn't avoid looking at her cleavage.

I just have to find a way to make sure she can't resist me this time.

After dressing quickly, she crept out into the living room and crossed to Alexi's door. She was fully expecting the room to be dark and Alexi to be sound asleep, so it took her a minute, when she let herself quietly into the room, to realize that she was seeing what she thought she was seeing by the soft subdued light of a single floor lamp.

The bed had been turned down, the sheets and blankets were in tangles, and in the middle of them was Alexi, lying face down and nude, her gorgeous ass—the object of many of Blayne's imaginings—rising and falling in a rhythm as familiar as time.

Blayne let go of the doorknob and the door clicked shut, and the sound was loud. Loud enough that Alexi's head swiveled to investigate. It was only then that Blayne saw the beautiful blond woman lying beneath Alexi, head thrown back in abandon, her body moving in counterpoint to the sway of Alexi's hips.

Alexi froze, disbelief replacing the hazy look of desire and arousal on her face.

Blayne felt as though she'd been slapped. In the long seconds that followed, she memorized every detail of that wretched tableau, and suddenly it all made sense. *No wonder she didn't want me.* The woman Alexi was fucking was tall and thin and beautiful and blond, and nothing at all like her. *If that's what turns her on, I haven't a chance. And never had. I could throw myself at her for the next ten years and it wouldn't matter.*

She felt like a fool. A frustrated, silly fool. Her bruised ego demanded satisfaction—some semblance of justice. Her Irish temper flared red-hot and her hands clenched into fists. "So I see there indeed *is* something…some*one*…who can get your mind on fucking and off of protecting me."

"Blayne…I…I…" Alexi was breathing hard, and so was the blonde.

"*So* sorry to interrupt," Blayne told the stranger beneath Alexi, her voice laden with sarcasm. "But I'm sure you'll still get paid handsomely."

"Well, *that's* quite uncalled for," Kristy responded. "Alexi, will you please tell this woman—"

"Kristy," Alexi cut her off. "I am sorry for this." She shifted her body off the model and covered her with a sheet as she did so. Then she reached for her robe, which had been thrown over a chair, and put it on. "I am afraid I must beg your indulgence and ask you to leave."

"Don't bother on my account," Blayne spat angrily. "I'm sure that if someone broke in and put a gun to my head tonight you'd jump right up off of her and be Johnny-on-the-spot, no problem."

Alexi froze and her face became stone. They glared at each other, Kristy all but forgotten until she spoke.

"Well, there is obviously some drama going on here that I don't wish to be a part of." She slipped out of bed and donned her coat and boots as Blayne and Alexi continued to stare at each other, Blayne seething with anger and Alexi's face a mask. "Work it out, ladies." She crossed to Alexi and kissed her soundly on the mouth. "You have my number. I'll let myself out."

"Sorry to spoil your fun." Blayne folded her arms angrily over her chest after Kristy had departed. "But I guess I see now why you had no interest in any of *my* efforts to get you into bed. Why didn't you just tell me I'm not your type? Why let me keep making a fucking *fool* of myself? Or does that *do* it for you?"

"Whether you are my type or not is irrelevant. What are you doing in my room?" Alexi leaned against the bedpost, hands in the pockets of her robe. It took every ounce of self-control not to show what she was feeling, which was an overwhelming riot of anger, embarrassment, frustration, and arousal. Her hands were trembling, but outwardly she appeared the picture of cool nonchalance.

"I...I..." Blayne sputtered, throwing her hands up in the air. "I can't believe you're going to act all indignant! You're supposed to be protecting me! Not fucking some whore in the next room!"

"Keep your voice down. My guest was a friend, and you were extremely rude to her. And I have not for an instant shirked my responsibilities. It is you who forgot your place and came in uninvited."

"I walked in because I couldn't sleep. And I thought you'd rather I not go out alone." Blayne began to pace as she talked, from door to window and back again, giving Alexi and the bed a wide berth. "But I can see you don't give a shit one way or the other, really. It's all just a fucking job to you, and that's all it's ever been."

"I have told you from the beginning that I am here to protect you, and that has to be the entirety of our association," Alexi said calmly. "That you chose to believe otherwise was your fault, not mine."

Blayne diverted from the path she was wearing in the carpet and crossed to the bed, stopping two feet from Alexi. "Then why act at times as though you wanted more? I know you did."

"I am as human as anyone." Alexi shrugged. "A woman keeps throwing herself at me as you have done, it will make me sexually aroused, yes. So it should come as no surprise that I found it necessary to call a friend."

"Someone obviously more to your liking than what was being offered to you. God, I was such a fool!" Blayne snorted in disgust. "Well don't worry. I get the picture now. You won't have to worry about me thinking *twice* about it, ever again."

"I think it best for you to return to your own room now, Blayne."

"I couldn't agree more." Blayne crossed to the door and threw it open with such force it banged against the wall. "Think you can keep your pants on long enough to keep me alive?" she shot back over her shoulder but was gone without waiting for a reply.

Alexi slumped down onto the bed as soon as she was alone. *Damn it. What a nightmare.* She should be grateful that Blayne had finally gotten the message and would no longer be spending every waking moment trying to get her in bed. It would make her life a lot easier.

She slammed her fist hard against the mattress. But she wasn't grateful. Or relieved. Or any of those things that she should be. For she had realized something quite unsettling in that moment before Blayne had interrupted them.

Kristy had been Kristy, unabashedly eager and willing to submit to whatever Alexi had in mind. Kristy had never failed to satisfy her thoroughly and completely, countless times and in countless ways. But as she'd moved atop the blond model, all Alexi could think about was Blayne. The body she wanted wasn't this one. For the first time in a very long time, her need for sex wasn't about coming. It was about the person. She wanted to be touching Blayne. Only Blayne would do.

Ridiculous. Just fuck her, and you'll feel better. You always feel better. She had closed her eyes as their bodies pressed together and warm flesh met warm flesh. Unusual, for it was the look on a woman's face as she came that usually got her most excited. That and her first touch of the wetness between a woman's legs, the measure of her ability to excite and arouse. That part was never a disappointment, for she made them wait for that moment until they could wait no longer.

But she knew inherently that she had no chance of coming tonight unless she closed her eyes. And she prayed that Kristy would keep silent. For she needed to imagine it was Blayne's body beneath hers, Blayne's legs around her, Blayne's mouth on her and…

She began to rock her hips. *Blayne. This is what you want. This is what you need.* She repeated it to herself with each pistoning of her pelvis as she tried to imagine how Blayne would look in the throes of passion. But her body would accept no substitute, and she was just realizing that when the real Blayne had interrupted them.

She had hated seeing the look of hurt and disappointment on Blayne's face as she discovered them, and realization struck. It pained her terribly to have caused that look. But she was stung by Blayne's remarks.

"I'm sure that if someone broke in and put a gun to my head tonight you'd jump right up off of her and be Johnny-on-the-spot, no problem."

The words had cut deep because they had brought back every detail of that awful night that still haunted her. It was for the best that they would be distant from each other now, over this, she decided. She had hurt Blayne, and Blayne had hurt her back, and the damage could not be undone. Perhaps it would somehow make the unbearable more bearable. *How could it feel any worse?*

She took off her robe and slipped under the covers, knowing full well that sleep would be long elusive. She could smell sex in the air, and it made her body ache for Blayne.

Tomorrow they would be different with each other. She would be polite, and courteous, the only thing she could be. She had done nothing wrong and had nothing to apologize for. And what about Blayne? *She will keep you at arm's length. As it should be. As it has to be. You will have the relationship you should have had all along. And that will help you keep her alive.*

It all sounded well and good, but it made her unbelievably sad.

❖

Blayne was so anxious to get out of the loathsome black dress that she tore it getting it off. Didn't matter, as she never intended to wear it again. It would remind her too much of her foolish, misguided efforts to gain the attention of a guarded, emotionless playgirl. A woman who had not an ounce of compassion. Alexi had brought another woman into their suite after turning her down flat not an hour before.

Blayne was furious, and all the more so because she had allowed Alexi to make her feel less than *enough. Never again*, she vowed. *Never again.*

She allowed herself to cry so that she would be over and done with it. She didn't want to try to understand why Alexi's actions had hurt her so deeply and mattered much more than they probably should.

She tried to accept that it was not to be. *She can have anyone she wants.*

And she tried vainly to tell herself not to take it personally. *You're just not her type, and you can't help that. If she's that damn superficial, fuck her.*

CHAPTER TWENTY

V asiliki Nikolos?" the voice was American, and unfamiliar. Vaso cradled the phone in the crook of her neck while she tried to wipe the grease from her hands with an old torn T-shirt. The carburetor from her aged Triumph motorcycle was in pieces, spread out on the newspaper that dominated the living room floor of her traditional English cottage. "Speaking. Who is this?"

"Miss Nikolos, my name is George Dombrowski, and I am a special agent with the Federal Bureau of Investigation in Chicago. I am calling about your sister Alexi. Have you heard from her recently?"

Vaso didn't answer immediately. "I have nothing to say to you, sir. But if you have something you wish to tell me, I will listen."

"Very well. I understand your reluctance to share information over the phone with a stranger," Dombrowski replied. "So I appreciate your being willing to hear me out."

"Please be brief and to the point."

"Your sister is protecting a witness in a very sensitive case and is currently in London," Dombrowski said. "We have lost touch with her and have been unable to relay three very important messages to her, which we are hoping you can do for us if she contacts you."

Vaso snatched up a pen and paper from her kitchen counter. "I am listening."

"The first is, the leak has been plugged."

"The leak has been plugged," Vaso repeated as she wrote down the phrase.

"Correct. Second, Theo sends his regards and asks that you call this number." Dombrowski then recited his own cell phone number, twice, and had Vaso read it back to him.

"That's my number," Dombrowski told her. "Special Agent George Dombrowski. Please tell her I have an urgent message for the witness about Claudia. Got all that?"

"Yes," Vaso answered. "Anything else?"

"That's all. I appreciate very much your taking all this down."

"Of course, I can make no promises she will ever get it."

"I understand. Thank you for your time. I would ask that you please call me at that number if you think or hear of anything that may help us find her."

"Good-bye, Mr. Dombrowski."

Vaso sank down into a kitchen chair and stared down at her notes. If Alexi was in London, she was no doubt staying at a hotel, and there were three hotels Vaso knew she liked. The problem was, she also knew her sister sometimes traveled anonymously. How would she find her if she had checked in under another name?

Vittorio Cinzano had results within hours of returning home. His boys had already tracked Blayne Keller and her companion to the Toronto airport, through the Subaru license plate and a well-placed bribe within the Ontario Provincial Police. But the trail had turned cold there.

So he'd poured more money and men into the endeavor, and made some threats, and they'd found a British Air gate attendant who was happy to take their money and volunteer what he knew. He told them about the American government's interest in two women who'd taken a flight to London.

"Have we found out who this woman is with her?" Vittorio asked the dour-faced captain who faced him across his desk. "She's what, FBI? Marshal? What?"

"We don't know for sure. Fletcher never gave us her name if he knew it, and looks like the passports they used were bogus. No records on either of the names."

"What's happening in London?" Vittorio rapped his knuckle on the desk. Once. Twice.

"We got calls going, checking hotels. Guys at the airport. Nothing yet, but it doesn't look good. We just don't have the contacts there, and security's real tight."

Vittorio slammed his fist down on the desk. "Then we're going to have to talk to the other guy," he decided. "He's a sure bet. He'll know where she is. Get on it."

His captain visibly blanched at the suggestion but said nothing.

Vittorio poured himself another glass of Glenlivet and considered his options as he sipped. He had lots of friends in Europe. Time to call in a few favors.

❖

The tension between Alexi and Blayne was so thick the next morning that neither sought eye contact or initiated any conversation beyond a polite *good morning.*

For Blayne, all the fun and congenial companionship of their first day in London had been spoiled by the evening that had followed, and her bruised ego had erased the desire for more light-hearted sightseeing. So she lingered over coffee on their balcony, silent and stoic, looking out across the expanse of Hyde Park and wondering how she could have been so damned blind and stupid.

She felt wholly inadequate, and sad to the core. And furious at herself that she had so quickly made more of their relationship in her mind than there ever really was. She had started to fall for Alexi, and fall hard. *Stupid. Stupid. Stupid. You kept telling yourself it was all about getting laid, and all the while you were letting her under your skin in a very big way. What a fool.*

She knew one thing. Continuing on like this until the trial would be agony. *I can't keep living like this. She may not want me, but I still want her. Even after last night. I still want her so damn bad.*

She knew she'd said some hurtful things when she'd walked in on Alexi, and in the bright light of morning she had begun to regret her angry comments. It wasn't like her at all. *I have no ties on her. None. And she really had every right to do what she did.* The fact that Alexi had waited after she should have been asleep…and had brought the woman to the suite, so she could still protect Blayne…well, it had actually been a pretty discreet and considerate way to do what she did. *She's risked her life repeatedly for me. I had no right to accuse her of not taking her responsibilities seriously.*

Inside, in the living room, Alexi stared miserably into a cup of cold coffee, bemoaning the loss of what had become welcome and engaging company. She wasn't close to many people, but she had come to respect and enjoy Blayne as an individual and friend. And she was reluctant to let go of that. Not to mention her attraction to Blayne, which burned like a fire within her. *What the hell do I do with these feelings?*

She knew one thing she could not do—stay another moment in this room with the woman she had hurt, the two of them barely speaking. She needed to clear her head and come up with a sensible plan for how she was going to manage this assignment. Perhaps she actually couldn't manage it. Perhaps she needed to replace herself. She knew a few trustworthy people in private security. Perhaps she could hire some muscle and run the assignment at a distance.

She allowed that thought to settle. It was a good idea. She could have a couple of bodyguards taking Blayne wherever she wanted to go in London or even around Europe. Keeping her moving was a good plan. Alexi could monitor them, staying within reach. If she could find the right people today, she could check out of the hotel and into another one not too far away. She could even take a day or two out of London and visit her sister. York was only two hours away by train and it was time she caught up with Vaso. Relieved to have a plan, she stepped out onto the balcony and cleared her throat to alert Blayne to her presence. "I need to run a quick errand and I would appreciate it if you would accompany me so that I can keep an eye on you. It will not take long, and you can remain in the taxi."

"Fine," Blayne responded. "You want to leave right now?"

"As soon as convenient, yes."

Blayne got to her feet but avoided looking at Alexi. She seemed beaten down, like a dark cloud was hovering just above her head. Alexi regretted the loss of that spark that had seemed an integral part of Blayne's personality.

"You're calling the shots," Blayne said dully. "Lead on."

Alexi gave the taxi driver an address, and Blayne stared out the window as they rode, making none of the excited observations that had peppered their sojourns the day before.

When they parked in front of a florist, Blayne took the first interest in their errand, watching Alexi intently as she exited the cab and went to stand in front of the shop next door, a paper-goods establishment that advertised personalized stationery in the front window.

Alexi observed several people passing by before she stopped one, a young college-age man dressed in a rugby shirt and jeans and laden with a backpack full of books. She said a few words to him and he nodded. She spoke to him some more and then handed him something—money, it looked like. The man smiled and went into the florist shop while Alexi waited where she was until he came back outside and gave her an okay sign.

She returned to the taxi and told the driver to return them to their hotel, and silence fell between the women again until they got back to their room.

"Well, that was in incredibly poor taste, to drag me along on that little errand," Blayne glowered as soon as they were alone. "Send her flowers to say you were sorry you got interrupted?"

"What?" It took Alexi a moment to get a handle on Blayne's anger. "Oh. No. I was sending a message to my sister. I may visit her while we are in England."

"Oh." Blayne's fury dissipated. *Stop being such an ass.* She stood where she was a moment, chewing her lower lip. "Alexi, can we sit, please?"

"Of course."

Blayne chose one end of the couch, Alexi the matching chair four feet away.

"I...I'm sorry about last night," Blayne said. "I shouldn't have entered your room without knocking. I shouldn't have treated your friend so rudely. And I most definitely should not have accused you of ever neglecting your responsibilities in any way. I owe my life to you."

"Apology accepted," Alexi said. "Blayne, I regret that you had to see what you did. And for whatever it is worth, I never intended to hurt you."

Blayne shrugged. "I'm a big girl. You made it very clear you were not interested in me, and I pushed you and pushed you."

"I think that neither and both of us is to blame. Perhaps I made allowances I should not have. Perhaps I was not clear enough." Alexi sat back in the chair and crossed her legs.

"It's clear enough now." Blayne let out a lengthy sigh. "I have to admit I feel rather foolish to have pursued you so."

"Please, there is nothing to feel foolish about. You were acting on your feelings, whatever those may be. It has been a terribly trying period for you. Perhaps it was your way of dealing with it all. A distraction. That would be natural."

Blayne looked directly at Alexi. "The way that I feel about you has nothing to do with my situation. I know you've insinuated that before—that I have some crush on you or something because you're protecting me." She took a deep breath and tried to stop her hands from shaking. "But that's not what it is. I'm sorry you don't return my feelings, Alexi. But they are *real* feelings. And they are more than about just sex." She got up then and began pacing, afraid she had said too much. "Look, it's my problem and I'm dealing with it."

Almost without thinking, Alexi went to her and put her hands on her shoulders to stop her from pacing. She hated seeing Blayne so miserable, but once she was touching her and looking into her eyes, all she could think about was how much she wanted to kiss her. She fought the impulse and made sure that none of her turmoil could be seen on her face. "How can I make this situation easier for you?"

Blayne gave her a rueful smile. "Touching me like that isn't helping."

"I'm sorry." Alexi dropped her hands and stepped back.

"Telling me that you forgive me for the hurtful things I said will make me feel better."

"I do forgive you," Alexi said without hesitation. "I forgave you before you left the room last night. I just want you to understand that your well-being and your happiness are important to me. I miss your smile."

"Thank you. And I appreciate your concern, but I'll be fine. Just need a little time to…" She looked down at her feet. *To come to terms with the fact that I can't have you. How can I smile about that?* "I just need some time."

"Shall I leave you alone?" It would give her the opportunity to make some calls, even meet any prospect who happened to be in London.

No. Never. "I'm not very good company today. I think I would rather just stay in, if you don't mind." Blayne looked out of the large glass doors that led to the balcony. "You can do as you like. See your friend. Whatever. I'll be safe here, I'm sure." She said this with no malice or anger whatsoever. Only calm resignation.

"I am not going anywhere, Blayne."

"Your choice." Blayne opened the doors and stepped out onto the balcony, ending the conversation.

The violets were delivered at four p.m. and came from the florist just down the street from Vaso's cottage on the outskirts of York. It was a close-knit neighborhood, so she had a passing acquaintance with the young deliveryman. She had bested him last month in a drinking contest at the local pub, and he had been begging for a rematch.

"Got a sweetheart, Vaso?" he inquired good-naturedly as he handed her the plant.

"Plenty!"

"Shy one, you," he responded, and that got a laugh. "Going to give me another go soon?"

"Things to do now," she dismissed him and closed the door.

There was no card with the flowers. She didn't need one. Violets had been their signal since Alexi had joined WITSEC. Vaso almost laughed out loud. The timing could not be more perfect, but they had always been oddly connected in that regard. She had been thinking a great deal about Alexi ever since that phone call, and she'd half expected her sister to sense this. *What are you up to now?*

She went into her room and threw some things into an overnight bag. She would take the morning train to London, she decided. Run a few errands and perhaps spend a few hours with one of the women she knew there before she met Alexi at the jazz club.

George Dombrowski arrived at Gatwick Airport at eight a.m. and immediately checked his cell phone for messages. None. He made it through customs and retrieved his bag, and found the train that went to London's Kings Cross Station, where he could catch the GNER northbound train to York.

He had never been to Europe before, but now was no time to act the tourist and he had no inclination to. He had grown fond of Blayne Keller, kind of like a daughter, and he wanted to do what he could to keep her safe. He saw virtually nothing of the British countryside beyond the impression that everything was very green and the houses were old and small. He was too occupied planning for all the likely contingencies of his visit.

❖

During another room-service breakfast that Blayne barely touched, Alexi decided it was time to take drastic action to try to break Blayne's funk. She just couldn't tolerate another day watching the sadness drag her down and crush her spirit. From the circles under Blayne's eyes and her haunted expression it was obvious she hadn't slept well, and she seemed motivated to do nothing but retreat into silence.

It pained Alexi to see the sadness that had descended on one of the most vivacious and vibrant women she had ever had the pleasure to know. And it grieved her deeply to know that she was the cause of it. Throughout the previous day she had wanted to hold Blayne. Comfort her. Kiss away her worries and her fears. Tell her what a desirable woman she was and how hard it was to resist her. Anything to put the smile back on her face.

But Blayne had remained on the balcony, determined on her solitude, until it grew too cold for her to stay outside. Then she had retreated to her room, letting it be known she wanted to be alone.

"We should get some fresh air," Alexi suggested as Blayne rose to shower and dress after picking at a slice of toast. "It will distract you from your troubles."

Blayne forced a half-smile. "Not if you are with me, it won't." She continued on to her bedroom but paused at the door. "But it's fine, Alexi. I'll go. Whatever you like."

Blayne waited until she was alone in the shower, immersed in the pounding spray, to let loose the pain of loss and jealousy that was crippling her with a good cry.

Being with Alexi now was torture.

Chapter Twenty-one

The Serendipity club was packed with people, and there was a murmur of ambient noise beneath the smooth jazz being played by a combo at the front of the room. As they walked past tables, Blayne caught snatches of quiet conversation, laughter, the clink of wineglasses or clatter of cutlery.

Alexi had requested a quiet booth off to one side, where she could get a good view of the front entrance. They were still getting settled when a svelte redhead about Alexi's age approached their table, arms outstretched. She was fashionably overdressed in a clingy designer cocktail dress in aubergine.

"Alexi! You should have called to say you were coming!"

Alexi stood and embraced the woman, kissing her once on each cheek. "An impulse, Esther. Or I would have." She turned to Blayne but kept one arm loosely draped around the stranger's waist. "May I introduce Fiona Murphy, an American business associate. Fiona, this is Esther Wells, our host. She owns Serendipity."

Blayne nodded politely and wished again that she hadn't agreed to leave their suite for dinner. "Miss Wells." She fought back a ripple of jealousy.

"Esther, please." The redhead returned her attention to Alexi. "Will you grace us tonight?" She tilted her head toward the four-piece ensemble currently entertaining her patrons and smiled. "I'm sure they'd love it. And they're nearly worthy of you."

"We will see. Perhaps."

"Wonderful. I will come back and convince you once you've eaten." Esther released Alexi and bid them both *bon appétit*, then departed to mingle with her other guests.

"What did she mean?" Blayne asked as Alexi regained her seat and a waiter arrived with drinks and appetizers, followed by another who took their food order.

"Esther is kind enough to indulge me when I am in the mood to play," Alexi explained. "You asked me once what my hobbies were. I suppose that jazz qualifies."

"You play? What instrument?"

"Alto saxophone."

For the first time in many hours, Blayne's demeanor perked up. "Are you any good?"

Alexi shrugged. "I suppose that is a matter of opinion."

"Well, I must admit you've made me curious now. I wouldn't mind hearing you play."

"If you like." Alexi really had not intended to take the stage, but if it might bring a smile to Blayne's face that was reason enough. Losing herself in jazz was also one of the best ways she knew for expressing feelings that she needed to get a handle on, so perhaps it was a good prescription for her tonight as well.

As the evening progressed, she was happy to see that Blayne seemed to be enjoying herself and was at least sampling some of the dishes she had ordered for them both. So when Esther came back around as they were having their coffee, she acquiesced and agreed to join the combo for a number.

The serious young man on sax readily gave up his instrument, and as she cleaned the mouthpiece and prepared to play she briefed the pianist, bass player, and drummer about the type of arrangement she had in mind.

It was a familiar standard—classic Cole Porter—its refrain so instantly recognizable that Blayne knew it immediately. "Easy to Love." And Alexi played it meaningfully, the rich tone of the sax so full of emotion that it startled Blayne in its honest intensity. It was everything that Alexi did not allow herself to be, all raw feeling. Her fingers danced skillfully over the keys, sultry and soulful one minute, desperately melancholic the next.

Blayne couldn't help but wonder whether there was a reason Alexi had chosen that particular song. She wanted so much to believe that Alexi was playing for her, telling her with her music what she could never say in words. *Dream on. I'm sure it's just a song she likes and knows well.*

The whole place had grown quiet, so quiet that when she finished, the sudden onslaught of applause was deafening. Blayne clapped along with the others and watched in fascination as Alexi seemed almost to come out of a trance, smiling somewhat sheepishly as she handed the sax back to its owner and returned to their table.

She opened her mouth to compliment Alexi as she sat down, but a stranger beat her to it.

"*Iperohi opos panda*," came the rich low voice from behind her. "Wonderful, as always." The roguishly handsome owner of the voice stepped around the column that had been concealing her and revealed herself.

Blayne stared, disbelieving. There were quite a number of differences. The stranger had much shorter hair, and it was a lighter shade of brown, but there was the same dramatic widow's peak. Her skin was a bit darker. Her androgynous physique was even more muscular than Alexi's and she was at least three inches taller. But much of the rest was the same. The angular face, strong jaw, high cheekbones. Long dark eyelashes and full eyebrows framed the same deep blue eyes. The straight nose and rosy red lips were nearly identical. But when she smiled, she looked more…devilish, somehow.

Alexi and the stranger kissed and embraced. Blayne could see from the emotion in their faces and eyes that the two were close and the reunion sweet.

After they had exchanged a few sentences in Greek, Alexi took a step toward the table and said, "Blayne Keller, may I introduce my sister, Vasiliki—Vaso—Nikolos."

Your very attractively butchy sister Vaso. "I would never have guessed." Blayne offered her hand. It did not escape her notice that Alexi had introduced her by her real name, and she wondered whether it had been a slip-up, or intentional. "Very pleased to meet you, Vaso."

Vaso took her hand and held it between both of hers while she appraised Blayne with an appreciative smile and unnerving direct eye contact that felt entirely too intimate. "The pleasure is all mine, Miss Keller."

Alexi said something to Vaso in Greek that seemed to startle her and she studied Blayne, then asked Alexi something in Greek. When Alexi nodded, Vaso let go of Blayne's hand and that fire in her eyes—that glint of attraction—disappeared.

That sounded an awful lot like a warning. Blayne would have given anything at that moment to know exactly what the two of them had said.

"Let us sit, shall we?" Alexi said, and they settled into the circular booth, Alexi in the middle.

"Please excuse my rudeness in speaking to my sister in a language you do not understand," Vaso said. "But I have some urgent family matters that I must discuss with her, so I am afraid I must beg your indulgence for another few minutes."

"Certainly," Blayne answered. "Please."

Vaso spoke for a few minutes, with Alexi interrupting now and then to ask a question. They were speaking low, and Blayne made a point of appearing to be focused on the jazz combo. But she was really listening intently to them. It was amazing how similar their voices were. She could hardly tell them apart. And she really liked the sound of Greek. It had a kind of musical quality to it, she decided…kind of romantic-sounding…

I swore she just said Dombrowski.

The next word she recognized popped out of their conversation as though it had been amplified. Perhaps because her brain was so starved to hear it. *Claudia.*

She turned in the seat to face them. "What do you know about Claudia?"

Vaso looked chagrined. Alexi frowned.

"Tell me, Alexi."

"Someone claiming to be Agent Dombrowski has contacted my sister with some messages for me. Messages from Theo Lang. He is apparently all right."

"Great. What about Claudia?" Blayne persisted.

"He said he has news about Claudia. I do not know what it is."

"Well, let's go! Let's call him!" Blayne started to get up, but Alexi placed a hand on her arm.

"Wait, please." She withdrew her hand as Blayne sank back into the seat. "This may be a trap to try to find out where we are. I have to think about the best way to proceed before we do anything. But I assure you I will find out about Claudia, if there is news of her. And as soon as possible."

Vaso pulled a cell phone from her belt and Alexi accepted it with a nod of thanks and stuck it into her pocket. Blayne watched her all the while, eyeing the phone greedily.

"Soon, Blayne. But not here. We should return to the hotel." She turned to Vaso. "Come with us?"

"I had planned on it," Vaso reached behind Blayne for the small bag she had stashed by the column.

They caught a cab to the hotel, Alexi seated once more between Blayne and her sister.

"So, what do you do, Vaso?" Blayne asked politely.

"Get into mischief at every opportunity." Vaso leaned forward so she could smile at Blayne past her sister. "What about you?" She still seemed intently interested in Blayne, but her expression radiated more curiosity now than heat.

"I see you are just like your sister in your ability to deflect personal questions," Blayne observed. "And I'm between jobs at the moment. I guess you could say I'm between *lives* at the moment."

"I see. I figured that my sister was working. You are"—she glanced at the cab driver—"with the program, then?"

Alexi answered for Blayne. "Yes and no. It is a rather long story and not for retelling."

"Of course," Vaso replied agreeably. "As you wish."

Once they got back to the suite, Alexi pointed Vaso toward her bedroom. "We are in there, if you would care to drop your bag."

Vaso took the hint and left Alexi and Blayne alone. They stood three feet apart, staring at each other.

"When are you going to call about Claudia?" Blayne demanded.

"Probably tonight. But I would like you to try to sleep now," Alexi said. "There are things I need to talk about with my sister, and I must consider every risk before I make any calls. I promise I will come and inform you immediately when I learn anything about your friend."

"I doubt I can sleep until I hear something."

Blayne's lower lip stuck out in a pout. Staring at it, Alexi felt a rush of butterflies in her stomach. *I wish you would not do that with your lips. Damn, but it makes me want to kiss you. So much. We cannot stand here like this or I will.*

"Please try."

Blayne sighed. It was a sigh of forced resignation, but to Alexi, it sounded sensually breathy, like a sigh of sexual satisfaction. "I'll be in my room."

Blayne looked at her oddly before departing, like she knew how nearly she had been kissed. Unsettled, Alexi poured two whiskeys from the minibar. Blayne was beginning to read her a little too well. She carried the drinks to the couch, where Vaso joined her, and they spoke in Greek, but the occasional English or French word crept in as well.

"I see why you asked me not to set my sights on this one. It is rather clear from the way you are with each other." Vaso leaned back and crossed her legs. "And how is that possible, since you are protecting her, by the way?"

"Nothing has happened between us." Alexi sipped at her whiskey. "But it nearly has."

Vaso kept silent. It was a long while before Alexi spoke again. "She is different, Vaso. Different from anyone I have ever met."

"I see that she is. I do not know that I have ever seen you look at a woman the way you have been looking at her. Were you playing that song for her?"

"Yes," Alexi admitted. Several minutes passed before she volunteered any more. "I have developed feelings for her. But I do not honestly know what to do with them. It is impossible to have anything with her."

"I imagine this is bringing up memories of…that night," Vaso said gently.

Alexi narrowed her eyes in pain. "That is precisely why nothing can ever happen between us."

"You will not let history repeat itself, I am certain."

"No. I will not."

There was another long silence. Vaso reached over and put a hand on Alexi's shoulder. "How can I help?"

"You came when I asked you to," Alexi replied, putting her own hand on her sister's. "As you always do."

"Of course."

Alexi got them two more whiskeys. She downed half of hers before she spoke again. "It has been…actually physically *painful* to be around her, I want her so much. And she has been flirting with me and trying to get me into bed for days."

Vaso's eyebrow lifted, but she made no comment.

"So when we got in last night, after she went to bed, I called a woman I know and invited her up. For a quick fuck, you know. Get it taken care of."

"Yes. And?"

"She walked in on us." Alexi sat hunched forward, her legs apart and elbows on her knees. She cradled her glass in both hands.

Vaso frowned. "I am sure that was awkward."

"Yes. I think perhaps it is for the best, actually, because she is no longer throwing herself at me." Alexi took another long drink of whiskey.

"But you miss it."

"And worse," Alexi said. "I…I could not…" She shook her head. "I wanted *her* last night. Only her."

Vaso leaned forward so that Alexi would look her in the eyes. "Serious, then."

Alexi shrugged. "It does not matter. It is what it is. It will pass."

"How long will you be watching over her?"

Alexi leaned back and exhaled a long, deep breath. *However long, it will not be nearly long enough.* "Difficult to say. Before you arrived I was thinking about replacing myself. I will learn more when I make that phone call."

"What of that? What do you make of the messages I brought you?" Vaso asked. "Is it good news?"

"Perhaps. We shall see."

"Can you tell me who is this Claudia?"

"A close friend of Blayne's," Alexi explained. "She has been missing for several days in connection with the same case."

"That is why she was so anxious for you to make the call. Why have you not?"

Alexi got up and walked to the doors to the balcony. She looked out at the passing traffic below. "I will. It sounds legitimate. This has just been a very difficult assignment. Many close calls, and it has made me especially cautious."

"Perhaps now is not the time to bring it up, but I thought that you were through with all of this, Alexi."

She'd wondered when Vaso was going to ask her about going back into WITSEC.

"I have reasons."

"I am certain you do." Vaso did not press. "I have not known you to bring a witness to Europe before."

"No. It is not usually done." A reluctant smile played at the edge of her mouth as the memory of their first pleasant day sightseeing popped into her head. Blayne's enthusiasm had made her see old familiar sights with new eyes. *It is all about the company you keep sometimes.* "But then, nothing about this case is typical."

"Can you come to York and stay with me?"

Alexi returned to the couch and resumed her seat. "Probably not wise. It is possible that those after Blayne might know I am with her, and also possible they could find you and watch you to see whether I show up. Unlikely, I think. But better we do not."

"As you wish. I will be happy to stay here as long as you like. I have no plans, and you know that I have missed you."

"And I you. It will be nice to have you with us for a while. Perhaps it may help ease the tension to have another person around." *Tension is an understatement.* Alexi stared at the door to the second bedroom, wondering what Blayne was up to on the other side. *Probably not sleeping. Thinking about Claudia? Or about last night? Damn it, but I wish you had not walked in on me like that. I know that hurt you, I saw it in your eyes, but what can I do now?*

As if in answer, the door cracked opened and Blayne leaned out, still dressed. "I take it you haven't called yet."

"I told you I would inform you immediately," Alexi gently reminded her. But the pain of anxious waiting was written so clearly on Blayne's face, it seemed callous to deny her any longer.

Alexi reached into her pocket for Vaso's phone. "All right. I hope the news is good." She turned to her sister and asked her in Greek for the number. Once it was repeated back to her in the same language, she headed for her bedroom to make the call.

Blayne's voice caught her at the door. "Is it Agent Dombrowski you're calling?"

She paused. "Yes."

"Give him my regards, please. I liked him."

"I shall."

He answered on the second ring. "Dombrowski."

Alexi closed the door and moved to the window. "Agent Dombrowski, this is Alexi Nikolos."

"Great! And it's George. Thank you for calling, Alexi. May I call you Alexi?"

"Yes. Please make it brief, if you will. I do not want to stay on long."

"I understand. Theo Lang is in the hospital with a broken jaw and assorted other injuries, but is on the mend. I'm acting on his behalf. Paul Fletcher is in FBI custody. He's the leak and is cooperating. The jerk says he pushed you out of WITSEC on orders from the mob. Also… Vittorio Cinzano is out of jail, we couldn't hold him without Keller."

Alexi absorbed this news without comment. "And Claudia Cluzet?"

"She and her father are in protective custody. They were in hiding. Both are well."

"Blayne will be most happy to hear that. By the way, she said to send her regards to you."

"Hey, that's great," Dombrowski replied. "Please give her mine. I got to feeling rather protective of her—I mean, more than usual, you know?"

Yes, I certainly do know. "She is a unique individual."

"That she is. Alexi, I have an offer for her from Theo."

Alexi's senses went on alert. "Yes?"

"Claudia and Philippe Cluzet have been accepted into WITSEC. They'll be sent to orientation within the week. If Blayne wants to see them before they're relocated, she has to get back here *now*."

"Is that the offer?" Alexi knew it wasn't, but she wanted Dombrowski to spell it out.

"Only part. Theo will relocate Blayne with them, and let them have some say in where they're placed, if she comes back and agrees to enter the program."

"I see."

"There will be a preliminary hearing for Cinzano in a couple of weeks. They need her for that or they won't have enough to charge him with anything substantial."

"I will relay the offer to her."

"One more thing. I'm in England. Here to help escort her back, provided she accepts as Theo hopes she will."

"Exactly *where* are you, Agent Dombrowski?"

"At a hotel near your sister's cottage," he answered. "Since she's not been home all day, can I presume she is with you?"

"I will talk to Blayne and call you back." She hung up the phone and lingered in the room for a few minutes, processing what she had just heard. She had a feeling that Blayne might take the offer. Not just to see Claudia, but also because things between the two of them had become so strained. A big part of her did not want to face the prospect of never seeing Blayne again, regardless of what might be the best course of action for both of them.

Blayne was pacing just outside the door. Vaso, still seated on the couch, was watching her.

"Well?" Blayne froze in her tracks as soon as she saw Alexi emerge.

"Claudia and her father are both well, and safe. They were in hiding and are now in protective custody."

Blayne felt a wave of euphoria and relief wash over her. "Thank God. Thank God." *I knew nothing could have happened to you without me knowing it, Claud. I knew it.*

"She and Philippe have been accepted into the Witness Protection Program," Alexi informed her.

"What? What did you say?" Blayne was still rejoicing in the knowledge that Claudia was alive and well. The news she and her father were going into WITSEC was a shock she wasn't prepared for.

"They are in the program and will be relocated very soon."

"But…why? Claudia didn't see anything! And Philippe wasn't even there!" It didn't make sense.

"I do not know the details," Alexi said. "But I would say that they must have information that makes them important witnesses."

Blayne considered this. "Not Claudia. I would know."

"Her father, then, perhaps," Alexi said. "But you know what this means, do you not?"

Blayne looked at her questioningly.

"Once they are relocated, you will not be able to see either of them again."

Blayne felt as though she had been punched in the stomach. The thought of having regained Claudia only to lose her in the same instant was intolerable.

"I am to relay an offer to you that you probably will wish to consider." Alexi kept her voice even, but her heart began to beat faster at the knowledge that Blayne's answer would decide how much longer they would be a part of each other's lives. "If you wish to see them, we need to return to the States immediately."

"And?" Blayne could tell there was more.

"They need your testimony in a hearing that is coming up soon. Theo is willing to relocate you *with* Claudia and Philippe—and give you some say in where that will be—if you go back now and enter the program."

Blayne sank into a nearby chair, her mind racing.

"One other thing, Blayne," Alexi said. "Agent Dombrowski is here in England. He will accompany us if you decide to go back. I believe you will be quite safe."

Safe. And with Claudia. As much as she abhorred the idea of putting her fate in the hands of others again, the idea of starting over somewhere was eminently more attractive if Claudia and Philippe were part of that scenario. *Either way, Alexi will be out of your life soon. Nothing you can do to change that.*

"What do you think I should do?" Blayne prayed for Alexi to voice some objection to the offer, give her some reason for the two of them to remain together. It would be torture to remain as they were, but a sweet torture that was preferable to the pain of separation.

"That is something only you can determine."

A lengthy silence descended as Blayne considered her options. *She doesn't want you, idiot. Face it. Deal with it. Get over it and move on. This way, you will at least have Claudia. You won't be alone.*

Her decision made, she got to her feet and asked, "When will we leave?"

CHAPTER TWENTY-TWO

B layne could remember several times in her life when she was keenly aware of being at a crossroads. When she felt she was rolling the dice and the stakes were unbearably high. This was such a time, and the weight of her choices felt crushing.

You've made your decision and now you will live with it. Time will help you to forget her. It has to.

She had already packed the night before. It was something to do instead of lying in bed with her mind racing over the events of the past few days. The bombing on the plane, and the chase at the lodge, and even the image of Alexi in bed with another woman. She didn't dwell on her most difficult memories, but lingered instead on the more serene and heated moments. Dinner together. The backgammon game. Sightseeing. *Les Miserables.*

Shortly after dawn, when she could no longer pretend that sleep might creep up on her, she threw on a robe and went out in search of coffee.

Vaso was seated on the couch, fully dressed, reading the morning paper.

"I hope there is enough of that for two." Blayne nodded toward the room service coffeepot on the table beside Vaso's elbow.

"Of course," Vaso replied congenially as she reached for a clean cup and poured. "Please, join me?"

"Thank you." Blayne took a seat beside her and accepted the aromatic brew gratefully.

"Could you not sleep?"

Blayne shook her head. "Too much drama in my life at the moment."

"You do not have to tell a Greek about drama. We invented the concept." That got the smile she had hoped for. "And drama is the reason I am about to dash home on the train to pick up my passport and pack a bag."

Blayne's smile grew a little wider. "It's great that you can come."

"I don't get to see enough of my sister, so this is a chance."

"Yes, well, while you two are catching up, you can tell your sister that I don't think I've ever met a more…more…"

"Infuriatingly complex and unemotional individual?" Vaso suggested.

Blayne nearly choked on her coffee. She looked up to find Vaso grinning conspiratorially at her. "Exactly. I knew I liked you."

"Of course. Everyone does."

Blayne sipped her coffee and studied Alexi's cocky near-twin. "Has she always been so…controlled? Perhaps that's not the right word."

"Alexi is a…difficult person to get close to, and always has been that," Vaso replied, her demeanor suddenly serious. "But it does not mean that meaningful emotions are not there, just that they are expertly hidden. You have to look hard to see them."

Blayne absorbed this. "Are you trying to tell me something?"

"My sister has always found it difficult to trust. To allow someone into her heart," Vaso replied. "She has perfected a number of techniques for distancing herself from emotions. Most frequently, she uses sex as a way to convince herself that any attraction is all about a physical need, rather than anything deeper."

"And you're telling me this because?"

"Because I think it important for you to know that she feels a lot more for you than she can express. So much that she thought that bedding another woman would help her deal with it. But it had quite the reverse effect—I think it only made her realize how important you have become to her."

Blayne froze, her coffee cup halfway to her mouth. "She told you that?"

"And undoubtedly she would be displeased that I have repeated it to you," Vaso said. "But I feel compelled to tell you what she cannot. I feel it is in her best interest that you know she returns your feelings. She just believes she is not in any position to do anything about them."

"She…returns my feelings?" Blayne felt her cheeks warm from embarrassment. *Is it that obvious?*

"You care a great deal for her, do you not?" Vaso asked.

So much so that I can't bear the thought of being apart from her. "Yes. I do. I…I think I'm in love with her."

The words had barely left her mouth when the door to Alexi's bedroom opened and the subject of their discussion appeared, her hair tousled from sleep and her eyes only half open. She jumped a little, startled to see them both already up and sharing coffee, with guilty expressions that told her they had been in the midst of talking about her when she had interrupted them.

"Good morning," Blayne said.

"Did you get any rest?" Vaso chimed in.

Alexi asked Vaso, in Greek, what they had been talking about. Vaso grinned a not-so-innocent grin and replied, also in Greek, that they had merely been exchanging pleasantries, nothing more, and that she should stop being so paranoid.

"Speak English, please." Blayne frowned.

"She wanted to know what we were talking about," Vaso volunteered. "I told her it was nothing she needed to concern herself with." She winked surreptitiously at Blayne and then glanced at her watch. "I should get going if I am to make it back here by the time our flight leaves."

As Vaso gathered her keys, coat, and bag, Alexi and Blayne watched in silence.

"Would you like some coffee?" Blayne offered once Vaso had departed for the train station. "I think there's a cup left, and I can order some more from room service."

Alexi shook her head. They had one day left together in London, and she wanted to make it one to remember for both of them. "We should not waste your last day here. I say we get dressed, have a proper breakfast, and then see whatever sights we have missed so far. What do you say?"

"I say that sounds wonderful," Blayne replied in a voice so soft that Alexi barely heard her.

As though through some unspoken covenant, the two of them seemed determined to put on their best faces for their last hours alone. After a leisurely breakfast, they strolled through the British Library, marveling at the Magna Carta and comparing literature and music preferences as they examined Handel's handwritten *Messiah,* an in-progress Beatles' lyric, a Gutenberg Bible, and Lewis Carroll's *Alice's Adventures Under Ground.*

After a boat ride on the river Thames, they stopped for a late lunch of dim sum in Chinatown, then took a ride on the London Eye observation wheel. At every turn, Alexi found herself watching Blayne much more than the scenery, relishing her company and fighting the constant urge to kiss her.

Blayne, for her part, tried not to think about what would happen after today. She wanted to live fully in the moment, implanting every second of the day forever in her mind. She found herself thinking time and time again about Vaso's words and praying there was some truth to the revelation that Alexi cared about her much more than she was willing to acknowledge or show.

Long before she was ready, it was time to pick up their luggage and head to the airport, where Vaso and Special Agent Dombrowski would be waiting for them. The taxi ride to Gatwick seemed much too short. "What will happen when we get to Chicago?" she asked.

"I am not certain." Alexi had wondered the same, but she had not wished to go into such details over a cell phone line. "Agent Dombrowski should have an idea of how Theo wishes to proceed."

Blayne looked over at Alexi and forced herself to ask the question. "Will you still be with me?"

Alexi could see in Blayne's eyes the same torment she herself was feeling. "I do not know. If…if there is a choice in the matter, do you wish me to be?"

"Of course!" Blayne answered without hesitation. *It may be torture, but it is apparently a torture I want to experience as long as possible.*

"Then I hope there is a such a choice. For I wish the same."

Blayne reached over and took Alexi's hand in hers as the sign for the airport turnoff came into view.

Alexi laced her fingers through Blayne's and they held tight to each other until the cab pulled to a stop and the driver got out to retrieve their bags.

Two hours later they were over the Atlantic, headed home.

❖

Selma Lang looked in on her husband and was happy to find him sleeping soundly in the hospital bed they had delivered that afternoon and set up in the den. He had gotten only fitful rest at the hospital, so he was ecstatic to be home.

Something else had also lifted his spirits, but Selma knew better than to ask. When she passed a comment about his mood, he told her he'd had very good news about a witness in his program and that was all he could say.

Selma didn't want to know anyway. She was just happy to have him home in one piece getting a decent sleep. He had hardly stirred in the last two hours, and she was reluctant to leave him, even for a quick trip to the drugstore. With his face wired like that anything could happen. But she needed to go if she was going to—the store closed at ten, and it was already nine thirty. The trip there and back would take her only fifteen minutes, and it *was* Theo who had insisted he needed new batteries for the remote *tonight*. He just knew he'd be up in the night channel-surfing. Selma paused at the door, wondering if she should wait. She would feel a lot better leaving him to run errands once the nurse they'd hired reported for duty in the morning.

Feeling a little silly about her nerves, she crept to the bedside and kissed Theo lightly on the cheek. She would get the batteries because that's what he wanted, but it was the last time she was letting him out of her sight until he was better. She started to go, but stopped long enough to pen a short note that she laid on his chest in case he woke up.

> *Gone to get your batteries. Be right back.*
> *XXX*

As soon as she was out of sight around the corner, Cinzano's men moved in.

❖

"What's going to happen when we get back?" Blayne asked Agent Dombrowski.

She was still disappointed that she'd ended up seated next to him on the plane while Alexi was across the aisle, one row back. But she hadn't complained. Vaso had decided to make the trip with them, so it was natural for the sisters to sit together.

"There's a new safe house. It's a two-story older home. Quiet neighborhood. Theo says you'll stay there until the preliminary hearing, which will be in two or three weeks, probably."

"Who'll be guarding me?"

"Theo was sure you'd want it to be Alexi after what happened at the lodge. Is he right?"

She nodded. "Absolutely."

"Well, I'm prepared to fill in for her when she needs a break," Dombrowski said. "Any time you have to leave the house, there'll always be at least two people with you. Probably she and I, but we can call in another marshal if we need to."

"I'm glad you've been reassigned to my case, Agent Dombrowski," Blayne told him. And that was the truth.

"Call me George. Please. Well, it's routine to take an agent out of rotation when he discharges his weapon," Dombrowski said. "But everything checked out fine, and I was happy to get another chance on your detail."

Blayne gave him a quick smile, then glanced across the aisle at Alexi. She was talking to her sister in a low voice. Greek again. Their eyes met, and Alexi gave her a little nod and a half-smile. A smile that said *yeah, I'd rather be sitting with you too.* Blayne was certain of it.

"You'll be guarding me at least until the hearing," she said.

Alexi smiled. "Good."

The flight attendant came around with their drinks and Dombrowski continued once she'd moved away. "They're going to bring Claudia and Philippe up from Indianapolis probably tomorrow, though it might be the next day. They'll be staying with you, with their own U.S. marshals, until the hearing."

"At the same house?" Blayne worried about what kind of target that would make.

"You'll be on the top floor, marshals below. After the hearing, you all officially get oriented at a WITSEC facility. That's where you get your new IDs and they brief you. Takes about a week. Then on to your new location and new jobs. You'll come back to Chicago for the trials. That will be a few months away, probably."

"And we're supposed to get a say in where we go, right?"

"Theo says you can choose between Pacific Northwest, New England, or Florida Panhandle." Dombrowski's hand was so large it fully enveloped his plastic cup. Every time he took a drink Blayne imagined him as a magician with a disappearing cup.

"Claudia and I will both vote against Florida, I think," she predicted. "We've talked about living there. Too hot. I bet she says New England or the Pacific Northwest. I'd be happy with either."

"Your inspector will be trying to find travel agency jobs for you. Or something as similar as possible," Dombrowski said. "I really don't know much more than that, I'm afraid. Alexi can tell you about the fine details of relocating. I'm just conveying what Theo wanted me to."

"I like him," Blayne decided. "I was sorry to hear he got hurt."

"He's tough. He'll be back at the office in a month or two. And frankly, you'd barely know he's been ordered to take it easy. He's been on the phone with me every few hours, seems like."

There were three men on the job, dressed in identical navy overalls. The van they drove bore bogus license plates and removable magnetic signs on the side that advertised a carpet cleaning service. The design of Theo Lang's upscale residence and curved drive worked to their advantage, for they could park where they could not be seen from the street.

The largest of the three men removed a rolled-up rug from the back of the van and carried it on his shoulder to the house while one of the others gained entry through a rear door. Lang woke up when they pulled him from his bed, but the carpet effectively muffled his cries, and they had him in the van without complications and were on their way within a scant few minutes. They took him to a deserted warehouse where Rosco Rosetti was waiting, and sat him on a battered office chair with wheels.

Theo's heart was drumming against his chest and he wheezed loudly, trying to catch his breath. His forced exertions demanded more oxygen than he could comfortably suck in through his nose and broken teeth, and he wished he had the wire cutters that had thus far never been out of arm's reach.

The man who addressed him was a fortyish brute in a dark suit, with a malevolent smile that gave him the creeps. He walked around and stood behind him, placed his hand on his shoulder, and squeezed hard enough to make him cringe.

"Looks to me like you're in a lot of discomfort, Mr. Lang. So let's make this as fast and as painless as possible." He paced slowly around to stand in front of Theo. "What we're going to do here is negotiate. You give us what we need, we get you back to the comfort of your bed. Simple, right?"

❖

"Have you heard anything at all I have said?" Vaso said, with not the slightest inference of irritation or displeasure.

Alexi, who had not taken her eyes off Blayne once in at least four or five minutes, nodded. "Everything. Family gossip, sexual escapades, speeding tickets and all."

"So you will be guarding her when you get to Chicago?"

"Yes. Apparently so. For at least a couple of weeks." She shifted her gaze to Vaso. "Will you be going back right away?"

There was no hint of plea in her question, but Vaso knew her sister well enough to understand what she was asking. Vaso had decided, as she watched the unfolding events in London, that she might be needed company for her sister, so she'd had Alexi book a fourth seat on the flight to Chicago.

Alexi's inquiry confirmed that she was appreciative and wanted her to remain close by. But she would not request it. Vaso knew it was nearly impossible for Alexi to seek personal favors of anyone.

"I will stay for a while," she said. "Nothing urgent that needs to be done at home, and it has been a long time since I have been to the U.S. Not since the last time I came over to see you, as a matter of fact. Do you still have your apartment?"

"No. I gave it up when I left."

"Then I will book a hotel. I am certain I can find things to amuse me until you have some free time."

"No doubt you can." Alexi had to smile at the understatement. Vaso viewed every place she visited as a playground, with a new landscape of women to seduce and other potential opportunities for hedonistic pursuits. Just as Alexi always had too. At the moment, however, she had no interest in any woman but Blayne.

"But of course I will always be available to you, if you need to talk or whatever."

Alexi placed a hand on Vaso's knee. "I know that. And I am grateful."

Vaso lowered her voice. "You are planning to guard her for a few weeks, then walk away?"

"I have no choice. It's for her own protection." Alexi paused. Hearing Vaso say the words *walk away* stabbed at her heart. "I do not know what I will do without her, Vaso. The mere thought…it is like an emptiness has opened up inside of me."

Vaso offered a comforting embrace and, with a brief hesitant look in Blayne's direction to ascertain she was unobserved, Alexi accepted. She was never one for tears, so it came as a shock to both of them when she found herself sobbing wordlessly into her sister's shoulder.

❖

Theo's jaw ached and he was freezing, dressed only in his flannel pajamas in the drafty, unheated warehouse. But his body was at the moment so pumped full of adrenaline that he could ignore the pain and discomfort. He knew he was in some serious shit, because the mob rarely risked the heat that would come crashing down on them if they messed with someone in his position.

When he didn't immediately agree to his captor's demand to negotiate, the man reached over, grabbed his skull, and nodded his already hurting head for him. "Good," he said, smiling that awful smile again. "So we agree."

Theo did not respond.

"The way I see it," the stranger continued, "you can give me Keller's location and I can guarantee that you get to see your son celebrate his birthday next week…"

Though he had been determined to keep silent, the threat loosened Theo's tongue. "Leave my son out of this," he replied angrily.

"Give me her location and your son will never know how close he came to dying."

"I don't know where she is."

"How fortunate that we know exactly where your son is as we speak." The stranger pulled a cell phone out of his pocket and flipped it open. "Know what's also fortunate? Whether he gets the thumbs up or down is only a button away."

Theo pictured his son, asleep in a modest ranch home on the south side of Chicago, wife curled up by his side and his two boys in their bunk beds down the hall. Beads of perspiration dotted his forehead, despite the chill in the air. He could take whatever punishment they gave to him personally, he was certain of it. But this was another matter altogether.

"Do you think you know now?" The man toyed with the phone in his hand, caressing it like a lover.

Theo's helpless fury boiled over. "Why should I fucking believe you?" he snarled, so vehemently that several of the stitches in his mouth and jaw gave way.

"You ready to find out if it's true?" the stranger replied. "Say the word and I press the button." Laughing, he said to the others, "How poetic! He wants to execute his son."

"Fuck you, you son of a bitch," Theo screamed, spitting blood and saliva through his broken teeth. "Fuck you!" He rose up out of the chair and started toward the man, but two of the goons in overalls grabbed him and shoved him roughly to his knees.

"I'll tell you! I'll fucking tell you! Just leave my son alone!" He broke down then, crying in fear and frustration, more angry than he had ever been. "You hear me, you son of a bitch? Just leave my son alone!"

"I already told you I'd leave him alone. Just tell me where Keller is, and we can all be on our way."

He had already resigned himself to tell them, but it still took an effort to volunteer the information that he knew would trade Blayne's life for that of his son. "She's coming in by plane tomorrow and will be taken to a safe house." He told them the address, cursing himself for his weakness, feeling relief and disgust in equal measure.

"I don't like to be lied to," the man said, studying Theo's face. "Should the address be incorrect, both your son and your grandsons will pay for that lie."

"It's the truth," he spat, hanging his head in shame. Then, more to himself than to them, he mumbled, "Now let me go home, please."

"Yes, of course," the man replied. "I told you I would take you home." He gestured to one of the men in overalls who was standing behind Lang. "Take him home."

The man pulled out a gun, aimed it at the back of Theo's head, and fired.

CHAPTER TWENTY-THREE

A lexi." Blayne bit her lower lip nervously. "I need to know something."

"And what is that?"

"Vaso told me that...that you have feelings for me."

Alexi exhaled a long breath and a look came over her face that said *I am so going to kill her for that.* Blayne didn't wait for one of her noncommittal answers. There was too much she needed to say.

Trying to keep her emotions level, she reached for the remote and switched off the television, then moved the pizza box so there was nothing in between them. She faced Alexi, one leg tucked under her body, her arm resting along the back of the couch.

Alexi, without thinking, mimicked her posture, so that their fingers were nearly touching. Their body language said that it was time for a talk. An intimate talk, acknowledgment that time between them was short and there were things that needed to be said and there could be no more running away. They had the safe house to themselves. Dombrowski had gone back to his hotel to catch a few hours' sleep and wouldn't return until the next morning.

It had been a long day. Alexi was fatigued to the core, but she had managed to get a nap after dropping Vaso at the Fairmont Hotel and picking up a few essentials, like a cell phone and another Beretta 92F and additional ammunition for her revolver. She had expected Blayne to be sleeping already, especially after finding her eating pizza with Dombrowski on the couch in the living room, the television blaring ancient *Rocky and Bullwinkle* cartoons. Instead their star witness was wide-awake and wanted to talk.

Alexi looked longingly at the stairs that led to her bedroom. *Just a few more nights with her, and then she will be out of my life.* She promptly ruined any comfort she might have taken in that thought by imagining what it would be like to lie beside Blayne, spooning her from behind, bodies breathing in unison as slumber claimed them. She glanced sideways at Blayne and knew her distraction level must be obvious. Somehow Blayne could read her as others could not.

"Alexi. The thing is…" Blayne's voice emerged a half-note higher than normal. "I…I had come to the conclusion…after I interrupted you, with your friend…" She couldn't look at Alexi. "That you'd been turning me down because I wasn't your type. I mean, she was beautiful. Blond…thin—"

"Blayne, you are a beautiful woman," Alexi interrupted, but Blayne held up a hand to stop her.

"Please, let me get this out?"

"All right."

"I admit I had a hard time with it. I was pretty up front about what *I* wanted. And I also just couldn't really understand it, because I mean, there were…*are*…definitely an abundance of sparks between us. Something special." Blayne stole a glance at Alexi for confirmation of this, and her heart soared to see Alexi's eyes moist with emotion. It gave her courage to continue.

"Vaso said that…sleeping with that woman was kind of your way to try to get me out of your system. But it didn't succeed in doing that at all. Was she right?"

Alexi couldn't look at Blayne, because she was certain Blayne would see the depth of her true feelings in her eyes. Instead, she stared at their hands, so close together on the back of the couch that if she leaned forward only slightly she could bring their fingers together. She longed for some physical contact, *any* physical contact, but would not allow herself to initiate even that. She felt that if she touched Blayne right now, she would be taking a step toward something inexorable— life-altering, a step she could not retreat from.

Blayne's candor made her realize with startling clarity how very deeply the woman sitting beside her had penetrated all of her well-built and maintained defenses. She had come to mean more to her than anyone before, and Alexi's ability to push her away was crumbling fast. *It is true, Blayne,* she wanted to say. *No woman can replace you. No woman can make me forget you.*

She knew she had a choice to make. Here and now. And she had to make it fast. She could go on living as she always had. Safe in her emotional distance from the rest of the world. Or she could take that one big risk she had always avoided. *What the hell am I going to do?* She had no immediate answers. Her head was spinning. But she realized that at the very least, she had to let Blayne know that yes, Vaso had been right. *I only want you.*

When she finally answered Blayne's question, it was only with a slight nod of her head.

"I know that you think that any relationship with me will compromise you doing your job..." Blayne edged closer and placed her hand on top of Alexi's. "But it doesn't have to, you know. It doesn't. No one will ever know, if that's what you're worried about. And I know that no matter *what*, you'd never let anything happen to me if you could prevent it."

A very long silence fell between them. Alexi tried to calm the pounding of her heart with deep, even breaths, but she felt not at all in control of her runaway emotions. Blayne's hand atop hers was driving her crazy. It begged to be caressed. It invited her to give in to the overwhelming urge to pull Blayne close and kiss her.

She felt as though kissing Blayne would tilt her world right again and bring everything back into focus. But she feared the repercussions of giving in to that impulse. *You are absolutely right. No matter what, I will not let anything happen to you. Even if that means I cannot have you.*

"It is impossible, Blayne. I am sorry."

"*Why*, Alexi? There's more to it, isn't there? Something you're not telling me?"

She hated to talk about it. Hated even thinking about it. But when she looked into Blayne's eyes she knew she had to erase the doubt she saw there. She had to let Blayne know just how much she wanted them to be together, even if it could never be so. Blayne deserved that much.

"This is my first WITSEC assignment in many months," Alexi began tentatively. "I left my job because...because of what happened to the last witness I was assigned to protect."

She slipped her hand from underneath Blayne's and got to her feet. A sudden restlessness came over her as the memory of that night became vivid again in her mind. She began to pace.

"Her name was Sofia Galletti, and she was married to a man who was very high up in the Salvatore crime family."

She heard Blayne's startled gasp. "That's the same—"

"Yes. Vittorio Cinzano is a Salvatore underboss. Sofia was married, very young, to the previous underboss…the man Cinzano replaced." Alexi let this information sink in before she continued. "Her husband was a bastard. He beat her. Cheated on her. Made her life a living hell. But there is no such thing as divorce when you are married to one of them. Her only way out was to disappear. And she needed WITSEC for that. So she called us and offered to turn on her husband."

She paced some more. "I protected her for two months, through her husband's trial. He was sentenced to life without parole." She paused and met Blayne's eyes, needing their calm harbor. "We were attracted to each other, and she tried again and again to…to get me to have sex with her."

Blayne nodded, understanding beginning to dawn.

"I put her off, though it was not easy, during the entirety of my time assigned to protect her," Alexi continued, turning away to stare out the window into the darkness beyond. "After the trial, she was assigned to another marshal, one from the district where she was to be relocated. But she would not go. She said that she had fallen in love with me and wanted to be with me."

"Were you in love with her?" Blayne asked.

"No." Alexi folded her arms and shook her head. "Not in love. But she was a lovely woman. Sweet. Vibrant. Caring. Certainly not at all deserving of the life she had been forced to endure."

"You cared about her," Blayne said.

"Yes. It got personal and I did have feelings for her," Alexi admitted. "Anyway. She called me a couple of nights after the trial ended. We had said good-bye to each other and she was due to leave for orientation the next morning. But instead, she slipped out of the motel where her new marshal was guarding her and telephoned me. She asked me to meet her at the safe house where we had stayed. Said she needed to talk."

Alexi wasn't sure she could tell the rest. She had only relayed the full story once before, to Vaso. Oh sure, she had repeated all the relevant details to a variety of local and federal officials during the investigation that had followed the shooting. But only Vaso had known about her feelings, her uncertainties, and her guilt.

"She begged me to take her away somewhere," she said finally, an ache tearing at her chest as the past came to life again in her mind. "Told me that she loved me and could not be happy without me. Pleaded with me to love her. To make love to her."

She wanted to remember those loving moments that had followed, but her mind seized upon the image of Sofia's naked body slumped in the corner, surrounded by red, and she could not shake the memory.

"I told her that it could not be as she wished. That no future was possible with me, because I did not return her feelings in kind. I told her that I cared about her, but I did not love her." She took a deep breath and let it out. "She cried. We talked some more. She asked me again to make love to her, to give her one evening to remember. I was not assigned to her anymore, so I let myself believe it would be all right."

Pacing the room, she recited the rest of the story as she had for the official record, with a voice as cold as Sofia's lifeless body. They had fallen asleep and Sofia had later awakened her after hearing a noise downstairs. Alexi had investigated. Heard shots. Run upstairs, only to be knocked out. When she had regained consciousness, she found Sofia Galletti dead and the men responsible gone.

She wondered now whether it was Fletcher who had tipped the mob on where they might find Sofia. Most likely, yes. But that knowledge did nothing to assuage her own guilt.

"Why didn't you tell me this before?" Blayne's voice from behind startled her, she had been so lost in reliving the past.

"It is not something I care to revisit," Alexi responded simply. "But I felt you should know now."

"It explains a lot. I'm sorry that it…that it haunts you so."

You are a very perceptive woman. Alexi turned to face Blayne squarely. "I wanted you to know because you *have* become very important to me. Just as Vaso told you. I wish that there could be more, but you now know why I can never let that happen."

"Not even after you stop protecting me?" Blayne asked.

Alexi returned to her seat on the couch and gave her a rueful smile. "Blayne, I am not the one you want. I am afraid I have no experience at all at relationships. I have avoided them all of my life."

Blayne cocked her head and looked at her curiously.

"Why? Do you know?"

She shrugged and stared at the floor. "I have not thought too much about it."

Blayne studied her face. "If you'll pardon my saying so, perhaps it's time you did. Because I think you're throwing away something very precious here. I think we could be great together."

Alexi ran her hand absently through her hair. She couldn't meet Blayne's eyes. She wanted to say the old familiar refrain she had repeated to every woman who had ever said anything like that to her: *I am not what you want. I cannot make you happy for long. I don't know how to do relationships.* But she could not say those words with any conviction right now. Not to Blayne. They were only tired excuses, worn thin from being repeated so many times.

Admit it. You are not pushing her away anymore because of some noble devotion to duty, or because of Sofia, or even because it is just what you always do. You are afraid. That is all. Heaven forbid you allow hope in your life. That would mean you would have to stop running from any kind of real and meaningful intimacy in your life. Alexi lifted her head and met Blayne's eyes. *Ironic, is it not, that I would gladly take a bullet for you but I struggle so to gather the courage to risk my heart to you.*

She knew it was probably fruitless to be considering what she was considering. *Is it possible? Can we be together? No,* she decided. *We will all probably be leaving here in a few hours. The course has been set and the clock is ticking. It is far too late to be thinking that there is a way to make this possible.*

"It cannot happen between us, Blayne. We just need to accept that."

Blayne was looking at her with such hurt and such *longing,* such *need,* that her body, totally of its own accord, leaned ever so slightly in Blayne's direction. She could drown in the depths of those eyes, pulled in by the gravity of emotion and want she saw there. The desire to kiss her, to convey to her what she could not say in words, had never been greater or more difficult to resist.

But the image of Sofia's dead body rose again in her mind, and she stood abruptly, breaking eye contact. Struggled to breathe. "You need to go upstairs, Blayne." Her voice was a harsh whisper. A ragged plea. *"Please."*

"Are you absolutely certain that is what you want?"

"It is what has to be," Alexi answered. She didn't watch Blayne stand; she didn't want to see her walk away.

The briefest touch of Blayne's hand on her shoulder as she passed by was almost more than she could cope with. As soon as she was alone, she poured herself a whiskey, doused the lights, and allowed herself to grieve. For Sofia. For what could never be. She was emotionally and physically exhausted. And totally at a loss wondering how she could fill the void in her life that would be left when Blayne was gone.

❖

Vittorio answered his cell phone instantly, though it was well after midnight. He had been waiting for hours for this call.

"There is only one person with her and the lights are all out."

"Excellent," Vittorio replied. "We are leaving now." He ended the call and reached for his coat. His bodyguard rose from the chair opposite his desk and they headed for the car they had acquired for the night.

His bodyguard was one of the few people close enough to Vittorio to risk offering any thought that might be taken as criticism. "Are you certain you want to be there yourself?"

Vittorio was not offended by the question because he knew it was asked out of genuine concern for his welfare, something rare in his world.

"There will be no more fuck-ups if I am there to see to it personally." He made sure his voice conveyed only a hint of the rage and frustration he felt at so many missed attempts on Blayne Keller's life. "And I must admit, I will not mind seeing her face when justice is served."

❖

An hour or so after retreating upstairs, Blayne was headed back down. She'd had a good cry, and then spent a restless half hour tossing and turning, and finally gave it up. She now had the sudden urge for some warm milk, like her mother had made for her as a child. She wondered whether her craving was more psychological than physical in origin. All she knew, all she could think about, was that she would soon never again see the woman who had finally captured her heart. And there wasn't a damn thing she could do about it.

She felt wretched. Lost. Empty inside. And sad to the very core of her being.

It was an old house, and a couple of steps in the middle of the staircase creaked as she descended. She winced as she hit each one, praying the noise wouldn't wake Alexi. The house was dark, but there was enough ambient light coming in through the living room picture windows that when she reached the bottom step and turned toward the kitchen she could see a silhouette in the big chair beside the couch.

Her heart jump-started in alarm, but then she heard the clink of ice in a glass from that direction and realized it was Alexi. She could not see her face, but she could feel her intense scrutiny.

Alexi could not look away. Blayne was wearing a snug tank top and French-cut panties that left almost nothing to the imagination. She had paused right where a shaft of light from the street lamp outside could cast her breasts and hips and thighs with seductive shadows that invited closer inspection.

Alexi stifled a moan of pleasure at the sight and downed a long gulp of whiskey. She had been doing nothing but imagining Blayne in something similar, or less, for the last hour. She had fantasized about kissing her. Sweetly. Hungrily. Torturing herself. And her imaginings had been so vivid that it was too much...just *too much*...to see her only a few yards away, looking like *that*.

Alexi could not help herself. She was drawn inexorably to Blayne because it was no longer about *wanting* to kiss her. She *had* to go to her. It was an act of desperation. The only thing she knew to do to stop the hurting. She deposited her glass on the table beside her elbow and got to her feet, approaching her slowly, without a word.

As Alexi came closer, Blayne could see that she was still wearing her jeans and black T-shirt, but it was not until she stood facing her, with only a foot or so between their bodies, that her expression took shape in the darkness. An expression that she suspected mirrored her own. Hungry. Driven. Her eyes heavy lidded with unmasked desire. The muscles in her chiseled jaw clenching and unclenching as though she was wrestling to contain a wellspring of feeling. She was staring at Blayne's mouth, and her rapid breathing seemed unnaturally loud.

Blayne glanced down at Alexi's hands. They were clenched into fists at her sides.

This is all that she can do. As far as she can go. But she needs more, and so do I.

As their eyes met again, Blayne brought her right hand up slowly, afraid that any sudden movement would spook Alexi away, like a sudden noise would make a deer bolt for the woods.

She touched her fingertips to Alexi's lips. Tentatively at first. Lightly traced the outline of the mouth she had stared at for hours and dreamed of for days. Then she pressed softly against the fullness of that ripe lower lip, and when she felt the softness give, and part, ever so slightly, she insinuated her thumb fractionally and heard Alexi's sharp intake of breath.

Alexi's fists gentled as they rose to cup Blayne's face. Her heart clenched at the first touch of that soft skin beneath her hands, and the face before her blurred in a shimmer of unexpected tears.

She blinked them away and pulled Blayne's face to hers, and kissed her.

CHAPTER TWENTY-FOUR

Blayne knew when Alexi's hands found her face that she was about to be kissed, and her whole body reacted to the realization. Her skin felt flushed, her knees went weak, and an electrifying jolt of arousal shot through her, culminating in her groin. Time seemed to stand still for a moment as they stared into each other's eyes. Expectant. Anxious. Nervous as hell. She could see everything in Alexi's eyes that she herself was feeling.

So when Alexi finally leaned forward and brought their mouths together, it felt as though a long-simmering thirst was finally being quenched. All she could think and feel and know was *finally*. And *soft*. *So soft*. Alexi's lips were far softer even than she had imagined when she had lost herself in daydreams of this moment.

Alexi skimmed her lips lightly over Blayne's, barely touching at all, an exquisitely gentle introduction of their mouths to each other. Seductive. Elusive. A minute of that, then her fingertips urged their faces closer as she brought their mouths more firmly into contact.

She kissed Blayne slowly, languidly, taking her time. She nipped lightly at her lower lip and teased her with the tip of her tongue, urging her lips apart, then retreating whenever Blayne complied.

Blayne felt a pressure building within her, a maddening pressure to be closer, to let go of the passion that consumed her, but she allowed Alexi to set the pace and depth and type of contact. Her blood was roaring in her ears and she was a breath away from begging by the time Alexi slipped one hand possessively around the back of her neck and wrapped the other around her waist.

As Alexi brought their bodies forcefully together, her tongue thrust into Blayne's mouth to wetly claim her, and the sudden overload of sensations sent a shudder through Blayne's body that rocked them both.

Blayne moaned into their enjoined mouths as Alexi's hand descended to cup her ass. She wrapped her arms around Alexi and felt more than heard her answer—a deep groan from the back of her throat. The primal sound fueled her arousal even higher and she would have sagged at the knees if Alexi hadn't walked her suddenly back against the wall.

Pinned there, she cried out softly as Alexi continued to kiss her—hard, and wet, their tongues battling for domination. The hand that had been on her ass stroked slowly up her side and beneath her tank top to lightly caress the swell of her breast. She surrendered to the thrill of the touch, opening her legs to invite Alexi's thigh between them, an offer immediately accepted with a thrust of her hips and another low groan.

She clutched Alexi tighter, fingernails raking over her back just shy of drawing blood. Her body was on fire. She moved her pelvis against Alexi's thigh and nipped at her lower lip hard enough to leave a bruise. That elicited another unintelligible answering sound of pleasure and a teasing play of fingertips along her painfully erect nipple.

The only thought that made it through her haze of physical rapture was the realization that she could possibly come like this, probably *would* come like this. But just as the knowledge struck her, the loud slam of a car door snapped her back to awareness, and an instant later, she found herself standing alone.

Alexi was already peering carefully out the front window.

Blayne remained where she was, heart pounding, trying to clear her head. *Christ.* She was so damn turned on she couldn't see straight. But when Alexi returned to her side, it was immediately obvious that she had regained more control of her body and emotions than Blayne had. Her half-lidded look had been replaced by the much more familiar visage of the alert U.S. marshal in charge of keeping her alive.

With a sudden sickening clarity, she knew why Alexi had been resisting her with such determination. *There is no way I could be making rational decisions right now, much less take responsibility for someone else's life.*

"It was nothing. A neighbor girl, coming home from a date," Alexi told her. Before she could say anything, Alexi put a hand gently, lovingly to her lips, ending their moment the way it had begun. "But I must not forget again, even for a moment, what I am here for. Please go upstairs."

Blayne knew she could not object. She sighed and with a reluctant nod of acquiescence, went up to her room.

❖

Vittorio arrived at the safe house a little before two a.m. All the homes in the neighborhood were dark, the only illumination provided by the rare streetlights, one of which was almost directly in front of their destination. They parked behind a dark sedan halfway down the block, and the driver of the sedan got out and joined them.

"I think the one you want is upstairs," he said. "She came to the window on this side of the house before the light went out. Not sure about the other, a tasty-lookin' broad with dark hair. The house has been dark ninety minutes or so."

Vittorio dismissed him with a nod of satisfaction. "Your work is done. Go home."

He pulled out his gun and screwed on a silencer. His bodyguard did the same.

"You take downstairs. I'll go up," Vittorio said.

They headed toward the safe house, keeping in the shadows. Vittorio could always depend on his man's expertise at quick and quiet forced entry. Tonight was no exception. They got in through the back door, and there was enough light to make out they were in the kitchen. After a moment's pause to listen, they advanced, bodyguard in the lead, to the door to the living room. They paused there again to briefly listen, then Vittorio gestured his man toward the front bedroom, while he crossed silently to the stairs and began to climb.

Still several steps from the top, he froze at a sudden and unexpected noise from the tread beneath his feet. He listened for a moment, then continued upward, cringing when another did the same.

Blayne's heart picked up when she recognized the creak of the stair. *Alexi's awake too. And coming up to see me.* But even as the thought hit her, she realized that something was amiss. *That second creak was much too slow.* Her heart became a loud jackhammer.

She had taken note of the two noisy stairs soon after they had arrived. They reminded her of the steps that had led from the family pub back home, up to their apartment. Four in a row, so noisy she could never sneak in after curfew. *It's not her. It's someone else, and they're sneaking up.* A cold stab of fear went through her when a dark silhouette, too big and bulky to be Alexi, materialized in her doorway.

Vittorio paused. He could just barely make out the dark shape in the bed. He raised his gun to fire, and just as he did, the figure sat up. It startled him so much that he hesitated for an instant before he pulled the trigger. As the gun went off, the figure rolled to the side and landed with a loud thud on the floor.

❖

Alexi was suspended in the netherworld between sleep and wakefulness, tucked into the crook of the couch, when a sound penetrated her consciousness. Something heavy had hit the floor upstairs. Her heart went into her throat. *Blayne.* She scrambled up, automatically reaching for her guns. The .357 Magnum she tucked into the back of her jeans. The Beretta she gripped tightly in her right hand. She listened intently for a split second as she got her bearings, then she bolted up the stairs.

As she neared the top, she spotted the dark silhouette of a man in Blayne's room, roughly framed by the doorway. Just as she caught sight of him, he raised his arm.

Vittorio took a step to his right to get a better shot. As he moved, he heard the loud report of a shot fired close behind him and felt the searing sting of a bullet as it pierced his right shoulder. *Fuck.* The gun in his hand clattered to the floor.

He bent to retrieve it, ignoring the pain, both hands groping in the darkness beside the end of the bed. Alexi saw the silhouette double over but not go down, so she tightened her trigger finger to fire again.

Blayne saw the flash of Alexi's gun as it went off, then, behind the slim silhouette that had fired it, she saw a hulking shadow coming up the stairs. "Alexi! Behind you!"

At Blayne's screamed warning, Alexi wheeled and fired. She caught Cinzano's man on the stairway just as he depressed the trigger of his weapon. His bullet missed her head by inches.

The bodyguard cartwheeled backward, tumbling back down the stairs, spewing brain matter and blood in a wide arc along the opposite wall until he landed in a heap at the bottom.

Cinzano found his gun just as Blayne shouted her warning, and in the time it took Alexi to kill his bodyguard, he had closed the distance to Blayne. Crouching, Alexi kept her gun trained on the large dark silhouette as she moved into the room. The man was slightly hunched over, and Blayne, she was certain, was sitting up at his feet.

"I have my gun to her head," he said. "Turn on the light."

When Alexi hit the light switch, she found Vittorio Cinzano standing over Blayne, one of his hands tightly gripping her hair. With the other, he held his gun to her temple.

Blayne was breathing so hard she was nearly hyperventilating, and her eyes were wide in shock and fear.

Alexi and the man she hated stared at each other. Neither showed any outward sign of recognition or surprise but for a quickly masked widening of Cinzano's eyes.

"So. Nikolos. We meet again." Vittorio's level voice belied his shock. "But you have your clothes on this time. What's the matter, won't fuck them unless they're married to the mob?" He yanked on Blayne's hair to pull her face his way, and glanced down at her. "But if you ask me, I think this one is worth fucking."

Alexi kept her Beretta trained on Cinzano's head. The muscles in her jaw and cheeks were tight with fury. "Let her go, Cinzano, or I'll—"

"Or what?" he barked. "I can have her brain on the wall before you finish that threat."

"Don't make it worse for yourself." Alexi lined up his temple through her sights and pictured his brain instead defiling the room. "If you shoot her, I will either kill you or testify against you and make sure you rot in jail. You are a dead man one way or the other."

The sounds of sirens could be heard in the distance.

"I'm not going to shoot her just yet," Cinzano said. "She's my ticket out of here."

He jerked Blayne's hair again and she cried out in pain. "You've caused me a lot of trouble, bitch. But no more."

"Listen. Take me instead," Alexi said. "I'm much more valuable to you than she is."

Cinzano smiled. "Is she worth that much to you? Then apparently there is more to this after all. Maybe you *have* fucked her! In that case, I'll take you both. Now, put the gun down or I'll blow her head off!" He shoved the end of his weapon hard against Blayne's temple. "We're getting out of here."

Blayne's cold fear turned to abject terror when she saw Alexi slowly place her gun on the floor. "Alexi! No!" she screamed, and jerked hard against Cinzano's hand, trying to free herself.

His attention was broken at that moment because his captive was suddenly making a ruckus and he could barely keep hold of her short hair. His wounded shoulder hurt like a son of a bitch, but he was not about to let it show. He didn't notice Nikolos reach behind her with her other hand to retrieve her revolver. Not in time.

Her bullet pierced his right hand and then continued on into his stomach. He dropped his gun and crashed backward against the wall.

Alexi kicked the gun away and scrambled forward, grabbing Blayne's arm to pull her out of Cinzano's reach, all the while keeping her gun on him.

The sirens were getting louder.

"Are you all right?" she asked over her shoulder.

"Yes. Yes, I'm okay," Blayne's voice was tight and breathy. She was shaking and her heart was pounding, but it was beginning to sink in that they were safe.

Cinzano groaned. His eyes were open and he was still moving, his good hand clutching weakly at the hole in his stomach.

Alexi made sure his gun was well out of reach, then pulled her cell phone out of her pocket and hit the speed dial she had programmed with Dombrowski's number. As she waited for him to answer, she said, "Why don't you get dressed, Blayne. There will be people all over this place within five minutes."

It didn't take even that long. The police arrived in two, and the FBI and paramedics were not far behind. Cinzano, still alive, was taken to the nearest hospital. Alexi and Blayne were immediately separated and taken by Chicago PD squad cars downtown for their statements.

As she rode to the station, Alexi reflected on what was to come. She had finally gotten the opportunity to bring Sofia's killer to justice, which was the main reason she had agreed to take on a case involving the Salvatore family. But she felt little satisfaction at the moment. Somewhere along the way, her priorities had changed, and the case had become all about Blayne.

Alexi knew it right away, but it would be several more hours before Blayne learned that they might never see each other again.

Chapter Twenty-five

The police station they took Blayne to this time was nicer than the one she spent most of a day in after Aldo Martinelli's murder. Newer, with padded chairs in the interview rooms and radically better coffee. And now that she knew something of what to expect, the experience wasn't quite so harrowing.

She was questioned for two hours by Chicago PD detectives, and two hours more by FBI special agents she had never met before. Then Agent Dombrowski came to see her, with a large bag of cheeseburgers and fries and all sorts of news. He told her that Theodore Lang was missing, taken in his sleep from his bed. It was all over the TV and radio. The mob was suspected in his disappearance. Vittorio Cinzano would survive and face several new charges, many involving the attempts on her life, so she would now be testifying in several trials.

In other words, he said, it was more vital than ever that she enter WITSEC. She would remain under guard by U.S. marshals in Chicago until the preliminary hearings. Then, like he'd said before, she would go through her orientation and be relocated with the Cluzets, coming back for the trials as needed.

"Where are Claudia and Philippe now?" she asked.

"In light of what's happened, the guy who's filling in for Theo decided they're safer where they are, in Indianapolis, until the hearings. They'll only be brought back here for their court appearance."

"Will Alexi guard me until the hearings?" Blayne asked.

Dombrowski frowned. "No. Though she wanted to. Created quite a stink in there about it earlier, actually." He rolled his eyes toward one of the other interview rooms. "But WITSEC is like the FBI. If a marshal discharges their weapon, they're put on temporary leave while there is an investigation. That can take some time in a case like this one. You'll probably be relocated before she is returned to duty."

The news sank in, and a cold dark cloud settled around Blayne. She and Alexi likely wouldn't be spending any more time alone together. "Can I see her now? Is she down the hall?"

He shook his head. "Sorry, no. She's gone to the WITSEC offices to see if she can help in the search for Theo."

"When can I see her?" Blayne asked.

"I'm afraid I can't answer that," Dombrowski said gently.

Why the hell didn't I get the number of her new cell phone? "Do you have her number?"

"Blayne, I'm sorry. I can't give that to you. We're not allowed to." Dombrowski's expression made it clear he wished it were different. "I know you two are close, and she probably wouldn't mind. But it's against the rules."

Blayne felt a moment of panic. *And she won't know where I am, will she? Not if she's off the case. So she won't be able to contact me. Fuck.* But then she remembered Vaso. *The Fairmont, that was the name of the hotel.* She'd be able to reach Alexi through Vaso, if through no other way.

"That's okay. I'll just call Vaso. Is there a phone here I can use?"

Dombrowski leaned over and laid a hand on her forearm. "You can't make any calls until they're done questioning you. And the calls you make after that will be screened, just so you know. So you can't give out any information about where you are, what your new name is, or how you can be contacted."

"Jesus." *I can't even talk to her anymore without someone listening in?*

"Yeah, I know. A real bitch. And much as I wish I could help you get adjusted and everything, I won't see you after today, either. You'll be taken to a new safe house and under the exclusive protection of the marshals from now on. Your new WITSEC inspector is flying in today to take charge of you."

Everything seemed to be happening incredibly fast. *If I had known last night was going to be our last night together...for however long, maybe forever...I would have...should have...* But then again, after some thought, she decided she would have done nothing differently. At least she had the kiss to remember. And remember she would. *Damn, what a kiss. Best kiss ever.*

"You know, I didn't expect a smile like that at the news I'm not going to see you any more." Dombrowski jutted out his lower lip in an exaggerated pout.

"Oh, George." Blayne smiled at him. "I *will* miss you. And I'll never forget what you've done for me. My mind was just on something else."

"I know you have a lot to think about. Stick to the positive—you'll see your friend Claudia soon."

"Yes. And I'm really looking forward to that."

Dombrowski stood. "Have to go now, I'm afraid. They'll be in to talk to you some more."

She got to her feet and gave him a hug, and he hugged her back. "I just want you to know, I think you're a brave woman, Blayne," he said. "And you're doing the right thing agreeing to testify."

After more questioning, she was introduced to her new WITSEC inspector, a tall, no-nonsense ex-Marine, who formally briefed her on what to expect during her orientation. He said her relocation choices would be taken into consideration, along with Claudia and Philippe's, but the exact destination would be withheld from all of them until they were moved.

After meeting with him, she was introduced to the three local U.S. marshals who would take turns guarding her until the pretrial hearings—two men and one woman, a married mother of two. All seemed pleasant enough, and capable.

They arrived at the new safe house in midafternoon. It was a condo this time, with two bedrooms and modern furnishings. She was finally allowed to make a phone call, but one of the marshals was seated on the other end of the couch, listening to every word.

She got the Fairmont and the front desk put her through.

"Vaso?" she said, when the phone was answered in Greek.

"Yes, who is speaking?"

"It's Blayne, Vaso."

"Ah! Blayne! How are you? I have been hearing all about it on the news!"

"I'm okay. It's on the news?" She reached for the remote to the television and turned it on.

"Yes. On CNN and the local stations. How is Alexi?"

Blayne had started to surf through the channels with the sound muted, but at the mention of Alexi's name she paused. "You haven't heard from her?"

"No, should I have?"

"Well, I thought you would have," Blayne answered. "But maybe she's still at WITSEC headquarters. Dombrowski told me she went down there to try to help in the search for Theo Lang. Her boss," she added. "He's missing."

"Yes, that is also on the news. Well, I have not heard from her yet. But I would expect her to call me when she is able to."

"They won't give me her cell phone number," Blayne said. "So I can't call her. Will you tell her...tell her..." She looked over at the marshal, who was feigning interest in a magazine. *Shit. What do I tell her?*

"Tell her I hope I'll get another chance to talk to her. Tell her...I'll never forget her." Blayne gripped the phone tighter. It wasn't what she really wanted to say, but it felt wrong to say that now, with someone listening. Too important to be passed along secondhand, but better secondhand than not at all.

"I will do that, of course." Vaso sounded so much like Alexi that it almost hurt to hear her voice. "I am certain that she will also never forget you."

I so want to believe you're right. She worked up her courage. It needed to be said. She feared too much she might never get another chance, and Alexi would never know.

"And Vaso, please tell Alexi...that I love her. Very much. Will you tell her that?"

"I will be most happy to. As soon as she contacts me."

❖

Alexi appeared at Vaso's door three hours later, looking haggard but acting like she was half wired on speed or caffeine. "Good thinking, getting a suite," she said in Greek as she breezed by, suitcase in each hand. "Which?" She waited for Vaso to point toward the bedroom on the right, then continued on into it to get rid of her bags.

She reemerged a minute later and glanced around approvingly.

"So I presume you have been listening to the news?" She said it lightly as she crossed to the bathroom.

"I am sorry about Theo Lang," Vaso said. "Has there been any news?"

Alexi shook her head. "Nothing yet. And I doubt they will find anything. It is how Cinzano found us, I think. But I am certain Theo did not give it up easily."

"I am sorry, Alexi. Were you close to him?"

"I am not close to anyone, Vaso," she answered ruefully as she crossed to the couch and took a seat. "You know that."

Vaso thought the statement very telling. She sat down beside her sister. "She called here earlier, looking for you."

Alexi's forced nonchalance evaporated, and suddenly, all of her loneliness and worry and anxiety could be seen on her face and heard in her voice. It was like a switch in her had been flipped. "What did she say? Was she all right?"

"She said she is okay. Disappointed that I had not talked to you. She wanted me to tell you that she hopes that she gets another chance to talk with you."

Alexi nodded and a smile lifted one corner of her mouth. "I hope that too."

"She also wanted me to tell you that she will never forget you," Vaso added, gratified to see her sister's smile grow at the news.

"Did she?"

"Indeed. I told her I was certain you would not forget her, either."

Alexi's eyes narrowed. "Taking liberties, are we not?"

"You have told me how you feel about her," Vaso placed a hand on her sister's shoulder. "And I am happy that you do. Because she also asked me to please tell you that she loves you. Very much."

Alexi's eyes grew moist at the news. "I...I had wondered..." she stuttered. "I mean, do you think she..."

"Yes, Alexi." Vaso tightened her grip on her sister's shoulder. "She meant exactly what you want her to mean. So what are you going to do about it?"

Alexi got up and began to pace. "I have not the first idea, Vaso. Not the first idea." *I just know the thought of being without her is excruciating.*

❖

Blayne tried the Fairmont repeatedly but Alexi was never there when she called, and Vaso seldom was either. Time dragged and she grew a little sadder by the day, with no word from Alexi and no idea of how her declaration of love really had been received. Her days were spent watching television, playing cards with the marshals, or being prepped for her testimony. The only people she saw were law enforcement types or lawyers, and she was beginning to go a little stir crazy.

When she got hold of Vaso she learned that Alexi was staying there, but was out at that moment.

"How did she react to my messages?" Blayne asked.

"She was very pleased to get them. As I told you, Blayne, she feels more for you than she will acknowledge."

"But she didn't leave any message for me, did she?"

"I think she hopes to talk to you herself," Vaso answered, staring pointedly at Alexi as she spoke. "Perhaps the next time you call she will be in."

Alexi glared back.

"I hope so," Blayne said. "I never know when they're going to let me use the phone. Well, tell her I called again, will you? And that I miss her and hope like hell that I'll get to see her again?"

"I will, Blayne." As soon as she hung up the phone, Vaso punched her sister lightly in the arm. "I am going to make you wait awhile to hear what she had to say this time, as punishment for your cowardice."

CHAPTER TWENTY-SIX

Three weeks later, the day before she was to testify, Blayne's gloomy outlook lifted in an instant when the knock at the front door turned out not to be the usual shift of marshals, but Claudia and Philippe.

"Blayne!"

"Claud!"

They both shrieked and ran headlong into each other's arms, meeting in a fierce embrace that almost knocked the wind out of both of them. Neither was anxious to part, and they were both so excited they talked over each other.

"How are you?"

"My God, I thought you were dead!"

"Where have you been?"

"They wouldn't tell us anything!"

It was all questions and exclamations, no answers, and suddenly both of them realized it and burst into relieved laughter.

"I've missed you so much," Blayne said, holding Claudia at arm's length to get a good look at her, but unwilling to let her go completely.

"Me too. We heard about Joyce, but nothing after that. I was afraid you were dead."

At the mention of *we*, Blayne for the first time looked over at Philippe, standing off to the side, near the door, watching them. He looked as though he had lost ten pounds and aged ten years, and it was then Blayne realized he had indeed known much more about the mob than he had ever let on.

She went to him and saw tears in his eyes before he hung his head in shame. He had been like a second father to her, and it hurt her to see him in such pain. She hugged him. "It's wonderful to see you, Philippe."

He hugged her back. "I'm sorry, Blayne. I don't know what to say, I—"

"Nothing to say now, Philippe. Let's enjoy being alive, and being together."

"So we've been hiding out in a motel in Indianapolis," Claudia said. "Spill. What have you been up to?"

It took a couple of hours for Blayne to provide a blow-by-blow recounting of every attempt on her life and every near miss between her and Alexi. Throughout the retelling, she described Alexi in such vivid detail that Claudia was able to absolutely picture the two of them together by the time their kiss was described.

She could see it all so well, in fact, that she asked Blayne to describe it again the next day as they waited in a small room near the courtroom to testify at Cinzano's pretrial hearing.

"Holy crap, how hot!" she summarized with slightly less than her usual aplomb. "I think I need a cold shower!"

"God, Claud, that kiss just sealed the deal for me. I mean…"

"You really have it serious bad for her, honey. I mean, great for you, but *not,* right?"

"You know it. I don't even know if I'm ever even going to see her or talk to her again."

They were seated on a pair of folding chairs, Blayne dressed in khaki pants and a navy blouse, and Claudia in a black skirt and pale yellow cashmere sweater. Though she maintained her side of the conversation, Blayne kept her eyes on the window in the room's only door. The marshal positioned just outside partially obscured her view, but she still could get a good look at the people passing by outside, going into the courtroom. *Please. Please.*

She had nearly given up when she saw them. Alexi and Vaso. So quick she might have imagined it. But she knew she had not. "They just went by!" She shot to her feet and hurried to the door, hoping for a glimpse of them among the crowd milling around in the hall. Nothing.

"They?" Claudia said.

"Alexi and her sister." Blayne prayed for them to find a reason to retrace their steps and reappear in her limited view. "Who is very much your type, by the way."

"What do you mean, my type?" Claudia said.

"Charming. Cocky. Sexy as hell, and very flirtatious. I like her. Kind of a tell-it-like-it-is type, which *you* definitely need."

"Cute?" Claudia asked.

"Well, I've described Alexi and I know you've got a good picture in your head of her, right?" Blayne kept talking to Claudia, but her eyes never strayed from the window.

"*Oh* yeah," Claudia said. "From your description, I'd go for her myself if you weren't already crazy about her."

"Well, Vaso looks exactly like her, just butchier. Great butchier. Like I said, just your type."

"And you said they just went by?" Claudia got up to join Blayne at the window. "What's Vaso wearing?"

"How the hell should I know?" Blayne said. "You know who *I* was looking at. Alexi has black pants, a white shirt, and her black leather coat on. One of my favorite looks for her, by the way. Very hot."

"So what else do you know about—" Claudia began, but Blayne cut her off.

"There they are! Over there!" She pointed toward a small crowd of people near the elevators. They partially obscured Alexi, in profile, talking to Vaso, who had her back to them. Vaso was wearing jeans, black boots, and a black leather jacket.

"Oh my God, Alexi *is* hot!" Claudia said. "*Very hot!*"

"I told you." Blayne tried waving in their direction in the hope of attracting Alexi's attention, but they were too far away.

"Is that her sister she's talking to?"

"Yeah, that's Vaso."

"I wish she'd turn around."

Blayne waved again, and this time, though she had been looking in completely the wrong direction, Alexi turned as though she had some sense that Blayne was there and looked right at her. Blayne's hand froze briefly where it was when their eyes met, still held high in the air.

Alexi raised her hand in greeting, said something to Vaso, and then headed straight for her.

Butterflies crowded her stomach, and she suddenly found it difficult to breathe.

Alexi exchanged a few words with the marshal who was guarding the room, and Blayne could tell from their body language that they knew each other. Something Alexi said made the guy laugh, and he nodded and reached around behind him, opening the door to admit her.

Blayne and Claudia backed up a few feet so that Alexi could step in and shut the door again. As soon as she was inside, Blayne threw her arms around Alexi and hugged her. A mix of emotions—relief, happiness, hope—poured through her and warmed her from within. She clutched fiercely at Alexi, wishing time to freeze.

A bit startled at first, Alexi adjusted quickly and hugged her back. Their reunion felt wonderful, but it was bittersweet, too, for she knew that the joy of this hello would be followed all too quickly with another good-bye, the next one probably their last.

"I've missed you. So much," Blayne said. "I was afraid I'd never see you again."

"I am here."

"Oh! Sorry, how rude." She released Alexi and turned toward Claudia. "Claud, this is Alexi. Alexi, may I introduce Claudia."

"I am very pleased to meet you, Claudia."

They shook hands warmly.

"Same here, Alexi. Thank you for taking such good care of Blayne."

Alexi smiled. "It was my job, but also my pleasure. May I ask you for a favor?"

"Sure thing."

"Would you mind giving us a few minutes? There is a bench just outside where the marshal can watch you."

"Oh! Of course! Most happy to!" Claudia looked so eager to leave them alone that both Blayne and Alexi chuckled.

But as soon as she'd gone, the laughter faded, replaced by uncertainty.

"Shall we sit?" Alexi offered. She felt edgy and nervous, unsure about how to react. She had been thinking about this for days and had rehearsed in her mind the things that she should say, and how she should act, to make it easiest for the both of them. But now that she was here, facing Blayne, she wasn't at all certain she could keep control of her emotions.

"How are you?" she asked as they settled into a pair of folding chairs.

Blayne thought about how to answer. If she were to respond

honestly, from her gut, she would say she was miserable. That their separation had been unbearable. Intolerable. That without Alexi in her life, there was very little joy at all. That she needed her, more than she needed air and water. But she had already told Alexi how she felt about her, to no avail. What would such a declaration accomplish now?

"I tried several times to reach you, but you were never there. And there were never any messages from you." There was no reproach in Blayne's voice, only sadness.

"Yes, I am very sorry about that," Alexi replied, not meeting her eyes. "I have been very busy." She thought of the countless times she had flipped open her cell phone and stared at it, battling with herself. *I desperately wanted to call you, Blayne, just to hear your voice. Or even just to know you were there. Hear you breathe. Feel some connection to you.* She felt an obligation to continue hiding how she felt for both their sakes, but with every passing moment it was getting more and more difficult to maintain her charade.

"Any word about Theo?"

"No. I am afraid not. And that worries me."

"I'm sorry."

A silence elapsed between them.

"They're going to take me away after I testify. Send me off to orientation," Blayne said at last. *Please, Alexi. Please tell me at least that you don't want to see me go. That you will feel my absence as keenly as I will feel yours. At least give me that.* She had her hands in her lap, and she was fidgeting nervously, picking at unseen lint on her new pants.

"Yes, I am aware of that." Alexi reached over and stilled Blayne's hand by placing her own hand on top of it. She felt a growing panic over the imminence of their separation. The words *they are going to take me away* made it suddenly much too real. It was becoming impossible to continue acting normally. She couldn't meet Blayne's eyes. Couldn't let her see it. *Change the subject.* "How are you holding up?"

"Honestly? I'm glad to be back with Claudia and Philippe, but I can't imagine never seeing you again." Blayne turned her hand over and interlaced her fingers with Alexi's. "Never talking to you. Not knowing where you are, and how you are."

She tried to memorize the feel of Alexi's hand. She stared down at it. Strong, calloused hands, a bit larger than her own. She never thought she could feel such comfort, such strength, in so simple a physical connection. She held on tightly, afraid that the moment she let go, Alexi would vanish, like a ghost.

All Alexi wanted to do at that moment was to hold Blayne, to stand up and embrace her fully and try to calm her fears. But she knew that she could not. The entirety of her attention was focused on their enjoined hands, and a part of her wished that Blayne would let go, because she wasn't sure that she could.

"I guess this is where I am supposed to tell you that it is all for the best." She tried to sound nonchalant as she said it, but it came out angry and frustrated. She hated having no control whatsoever over the situation.

The statement, and the tone of it, seemed to invite a question. Blayne heard a small crack in Alexi's absolute certainty, a hint of her inner feelings, and she seized upon it. "You said what you are supposed to tell me. What if you tell me something you aren't supposed to...for a change?"

"Blayne, there is so much I would like to tell you, so much I need to tell you. But I do not know that I can." Alexi reluctantly disengaged from her, stood, and began to pace, running her hand repeatedly through her hair.

"This may be—probably *will* be the last time we see each other," Blayne pleaded. She could see from Alexi's rapid loss of composure that her feelings were very near the surface. *Please let me in. Please.* "Time is short, so if you have something to say you better say it. Because they'll be coming for me any minute."

After several more seconds of restless pacing, Alexi returned to the chair beside Blayne and took her hand again. She was past frustration now. The desperation over losing Blayne was beginning to make itself felt as a very real pain in her gut. She stared at the clock on the wall, watched the red second hand sweeping them too quickly toward their final good-bye.

"I find it hard to imagine my world without you in it. I find it hard to imagine never seeing you smile again, never kissing you again. Never..." She looked at the floor and shook her head. She was admitting all of this to herself as much as she was to Blayne. "Damn it. You do not need to hear this and I should not be saying it."

"I do need to hear it, Alexi," Blayne said. "I needed to hear it or I would have gone crazy thinking it was just me."

"So now you know." Alexi's voice shook. She was relieved to have finally opened up to Blayne about her feelings. There was some comfort in knowing what was between them was mutual. But it did nothing whatsoever to ease her frustration over the situation. "Are you happy? Has my telling you changed anything? No. It has not. You still have to disappear, and I am acting very unprofessionally."

"Has nothing changed? Really? You don't think our sharing how we feel about each other changes things?" Blayne asked.

"Everything and nothing has changed, and we both need to find a way to deal with that," Alexi said. *You have made me feel this way, made me fall in love with you, and for what?* She felt anger and sadness, and even a little frustration with Blayne. *You've put me in a compromised position, one I am not familiar with—having to feel, and having to admit to these feelings...and now what am I to do with that?*

"Tell me how I'm going to do that, Alexi. You're the expert at this. How do I just forget you and go on?"

Alexi was silent for a long minute, surprised by Blayne's words. Her voice was so quiet when she answered that Blayne had to strain to hear her. "I am anything but an expert at this. I have never felt anything remotely similar, so I do not have the answers you need. I cannot even answer for myself."

Blayne's jaw dropped. "Is that really true?"

"Why do you ask me if this is true? Do you think I am looking for ways to make this more difficult? Nothing could be further from the truth, and I realize this admission will only make it more difficult, but you make me *feel* and I do not know what else to do with it but admit to it."

"I wish you had told me this sooner," Blayne said.

"And I wish it had been possible, but your safety was not something I was going to compromise by putting us both in a vulnerable position. I get paid to keep you alive, not to feel."

And that has been the story of my life. Being paid not to feel anything. Alexi felt suddenly defeated, as if too many of her choices had been the wrong ones.

"But you're not protecting me anymore." Blayne could not disguise her exasperation. "Isn't there some way we can be together?"

"If only you knew how often I have thought about it, trying to find a way. I am afraid that it is just not possible. Your safety cannot be compromised." The thought of anything happening to Blayne filled her with a cold kind of terror so profound she had no defense or experience against it.

Alexi looked her in the eyes, and Blayne could see she was fighting back tears. "I will not allow anything to happen to you," she said. "And definitely not because of me."

❖

Claudia had no problem at all giving Blayne and Alexi some alone time. She was happy to give Blayne the opportunity to be with the woman who had come to mean so much to her, and it also meant she might get the opportunity to get a better look at Vaso, if she was still hanging around.

And happily, she was. Vaso was leaning against the opposite wall, looking slightly bored, but when she spotted Claudia, she straightened and raised an eyebrow in appreciative surprise. Her gaze trailed slowly up and down Claudia's body.

Claudia tried not to squirm under the scrutiny, but it was no easy task. Vaso was everything Blayne had described, and then some. Strikingly handsome, she seemed to embody sexual appeal, and she didn't have to work at it at all. Though her overt and insolent ogling was a bit disconcerting, Claudia was determined not to show her discomfort. She stared right back.

Vaso smiled rakishly at her boldness and, after a moment, came over and joined her on the bench. "Are you nervous?" she asked.

It was not the opening line she had expected, and it came as a pleasant surprise that Vaso would express regard for her current situation. In fact, she was indeed a bit anxious about her upcoming testimony. "Yes. A little."

"Maybe I can change that." Vaso leaned back, crossed her legs, and stretched her arm along the back of the bench, looking every bit like she was settling in for an extended visit with an old friend.

"Oh? What would make you think so?"

"The fact that I know that you would want me to," Vaso stated confidently.

"Oh really?" Claudia bandied back. "What makes you so sure?"

"Because of the way that you're looking at me."

Claudia couldn't help but smile. "You're just like Blayne said you were. Have you always been this arrogant?"

Vaso seemed to consider the question. "Come to think of it, yes."

That elicited a laugh. "And how often does it work for you?"

"I have not been disappointed yet," Vaso replied matter-of-factly.

Claudia was a little annoyed that she found Vaso's self-assuredness so compelling. "Okay, Miss God's-gift-to-women, let's say hypothetically I do want you to make me less nervous. What do you have in mind? Think you can charm the pants off me?"

"Now that is something I would like to try." Vaso leered at the expanse of Claudia's legs exposed by her skirt. "You have a beautiful body."

"Don't hold your breath," Claudia responded. She tried not to fidget, but with Vaso's gaze on her, it was difficult not to.

"Are you saying that it is not possible, or just not possible for me?" Vaso countered.

"I'm still deciding that. And by the way, I'm still nervous. Your witty repartee isn't helping a bit."

Vaso leaned in closer and lowered her voice so the marshal could not overhear. "Yes, but I am sure your nerves have more to do with me right now. You can deny it but frankly you should not bother."

Claudia laughed but could not stop the flush of embarrassment that warmed her cheeks.

"I see I am right," Vaso stated.

"You're delusional."

"Hardly. I see it in your eyes."

"Perhaps I will be the first woman who turns you down," Claudia threatened with as much nonchalance as she could muster. But try as she might, she didn't sound convincing, even to herself.

"Perhaps you shouldn't hold *your* breath," Vaso replied.

"God, you are too much. Do you have any redeeming features whatsoever?"

Vaso pursed her lips as though seriously contemplating her answer. "Hmm…give me a few…days…" She grinned mischievously. "And I'll come up with something."

Claudia laughed again. She was enjoying the playful banter far too much. "Oh? You give women a few days? You don't strike me as the type."

"I do not know what type I am, but I am certain I am *your* type."

"You're impossible! Your type is probably anything with a pulse," Claudia said. *God, you're dangerous. Seriously dangerous.* "Where's your scorecard? Long full by now, I bet. Or don't you take notice of names?"

"This is where you are wrong," Vaso said. "My scorecard includes only beautiful, responsive, and hard-to-get women, *Claudia.*"

The way that Vaso said her name sounded so incredibly intimate that Claudia felt as though she had just been undressed. "Yes, indeed. You are definitely everything that Blayne said you were. But for some ungodly reason I like you anyway." Vaso had certainly made her forget for a moment where she was and why she was there. "Although you are undoubtedly the cockiest woman I have ever met, you do have a certain charm. We might have had fun together. Pity I'm about to disappear."

"We are already having fun." Vaso shifted her body a little closer to Claudia's. "Are you saying that you would have liked to see me again?"

Their proximity was deliciously unnerving. "Well, perhaps...I mean..."

"This sounds like more than just perhaps," Vaso replied, inching even nearer.

"Don't get so full of yourself. I haven't decided whether you deserve me," she managed.

"I have no doubt that we deserve each other."

Claudia half wished she didn't find Vaso's low rich voice and melodious Greek accent quite so irresistible. "Well, I'm a real prize. Saved for the select few."

Vaso laughed. "Go ahead, be honest with yourself. I am sure you will find it freeing."

Her audacity was absolutely disarming. "I am so completely torn between wanting to kiss you and slap you into next week."

"I will take curtain number one, please," Vaso said. "Of course, you can always slap me and then kiss me to make it better."

"I think you have already been kissed far too much by too many women," Claudia concluded.

"You think too much. How about acting on some of those impulses?"

"Not a chance. Even if we weren't surrounded by people. I'm not quite that easy."

"Maybe not, but you want to finish this, and I know that we will." Vaso's demeanor was one of absolute confidence this would be the case.

"And how in the world do you know that?"

"I always finish what I start." Vaso uncrossed her legs and edged over the final inches so that their bodies were touching.

"And how and where do you think we'll get the opportunity to finish this?" Claudia was deliciously aware of the warmth of Vaso's thigh against hers, though she made no outward sign of it. "I'm about to go in to testify, and then I'll be spirited away from here, to a new life and a new identity."

Vaso shrugged. "I do not know when or where, but I know that I have to find a way."

"Have to?" Claudia tilted her head and studied Vaso, intrigued. "After just talking to me for these few minutes? Or won't your ego take it well otherwise?"

"Has it only been minutes? It seems like I have been wanting to kiss you far longer than that." Though it sounded every bit an overused pick-up line, it seemed original and entirely heartfelt when Vaso said it, and Claudia found herself wanting to believe it was so.

But just then, a bailiff emerged from the courtroom down the hall and headed straight for her. Evidently it was her turn to take the stand.

"Well, Blayne said you were charming, and you certainly are that," she concluded as she got to her feet. She looked down at Vaso with a frown of regret. "And she said you were my type, and I am forced to admit she is right about that too. It really is a damn shame we couldn't have met under slightly more accommodating circumstances."

"Do not consider this concluded, Claudia," Vaso replied confidently. "You never know what the future holds."

❖

Despite Vaso's optimistic declaration, Blayne and Claudia did not get the chance to see Alexi and Vaso again before their orientation and relocation, a fact that depressed the hell out of both of them.

They were settled into a new duplex in a suburb of Portland, Oregon, Philippe in one half and Claudia and Blayne in the other, and their new WITSEC inspector helped the women both get jobs at a travel agency that was not so different from the Balmy Breezes.

Their lives and routines were soon much the same as they had been before Martinelli's death. But it didn't feel at all that way to Blayne. She felt incomplete now, without Alexi, and she wondered whether anything could ever fill the void caused by their separation.

She missed Alexi so much that she even went so far as to telephone the Fairmont one day, totally against the rules, some two weeks after they were resettled. But the Nikolos sisters had checked out, leaving no forwarding address.

That's that, then, she told herself as she hung up the phone. *You'll just have to try to forget her and move on.* It felt like an impossible task.

CHAPTER TWENTY-SEVEN

B layne was having a particularly bad day. A young couple, about to get married, came in to book a romantic honeymoon in London, and she had to smile and act all helpful and pleasant when the whole experience made her feel desperately lonely for Alexi. Long after they'd gone, she remained hunched over her desk, staring at brochures advertising all the attractions they had been to, so absorbed in her own thoughts that she didn't notice that Claudia had stopped talking, mid-sentence, to the businessman she was booking a flight for.

A shadow fell across her desk as a familiar voice broke the ensuing quiet.

"I would like to book a trip for two to Fiji, please. By way of Greece."

For a moment, she didn't dare look up. Afraid she had imagined it. Afraid to believe that Alexi was really there. But her heart was about to break out of her chest. She knew it was for real.

"That is, if you would like to, of course," the voice added uncertainly.

She looked up and found Alexi regarding her with an expectant expression. But Blayne was so shocked she couldn't breathe. Couldn't move. Couldn't speak. She knew she must look a bit idiotic, with her mouth hanging open like she could feel that it was.

But she couldn't help it. Her surreal, off-its-axis life had suddenly tilted sharply again, and she didn't dare believe it was true. *She's here. She's really here. For me. Three feet away. And God, more gorgeous than ever.* Her stomach knotted and her vision swam—she wanted to rush into Alexi's arms but she didn't at all feel capable of standing.

"I had hoped you would look rather more pleased to see me." There was a twinkle in Alexi's eyes and a smile on her face, so she'd obviously read Blayne right and concluded that her temporary mute paralysis was a good thing. "May I sit?" She asked it casually, as though stopping by like this was something that she did every day.

Blayne found the wherewithal to move enough to shake her head, but that was about all she could manage.

"No?" Alexi stiffened, and a pained expression replaced her bemused one.

Blayne shook her head again and finally managed to find her voice. "No sitting until you hold me."

Alexi grinned broadly as relief washed over her face. "Happily done!"

She came around the desk, drew Blayne to her feet, and they embraced long and fiercely.

"God. I can't believe you're here," Blayne whispered into Alexi's neck. "How are you here? No, wait—that doesn't matter." She loosened her grip just enough to drink in her face. "Why are you here?"

"I told you. I am here to invite you to come with me to Fiji, if that is still where you want to go most in the world. The destination does not matter to me. As long as I am with you."

"Where I want to go most in the world is anywhere you are," Blayne answered.

"Then apparently we have some things to talk about. When do you get off work?"

"She can leave now," Claudia interjected, which made them both laugh. "Hey, Alexi."

"Hello, Claudia."

"Didn't happen to bring your sister along, did you?"

"No, but she sends her regards to you. She asked me to tell you that she still intends to finish what she started. Said you would understand."

"She did, did she?" Claudia smiled broadly at the news.

"Can you really leave now?" Alexi asked, her arm still encircling Blayne's waist.

"Only a half hour left, and I have no one else booked. If Claud's willing to cover, I don't see why not."

"Let us go, then?"

Blayne was surprised to see Alexi head for the sleek Ducati

Monster that was parked in front of the agency. She picked up one of the helmets sitting on the seat and handed it to Blayne. "This is all right, is it not?"

"Sure! It's great! Do you want directions to the house?"

"Later," Alexi answered, as she put the other helmet on. "I have something else in mind first, if you will trust me?"

"Such a question. Of course!" Blayne nearly shouted, her glee boiling over. "Anything you want! Everything!"

Soon after, with Blayne snuggled tight against her back, Alexi was speeding along the Sunset Highway toward the ocean.

Motorcycles were her favorite way to travel, but Alexi began to have regrets about her decision almost at once. It was wonderful to have Blayne so close, their hips glued together and Blayne's arms around her waist, hugging her tight. But it was a little too wonderful when Blayne's hands began to stray, caressing her thighs lightly as they sped along.

She had been thinking about Blayne's hands on her body for weeks. After the hearings, she'd taken a leave of absence from WITSEC and insisted Vaso accompany her on a trip, intending to get her mind off Blayne. They went to the south of France, where there were warm beaches and endless parties and an unlimited supply of willing women to bed.

But once they were there, she had soon realized that nothing and no one could keep her from missing Blayne with every fiber of her being. She felt lost and adrift without her. Blayne had touched a part of her that no woman ever had, and Alexi had no idea how she would ever be able to return to the way she'd lived her life in the past. To solitude and emotional isolation.

She had suffered for three weeks before she telephoned George Dombrowski and asked him for a favor. At first, he claimed he could not help her, but she knew how much he had come to care for Blayne, so she told him honestly what her plans were and asked him to try.

It took him four hours to get the information she needed. She was on the next plane back to the States. And now, here she was, legs open to straddle the bike, a very vulnerable and accessible position to be in, and Blayne's hands were teasing, taunting, going near, but not too near. The vibration from the powerful motor was only adding to the stimulation.

By the time they reached the coast, her body was ablaze with arousal, and she ached to be in a position where she could begin to give back as good as she had gotten. The desire to touch Blayne had never been more overwhelming.

They arrived at the ocean almost an hour before twilight, so they had plenty of time to find a good place to watch the sun set. Alexi took Blayne's hand and led her to a secluded stretch of beach, away from the smattering of others who were there for the same purpose. She got comfortable and invited Blayne to sit between her legs in the circle of her embrace—their positions on the bike, only reversed. This time, she would be the one able to taunt and tease and arouse.

They snuggled in, bodies tight together and faces touching, and watched the sky turn orange and red and purple. Alexi slipped her hands beneath Blayne's jacket and lightly stroked her stomach through the thin green sweater she wore—a sweater she recognized as having been purchased during their shopping spree in Harrods. Every now and then, she would lightly trail her fingertips down along Blayne's thighs, mimicking the torment she had been put through on the highway.

When she felt Blayne's body shift slightly beneath her hands and heard her sudden intake of breath, Alexi kissed her cheek, her neck. Soft, sweet kisses, introducing their bodies to each other. Kisses meant to promise, and to excite.

It was a quiet, peaceful setting, but Blayne's heart was beating a mile a minute from the thrill of Alexi's touch, and from having Alexi's body wrapped tightly around her own. "I can hardly believe we're really here," she whispered almost reverently. "It's like a dream."

"A dream come true," Alexi murmured between kisses.

"It feels so wonderful to have you hold me. Touch me. To be able to touch *you. Finally.* God, what you are doing to me." She arched her neck to allow Alexi's mouth a wider landscape to explore, moaning when Alexi's tongue and teeth nipped and tasted the soft pale flesh beneath her jaw.

"It has been torture for me too," Alexi whispered back. "So very much, I have wanted to touch you. So very much." She ached to slip her hands up under Blayne's sweater, to feel the soft skin beneath, but she wanted to take things slowly. Drive Blayne crazy with desire, and revel in and relish every moment herself.

Blayne closed her eyes and took a few deep breaths, trying to calm her runaway heart. She was nervous and excited and a little terrified too. She'd never wanted anything or anyone this much. Not nearly. And everything that Alexi was doing was only sending her higher by the second. "If you keep that up, we're going to very soon be in a position that will either get us an audience, or arrested."

Alexi chuckled against her neck. "Will we? And what position are you seeing us in?"

"A compromising position," Blayne answered. "Specifically? You on top of me, kissing me like you kissed me the first time."

A low growl in the back of Alexi's throat told Blayne what she thought of that particular image.

"You keep putting pictures like that into my head and I may not be able to take you to dinner as I had planned." Alexi wrapped her arms tightly around Blayne's waist again and hugged her close.

"We've got lots of time," Blayne said. "Tomorrow's Saturday and I don't have to work. I'd like to…you know…"

"I know," Alexi whispered in her ear. "Slow. Make it last. Make it perfect."

Blayne lifted her hand to caress the face that rested against hers. "Exactly."

"Shall we find a nice place for dinner, then, and flirt some more? I can flirt back now, you know," Alexi said.

"Prove it," Blayne challenged as she jumped to her feet and offered a hand to Alexi.

Alexi allowed herself to be pulled up, and she kept hold of Blayne's hand as they headed toward the bike. "Fair warning, however," she said when they neared the Ducati. "If you put your hands on my thighs again like you did, I am going to have to pull over and do something about it, and you are going to be one very hungry woman."

Blayne laughed. "It'll take every ounce of willpower I have, but I'll be on my best behavior. For now. After dinner, all bets are off."

"I will hold you to that."

❖

They found a romantic seafood restaurant a little ways down the coast, and Alexi made sure they were given a private candlelit table that overlooked the ocean. While they waited for their fish, they sipped white Lambrusco and grinned at each other like teenagers on a first date.

Alexi raised her glass and waited for Blayne to raise hers. "To your beautiful smile. The smile that brought you to me."

"That's lovely," Blayne said, her face warming from the unexpected compliment. "Thank you." She was quiet for a few moments. "You know, I thought for a long time that you weren't interested in me. That I wasn't your type. I know you can have any woman you want."

Alexi leaned over to touch her cheek. "You are a very beautiful woman, Blayne, and very much my type."

Blayne took another long sip of wine to try to calm her nerves. The way that Alexi was looking at her was doing all sorts of marvelous things to her insides. "Good to know."

"I thought I made that clear when I kissed you," Alexi said gently. "I just had to. You left me no option."

"I hoped you felt that way." Blayne responded. "But I guess I wasn't sure. I had been really throwing myself at you. And like you said…you're only human."

"Yes, I am only human, and when a beautiful woman throws herself at me it is very difficult to resist. I did it only because I had to, not because I wanted to."

Blayne caught her lower lip between her teeth and glanced at Alexi expectantly. "And now? What do you want now, Alexi?"

Alexi leaned forward again, placed a hand on Blayne's, and looked into her eyes. "Right now I want to kiss you. Right now I want to do what I have to do."

Blayne's skin tingled at the memory of how the last kiss had made her feel. "Can I take a rain check on that? Perhaps for dessert, somewhere more private?"

"I have never looked forward to dessert before like I do now."

The waiter interrupted them with their meals, and it took only a few forkfuls for them to both realize they were virtually bolting down their food. They looked at each other and broke up laughing.

"I wish I could say that it is good, but I have not tasted a thing," Alexi said. "So how is yours?"

"I'm eating only because I think we'll need sustenance later," Blayne replied.

"Why? Do you have plans?"

Blayne nodded her head slowly and deliberately. "Oh, yeah. I intend to keep you much too busy to eat."

Alexi raised an eyebrow in amusement. "Do tell."

Blayne put her hand on Alexi's thigh under the table. "I'd rather show than tell."

"I would rather you do that too," Alexi responded, her voice tight.

"You know, I am suddenly feeling very full. Can't eat another bite." Blayne licked her lips. "Unless of course, you'd like me to nibble on you. That can be arranged."

"Would you like to move on to dessert?"

"Now that, I definitely have an appetite for."

Alexi turned to find the waiter. "Check, please!"

They settled the bill and headed for the bike, which was parked behind the restaurant, away from traffic and the attention of anyone passing by. Alexi reached for the helmets, but Blayne grabbed her by the lapels of her jacket and yanked her close.

"Can't wait anymore," she rasped before pulling Alexi's lips forcefully to hers.

This kiss began where the first left off, hungry and full of need, the outcome of long hours and days and weeks of wanting what was now not only possible, but finally within reach.

Blayne nipped and tugged at Alexi's lips, and stroked them with her tongue, and Alexi answered with equal passion, thrusting her tongue into Blayne's mouth to claim and explore the welcoming warmth.

Blayne's arms went around Alexi's neck, and Alexi's hands went to Blayne's ass, and their bodies came together in a rush of heavy breathing and low moans as the kiss went on and on and on. They remained like that until the lights of a car swept over them as it parked nearby, jolting them back to reality.

"Christ," Alexi panted as they broke apart. "How the hell am I ever going to be able to drive us anywhere?"

Blayne traced a hand lightly down the center of Alexi's chest. "Oh, I'm confident you can get us somewhere we can continue this."

"I am glad you are confident." Alexi reached for the helmets with an unsteady hand. Her body was so painfully aroused she worried the vibrations of the bike might push her over the edge.

They put on the helmets and mounted the bike, Alexi struggling to focus on driving and not on the feel of Blayne snuggled up behind her. She knew it was impossible—Blayne was wearing a jacket, and so was she—but she swore she could feel Blayne's nipples against her back.

They had gone only a few miles up the coast when Blayne's hands slipped from her waist to her crotch. It was only a light brushing tease of a caress, but it shattered the small amount of focus Alexi had garnered. She swerved into the next motel they passed, a collection of beachfront bungalows that advertised a scenic view, in-room Jacuzzis, and privacy.

As soon as she stopped the bike, she glanced over her shoulder and said in a voice that was not hers, "All right?"

"Perfect."

Blayne stuck close as Alexi registered, requesting their nicest accommodations.

"How many nights?" the clerk asked.

Alexi looked to Blayne for the answer.

"Two nights," she replied. "You have room service, right?"

"Yes, of course," the man replied cheerily. "We can deliver from any of the area restaurants. Twenty-four hours. Menus are in the rooms."

"Great!" Blayne tried for a casual air but found Alexi staring at her with what could only be described as a wolfish grin. *Dear God. Get me into that room right now.* "Ready?" she asked, as seductively as she could manage with Alexi looking at her like that.

Alexi only nodded, very slowly, with that grin getting just a little wider, and Blayne swore she could see her pupils dilate right there, the vivid blue rings shrinking as Alexi's hunger reached out and enveloped her.

They left for the room, Alexi moving ahead to politely open doors, her hand resting on Blayne's lower back as they walked. Blayne felt light-headed from nerves and excitement, the thundering of her heart loud in her ears. She found it incredibly hard to take a deep breath. Her body was thrumming as every nerve ending sang out for Alexi's touch.

For weeks they had been wanting, craving, needing. Desire growing by the day without hope of fulfillment. And now they were here, and she surely could never remember ever being this incredibly turned on and fearful at the same time. *Please don't let me do anything to disappoint her. Please. She means far too much.*

Alexi's body seemed charged by electricity, as though every sense had been acutely and profoundly heightened to appreciate such a long-awaited moment. She walked beside Blayne, her nostrils flaring to catch another whiff of her perfume, a hint of citrus with undertones of earthy, musky sensuality. *That's her, her essence.*

It fed her and sent her higher, as had the look in Blayne's eyes when she turned to her, back at the desk. *After making it clear we are going to be in here touching each other for the next forty-eight hours or so. Jesus.* The look in Blayne's eyes had been one of open and unfettered desire as deep as her own.

Alexi had felt arousal before, certainly, but these feelings that Blayne stirred up in her were overwhelming. And unfamiliar. A mixture of unmatched excitement and absolute terror. She used sex as a means of satisfying a physical need, never her emotions. This was an unfamiliar arena, and she was involved in a very scary challenge she desperately did not want to lose.

She was a passionate lover, accomplished at giving and confident in her abilities to arouse and satisfy. Showing a woman she was horny for her was easy. But she had little experience at taking…or at showing someone how she *felt* about them with sex. And what she felt for Blayne…she couldn't put into words. So she knew of no other way to tell her than through touch.

❖

It was a lovely room, with a king-sized bed facing the ocean, and privacy blinds that allowed the occupants a splendid view while affording them complete protection from prying eyes.

"Would you like some…wine? Or music? Or…" Alexi stood just inside the door, watching as Blayne checked out the view and the Jacuzzi.

"No, thank you." Blayne crossed to the bed and sat on one corner, bouncing up and down once or twice as though checking out the durability of the mattress. Her expression changed from playful to serious. "All I want, all I need, is the beautiful woman I see standing before me," she said softly. "Who I very much wish would get over here and kiss me. Since there is nothing to interrupt us this time."

Alexi bit back her nervous apprehension and slowly approached the bed. Her chest rose and fell and she sucked in air, desperate to calm her raging heart. Blayne's gaze traveled up and down the length of her body, lingering here and there with undisguised appreciation for the way she moved.

"I love your body." Blayne sighed. She opened her legs to invite Alexi in between them, and looked up at her as they embraced. "You have no idea how many times I just *watched* you and thought…Oh, how I wish!"

Alexi smiled and brought her hands up to frame Blayne's face. "I have a very good idea, as a matter of fact."

She lowered her mouth to Blayne's, kissing her with exquisite tenderness, savoring the sweet softness, the easy submission to the strokes of her tongue. Blayne opened to her like a flower, drawing her in, deepening the kiss until it roared hot and wet.

"Blayne," she panted, pulling back slightly as her self-control threatened to snap. *Slow. Slow.* Jaws clenched in determination. "You are driving me wild. It is so hard to…take time, but I want to."

"And we will," Blayne whispered breathily. "I want us to explore each other thoroughly…" She tilted her head to kiss Alexi on the neck. "Find every sensitive spot…" More kisses and gentle nips. "See how very much we can climb. And climb." More nips and bites and sweet tongue caresses. "Higher and higher…" Her hands threaded through Alexi's hair, pulling her head back slightly to expose more of her neck for kissing.

Alexi moaned as a pressure began to build in her chest, an ache so profound it felt as though it would smother her. "*Please.* I have to feel your body." In response, she felt Blayne's hands on hers.

"I want you to undress me. Slowly." Blayne's breathing was ragged, uneven, just as Alexi's was. Her hands guided Alexi's to the bottom of her sweater, and together they pulled it up and over her head.

She shivered slightly as Alexi's gaze settled on her black lace bra. "Happy with what you see?"

Alexi brought her hand up and lightly traced the silk and lace with her fingertips, skirting around the rigid peaks of nipples that strained against the sheer fabric. Her voice was hoarse, as though she had just awakened. "Very much. You are incredibly sexy."

"Pants next?" Blayne wanted to sound confident and cavalier, but her voice and shaking hands betrayed her nerves.

As she looked into Blayne's eyes, Alexi slowly caressed the undersides of Blayne's breasts through her bra, then trailed lightly down her sides, across her stomach, and to her belt. She unfastened it, then slipped her fingers into the waistband of the black dress slacks, marveling at the soft skin beneath. She unfastened the button, then slowly unzipped. She looked down.

Blayne was wearing black silk panties, low cut and very brief.

Alexi's mouth watered at the sight. "Beautiful. So beautiful. Lie back," she said hoarsely.

Blayne reclined on the bed and lifted her hips so that Alexi could remove her pants. Socks were next. She was in just her bra and panties now, and Alexi's eyes drifted to the apex of her legs as she opened them enticingly, and took notice of the dark circle of dampness.

The sight sent a hot flash of desire through her that chipped away at the restraint she was barely maintaining. And how she loved the look in Blayne's eyes right now. Wanton. That was the word for it. She climbed up onto the bed, and over Blayne, and spent a very long moment letting her eyes feast on the body beneath her before she lowered herself onto Blayne and kissed her again.

She pushed her tongue into Blayne's mouth and inserted one thigh between her legs, and then her hips began to move of their own accord. Blayne sucked on her tongue and began to moan softly as her hips matched Alexi's movements, thrust for thrust.

The pressure for release was incredible. *Take it slow. Take it slow.*

"You next," Blayne panted, out of breath. She reached between their bodies for the buttons on Alexi's shirt. "Have to feel you, against me."

Alexi rolled off her and lay on her side to allow her access. Blayne's nimble fingers quickly went to work, freeing her from her clothes. As her body was revealed, Alexi watched Blayne's face, heard her gasp of pleasure at the sight of her nearly transparent bra, which allowed a clear view of her dark areolas through the sheer cream-colored fabric.

Blayne sucked in air through slightly parted, swollen lips, playing her fingers over Alexi's nipples and watching them respond. The look in her eyes and the thrill of her touch drove Alexi ever closer to the limit of her endurance. She pushed Blayne's hand down to the clasp of her low-cut jeans, and Blayne let out a soft moan of approval while she popped the button and pulled the zipper down.

Her gaze drank in the soft, bronzed skin and the hint of dark hair peeking out from the top of the panties, a brief triangle of sheer fabric that matched Alexi's bra. "God, so wonderful. So hot." Her eyes returned to Alexi's. "Sit up. I really need you naked."

Alexi did as instructed, and Blayne slowly pulled off her jeans, running her hands firmly down the expanse of muscled thighs and calves. Then she shifted to straddle Alexi before slipping her hands beneath Alexi's blouse. She slid the garment slowly off Alexi's shoulders, then reached around to unclasp her bra.

Alexi's breasts were not overly large but were beautifully shaped and well proportioned to her lean, trim torso. The nipples were dark and fiercely rigid. Blayne's hands splayed to take both of them in, and as she did, she threw her head back in ecstasy and let out a long, low growl of pleasure.

Blayne's hands on her breasts were torturously light and maddeningly slow in their explorations. Every brush of a fingertip against one of her nipples sent a pulse of pleasure to her groin. The sighs and moans that Blayne was making, and the way her body was beginning to move, were driving Alexi insane with raw and desperate *need*.

"The sounds that you make…" It was a struggle to form words, but she wanted so badly to let Blayne know what she was feeling. "When I touch you…they *move* me. They reach deep within me and turn me inside out."

"That's a good thing, right?"

Blayne met her eyes, and the smolder in her expression made it clear the question was purely rhetorical. Alexi nodded anyway as she reached behind Blayne to unfasten her bra. Her heartbeat double-timed and the throbbing between her legs grew stronger as Blayne's breasts were revealed to her. So different from her own—larger, and the skin so pale and delicate. The nipples dark pink, in bold attention, and demanding her mouth.

She pulled Blayne's body close and danced her mouth and tongue wetly over her right breast, then left, caressing the soft swell and pausing for gentle, quick nips at each nipple, eliciting more whimpers and sighs.

"Harder," Blayne gasped. "*More*, Alexi. *Please*. Suck me."

Her hands entwined in Alexi's hair and caressed her scalp with firm purpose, urging her on, and Alexi gave her what she asked for. The sensations of Alexi's mouth on her breast let loose a surge of wetness between her thighs.

Alexi felt Blayne's arousal coat her stomach as she feasted on one breast, then the other. The combination of all the different types of sensations made her feel almost dangerously overstimulated. Her body wanted to rush, to drive to completion, and it was hard not to give in.

Blayne's hands moved from Alexi's hair to her face and tilted it upward, and Blayne's mouth descended on hers for another scorching kiss. Blayne was breathing so hard it seemed as though she was already well on the road to orgasm, solely from the contact of their bodies and mouths.

"Nothing between us," Alexi managed when they finally parted to breathe. She slipped her hands within the confines of Blayne's panties to roughly massage her ass.

"No barriers anymore," Blayne agreed, lifting herself so that Alexi could slide the panties down and away.

Blayne returned the favor and eased Alexi's panties off, and they lay side by side for a moment, not touching, relishing their first opportunity to gaze upon and admire the body each was being offered.

"Tell me what you like." Alexi reached a hand out and ran it lovingly, wonderingly over Blayne, memorizing all the places that drew sighs and shudders.

"Anything you do…everything you do…" Blayne's voice was tight. "Feels unbelievable. Like nothing I have ever felt. Ten times *more…*"

"So damn intense," Alexi agreed.

"Yes. Intense. I can't believe how much you turn me on. It's…it's a pain, in my chest, in my…" She reached for Alexi's hand and placed it over her sex. "Just touch me, Alexi. I need it. I need *you*—so damn much. I can't stand waiting another minute. Another second."

Alexi shifted until she was lying half atop Blayne, and her hand parted Blayne's legs while she claimed her mouth in a crush of lips. The kiss gentled, however, as Alexi's fingers slipped into the soft, silky folds of her sex.

Blayne let out a startled cry when Alexi's fingers smoothed lightly over her swollen clit and continued on, to dip into her abundant wetness and spread it with caresses liberally over the surrounding flesh.

"For me," Alexi grunted, half in wonder, half in proprietary claim.

"Yes, Alexi." Blayne sighed, eyes shut as she began to push against Alexi's hand. "All for you. Only for you."

Alexi watched Blayne intently while she stroked her, unhurriedly building her higher and higher. Varying the speed and pressure of her touch in response to the buck of her hips and the sounds that escaped her, and the tightening of the muscles in her face and body.

She made it last, bringing Blayne close to orgasm again and again, only to retreat a beat or two, until she felt fingernails digging into her back and hips fierce against her hand. Blayne's face was flushed with need, lower lip darkly bruised where it was captured between her teeth.

Only then did she penetrate her, finding her open and ready, eager to be filled. Sliding two fingers inside, she pressed her thumb along the hard swollen ridge of Blayne's clit and replicated the movement she had learned bringing her so close. The renewed contact sent her crashing over the edge.

It took Blayne several moments to get her breathing back to normal. She clutched tight to Alexi, and Alexi to her, as the spasms from her climax subsided. When they did, she kissed Alexi, sweet kisses along her neck, cheek, shoulder, anywhere in reach, and soon the kisses turned fevered.

"You asked what I wanted," Blayne murmured. "What do you want? How do you want me to touch you?"

"I want you to…do whatever you wish to do," Alexi stammered. Her throat was suddenly dry, and every muscle in her body was taut in anticipation of Blayne's hands on her.

She rarely let anyone touch her intimately. It was far outside her comfort zone to surrender so—normally, she brought herself to climax, sometimes long after her sexual partner had departed. But over the past weeks, her body had come to need and want Blayne's touch as much as it wanted oxygen, and food, and the brilliant, blinding warmth of the sun.

"Then I want to try to make you feel the way you just made me feel," Blayne answered, gently pushing Alexi onto her stomach in the middle of the bed. "Tall order. That was pretty spectacular," she added with a grin. "But I want to see if I can learn your body as quickly as you learned mine."

Alexi closed her eyes as Blayne began a long and thorough mapping of the landscape of her body, with her hands, and lips, and tongue. She explored her with caresses from head to foot, concentrating on the areas that drew a hitch of breath, a thrust of pelvis, an unintelligible throaty hum or moan.

Alexi had a sensitive back, so Blayne lingered there, covering every inch with her mouth and her body while she fondled Alexi's ass, drifting every now and then between her legs to encourage her to spread them further, tantalizing teases of what was still to come.

After several long minutes of this torturous foreplay, Blayne urged Alexi onto her back to continue. Their eyes met. "I want you to watch me make love to you," Blayne whispered huskily. "I want to see in your eyes how I'm making you feel."

Alexi could only nod, no longer certain of her voice.

Blayne avoided her breasts and her fevered groin for several more minutes, heightening Alexi's arousal by finding sensitive places she herself had never really known she had—along her sides, her hands, her shoulders.

By the time Blayne's mouth descended on her breasts, Alexi had no further apprehensions about being touched. Or about how she would let Blayne know what she was feeling. Everything felt too right and too natural and too perfect to worry about such things now.

Blayne's tongue played over one of her nipples before her lips closed around it to lightly suck.

"So good," Alexi murmured, placing her hand on the back of Blayne's neck.

The pressure of her fingertips told Blayne what she wanted. Understanding at once, she varied the intensity of her bites and sucks in accordance with Alexi's subtle urgings. The insistent pulse between her legs throbbed louder and stronger with each suck, and grew yet again when she continued her attentions on the other breast. Alexi's hips rolled and pitched, her clit seeking direct stimulation, and Blayne's hand found its way to her thigh, and then her center.

Alexi closed her eyes, her body poised for a hard, heated stroking, but Blayne had other ideas. After several teasing passes of her hand, each so light that Alexi's pelvis rose to meet it, she finally dipped low enough to find her wetness. Blayne hummed her approval at what she encountered, and Alexi felt the sound as a vibration where Blayne's mouth was pleasuring her breast.

Without warning, Blayne withdrew and Alexi, feeling the loss profoundly, looked down to see why. She watched as Blayne put her fingers to her mouth, to taste her, all the while staring at her with the same flushed, hazy look on her face she'd had right before she had come.

"Mmm. Wonderful. I love how you taste." Blayne returned her

hand to Alexi's sex and resumed her slow, easy strokes and circles, but she kept her eyes on Alexi's face, watching her reactions. "Look at me. Show me how I make you feel."

When Alexi's eyes, and breathing, and other clues told Blayne that she was nearing climax, she slid down Alexi's body and put her mouth where her hand had been. Wrapping her arms around Alexi's thighs, she used her tongue and lips to stroke and suck her, until the body beneath her was writhing.

Alexi's arousal doubled and redoubled. Even when she thought she could not feel more, had no more room for sensations, Blayne sent her fractionally higher still. Blayne's mouth drove her past the point of no return, sent her to a place where her need for release was insistent and absolute. Nothing else mattered.

Blayne knew the moment and urged her to surrender to it. "Come for me. Now," she whispered, before flicking her tongue rapidly back and forth across Alexi's swollen clit.

Alexi's whole body clenched and rose up off the bed, and a choked cry escaped her lips when she climaxed.

Blayne slowly kissed her way back up the quivering flesh as it calmed. "You are so incredibly beautiful when you come."

"You are incredibly everything." Alexi drew her close. "Arousing. Sexy. Responsive. You make me feel…wonderful. Cherished. You give me reason to look forward to tomorrow."

Blayne loosened their embrace enough to raise up on one elbow so she could look down at Alexi. She traced a hand lightly over the flat plane of Alexi's stomach and abdomen. "I like the sound of that. Tomorrow, with you."

"I want you in my future, Blayne. In all of my tomorrows. I do not know how we will manage it. But I know I have found something very special with you. Something I should pursue, because I have not seen it before and may not again."

"I'm glad you've realized that," Blayne said. "Because I feel the same way too. I've felt lost without you these past weeks."

"And I you. My life has felt incomplete without you in it."

"Alexi…I don't want to jinx us being here together or anything, but I have to ask…what's changed? I mean, you said it was impossible." She bit her lip. "I guess maybe I'm a little afraid you'll change your mind."

"No, Blayne. No," Alexi quickly reassured her. She enfolded

Blayne in her arms and hugged her close. "I do take my job very seriously, as you know, and I could not do anything to jeopardize you while I was assigned to protect you. But...but I also have used my job as an excuse to keep from getting seriously involved with anyone. I see that now. The past made me afraid, and I let guilt about what happened with Sofia cloud my judgment."

Blayne caressed Alexi's stomach. "I think it's time to forgive yourself about Sofia."

"I do not know if I can. But I do know that the simple reality is, you are safer with me than without me. Involved with each other or not. I know I can protect you as well or better than anyone."

"That's wonderful news. So...when do you have to go back?" Blayne asked. "And how are we going to work this with you in Chicago and me in Portland now?"

"To be bluntly honest, Blayne, I should warn you that I have no experience at having a serious relationship. I am not very good at sorting out emotions and feelings and I have few skills in communicating them. That said, if you are willing to take a chance with me and see where this might lead, I am willing to do what I can to make it work and make you happy."

"That mean you are going to fly out frequently to see me?" The hand that was caressing Alexi's stomach began a slow trip south, stroking ever closer to her sex.

"It means that I am on an indefinite leave so that I can spend time with you," Alexi said. "I may go back, I may not. I really do not need to work, and there are a lot of other things I could do with my background that might also be interesting." She reached for Blayne's wrist and stopped her hand from any further advance toward her clit.

Blayne frowned in disappointment and looked at her.

"Do you want me, Blayne?" Alexi waited expectantly for her answer. "Even though I do not know whether I will be any good at this relationship thing at all?"

Blayne smiled and reached up to stroke her cheek with the back of her hand. "Of course I want you. I love you. And there is no pressure for you to *be* anything, or *say* anything, or *do* anything. Just be with me. We'll take it a day at a time, and figure it out together."

Alexi's face relaxed into a smile. "I am very happy to hear you say that."

"You know, I was about to show you how much I love you, until you stopped me." She started to reach between Alexi's thighs again, but Alexi's wolfish grin returned.

"First, Blayne, I must insist on my turn."

"Turn?"

Alexi rose up off the bed and looked down at her. "My turn. I have to taste you. And I have to make you come hard that way, just like you made me. And then we will order room service and have some sustenance. And then it will be your turn again to decide what and how and where. We have time for plenty of turns. Plenty."

"I think you are a bit too used to getting your own way." Blayne spread her legs and put her hand gently on the back of Alexi's head as she kissed her way down. "We'll have to work on that."

Alexi's mouth found her.

"But not today," Blayne murmured.

Stunned with joy, she closed her eyes and let Alexi take her back to the stratosphere.

About the Author

Kim Baldwin has been a writer for three decades, following up a twenty-year hitch in network news with a much more satisfying career penning lesbian fiction. She has published four novels with Bold Strokes Books: the intrigue/romances *Flight Risk* and *Hunter's Pursuit*, and the romances *Force of Nature* and *Whitewater Rendezvous*. She has also contributed short stories to three BSB anthologies: the Lambda Literary Award winning *Erotic Interludes 2: Stolen Moments*, *Erotic Interludes 3: Lessons in Love*, and *Erotic Interludes 4: Extreme Passions*. She lives in the north woods of Michigan.

Visit her Web site at www.kimbaldwin.com.

Books Available From Bold Strokes Books

More Than Paradise by Jennifer Fulton. Two women battle danger, risk all, and find in each other an unexpected ally and an unforgettable love. (978-1-933110-69-1)

Flight Risk by Kim Baldwin. For Blayne Keller, being in the wrong place at the wrong time just might turn out to be the best thing that ever happened to her. (978-1-933110-68-4)

Rebel's Quest, Supreme Constellations: Book Two by Gun Brooke. On a world torn by war, two women discover a love that defies all boundaries. (978-1-933110-67-7)

Punk and Zen by JD Glass. Angst, sex, love, rock. Trace, Candace, Francesca...Samantha. Losing control—and finding the truth within. BSB Victory Editions. (1-933110-66-X)

Stellium in Scorpio by Andrews & Austin. The passionate reuniting of two powerful women on the glitzy Las Vegas Strip, where everything is an illusion and love is a gamble. (1-933110-65-1)

When Dreams Tremble by Radclyffe. Two women whose lives turned out far differently than they'd once imagined discover that sometimes the shape of the future can only be found in the past. (1-933110-64-3)

The Devil Unleashed by Ali Vali. As the heat of violence rises, so does the passion. A Casey Clan crime saga. (1-933110-61-9)

Burning Dreams by Susan Smith. The chronicle of the challenges faced by a young drag king and an older woman who share a love "outside the bounds." (1-933110-62-7)

Fresh Tracks by Georgia Beers. Seven women, seven days. A lot can happen when old friends, lovers, and a new girl in town get together in the mountains. (1-933110-63-5)

The Empress and the Acolyte by Jane Fletcher. Jemeryl and Tevi fight to protect the very fabric of their world...time. Lyremouth Chronicles Book Three. (1-933110-60-0)

First Instinct by JLee Meyer. When high-stakes security fraud leads to murder, one woman flees for her life while another risks her heart to protect her. (1-933110-59-7)

Erotic Interludes 4: Extreme Passions. Thirty of today's hottest erotica writers set the pages aflame with love, lust, and steamy liaisons. (1-933110-58-9)

Storms of Change by Radclyffe. In the continuing saga of the Provincetown Tales, duty and love are at odds as Reese and Tory face their greatest challenge. (1-933110-57-0)

Unexpected Ties by Gina L. Dartt. With death before dessert, Kate Shannon and Nikki Harris are swept up in another tale of danger and romance. (1-933110-56-2)

Sleep of Reason by Rose Beecham. Nothing is as it seems when Detective Jude Devine finds herself caught up in a small-town soap opera. And her rocky relationship with forensic pathologist Dr. Mercy Westmoreland just got a lot harder. (1-933110-53-8)

Passion's Bright Fury by Radclyffe. When a trauma surgeon and a filmmaker become reluctant allies on the battleground between life and death, passion strikes without warning. (1-933110-54-6)

Broken Wings by L-J Baker. When Rye Woods, a fairy, meets the beautiful dryad Flora Withe, her libido, as squashed and hidden as her wings, reawakens along with her heart. (1-933110-55-4)

Combust the Sun by Andrews & Austin. A Richfield and Rivers mystery set in L.A. Murder among the stars. (1-933110-52-X)

Of Drag Kings and the Wheel of Fate by Susan Smith. A blind date in a drag club leads to an unlikely romance. (1-933110-51-1)

Tristaine Rises by Cate Culpepper. Brenna, Jesstin, and the Amazons of Tristaine face their greatest challenge for survival. (1-933110-50-3)

Too Close to Touch by Georgia Beers. Kylie O'Brien believes in true love and is willing to wait for it. It doesn't matter one damn bit that Gretchen, her new and off-limits boss, has a voice as rich and smooth as melted chocolate. It absolutely doesn't... (1-933110-47-3)

100th Generation by Justine Saracen. Ancient curses, modern-day villains, and a most intriguing woman who keeps appearing when least expected lead archeologist Valerie Foret on the adventure of her life. (1-933110-48-1)

Battle for Tristaine by Cate Culpepper. While Brenna struggles to find her place in the clan and the love between her and Jess grows, Tristaine is threatened with destruction. Second in the Tristaine series. (1-933110-49-X)

The Traitor and the Chalice by Jane Fletcher. Without allies to help them, Tevi and Jemeryl will have to risk all in the race to uncover the traitor and retrieve the chalice. The Lyremouth Chronicles Book Two. (1-933110-43-0)

Promising Hearts by Radclyffe. Dr. Vance Phelps lost everything in the War Between the States and arrives in New Hope, Montana, with no hope of happiness and no desire for anything except forgetting—until she meets Mae, a frontier madam. (1-933110-44-9)

Carly's Sound by Ali Vali. Poppy Valente and Julia Johnson form a bond of friendship that lays the foundation for something more, until Poppy's past comes back to haunt her—literally. A poignant romance about love and renewal. (1-933110-45-7)

Unexpected Sparks by Gina L. Dartt. Falling in love is challenging enough without adding murder to the mix. Kate Shannon's growing feelings for much younger Nikki Harris are complicated enough without the mystery of a fatal fire that Kate can't ignore. (1-933110-46-5)

Whitewater Rendezvous by Kim Baldwin. Two women on a wilderness kayak adventure—Chaz Herrick, a laid-back outdoorswoman, and Megan Maxwell, a workaholic news executive—discover that true love may be nothing at all like they imagined. (1-933110-38-4)

Erotic Interludes 3: Lessons in Love ed. by Radclyffe and Stacia Seaman. Sign on for a class in love…the best lesbian erotica writers take us to "school." (1-9331100-39-2)

Punk Like Me by JD Glass. Twenty-one-year-old Nina writes lyrics and plays guitar in the rock band Adam's Rib, and she doesn't always play by the rules. And oh yeah—she has a way with the girls. (1-933110-40-6)

The Clinic: Tristaine Book One by Cate Culpepper. Brenna, a prison medic, finds herself deeply conflicted by her growing feelings for her patient, Jesstin, a wild and rebellious warrior reputed to be descended from ancient Amazons. (1-933110-42-2)

The Exile and the Sorcerer by Jane Fletcher. First in the Lyremouth Chronicles. Tevi, wounded and adrift, arrives in the courtyard of a shy young sorcerer. Together they face monsters, magic, and the challenge of loving despite their differences. (1-933110-32-5)

Justice Served by Radclyffe. Lieutenant Rebecca Frye and her lover, Dr. Catherine Rawlings, embark on a deadly game of hide-and-seek with an underworld kingpin who traffics in human souls. (1-933110-15-5)

Justice in the Shadows by Radclyffe. In a shadow world of secrets and lies, Detective Sergeant Rebecca Frye and her lover, Dr. Catherine Rawlings, join forces in the elusive search for justice. (1-933110-03-1)

A Matter of Trust by Radclyffe. JT Sloan is a cybersleuth who doesn't like attachments. Michael Lassiter is leaving her husband, and she needs Sloan's expertise to safeguard her company. It should just be business—but it turns into much more. (1-933110-33-3)

Force of Nature by Kim Baldwin. From tornados to forest fires, the forces of nature conspire to bring Gable McCoy and Erin Richards close to danger, and closer to each other. (1-933110-23-6)

Stolen Moments: Erotic Interludes 2 by Stacia Seaman and Radclyffe, eds. Love on the run, in the office, in the shadows…Fast, furious, and almost too hot to handle. (1-933110-16-3)

Distant Shores, Silent Thunder by Radclyffe. Dr. Tory King—along with the women who love her—is forced to examine the boundaries of love, friendship, and the ties that transcend time. (1-933110-08-2)

Beyond the Breakwater by Radclyffe. One Provincetown summer, three women learn the true meaning of love, friendship, and family. (1-933110-06-6)

Safe Harbor by Radclyffe. A mysterious newcomer, a reclusive doctor, and a troubled gay teenager learn about love, friendship, and trust during one tumultuous summer in Provincetown. (1-933110-13-9)

Hunter's Pursuit by Kim Baldwin. A raging blizzard, a mountain hideaway, and a killer-for-hire set a scene for disaster—or desire—when Katarzyna Demetrious rescues a beautiful stranger. (1-933110-09-0)

Honor Reclaimed by Radclyffe. In the aftermath of 9/11, Secret Service Agent Cameron Roberts and Blair Powell close ranks with a trusted few to find the would-be assassins who nearly claimed Blair's life. (1-933110-18-X)

Honor Guards by Radclyffe. In a wild flight for their lives, the president's daughter and those who are sworn to protect her wage a desperate struggle for survival. (1-933110-01-5)

Love & Honor by Radclyffe. The president's daughter and her lover are faced with difficult choices as they battle a tangled web of Washington intrigue for...love and honor. (1-933110-10-4)

Honor Bound by Radclyffe. Secret Service Agent Cameron Roberts and Blair Powell face political intrigue, a clandestine threat to Blair's safety, and the seemingly irreconcilable personal differences that force them ever farther apart. (1-933110-20-1)

Above All, Honor by Radclyffe. Secret Service Agent Cameron Roberts fights her desire for the one woman she can't have—Blair Powell, the daughter of the president of the United States. (1-933110-04-X)